Without Trace

Without Trace

Katherine John

St. Martin's Press
New York

Library of Congress Cataloging-in-Publication Data

John, Katherine.
Without trace / Katherine John.
p.   cm.
"A Thomas Dunne book."
ISBN 0-312-13218-2
I. Title.
PR6060.0237W58   1995
823'.914—dc20   95-14714   CIP

First published in Great Britain by Random Century Group

First U.S. Edition: August 1995

10   9   8   7   6   5   4   3   2   1

To Trevor John

Acknowledgements

To John, Ralph, Sophie and Ross for their continual love and support, and for giving me the time to write this book.

To John Carey for a casual sentence that set me thinking.

To Sally Collis for typing it.

To Maria Brawn for reading it (even in the early stages).

And to Jennifer Price for her unstinting friendship and heroic endeavours to create order out of domestic chaos.

And most important of all, to my agent, Michael Thomas, and my editor, Rosie Cheetham, for their patience and forbearance with a new author.

Thank you

Without Trace

Prologue

The motorway was deserted. A tarnished pewter ribbon streaking across countryside drained grey by the indistinct light of a watery moon. The bushes that marked the boundary between road and farmland moved slightly in the chill night breeze, then, as headlights shot across the horizon, a figure moved forward, a darker shade amongst the shadows. It waited patiently at the side of the road, its white-gloved hands raised high as if in supplication. The solitary man seated behind the wheel of the small saloon car slowed the engine in response to the age-old gesture, then jammed the car decisively to a halt.

'I'm so sorry to trouble you, but my car went off the road about a mile back. Could you possibly give me a lift to the nearest town?' The voice that drifted in through the opened car window was cultured, polite.

'Of course. Get in.' The driver made a conscious effort to keep his reply casual and friendly, as though he were often flagged down by pierrots on the motorway at four in the morning. He reached across to the passenger door and unlocked it. 'Have you been to a fancy dress party?'

'Oh, yes, the costume . . .' The pierrot's laugh was shallow, artificial. 'My appearance must seem a trifle bizarre, to say the least.' The clown was detached, distant, as though the man or woman behind the mask of white greasepaint were merely intoning well-rehearsed, yet scarcely understood lines.

'Did you hurt yourself when your car left the road? Hit your head against the steering wheel, perhaps?'

The driver looked the pierrot over keenly with a professional eye.

'No, there's no injury. I am perfectly well, thank you.' The pierrot stepped into the car and settled himself comfortably in the passenger seat. Even under the inadequate car light, his costume appeared perfect in every detail. A consummate work of theatrical art and a very different affair to the rough ensembles that were hastily thrown together for the hospital balls, the driver decided.

The pierrot's black skullcap and loose pyjama suit were of a thick, dull satin, the front of the hat and the high-necked jacket ornamented by a single row of bushy, white silk pompoms. The whole effect was one of expense, managing somehow to suggest the unhurried wealth and luxury of another age. Crepe paper and cheap creased rayon lining would be more today's standard, even on the stage of the one ailing professional theatre that the town could boast. The driver looked up from the costume to the heavily made-up face. Was the pierrot really a pierrette? The height and build suggested a man, yet the voice was high-pitched, curiously feminine, almost as though it were an integral part of the disguise.

'I'm driving to the outskirts of town. Will that suit you?' the driver asked quickly, suddenly remembering why he was travelling on the motorway at such an ungodly hour.

'Yes. The outskirts will be fine. I'm sorry to put you to all this trouble.' The clown crossed his arms, slipping his hands into the wide sleeves of his suit like a pantomime Chinaman.

The driver turned the ignition key and reached for the gear stick, but the car didn't move forwards. A flash of cold steel darted upwards from the pierrot's hands. The driver stared in disbelief at the blade, watching transfixed as it moved inexorably towards him. He winced involuntarily as the sharp tip of the knife penetrated the soft skin of his throat just below his left ear. Then realization dawned. This was no dream. This was really happening. His hands flew upwards in a desperate attempt to wrest the weapon from the pierrot's hands, but the defence was too weak, too late. Before the driver's fingers even touched the knife, they fell limply, landing with a dull thud on the leather-gloved steering wheel.

The pierrot sat quietly for a moment watching the steady flow of blood that pumped out of the severed throat down on to the dead man's chest. Finally he withdrew his knife. It came easily. Wiping the blade clean between the gloved fingers of his left hand, he slid it back into the sheath that lay concealed beneath his sleeve.

He turned away from the rattling body, opened the car door and stepped out on to the harsh gravelly surface of the hard shoulder. Animal-like, he stood poised on tiptoe, his muscles stretched to their utmost, his face upturned, sniffing the air as though he were searching the atmosphere for an alien scent. All was quiet, peaceful.

He walked around to the driver's side of the car and wrenched open the door. The body slumped sideways out on to the road, landing awkwardly on its head. The pierrot linked his hands around the dead man's chest and began to drag him backwards, pushing the lolling head down onto the blood-soaked chest as though he were a child trying to mend a broken toy.

Panting with effort, he laboriously heaved his burden off the road, deep into the thick, tangled undergrowth which ran alongside the motorway. Soon his movements were lost amongst the rustlings of the bushes. The moon disappeared behind a bank of thick cloud. Far away on the eastern horizon a faint lighter tinge

9

to the sky heralded dawn, and the advent of the new day.

The light grew stronger, turning to silver, then gold, before the pierrot emerged from the hedge. He waded stiffly through the overgrown weeds, back up the bank to the parked car. His breath jerked spasmodically in quick, short gasps, and his hands trembled as they clutched an oddly-shaped bundle that he had made from the dead man's jacket. He laid his burden gently on the passenger seat of the car, slamming the door shut before walking around to the driver's side.

From the nearby woods came the first tentative notes of the morning's birdsong. They mingled with the quiet purr of the engine as the car slid off the hard shoulder on to the empty motorway. Within minutes it was no more than an insignificant speck on the horizon.

The landscape behind remained unchanged except for a darkly wet slick of gore that slimed off the road into the undergrowth. The gleam of gold on the eastern horizon intensified, lightening the sky to a translucent shade of opal. Rain began to fall. Slight at first, it became a downpour as the morning progressed. A heavy, cleansing rain that washed away the traces of blood and flesh, diluting the red stain to a mark that might have been anything. Cars arrived and sped past in the traffic lanes. Intermittent at first, they became a steady trickle that roared into a torrent with the advent of the rush hour.

The travellers who glanced casually out of their car windows never thought or wondered at the stain that marred the gravel on the hard shoulder. But they were the lucky ones. For them, journey's end was not yet in sight.

Chapter One

The telephone rang shrilly in the still atmosphere of the darkened bedroom. A tired hand groped its way out of the tangle of bedcovers and duvet, and fumbled vaguely in the direction of the bedside-table. There was a melodic crash, closely followed by the muttered sound of soft cursing.

'Dr Sherringham?'

'Which one?' Daisy grumbled sleepily.

'Dr Tim Sherringham.'

'Thank God for that!'

'I beg your pardon?'

'I'll get him for you,' Daisy snapped curtly. It was enough to have been woken from a deep and blissful sleep, without having to cope with a humourless telephone operator. 'Tim.' Daisy poked the huddle of bedclothes beside her. 'Tim!'

'No, not tonight. Please not tonight.' Tim buried his head under the pillow. 'They promised that they wouldn't do it to me. Not tonight!' he insisted. Ignoring his protests, Daisy scrabbled beneath the bedclothes until she found his hand. Wrapping his fingers firmly around the receiver, she left the bed and stumbled into the bathroom, to the accompaniment of Tim's muffled voice.

'Tell the hospital I'm ill. Dead! Anything! Daisy. Daisy!'

Why do I always do it? Daisy thought irritably. She was incredibly thirsty, dehydrated from the wine and vodka she had drunk earlier. She filled her toothglass with water from the cold tap before staring gloomily at her reflection in the mirror that hung above the wash-

11

basin. Her long, dark hair was dull, the curls and waves stiff from the setting lotion and lacquer she only wore on what Tim sardonically referred to as 'state occasions'. It would be hell trying to brush it out in the morning, she thought miserably, wondering just how many, or rather how few, hours away her morning would be.

She stood on tiptoe and peered at her eyes. They were already bloodshot, and there were thick, dark smudges underlining her lower lashes that had nothing to do with leftover mascara. She looked as exhausted as she felt. And she was operating at nine sharp. Assisting the hospital dragon, the one female consultant, who devoured housemen in the same way the other consultant surgeons devoured whisky.

'Damn, and double damn!' she murmured dismally as she jerked the cord that switched off the bathroom light, and wandered back into the bedroom.

'I'll second that.' Tim was out of bed, pulling on the white evening shirt that he had tossed on to the bedroom floor only an hour earlier.

'If you undid the buttons when you took it off, you wouldn't have to do that.'

'Do what?' Tim enquired mechanically.

'Pull your shirt on over your head.' Daisy watched her husband, feeling curiously detached for a moment. They were married. Had been for nearly six months, and she still couldn't get used to the fact.

What was it Judy had once said about Tim? 'He was too good to be true. Good-looking and good-natured. Still the clean-living, all-American boy, even though he hadn't set foot in America for fifteen years.' He even looked like the archetypal movie star hero. Six foot six inch frame, slim build, curling dark hair and devastatingly blue eyes . . .

'Stop looking at me like that.'

'Like what?' Daisy smiled up at him innocently.

12

'Like you want to get back into bed.'

'But I do. I really do.' She flung herself headlong on to the dishevelled duvet.

'I get the distinct impression you couldn't give a damn whether I get in with you or not.'

'I would care,' Daisy answered honestly, 'if I wasn't so very, very tired. Tell me, why do I always find your brother's parties so exhausting?'

'Because my brother is exhausting.' Tim ran his fingers impatiently through his hair as he glanced around the room. 'But exhausting or not, at this time in the morning I have to agree, big brother's got a point.'

'What point?' Daisy enquired sleepily.

'A point about having to get up in the middle of the night,' Tim snapped. 'It's downright uncivilized. Daisy, where are my pants?'

'Your trousers,' she corrected, 'are lying where you flung them, here, on my side of the bed.' He shook the bedcover, and his evening suit fell on to the floor.

'Do you know what Richard said to me last night?'

'No, I don't.' Daisy was just beginning to drift hazily into that pleasantly comfortable grey world somewhere between waking and sleeping.

'He said he's only had to get out of bed in the small hours once in the last ten years. And that was the night Joanna's father had his heart attack . . .'

Daisy groped her way back to consciousness. 'He's offered you a job again, hasn't he?'

An oppressive silence closed between them for a moment, then Tim answered her. 'He has, and from where I'm standing right now, it looks just the ticket,' he asserted defiantly.

'Taking rich men's blood pressure!' she expostulated. 'Spending every day listening to long lists of imaginary ills, just because the patient's wealthy enough to foot the bill in that over-developed, crassly-decorated mausoleum your brother calls a clinic.'

'It's not at all like that, you little socialist . . .'

'I know exactly what it's like,' she retorted heatedly. 'Well, you do what you want with your life, but leave me out of it. You're not going to turn me into your personal dogsbody as Richard's done to Joanna. I'm not going to waste my life hosting parties, and carrying out meaningless research for some cosmetic company on the top floor of the clinic. I'm staying right where I am . . .'

'A houseman for ever?' Tim enquired mildly.

'No, not a houseman for ever!' she exclaimed furiously. 'Damn you, Tim.'

'I love you when you're angry,' he whispered softly, taking the bitterness out of their argument. 'Your eyes blaze so beautifully.' He sat on the bed, pressing her back against the pillows and kissing her vehemently. 'We'll talk about this tomorrow . . .' He glanced at his watch '. . . today . . . Oh blast it, another time, when we're not so tired,' he finished, giving her another, shorter kiss.

'If we wait till then, we'll never talk,' she replied, smiling despite the anger that still scalded inside her.

'You never know, one day we may both be given the same day off.'

'Is that going to be the same day all geriatric consultants retire and we get promoted?' She knelt on the bed and locked her arms around his neck, pulling him back down next to her. 'Headache gone?' she asked. He nodded. 'Quite gone?' she persisted.

'Yes,' he murmured.

'In that case, as we've only just made up,' she whispered seductively, 'must you go? Right now? Right this minute?'

'Right now, right this minute,' he echoed, disentangling himself from her arms. 'Yesterday I pleaded

14

with Bassett. "Put Mrs Hawkins on the theatre list," I begged. "We can do a Caesarean this afternoon. A nice, quiet, calm operation." And what did the great man say? "No. Leave it until Monday," he said. And now what? I have to get up at . . .' He squinted sideways at his watch . . . 'three-forty in the morning, after a night on the tiles, to go and operate.'

'Are you sure you're in a fit state to drive?' Daisy asked, as she crawled back under the bedclothes.

'I didn't indulge myself as much as you, darling,' he replied pointedly. 'Besides, fit state or not, by the sound of it Hawkins junior won't wait any longer than the time it'll take me to get to the hospital.' He wrapped the duvet tightly around her. 'Breakfast at eight in the canteen?'

'You take me to such nice places.'

'Don't I just.' He paused for a second in the open doorway. 'Love you.'

'Love you too.'

The temptation to return to sleep was simply overwhelming. Daisy's eyelids drooped heavily, and she slid sweetly, effortlessly downwards, sensing rather than actually hearing Tim leave the room. Her final thoughts were of doctors and night calls.

Why hadn't they taken up farming or train driving? No. Train drivers had to work at night too, and so did farmers when their animals were sick. Their lives would be no different. Her mind drifted aimlessly, incoherently, for a few seconds, then there was nothing. A simple dreamless sleep that obliterated everything. Even Tim's absence in the bed beside her.

It was the alarm that woke her. It was buzzing angrily on the floor beside the bed. She hadn't even bothered to pick it up after she'd knocked it over during the night. Resisting the temptation to bury herself under the duvet for an extra minute or two, she sat up. Then, forcing herself to be strong, she determinedly opened her eyes and threw back the bedclothes.

Tim's maroon velvet bow tie lay on her dressing table next to a glittering bundle of her costume jewellery. Why was it too much effort to put things away at night? she wondered wearily as she stepped over her black taffeta evening dress on the way to the bathroom. Next time she'd find the energy. She really would. The sparkle and glamour of the evening looked cheap and tawdry in the cold light of morning. Like a persistent hangover it tainted the beginning of the new day.

Turning the shower on tepid she braced her muscles for the sensation of cool water on her skin. Her body as well as her mind was still heavily numbed by sleep. If her life could consist only of evenings and nights, the world would be perfect, she mused happily. She'd simply glide through beautifully quiet private times with Tim. But then perhaps even perfection would grow tedious. They'd stir themselves now and again to do the odd afternoon of work. Just one or two a week, preceded by long lazy mornings spent drinking coffee and reading the newspapers. Like Sundays in the old days, before patients, responsibilities and duty rosters had taken whole chunks out of their lives. But dreams were dreams, and reality was this never-ending ghastly effort. Shivering, she turned off the shower and reached for a towel.

Twenty minutes after getting out of bed, she locked the flat, took the lift down to the ground floor, and left the building through the main entrance. Jangling her car keys impatiently through her fingers, she searched the ranks of parked cars for her Fiat. There was only Tim's Mercedes.

'Blast him!' she cursed crossly. How dare he take the Fiat? He knew she hated driving his car. Besides, no self-respecting registrar should drive a Mercedes. The very idea was ridiculous. If his brother had to give

16

them a car instead of teaspoons for a wedding present, he should have given them an anonymous little runabout, not this gross, gleaming status symbol which she loathed driving and was petrified of scratching.

She opened the door angrily and tossed her bag into the back, before climbing into the driving seat. At least there wouldn't be too much traffic on the road at this time of morning. Another hour and it would be chaos. She jerked the seat forward, smiling at the thought of Tim folding his long legs into her Fiat. He invariably forgot to adjust the seat. The last time he'd done it, he'd twisted his knee and screamed at her, 'Damn you for being a midget!'

Consoled by the memory of Tim's discomfort, she turned on the ignition and crashed the gears. Muttering to herself, she tried again, and slowly, carefully, inched her way out of the parking bay on to the drive.

Once she reached the motorway slip road, Daisy forgot about the car and drove automatically. As Tim often commented, the Mercedes was built for motorways. She sat back in the driving seat and relaxed.

She knew full well it was childish of her to resent Richard for buying them the car. After all, Tim owed his brother a great deal. His education, the flat that had been a wedding present along with the car, and there was no disputing the fact that Richard would have given them a great deal more if Tim hadn't put a stop to it. When it came to money, Richard was generous to a fault. But his generosity did nothing to assuage Daisy's inferiority complex.

She had struggled into medicine the hard way, via comprehensive school and a comfortable, slightly shabby, middle class home. Nothing, not even the brief glamour of the annual college balls, had prepared her for the Sherringham life style.

First there was the vast Georgian mansion that still remained as much Tim's home as Richard's. She could never bring herself to breeze through its grand double doors and shout commands to the butler in the same careless way Tim did. But then she hadn't entirely managed to suppress her first overawed impression that everything in the Sherringham household, from the luxuriously tasteful decor, down to the elaborately staged dinner parties, belonged in one of the Sunday colour supplements.

Richard and Joanna existed in a superficially splendid and perfect world that allowed nothing distasteful, nothing obnoxious . . . nothing *real* to intrude. Their daily life would make a glossy, visually impressive, Hollywood film. But Daisy felt that she would have been happier watching from the stalls with an ice-cream and a packet of popcorn, rather than moving on to the set as one of the players.

She couldn't even blame her sense of isolation and unreality on Richard and Joanna. Neither of them had ever so much as hinted that she was different from any of the titled, wealthy, famous or infamous people who moved in and out of their household. Ignoring her socialist ideals and chain store clothes, they had welcomed her into the family with open, if slightly chilly, arms. And she soon realized that their lack of warmth was not restricted to her. They kept themselves detached and slightly distant from everyone. Except Tim. No one could ever be indifferent to Tim. But then Tim didn't fit into Richard's closed world. He had broken away. Or had he?

Doubts crept like cockroaches from the recesses of her mind. Didn't Tim always listen to Richard, even when his brother mocked the National Health Service hospital she and Tim worked in? The lack of funds that told in the outdated equipment and the long waiting lists they had to cope with every working day. The endless hours of duty, the constant fight against time that meant they had virtually no time to call their own.

And each caustically realistic observation that Richard made terrified her.

She pictured herself sucked into the Sherringham whirlpool, transformed into a beautician's ideal of the perfect woman. Immaculately styled hair, nails painted with varnish that never had the opportunity to chip, her better features heightened, transformed by layers of expertly applied make-up. Newly programmed to make the correct responses for each and every social occasion. Her career subjugated to Tim's, just as Joanna's aspirations in psychiatry had been cleared away to make way for Richard's own ambitions.

'But it's not the quantity of our private life that's important, dear brother. It's the quality.' Tim's laughter intruded into her grim fantasy. He'd said that the first time she'd heard Richard try to pressurize him into working at the Holbourne and Sherringham Clinic. But he hadn't said it again last night. Or if he had, she hadn't been around to hear him say it.

'Damn Joanna and her parties,' she muttered feelingly. She could even smell Joanna's astringent perfume in the car. 'Damn and double damn!'

Jerking herself sharply back to the present, she blew her horn furiously as a flashy red Porsche cut dangerously close in front of her. 'Idiot!' she mouthed briskly at the uncomprehending driver. Give a middle-aged man a sports car and he had to live up to the image, even if it meant killing himself and everyone else on the road.

Despondency followed in the wake of her brief flare of temper. She knew from bitter experience that her anger was pointless and, what was even worse, destructive. When she was with Tim, she was sure of him, his love for her, the life they had chosen to lead together. She was a fool to allow one of Richard and Joanna's empty, meaningless parties to upset her. She had to bury all her doubts. Be positive. Count the pluses in her present life with Tim, not worry about the minuses that might be lurking around the corner. Besides, what could she do if Tim did change? Threw in his lot with Richard and took a directorship in the Holbourne and Sherringham clinic?

She focused on the last weekend she and Tim had shared. Had it been a month, or two months ago? They had taken their boat down the coast and dropped anchor in a deserted cove for a couple of days . . . and nights. There had been no telephones, no bleepers, no Richard. Nothing except what they themselves had made of the brief holiday. Tim had been right, it was not the quantity of time they spent together. It was the quality.

She took the slip road off the motorway and drove up to the hospital. Confidently, she steered the Mercedes into one of the wide bays marked 'Registrars Only'. Tim may have driven her Fiat here, but he could damn well take the status symbol home. She lifted her bag off the back seat and locked the car door. Then, swinging her case wide, she swept through the main entrance towards the lift.

'Nice morning, Dr Sherringham.'

'Beautiful, John.' She smiled at the porter, as she pressed the lift button, then glanced at her watch. It wasn't quite eight. She wondered if Tim were waiting for her. Hospital nights had a nasty habit of extending into days, particularly on the maternity ward.

'Lazy people take lifts, active, health conscious ones take the stairs.'

'You can be healthy enough for both of us this morning, Judy,' Daisy yawned as she walked into the lift.

'I never said I was one of the active breed,' Judy answered, joining her. 'Merely commenting on their ways. Are you going to the canteen?' Daisy nodded. 'You look terrible,' Judy grinned cheerfully, pushing

20

the button for the tenth floor. 'Was the surgeons' barbecue really that wild?'

'Not the barbecue. Tim's brother's dinner party.'

'Ah, the eminent Dr Sherringham, as opposed to the two plebeian ones.'

'That's it.' Daisy braced herself for the shudder that all the hospital lifts gave when they reached their floor. 'Where are you this morning?'

'Antenatal clinic.' Judy stepped out of the lift and pushed the canteen door open. 'And you?'

'Theatre.'

'Not with . . .'

'Her Mightiness herself,' Daisy replied grimly, picking a none too clean tray from the stand. She looked around the tables. The place was half empty, and there was no sign of Tim. 'Can I buy you a coffee?' she asked Judy.

'You could, but then again, I think I'd prefer orange juice. At least that's covered by the Trade Descriptions Act. Where's Tim? He should be here soothing your fevered brow, considering the day you have ahead of you.'

'In Maternity. He had an emergency call last night, the Hawkins baby.'

'Poor Tim. Was it a very early call?' Judy commiserated.

'Four-ish, but when you've only been in bed an hour it seems earlier.'

'Don't I know it.' Judy picked up two plates of toast from the warming tray. 'Can I tempt you?'

'Errghh.'

'Do I take it that means "no thank you, dear friend"?' Judy enquired mildly. Suddenly she grasped Daisy's arm. 'Oh my God, watch out! Here comes pain personified.'

Daisy snatched her coffee and marched briskly to a

21

table at the far end of the canteen, Judy following at a smart pace.

'He's heading this way.'

'Isn't he always,' Daisy muttered through clenched teeth. 'The man's in love with you.'

'Or you,' Judy parried.

'Can't be me. I'm a married lady.'

'Since when has a little thing like Tim stopped a first-class menace like Eric Hedley?'

'Can I join you, girls?'

'We're not girls, we're doctors.' Judy slammed her coffee down on the table. 'And since you're already half-way into that chair, your question's superfluous.'

'Where's the blue-eyed boy this morning?' Eric asked snidely, scraping his polypropylene chair closer to the table.

'Whose blue-eyed boy?' Daisy demanded irritably.

'Whose blue-eyed boy do you think? Tim, of course. Every consultant's dream registrar.'

'Jealousy, dear Eric, doesn't become you,' Judy purred over-sweetly. 'We all know how you angled for Tim's post, but fortunately for the rest of us, the better man was appointed.'

'I wouldn't be too sure of that if I were you,' Eric retorted swiftly. 'I've just left the labour ward. Mrs Hawkins' waters broke at seven-thirty this morning, and already the baby's distressed.'

'But Tim's . . .' Daisy stared at Eric blankly.

'Tim's nowhere to be found,' Eric crowed. 'They've been paging him for . . .' he looked pointedly at his watch, '. . . thirty-five minutes, and although our esteemed registrar is on call, he's simply not responding.'

'But that's ridiculous,' Daisy protested. 'Tim left the flat early this morning.'

'Early this morning?' Eric raised a querying eyebrow. 'Well, wherever he is, it's not here. I've been on call

all night. Six emergencies and no help. It hasn't exactly been a picnic. And I'll tell you something else. They're calling Bassett out now, and if I were a consultant, I wouldn't be the least bit pleased to be dragged out of bed at this time in the morning just because my registrar was too bloody idle to respond to an emergency call.'

'Then it's just as well you'll never be a consultant,' Judy snarled protectively.

'Tim left before four this morning,' Daisy asserted forcefully. 'He must have reached here around four-thirty . . .'

'That's very clever of him considering he wasn't even called out until seven-thirty,' Eric sneered. 'Don't tell me, let me guess.' He looked Daisy straight in the eye. 'Can our golden boy be cheating on his wife?' he enquired coolly. 'Well, whether he is or he isn't, I'm sure there's nothing amiss that big brother can't solve. What it is to have the power of the medical mafia behind you.'

Blind fury welled within Daisy. She stared at Eric, watching the self-satisfied expression spread across his plump face. He looked just like a cat, gross and over-fed. Deliberately, she reached out for her coffee cup. Holding it by the handle, she swung it high in front of Eric's nose, tossing the contents full into his face. He screamed, but she didn't wait to find out whether the noise he made was born of pain, or shock. She pushed her chair back. It fell to the floor with a loud crash. Oblivious to the disturbance she'd created, she ran headlong out of the canteen.

'If that was anything other than hospital coffee, you'd be on your way to the burns unit,' Judy quipped, before chasing after Daisy. She caught up with her on the staircase. 'I thought you were the lazy one . . .'

'Please, Judy, no jokes. Not now.' Daisy begged.

23

'OK, no jokes.' Judy's face became serious. 'But do you mind telling me where you're going?'

'Maternity.'

'Do you think that's wise?' Judy laid a restraining hand on her friend's arm. 'If Tim's down there and really in trouble, he's not going to want you around.'

'If Tim's there and able to handle whatever's happening, he won't even know I'm close. But if he needs me . . .'

'I'll go with you.'

'Judy . . .'

'Come on, or we'll both be late for duty.'

'No, I'm sorry, Dr Sherringham, but Dr Tim Sherringham hasn't been here today. No, we didn't call him out before seven-thirty. No, there was no answer from your home number. I appreciate there must be some mistake, but I have a ward to run. If you'll excuse me . . .' The sister turned to her drugs trolley.

'The Hawkins baby?' Daisy asked the sister's back.

'The foetus is no longer viable.'

Calm, reasoned words of logic, articulated in the standard bedside manner. But Daisy wasn't in the mood for logic. She clenched her fists tightly, straining them impotently against the pockets of her white coat.

'Is there anything else?' The sister turned and looked pointedly at Daisy.

'No. Nothing. Thank you.' Daisy stepped aside, allowing the sister to rattle her trolley down the long corridor that led to the patients' beds.

'I heard Tim ask for Mrs Hawkins to be put on the theatre list yesterday.' Judy's voice intruded on Daisy's nightmare. 'No one can blame him for this. No one.'

'The baby's dead.' Daisy listened dully to her own words. 'And we're doctors. We take the losses along with the gains. Wasn't that what they taught us in medical school?'

'Look, there's nothing we can do here, and it's half eight already.' Judy steered Daisy towards the main corridor. 'If you don't get to the theatre and scrub up right now, there are going to be two Dr Sherringhams on the carpet.'

'Something must have happened to Tim. He'd never ignore a call.' Daisy's eyes scanned the corridor feverishly. 'He must be lying somewhere, hurt or . . .'

'If you go to the theatre, I'll organize a search of the hospital. As soon as he turns up, I'll get word to you, I promise.' Judy caught Daisy's hands in her own. 'He's probably picked up on another call,' she insisted firmly. 'You know Tim. Doctor first, husband second. I thought you'd have realized that when you married him.'

'You really think that's what's happened?' Daisy pleaded desperately.

'I'm certain,' Judy reassured her.

'And you'll get word to me as soon as you know where he is?'

'I promise. Now get going before the fireworks really start.'

Miss Palmer-Smith was on form that morning. By nine-fifteen, Daisy felt as though she, and the other house-men, were personally responsible for most of the deficiencies in the theatre, if not the hospital. Routine hernia followed routine appendicectomy with Daisy either mishearing or misinterpreting every command and question Miss Palmer-Smith tossed her way. And it didn't make things any easier when a chance remark reminded her that Miss Palmer-Smith was a personal friend of Richard's.

Minutes before the final patient on the morning's list was due to be wheeled into the theatre, Alan Cummins, Tim's counterpart in Paediatrics, peered in through the porthole. He stayed just long enough to catch Daisy's

25

attention and mouth, 'Tim's in the hospital,' before disappearing from sight. Where Daisy had felt merely incompetent before, she now felt positively idiotic. She dropped an instrument, backed into a nurse, and caught her hip awkwardly on a trolley. All in the space of less than five minutes.

'Are there any emergencies at the end of this list?'

'No, Miss Palmer-Smith,' Daisy muttered from behind her mask.

'Perhaps it's just as well, Dr Sherringham. If you'd stitch up.'

'Yes, Miss Palmer-Smith. Thank you,' Daisy replied automatically, not really knowing why she was being thankful. Gratitude for the end of the morning, perhaps?

Miss Palmer-Smith swept out of the theatre, and Daisy forced herself to concentrate on the patient on the table. A few minutes more and she'd see Tim. What on earth had happened to make him behave so stupidly? Had there been a crash on the motorway? Had Tim stayed with the injured driver? If so, why hadn't she seen him on the way in? This was the only General Hospital for miles, so why hadn't he booked in here? Unless he had taken whoever it was to Richard's clinic. Of course . . . the clinic. It was closer to town . . . Options crowded into her confused thoughts like pigeons scavenging for bread.

'How long do you want before I start bringing her round?' the anaesthetist enquired. Daisy glanced across to where Mike Edmunds sat, his slight figure half hidden by the clinical array of tubes and bottles that surrounded the patient's head.

'One minute more and I'll be through.' Already the tension was lifting. Miss Palmer-Smith was a first-class surgeon, Daisy allowed grudgingly, but the atmosphere she generated was anything but conducive to work. It wasn't good for either patients or staff.

Meticulously, Daisy knotted the final threads into the patient's abdomen.

'Very neat,' Mike commented appreciatively. 'Do you darn Tim's socks as well?'

'Sometimes,' Daisy replied absent-mindedly.

'By the way, I'm sorry about Tim's trouble. If there's anything I can do . . .'

'Thank you.' Daisy smiled across at him, relief flooding through her nerve endings. She was touched by the note of sincerity in Mike voice. And soon, very soon, she'd be with Tim. Would he be waiting for her in the surgeon's changing-room? She cut the final cord with a flourish. 'That's me finished.'

'I'll stay in post-op for a while.' Mike tilted the patient's head back. 'Go and get yourself a coffee. You look as though you need one.'

Alan, not Tim, was waiting for her in the surgeon's changing-room.

'Where's Tim?' Daisy demanded nervously as soon as she walked into the room.

'No one can find him,' Alan replied sheepishly. 'His car's in the car park . . .'

'Oh God!'

'Oh God what?'

'Do you mean the Mercedes parked in the registrars' bay?'

'Don't tell me. You put it there,' Alan groaned.

'Tim took the Fiat last night.' She stripped the rubber gloves from her hands and threw them in the bin.

'I'll check the car park one last time,' Alan said briskly. 'If he doesn't turn up soon, Bassett's going to have his head on a plate.' Of average height and plump, with fair freckled skin and vivid ginger hair, Alan was the life and soul of every hospital party. They all blessed him for his incredible sense of humour, his ability to see the funny side of every situation no matter how ghastly. But for the first time since she'd known him, Daisy couldn't see even a glimmer of a smile on his face.

'Alan, what do you think's happened to Tim?'

An uneasy silence hung in the air that said more than all the false reassurances Alan could have uttered. 'I wish I knew,' he hedged evasively.

Daisy turned and stared blankly into her locker. She didn't want anyone, not even Alan, to see just how close she was to breaking point.

'I didn't mean it that way.' Alan wrapped his arm awkwardly around Daisy's shoulders, and pulled her head down on to his chest. 'You really are worried, aren't you?'

'Wouldn't you be if it was Carol?' Daisy mumbled into the hairy tweed jacket he was wearing.

'There has to be a perfectly reasonable explanation for all of this, believe me . . .'

'Such as?' she demanded.

'He could have had an accident . . . gone off the road . . .'

'Someone would have found him by now,' she insisted. 'Besides, all motorway casualties are brought here . . .' She pushed her hands against his chest and looked into his eyes.

'I've checked casualty six times this morning,' he admitted shamefacedly, refusing to meet her questioning look.

'And he's not there?'

'He's not there,' Alan echoed helplessly, shaking his head. 'Daisy, what do you want to do?'

'I have to look for him.' She turned and pulled her skirt and blouse out of her locker. 'I have to do something . . . anything . . .' she finished on a note of high-pitched desperation. 'He left the flat before four and it's . . .' She checked the clock that hung above the theatre door, '. . . it's twelve-thirty now. Alan, it's been eight hours.'

'You can't make too much of that, Daisy. You know how easy it is to forget the time, especially if you're working. Tim could be caught up in an emergency of some kind.' He knew she didn't believe him. He didn't even believe himself.

'Look, I'll tell you what,' he said decisively. 'You finish changing, then telephone your flat. You never know, he may have gone back there, especially if he had a bump in the car.'

'And if he doesn't answer?'

'I'll drive you and Judy to the flat. We'll look out for him on the way, and what's the betting that he passes us. And then won't we feel fools?' Alan rubbed his hands briskly together and smiled at her warmly. 'Come on girl, we've got things to do. See you in the car park after you've changed.'

Daisy stripped off her gown, and dressed in record time. She knew full well that staff weren't supposed to leave the hospital during meal breaks, but she didn't even want to ask Alan if he'd cleared that with the office. If he had, all well and good. If he hadn't, they would have to ask, and that might mean refusal. It was a half-hour drive to the flat, and a half-hour back. And they had a bare three-quarters of an hour for lunch. But then it might not take them that long. If Alan was right, they would see Tim on the way.

She pulled her purse and car keys out of her bag, and walked out of the changing-room to the nearest pay phone. She dialled the number of the flat, then waited. The telephone rang hollowly in her ear. If Tim was there, he wasn't answering. Damn him! Shrugging her white hospital jacket over her shoulders, she walked out of the building into the car park. Alan was waiting for her, a small furrow of concern marking a narrow line between his bushy eyebrows.

29

'You telephoned.' It was a statement, not a question.
She nodded. 'He's not there, or else he's not answering.'

'Come on, then. If we're going to be back for afternoon clinic we'd best get moving.'

'Let's take the Mercedes,' Daisy suggested. 'If Tim sees it, he'll stop.'

'Good thinking.'

'You drive.' She threw the keys at Alan.

'I'm not driving your Merc,' he protested.

'I want to look out for Tim, and I can't do that and drive. Is Judy coming?'

'I told her we'd pick her up at the main entrance,' Alan replied, then, yielding to the anguished look on Daisy's face, he climbed reluctantly into the driving seat of Tim's car.

'You look left, I'll look right, and Alan, you keep your eyes on the road,' Judy ordered as she jumped into the back of the car.

'Yes, Ma'am.' The journey was a strain, with Judy and Alan's jokes growing thinner and more forced as they drew nearer to the flat. It was a relief all round when Alan finally turned into the driveway of the six-storey mock-Georgian block.

'I'll go and see if Tim's there.' Daisy opened the passenger door before Alan had even stopped the car. Shivering, despite the warmth of the spring sunshine that had followed the morning's rain, she stepped out into the fresh air. She didn't look along the ranks of parked cars . . . if the Fiat was there, then marvellous. And she'd find out soon enough. If it wasn't, so what? Its absence meant nothing. Tim could have broken down . . . crashed. She knew she was clinging to intangible threads of 'ifs' and 'maybes'.

'Wait!' Judy called. 'We'll come with you.'

Daisy walked quickly into the building with Judy

30

trailing her, while Alan parked the car. She moulded her lips into a wooden smile for the porter's benefit.

'You're back early, Dr Sherringham,' he said brightly, looking up from the newspaper spread out on his desk. 'No one sick today?'

'I've decided to ignore my patients and play truant, Fred,' she answered. 'We're looking for Tim. Have you seen him?'

'Not this morning, Doctor.' The old man whipped off his blue commissionaire's cap, and scratched his bald head thoughtfully. 'But then I'm not always at the desk. Between putting out the rubbish and seeing to the post . . .'

'Thanks, Fred,' Daisy interrupted abruptly, cutting him short. He wasn't always at his desk. She knew that. Tim could have come in at any time, and gone upstairs without Fred noticing. The list of 'maybes' was growing, both in number and intensity. Tim had to be in the flat. Daisy concentrated all her energies on a clear-cut image of her husband. He had to be there. He simply had to!

Judy called the lift. The doors clanged open as Alan walked into the foyer.

'Third?' he asked, walking into the lift.

'If you don't know by now, you never will.' Daisy thrust her hands deep into her pockets. She was shivering, but if the other two noticed it, they were tactful enough not to say anything.

'You've got my keys,' Daisy reminded Alan when they reached the flat door. He flicked around the ring until he found the right one, then inserted it into the lock. The door swung open slowly. Daisy flung it back on its hinges and stepped swiftly into the reception area. All the doors that led out of the small hallway were closed. She swayed for a moment, then laid her hand firmly on the brass handle of the living-room door, jerking the handle down, and almost kicking the door open with her foot.

The room yawned vacantly back at her. Her synthetic fur cape lay on one of the arms of the leather chesterfield where she had left it the night before. Tim's evening shoes stood in the middle of the pale grey carpet, his raincoat slung over the mahogany coffee table next to the glass wall that opened out on to the balcony.

She walked through the connecting doors that led into the formal dining-room. The high-backed chairs stood grouped around the antique Spanish dining-table. On the longest wall, spindly pink shells posed formally in a rock pool – Tim's first, and only, attempt at oil painting. She walked on through the kitchen into the inner hall that led to the two bedrooms and the bathroom. Everything was as she had left it that morning. Her taffeta dress lay on the floor. Tim's wardrobe door stood open, their towels hung limply on the bathroom rail.

'He's not in the spare bedroom or the study.' Judy looked anxiously into the master bedroom. 'Do you think he's been back since this morning?' Daisy shook her head. A depressing sense of anticlimax engulfed her. Anything, almost anything, would have been better than this cold emptiness.

'Well, he hasn't been back here and he didn't reach the hospital.' Alan looked in, his face fixed in a grimace of aggressive optimism. 'That narrows the field. The car must have broken down somewhere between here and the hospital.'

'For nine hours?' Daisy questioned flatly.

'If his car went off the road, he could be concussed. For all we know, he's still sitting in it now.' Alan, the calm, no nonsense medical man was taking over. 'There's obviously nothing here, so shall we go and look?'

32

Daisy followed Alan and Judy out of the apartment. Disturbing, half-formulated images whirled through her mind at breakneck speed. How was this going to end? What if the empty apartment was all she was going to be left with? What if she never saw Tim again? 'We'll find him, Daisy, don't worry. I promise you we'll find him.' A note of hysteria crept into Alan's voice. He, too, had been unnerved by the empty flat.

He brought the Mercedes round to the front of the building, and she and Judy climbed in.

'Look left, particularly when we get to the motorway,' Judy commanded as Alan turned the ignition key. 'There's a ditch at the side of the road. The car could have veered into it.'

Alan drove slowly down the inside lane. Occasionally a car hurtled past them, horn blaring, lights flashing, and once a group of teenagers drew alongside shouting insults through their open car windows.

'Get yourself a wheelchair, Grandad! You don't need a motor that can go.'

'What a waste of a set of moving wheels.'

'I'd never realized how monotonous this landscape was.' Judy shifted uncomfortably in her seat. 'Trees, hedgerows, fields. Trees, hedgerows, fields. Is there nothing else?'

'What's that?' Daisy screamed suddenly, her nerves wound to snapping point.

'What?' Alan screeched the car to a halt on the hard shoulder.

'That bundle over there. There's blood on it,' Daisy whispered.

'Take it easy.' Judy's hand groped for Daisy's.

'You two stay here. I'll go and look.' Alan left the car. Slamming the door shut with unnecessary vigour, he walked over to the extreme edge of the hard shoulder. Daisy watched numbly as he crouched low for a moment. He rose quickly, straightening himself

33

to his full height. Furiously he kicked whatever it was he'd been looking at down the embankment.

'Dead fox.' he muttered curtly as he re-entered the car.. 'If you ask me, we've all got a bad case of the jitters. Tim's going to laugh himself silly when he hears about this.'

'I hope so,' Daisy breathed fervently. 'I really hope so.'

The remainder of the journey passed without incident. Alan parked the Mercedes in the registrars' bay barely minutes before the two o'clock clinics were due to start. 'See you in the canteen after work?' he suggested.

'See you,' Judy agreed.

'And whoever hears from Tim first gets a message to the other two?' Alan's plea fell on deaf ears. Judy was already running towards Out-patients, while Daisy was searching through the rows of parked cars, looking for a small blue Fiat that wasn't there.

'Coffee after work,' Alan repeated, pressing the car keys into her hand.

'Thank you, Alan. I'd like that.'

'I'll ask in Casualty . . .'

'I'd rather do it myself, if you don't mind.'

He nodded. 'I understand.'

She turned her back on him and walked slowly towards the hospital buildings. There was something in the determined set of her shoulders, the curve of her neck, that tore into his consciousness.

'Blast Tim for giving her such a scare!' he thought irritably as he walked across the lawns to the children's annex.

Chapter Two

'And what time was it when Dr Sherringham left?'

'Sometime before four,' Daisy answered tersely. It was warm in Alan's tiny office, and there were far too many people there: two police sergeants; the chief surgeon, Mr Bassett, who was already looking vaguely apologetic for his earlier outburst against Tim; Judy, who simply wouldn't be put outside; and of course Alan and herself.

At six o'clock, after she and Alan had made a second fruitless visit to the apartment, she had finally capitulated and allowed him to call the police. It appeared to be the only thing left to do. The AA had received no accident reports that day for the stretch of motorway between the apartment and the hospital. Tim hadn't been admitted to their casualty department, or any other within a fifty-mile radius. And, most worrying of all, no one had heard from him in fourteen hours.

Alan had spent most of his tea break trying to persuade her to call the local police station, but she had refused, hoping against hope that even at that late hour Tim would walk into the canteen, an apology and a plausible explanation ready framed on his lips. 'I'm sorry, darling. I fell asleep behind the wheel of the car and went off the road. Didn't come round until half an hour ago.'

She'd look up at him and laugh, but there would be tears of sheer relief on her cheeks. Then she'd reach out and touch him, stroke the side of face . . . Only Tim hadn't returned. Instead, she and Alan had waited until the last possible moment before returning to their respective clinics.

She'd taken ten minutes out at five o'clock to telephone the Holbourne and Sherringham Clinic. Gritting her teeth, she'd forced herself to be polite to one of the talking beautician's heads that Richard employed to run the clinic's reception desk.

'It's Dr Daisy Sherringham here.' She'd introduced herself bluntly, cutting into the ritual 'Good afternoon. Holbourne and Sherringham Clinic. Can I help you?'

'Yes, Dr Sherringham.' There had been an edge to the carefully modulated tone that told her the dislike wasn't one-sided after all.

'Could I speak to Dr Richard Sherringham, please?'

'But didn't you know, Dr Sherringham,' the receptionist sounded surprised, 'Dr Richard, left for a lecture tour this morning. He's in New York tonight and . . .'

'Yes. Yes of course. I'd forgotten. How stupid of me.' Tim's disappearance had put everything else out of her mind. She'd only succeeded in giving the idiotic girl a chance to crow over her ignorance of family matters. Gripping the receiver tightly, she'd steeled herself to ask the question that lay uppermost in her mind.

'Has Dr Tim Sherringham been in the clinic today?'

'Why no, Dr Sherringham. Dr Tim hasn't been here. Should we have expected him? I've been on duty all day and the only doctor we have on the premises is the locum . . .'

'Fine. Thank you very much. Sorry to have troubled you.' Daisy had dropped the receiver back on to its hook, her imagination busy with the seeds of the story that the receptionist would undoubtedly nurture, and plant in selected areas of the town. 'Tim Sherringham and his wife don't even communicate with one another. My dear, can you imagine, she even telephoned me to ask if I'd seen him.'

She swore angrily under her breath, then picked up the telephone once more. Where Tim was concerned she had no pride, no pride at all. Her call was answered almost immediately.

'The Sherringham residence.'

'Hello Hare. It's Daisy.'

'Good evening, Dr Daisy.'

'Is Joanna in?'

'Her Ladyship flew out to her father's Italian villa this morning, Dr Daisy. I thought you knew. She did discuss her plans last evening.'

'Of course, Hare. How silly of me.' Hot, hopeless tears had welled behind her eyes. 'Tell me, has Tim been at the house today?'

'Not today, Dr Daisy. We haven't seen him since last night, or should I say this morning, when you left.'

'Fine, thank you, Hare. Goodbye.' Only it hadn't been fine. The last 'ifs' and 'maybes' had been torn out from under her. She longed to crawl into a corner of out-patients and hide until the whole nightmare ended. Tim would find her. Tim, with his strong arms, a smile crinkling the corners of his deep blue eyes.

She hadn't hidden, of course. That would have been infantile and she was an adult. She'd returned to her clinic, cleared her desk and waited until Alan had come looking for her. He'd driven her to the flat, then, when they hadn't found Tim, she'd asked him to do what he'd been pleading with her to do all afternoon. Call the police.

'You couldn't be more specific about time, could you, Doctor?' The sergeant gave her a small friendly smile. She had a vague recollection of seeing him somewhere before. Somewhere where he hadn't been a policeman. A patient, perhaps?

'Tim mentioned the time when he was dressing,' she murmured slowly, desperately trying to piece together the events of the previous night. The problem was, last night had merely been one of the many occasions she or Tim had been called out in the early hours. 'We'd been to a party,' she apologised. 'I was very tired.'

'Whose party was it, Dr Sherringham?' This was the second sergeant, the one who'd introduced himself as Collins, Peter Collins. Daisy had already marked him down as a cold bastard. He was just as polite as the first sergeant, but his brown eyes were frosty, appraising with no hint of inner warmth.

'It was a *bon voyage* party for Tim's brother,' she explained irritably, 'Richard Sherringham . . .'

'Dr Richard Sherringham? The doctor who runs the Holbourne and Sherringham Clinic?' She nodded, angry that she should go up in anyone's estimation, even this sergeant's, because of Richard's influence.

'What time did you get back from the party?' The first policeman, the one Alan had called Trevor, enquired gently.

'About two. We talked for a while, then we went to bed around two-thirty.'

'And the call came?' Peter Collins barked, taking control again.

She closed her eyes tightly against the memory of Tim standing at the foot of the bed pulling on his trousers, his evening shirt hanging loosely on his tall, slim frame. 'I have to get up at . . .' He'd squinted at his watch '. . . three-forty in the morning . . .'

'It was three-forty,' she said flatly.

'Three-forty. You're sure of that?'

'I'm sure.' Daisy opened her eyes and looked at Trevor. There was concern, and perhaps even a little sympathy, mirrored in his eyes.

'Could you tell us what your husband was wearing when he left?' Peter Collins' voice was authoritative. Calm, logical, he sounded just like the sister who'd told her and Judy that the Hawkins foetus was no longer viable. She found herself wondering why the system

38

bled the emotions out of some people, while leaving others intact.

'Your husband's clothes?' he pressed.

She forced herself to concentrate on his question.

'White silk evening shirt. Black trousers, evening trousers,' she added as an afterthought. 'No tie. It's still in our bedroom.'

'Coat?' Collins' pencil was poised over his notebook.

'He may have worn his overcoat.' She stumbled over her words, wishing she could sound as matter-of-fact as the sergeant, all the while hating this minute, cold-blooded dissection of her private life with Tim. 'He left his raincoat in the living-room.'

'Well, that gives us a description of your husband's clothes. Alan's given us a physical description as well as the make, model and number of the car he was driving. We should have something to tell you quite soon, doctor.' The first sergeant pocketed his pencil, and prepared to leave.

'Just a minute, Trevor.' Collins flicked back the pages of his notebook. 'Let's go through it all once again, shall we. I'm not quite sure of one or two points. Bit slow on the uptake,' he apologized flatly, without a trace of regret. 'Any errors of judgement are all on my part, of course, Mrs Sherringham.' He shot a sharp glance in Daisy's direction.

'Dr Sherringham,' Alan corrected for her.

'Quite.' Collins looked hard at Alan. 'Now, if we run through the facts one more time.'

'If you really think it will help.' Mr Bassett was bored. His whole day had been plagued by petty annoyances. To begin with, he'd had to get out of bed earlier than he'd done in years, and his effort had been wasted. The Hawkins baby had been long past saving by the time he'd reached the hospital, and to cap it all, his registrar had taken off without so much as a 'by your leave'. Sherringham wasn't exactly his idea of a perfect registrar, he was far too argumentative to warrant that description. But the man was capable and efficient. He could be left to get on with things . . . and with the decent golfing weather only just beginning . . .

Seemingly oblivious to Bassett's annoyance, Collins sat back in his chair.

'Now let me see,' he began in an irritatingly slow voice, 'it's three-forty in the morning and the telephone rings in your apartment, *Dr* Sherringham.' He looked to Daisy for confirmation.

'It was a little before that,' she snapped. 'Tim mentioned the time when he was dressing. He was up by then.'

'You answered the telephone?'

'It was on my side of the bed.'

'Presumably you spoke to whoever was at the other end.'

'Isn't it usual to speak to whoever rings you?' Her voice was brittle with sarcasm.

'Was it a man or a woman?' he continued blandly.

'A man . . . I think,' she added, her certainty wavering.

'Think again, Dr Sherringham,' Peter Collins insisted. 'This could be crucial.'

'It was a man,' she asserted. 'Definitely a man. All the night telephonists here are men.'

'But the telephone call didn't come from here,' Collins stressed quietly. 'Surely you must have realized that by now.'

'What do you mean?' she demanded. 'Of course it was a hospital telephonist. I took the call . . .'

'And I checked with the switchboard, Dr Sherringham.' Collins deliberately allowed his voice to linger over her name. 'You say your husband responded to a call that came in sometime around three-forty. But the hospital records are quite specific. He wasn't called out until seven-thirty.'

Seven-thirty! Eric Hedley grinning up at her in the canteen. Seven-thirty!

'Then it's true."

'What's true, Dr Sherringham?' Collins enquired sharply.

Daisy could have kicked herself. Why hadn't she stopped to consider for a moment before blurting out her thoughts?

'Eric . . . Eric Hedley, he's a houseman here.' Her voice was harsh, rasping. 'He told me this morning that Tim hadn't been called out until seven-thirty.'

'And you didn't believe him?' Collins looked carefully into her eyes.

'How could I,' she insisted, 'when I knew otherwise?'

'Then you really believe that the hospital called your husband out in the early hours of the morning.'

'I'm certain of it. I took the call myself. Tim mentioned the Hawkins case . . .'

'There's no record . . .'

'Damn the record!' she screamed in an eruption of pent-up emotion. 'Damn! Damn . . .'

'Daisy, it's all right. It's going to be all right.' Alan moved across and perched on the arm of her chair. He cradled her head gently, pulling her face down on to the hairy tweed jacket that she remembered from the morning. Only this time she didn't fight the touch of his hands on her shoulders. She closed her eyes and allowed the tears to fall unchecked. It was so easy to cry, not to think any more about Tim. About last night or the telephone call.

'Dr Sherringham has put up with more than enough for one day, Sergeant Collins,' Judy reprimanded sternly.

'It's the job of the police to establish the facts, Dr . . .'

'Osbourne, Judy Osbourne. And it is possible to establish facts in a civilized manner. Doctors do it all the time,' she said humourlessly.

41

'I think we've enough information to be getting on with, Peter. If Dr Tim Sherringham contacts any of you, you will let us know, won't you?'

'Of course we will, Sergeant . . . Joseph, isn't it?' Impatient to be gone, Bassett rose from his chair.

'Sergeant Trevor Joseph, or Sergeant Peter Collins,' Collins offered calmly, completely nonplussed by the effect his questioning had had on Daisy. 'If you telephone the station they'll get a message to one of us.'

'Or you could always call on Alan, of course,' Joseph smiled. 'He's never yet failed to get hold of me when he wants something done.'

'Thanks for coming, Trevor. I really appreciate it,' Alan replied.

'Any time.' Trevor opened the door. 'After all, I owe you enough favours.'

'Have you any thoughts on what may have happened to Tim Sherringham?' Bassett, hand on door handle, looked at the policemen as though he expected one of them to conjure Tim out of the air.

'We deal with missing persons every day, sir,' Collins answered blandly. 'People disappear for all sorts of reasons. Life suddenly gets on top of them, too much responsibility too soon.' He shrugged his shoulders.

'Believe me, that theory doesn't apply to Tim Sherringham,' Alan interrupted warmly.

'I wasn't speaking personally, Doctor,' Collins continued in a tired voice, as though he were bored with the whole affair. 'Everyone here is far better acquainted with Dr Sherringham than I am, and as such your conjectures about his sudden disappearance will be far more valid than mine. All I'm saying is that every day people walk out of apparently full and happy lives, and never return. The Salvation Army have tens of thousands of such cases on their books.'

'Teenage runaways,' Judy said scornfully. 'Tim Sherringham can hardly be classed as one of those.'

42

'Not everyone who vanishes is a teenager, Dr Osbourne. The Salvation Army will be the first to tell you that youngsters form only a small percentage of the missing persons on their lists. The lure of the bright lights and greener grass is there for everyone. Grown men meet grown women, they have affairs, and on occasion they find it simpler to walk out of one life and start another without waiting around long enough to make excuses . . .'

'Tim isn't having an affair!' Daisy lifted a tear-stained face and stared defiantly at Peter Collins.

'I'd be the last person to tell you he was,' the police-man answered patronizingly. 'What I am saying, to all of you,' he looked around the room, 'is that family, friends, colleagues . . . they frequently come hotfoot to the police with a story about a missing person, all of them fearing the worst, when often there's a perfectly obvious, logical explanation for the disappearance if only they'd look for it.'

'Dr Sherringham,' Trevor Joseph held out his hand to her. 'We've a good description of your husband, and the car he was driving. We'll find him soon. Please don't worry.'

'Thank you, Sergeant.' Daisy shook his hand. She was grateful to him for silencing Peter Collins, but she didn't believe a word he'd said about finding Tim soon.

'Do you have a recent photograph of your husband?' he asked, almost as an afterthought, as he was walking out through the door.

'I have some at home, in our flat.'

'Would you mind if I dropped by and picked one up? I'll ring first.'

'Not at all, Sergeant. Any time,' Daisy replied, the social automaton within her taking over.

The room emptied quickly. The police and Mr Bassett left. Alan walked with them as far as the main

43

entrance. He returned to find Judy sitting on the floor in front of Daisy, silently holding her hand.

'What do you two say to picking up a bottle and a take-away and going over to my place for dinner?' he suggested with forced enthusiasm.

'Carol would have a fit, and quite rightly so at this short notice,' Judy commented. 'Besides, I've already decided. Daisy and I are going up to my place for dinner.'

'A hospital flat?' Daisy made an effort to control the tremor in her voice. 'Thanks, but no thanks. I'm going home.' She knew full well that Alan and Judy were looking at one another behind her back and shaking their heads. 'If Tim's going anywhere, he's going home, and I want to be there when he walks in.' She fumbled for her bag and stood up, but the question hung unspoken between them. What if Tim didn't come back?

Judy braved the silence. 'I'll go with you. Believe me, any variation on the theme I had planned for this evening would be more than welcome.'

'Please don't take this the wrong way,' Daisy said insistently, 'but I'd rather be alone. I have to clean the flat, not to mention sleep. I'm going to need as much as I can get. I'm on duty this weekend.'

'Are you sure you'll be all right?' Alan eyed her with an expression she knew only too well. It was one all doctors used on their patients. Only she wasn't a patient. Not yet.

'If I feel the need to be with someone, you'll be the first people I call. I promise.'

'And you won't have to call very loud for me,' Judy interposed. 'I'll be in your spare room.'

'Judy!'

'I won't take no for an answer. I'm sick of hospital flats, and after this morning's reminder of how the other half lives, you simply won't keep me away. I'd love a bath in your guest bathroom.' Judy picked up her bag and walked to the door. 'First stop, my miserable hovel to grab my toothbrush, then it's your place. After you, Dr Sherringham.'

Ignoring Judy's attempts at cheerful chatter, Daisy crawled the Mercedes along the road home. Judy gently reminded her that they'd been over the road twice already that day, but she couldn't bring herself to pick up speed. She glanced sideways out of the window every few moments, searching for something . . . anything. But inevitably there was nothing.

Reluctantly she parked the car and walked up to the flat, Judy at her side, hope tugging at her nerve endings like a taut elastic band. Perhaps Tim had called? Left a message? Perhaps he'd come back to change his clothes?

But the same bleak emptiness greeted her when she walked through the front door. Nothing.

Judy moved tactfully into the spare room, announcing on the way that she was going to take that long, hot bath she'd promised herself. Left to her own devices, Daisy took off her coat and set about cleaning the flat. She carried the clothes littering the living-room through to their bedroom, and hung them neatly in their wardrobes. Then she made the bed, picking her own and Tim's clothes off the floor. His blue towelling bathrobe lay in a heap behind the bedroom door. She grasped it as a lifeline. Holding it close she sat on the bed. The smell of his cologne was embedded in the soft fibres. She fingered the broken loop of material that prevented Tim from hanging it up properly. She should have sewn it weeks ago . . . Then, like a flood-tide bursting through dam gates, the emotions she'd barely kept in check throughout the day crashed to the surface. Burying her face in the pillows, she sobbed, her fingers wrapped tightly around the sleeves of the robe. Where was he? Why had he gone? Last night had been no different to any other night. He loved her. His last words had been 'Love you'. Surely you knew, had some sort of warning, before your world turned upside-down.

Peter Collins' words sounded dully above her own despairing cries, 'Grown men meet grown women, they have affairs, and on occasion they find it simpler to walk out of one life and start another without waiting around long enough to make excuses . . .' Could that really have happened to Tim? Could he have met some-one else without her knowing, sensing, that he'd changed?

'If we don't eat, we could go to bed for a couple of hours.' Tim's face, suggestive, smiling, had looked round their bedroom door as soon as she had walked in yesterday evening.

'You'll be hungry,' she'd warned, warming to the idea.

'Not. in the way it counts. Here, woman,' he'd commanded.

She'd thrown her coat to the floor and had run to him, laughing. His black hair, wet from the shower, had been plastered to his forehead, and his skin had been damp, smelling faintly of soap. He could never wait long enough to dry himself properly.

'We'll eat at Richard's,' he'd said much later, pulling her naked body along the length of his.

'Pâté de foie gras, snails caviar, and peanuts,' she'd prophesied, snuggling close to him under the duvet.

'Not on your life. We'll raid the fridge. There's bound to be some real food in the house. We Sherringhams are a hungry lot.'

'Don't I know it.'

Their eyes had met and they'd both laughed. He'd loved her at that moment, she was sure of it. And that moment was their life together. Tim could never lie, never conceal his feelings. Richard was the cool one, the one who calculated the value of every smile, every friendship he made. Richard could always be trusted to show polite interest, no matter what his opinion of the person he was dealing with.

'Daisy? Daisy! Are you all right?' Judy's knocking broke into her reverie.

'Fine.' Daisy almost choked on the word.

'There's a policeman here to see you. Sergeant Joseph, the one Alan knows.'

'I'll be out in a minute,' Daisy answered impatiently, resenting the intrusion.

'I'll make some coffee.'

Daisy heard the kitchen door shut and the tap run. Judy was a good friend – not many people would have left her to her own devices this long, she realized gratefully. She dragged herself reluctantly off the bed and into the bathroom to wash her face. It was easy to resist the temptation to glance in the mirror. She knew she looked dreadful. There was no need to confirm it.

Sergeant Joseph was waiting for her in the living-room. Judy was still in the kitchen.

'Hello.' She spoke carefully, deliberately, striving to keep her voice steady and on an even keel.

'Hello again.' The policeman rose from his uncomfortable perch on the edge of the leather chesterfield as she walked in.

'You really can't place me, can you?' he asked, as she sat down in the chair opposite him.

'Please sit down.' She was grateful to him for making it easy for her, for the sensitivity that led him to camouflage his real purpose in coming to see her behind a barrage of small talk. 'I'm sorry, your face *is* familiar, but I can't remember where we met.'

'I was one of your patients. I had a . . .'

'Broken and lacerated legs.'

'You remember ailments, not people?' He lifted a

47

questioning eyebrow. There was a comical expression on his face that made her smile despite the misery that gnawed within her.

'Doctors are like that, I'm afraid.'

The door swung open and Judy walked in with a fully laden tray. 'Excuse my dress, or rather lack of it,' she apologized, swinging the sleeves of her kaftan wide as she laid the tray down on the table between them. 'If you don't mind, I won't stay. I have to dry my hair.' She patted the towel turban on her head.

'Thank you, Judy.'

'Don't go eating any biscuits,' she warned as she left the room. 'They're for him. Not you. We're going to eat later.'

'Yes, Mother,' Daisy retorted.

'I'm glad to see someone's looking after you.'

'Judy's a good friend,' Daisy replied. 'Coffee?'

'Yes, please. White, one sugar.'

Daisy reached out and poured two coffees, leaving her own black and unsugared. 'You're allowed to eat,' she reminded him, pointing at the chocolate biscuits Judy had arranged on a plate. He took one.

'Thank you, this is very civilized, and more than welcome after the day I've had, I can tell you.'

'You're not on duty?'

'No. I've finished. For tonight at least.'

'Thank you for coming to the hospital this afternoon.' She settled back into her chair. 'Alan told me you came as a personal favour to him. I know it should have been a raw young constable.'

'Think nothing of it,' he said quickly, embarrassed by her gratitude. 'Alan's always ready to do something for me whenever I need help. I'm only sorry that Peter was as heavy-handed as he was.'

'Heavy-handed, maybe,' she agreed dryly, 'but undoubtedly right. Don't most people disappear because they want to?'

48

'They're not usually doctors on emergency calls,' he commented uneasily. 'Look, I'd like to be frank with you. I shouldn't tell you this, but Peter's been through a rough time lately. He's a good policeman, but for once he's allowing his personal life to intrude into his work. His wife ran off with another man about a month back. She packed her bags and walked out one day when he was at work. No note, nothing. It took Peter just two days to track them down. They were in her sister's flat in London.'

'I'm sorry.' She wasn't in the least bit sorry. She'd taken an instant dislike to Peter Collins. Her sympathies lay with his wife, whoever she was. It couldn't have been easy being married to a man like that.

'Tell me,' Trevor cleared his throat nervously. He'd obviously been building up to this question through all the pleasantries. 'Does your husband ever work in Dr Richard Sherringham's clinic?'

'No,' she replied shortly. 'Tim and Richard are brothers and they're close. Richard's tried to get Tim to work in his clinic, but he hasn't succeeded yet. Why do you ask?'

'Because some pretty important patients frequent the Holbourne and Sherringham Clinic. And your brother-in-law is pretty important himself. He invites a few friends around for drinks and we all get a night's overtime.'

'I fail to see what Richard's lifestyle has to do with Tim's disappearance.'

'In an ideal world where everyone was treated equally it would have no significance. But we're corrupt enough to treat some people, important people,' he added, 'differently. The men upstairs jumped a little when Peter and I filed our report this afternoon.'

'And now you've come for Tim's photograph?'

He nodded. 'For the moment it will only be used

internally. If the decision is taken to go public, you'll be consulted.'

'Public?' She looked at him, mystified.

'The press, television coverage, that sort of thing.' The coffee-cup shook in her hand. She felt her safe, secure world slide out from under her. 'I'll look for the photograph.' She left her chair and walked over to the wall cupboard. 'These are the most recent pictures I have of Tim.' She handed him an envelope that had arrived from the developers only the week before.

'Nice boat,' he commented, as he flicked through the snapshots.

'Yes,' she answered curtly. A tidal wave of weariness suddenly overwhelmed her. She needed to be alone, to cry, to think, to sort out her battered feelings. She ran her hands over her aching head, wishing that he would go and leave her in peace. This sitting about making small talk, drinking coffee, it all seemed so pointless, so utterly ludicrous. Like worrying what clothes and hairstyle to wear to a funeral.

'I'll take these, if I may.' He picked out two close-ups of Tim's face. One had been taken on board their yacht. Tim was looking out to sea, his hair windblown, his face glowing in the cold sea air. The other had been taken in their dining-room, at a party they'd given to celebrate Tim's promotion to registrar. Alan Cummins had snapped them unawares. They were relaxing at the table, glasses in hand, eyes fixed on one another.

'When will I get them back?' she asked.

'As soon as we copy them.' He rose. 'I must be going.'

'You'll let me know the minute you find anything.'

'I promise. Try not to worry too much.'

'Thank you, Sergeant.' She showed him out impatiently, wanting silence. A peaceful silence in which the phone could ring, the door-bell sound, with Tim standing there.

'I'll be in touch.'

'Goodbye.' She closed the door, leaving him with the consoling thought that at least she wasn't alone. Judy Osbourne was with her. And Judy was a doctor.

'Is she cracking yet?' Peter Collins looked up expectantly at Trevor as he climbed into the car.

'She's on edge, but who wouldn't be,' Trevor replied, refusing to be needled by Peter's bantering tone. The last thing he wanted to do was provoke an argument. Peter had been as unpredictable as a rabid dog for the past couple of weeks.

'Is she alone?'

'Judy Osbourne is with her.'

'The frigid, liberated blonde we met in Cummins' office?'

'That's the one.'

'I know some medicine that would cure that doctor.' Peter started the car.

'Perhaps she doesn't need it,' Trevor suggested evenly.

'Her sort always need it, and never get it. That's why they're so bitchy.'

'And you're the bloke to give it to her?'

'I'm the one.'

They drove on for a short while in silence. Then Peter swung the car into a sudden screeching U-turn.

'What's up?' Trevor enquired mildly. Five years of working with Peter Collins had given him an immunity to even the most erratic extremes in his colleague's behaviour.

'We'll go back on the motorway. You never know.'

'The road's probably worn away. Every patrol car in the district has driven along it by now.'

'Very possibly.' Peter concentrated on the road for a few minutes. 'You know Daisy Sherringham's sort invariably do,' he observed acidly.

'Do what?' Irritation rose like bile in Trevor's throat. Peter could say what he liked about Judy Osbourne, but Daisy Sherringham was another matter. Tim Sherringham was already down in his books as a lucky man. It would be nice to think that someone would be as distraught about his disappearance as Daisy was about Tim's. But then, his chance had come and gone, a long time ago.

'Crack up, of course.' Peter's words bludgeoned into Trevor's thoughts.

'Leave off, will you, Peter,' he retorted with uncommon savagery. 'You've lived in a sewer for so long you don't even know how to come up for air any more.'

'Occupational hazard, old son.' Peter gave a short, mocking laugh. 'It happens to us all. Even you one day, believe me.'

Ignoring Peter's last remark, Trevor sat low in the passenger seat and watched the street lights flash by as they drove from the suburbs towards the main artery that led into the town. His Achilles heel in all this was Daisy Sherringham, and he knew it. He had fancied – no, not fancied – that was a word that applied to pub pick-ups and amateur prostitutes – he'd been attracted to her the very first time he'd set eyes on her, and the situation had been far from romantic. He'd been stretched out on a hard narrow couch in Casualty, trouserless, his battered legs naked in all their torn and bloody glory. Then she had walked into the spartan cubicle and the sun had come out from behind the clouds.

'Are you my angel of mercy?' he'd asked. The whole situation had been absurd. He, the hardened, experienced policeman, able to cope with whatever unsavoury episodes fate tossed his way, had flung out a hackneyed phrase more appropriate to a moonstruck schoolboy.

'I'm the houseman,' she'd replied quietly, in an off-hand manner that told him she was used to dealing with casual romantic banter from male patients. But he'd persisted, wanting to make her see that it wasn't casual. Not in his case.

'Do you mind telling me how you did this?' She'd prodded his leg gingerly with her forefinger.

'I got caught up in an argument. There was a car and a wall. I became stuck between the two, and, as you can see, I lost.'

'That'll teach you to stay in at night.' Her eyebrows had lifted slightly and she'd smiled at him. He'd never seen eyes like hers before, misty grey, with a trace of humour that made him smile himself, despite the pain that thrashed around inside him. Her dark hair had been pinned severely back, just as it was today. Yet he was sure, absolutely certain, that if she let it down it would be long, curling softly at the ends.

'Can you feel this?' She'd touched his right shin. He'd nodded, then a wave of nausea had washed over him. God, how he'd fought that sickness. The ignominy of needing to throw up in front of her.

'Sergeant Joseph is a policeman,' the nurse had chipped in. Strange, he'd thought the nurse good-looking before Daisy had walked into the cubicle; now he couldn't even remember what she looked like.

'Policeman or not, I think you'd better get him a bowl,' Daisy had said.

'We really should get together one night,' he'd blurted out when the nurse had left to empty the bowl. Daisy had glanced up at him coolly, shifting her gaze back from his face to his legs. 'I've got more man in my life than I can handle now, but thank you for the compliment, Sergeant Joseph.'

'More man . . . more man . . . more man . . .' The words echoed at him from the windscreen wipers. Drizzle, the bleak, shiny grey road, and a missing person's report. His present.

'Here you are, door-to-door service. Pick you up at eight tomorrow.'

'OK. Thanks, Peter.' Trevor shook himself out of the past. He was behaving like a lovesick fool. After all, how long had it been – six months? No, a year. He'd forgotten how long it had taken his legs to heal. He was day-dreaming about a girl he'd tried – and failed – to pick up over a year ago.

'What do you think's really happened to this guy, Peter?' he asked as he got out of the car.

'Beats me.' There was an inflexion in Peter's voice that said he didn't really care. 'On the surface, he appears to be a steady enough fellow. Hardly the sort you'd expect to clear off without a word to anyone. But then, you never can tell.'

'And if he hasn't cleared off?'

'You know the answer to that one as well as I do.' Peter's eyes narrowed against the orange glare of the streetlamps. 'There are enough junkies and pushers freaking out in this town to make your average Saturday night mugger look like Orphan Annie. But I'll tell you something for nothing.'

'What?'

'You and your bloody hospital connections have got us stuck with this one. It's my guess we're going to be the lucky sods landed with the legwork. The Sherringham connection has upset them upstairs, and whenever they're upset, we get a mess to clear up.'

'We'll see.'

'Sure you won't change your mind about that drink I offered to buy you?'

'No. No thanks. See you in the morning.'

Peter revved the engine and drove away as Trevor slammed the passenger door. Trevor stood on the pavement for a moment. He looked up at the darkened windows of his flat. This morning he'd been quite content with the two poky rooms, plus the bathroom and

54

kitchen, set over the grocer's shop. But then that had been before he'd seen the Sherringham apartment. So what was his problem? he asked himself angrily. Envy for what he couldn't have? Money on a scale that shrieked inheritance rather than earnings? He pushed his key into the lock of the side door. Then he remembered there was no food in his fridge. He'd have to go downstairs and forage. And what great delicacy lay in store for him tonight in Frank's freezer cabinet? Fish fingers? Beefburgers? A frozen dinner for one? His stomach wilted at the thought. Perhaps he wouldn't bother, just get himself a drink and watch TV until bedtime.

'To hell with it,' he exclaimed to the empty street. Was it any wonder he'd spent the last ten minutes dreaming about Daisy Sherringham? With his life the way it was, what else was there for him to do? He jerked his key out of the lock and began to walk down the street. He'd go to the local, eat a simulated pie, drink some beer, talk to the natives, and who knows, with luck he might avoid turning into a cold, self-sufficient, hard-bitten bastard like Peter. People needed friendship, time out for relaxation. Even policemen.

Just after two in the morning, Peter Collins left the warm, smoky back bar of the White Hart to begin his one-and-a-half mile walk home. On a summer evening it was a pleasant stroll. Leave the pub by way of the beer garden, down the rough wooden steps that led on to the beach, strike out along the shoreline of the curve of the bay that bit into the centre of the town, and into the house through the sandy yard that had once been part of the beach. No roads. Only sea and shore as near to its natural state as tourists, litter, sewage, and the town council allowed it to be.

He'd been taking this route for four weeks now, but never in daylight, only during the dark cold hours of early morning. Four weeks! Ever since that silly bitch Wendy had walked out on him. He'd been so bloody angry then . . . but that had been before common sense and Trevor had prevailed. After all, what would he have accomplished if he'd followed her to her sister's place? He'd only have lost control and gone for her, and that burk she'd run off with. She wasn't even worth that much effort.

He was better off without her. The only part of him she'd damaged was his pride. It had taken him barely a week of hard drinking to write her out of his life. He'd spent some of that time going through the cupboards of the neat suburban semi they'd lived in. He had collected all the important papers he could find; mortgage agreements, insurance policies, every last thread that tied them together; then he'd mailed her the lot. He found a solicitor, told him to arrange a divorce as quickly as possible, a divorce that would give Wendy everything he owned except his clothes and records. And told him to pass on the message that he'd see her in hell before he'd give her a penny more.

That had been it. He'd packed his bags and moved on without a backward glance. His married life was over. Enter Peter the wolf. Four weeks had been enough to show him that the only difference between Peter the wolf and Peter the married man was the absence of argument in his life. It had come as a pleasant, if not altogether unexpected surprise.

Within two days he'd rented the flat. He'd always fancied living next to the sea, but the old Edwardian houses had never been smart enough for Wendy. She'd wanted a garden, her own, not shared. A patio, fitted kitchen, fitted carpets, double glazing, regular mealtimes, twee evenings out with her dull boring friends in nice, plastic pubs, not the dives he frequented. God, how he'd quarrelled with that woman over the petty things she put such store by. He kicked a pebble into the waves that swished gently back and forth on the beach. The best thing she'd ever done was leave him, and the idiot who'd taken her on would soon find out just how shallow she really was. They deserved one another.

Thrusting his hands deep into the pockets of his padded anorak, he stood for a moment and looked out over the dark swaying sea. The lighthouse blinked steadily from the rocky promontory on his far left. In front of it, the moonlight picked out the ragged outline of the wired-off pier. Derelict, dangerous, it remained a testimony to the unpalatable fact that the town didn't have enough money to clear up all the rotting ruins left over from its past.

He walked on slowly. What was it about waves, water, the eternal movement of the sea, that cast a primitive, calming spell on men? Made them thoughtful, quieter? He stepped down to the shoreline, his footsteps mingling with the thick, sucking noises of the water swirling amongst the pebbles. Strange how soon life became a routine. Even a new life. He could easily have taken his car along the coast road that wound past his flat and the White Hart. No copper on the beat would dare stop a sergeant, least of all him, even if they knew he'd had a skinful of beer. But he'd come to like this walk home, even looked forward to it. It provided him with thinking time, and God only knew there was precious little of that during his day. And there wouldn't be while Trevor Joseph took on work that shouldn't be theirs, like this bloody Sherringham case.

Would Joseph ever grow up? Stop being so damned soft, trying to help out every Tom, Dick and Harry who asked for favours. They were attached to the drug squad, for God's sake, not Missing Persons. Not that anyone would know from the way Trevor behaved. A smile and a helping hand for every kid who fell off his bike. A couple of quid for blokes who were down on their luck. Last week it had been a ticket home for a runaway kid. There was no saving the man, he decided irritably. The whole town knew him for a soft touch. Soft in the head, more like it.

The grating noise of pebble hitting rock came from up ahead, and he stopped in his tracks. A shambling shadow was groping its way towards him. Small, stocky, loose-armed, it teetered precariously from rock to rock, bottle in hand. Then he heard the singing, harsh and unmelodious.

'I've got a luv-er-ly bunch of co-co-nuts . . .'

'Dare say you have, Andy,' he intoned in his bored, professional voice.

'Mister? That you, Mister?' A grimy face peered slit-eyed up at him.

'It is. Why are you here, and not tucked up at the shelter?'

'No room at the shelter, Mister. Not no more. There's never any room there. Too many on the streets. Times are hard. Awful hard. Shelter's full. First come first served, that's what the man said. Even a regular can't get in no more. I got to queue like the rest, and they queue too early, Mister. Honest.'

'You stayed out, Andy, didn't you? Stayed out until after they locked the doors?'

'Not me, Mister. I don't like sleeping rough. Not no more. I'm getting too old. I like bed. Bed's better than the beach, Mister. I know that.'

'Drunk, too. Where did you get the money?' Peter demanded.

'You know me, Mister, never got any money,' Andy whined. 'Where would I get money?'

'The same place you got this.' Peter grabbed the end of the bottle Andy was swinging. 'Are the Sally Army giving away free booze now? If they are, it's the first I've heard of it.'

'Found it, Mister. Honest. Found it.' Andy grovelled and cringed in a manner born of long habit. The pretence of humble subservience was more than Peter could bear. The filth, the rags, the lice, the smell he could cope with. But not the total lack of human dignity. It revolted him. Made him sick to the pit of his stomach.

'Keep your booze, Andy.' He suddenly released the end of the bottle. It swung round in Andy's loose grip, half the pitiful contents joining the slime on the rocks.

'Don't waste my booze, Mister,' Andy begged, jerking his head away sharply as if Peter had hit him. 'Please, Mister, don't waste my booze.'

'You've had enough, Andy, more than enough.' Peter took a step forward, then remembered he was a policeman. 'Seen any pushers on the beach today, Andy?'

'Not today, Mister. Not today.' Andy flopped limply on to the pebbles, legs spread out in front of him, arms straggling wide, head lolling like a rag doll's. 'But I'll tell you what I did see, Mister. Give me some change and I'll tell you.'

'Change for what? More booze?'

'Breakfast, Mister. Change for breakfast. For tea and toast. I can get tea and toast up at the day-centre for twenty pence. Only twenty pence, Mister. Please.' Again that grating whine.

Peter hitched up his anorak and fumbled in his trouser pocket. His hand closed over a coin and he flicked it on to Andy's lap.

'Bless you, Mister. You're a regular Mister. They're not all like you.'

'You saw something, Andy,' Peter reminded him irritably.

Andy looked over his shoulder as if he expected someone to creep up on him. Instinctively Peter glanced around too. There was only the moonlight, the light and shadow darkness of the beach. The neon glare of the town glimmering faintly on their left. The broken pier up ahead.

'Ghosts, Mister.' Andy's breath misted in the cool air. 'That's what I seen. Ghosts. They've come back. From when I was a kid. The ghosts've come back.'

'Andy!' Peter threw back his head and laughed. The sound echoed back, mingling with the crash of the waves. 'The only ghost here is the one in your head. It comes out of that.' He pointed at the bottle.

'No, Mister.' Andy craned his head as close as he could towards Peter without actually moving his body. His voice whimpered in awe. 'There's a ghost on the pier. In the show. Everyone knows about the show, Mister. There's no need to go to the Shelter no more, not with the theatre open again. It's warm there, Mister. Like it was a long time ago. When I was little. There's jokes and music again. People laughing, happy people, because the clown's back. You should see him, Mister, his white face, his suit . . . he's all black and shiny, like . . . like . . .' his voice slurred into a jumble of guttural sounds, 'like bags, Mister,' he shouted, grasping triumphantly at the image. 'Them black bags they keep clothes in at the shelter. And he sings, he sings awful pretty, Mister.' His filthy hand reached out and clawed at Peter's trousers, grasping tightly at his leg.

'I can get you in, Mister. I know how.' The grotesque offer wafted on the crest of Andy's fetid breath. Repelled by the man at his feet, Peter jerked his leg sharply, breaking Andy's grip. Andy fell face downwards on to the pebbles, but he continued mumbling. 'They trust Andy. They're my friends. They let me in. I don't need money. I can get you in too. I've got this.' His eyes lingered lovingly on the bottle clutched in his hand. 'We can go now, Mister, if you just help me up.' He stretched out his filthy paw. 'I'll show you the best seats. They're in the back. You can put your feet on

60

the chairs in front. We'll be like lords, Mister. Like
lords . . .' Andy's voice slurred, he began to relax, the
bottle slid sideways between his loosening fingers, then
rolled on to the pebbles, the last of its meagre contents
spilling out on the beach.

Peter stared down at Andy for a moment, then, without a trace of compassion, he rolled him over with his
foot. Andy was dead to the world, dead drunk. Peter
glanced up, measuring the distance between the sea,
and the line of debris and seaweed that lay on the
sand above Andy's head. The fool was lying about two
metres below the high-water mark, and the sea was
still coming in. Damned idiot. He could drown.

Quelling the revulsion he felt, Peter gritted his teeth
and edged his foot beneath the greasy shreds of clothing
that clung to Andy's emaciated body. Gingerly he
kicked the drunk backwards. His foot broke through
the rotting cloth. Damn it, he'd have to touch him after
all. There was no other way.

He left the down-and-out in the scant shelter of the
sea wall. It wasn't that cold. Andy could sleep it off on
the beach. It wouldn't be the first time.

Daisy stirred restlessly in her sleep. A cold draught
blowing across the bed had disturbed her. The current
of cold air wasn't enough to wake her, the powder that
Judy had mixed into her bedtime coffee saw to that,
but it was enough to break her pattern of sleep.

Then something familiar happened, something so
familiar she accepted it completely, unquestioningly. A
body slid into the bed behind her. Icy legs lay at the
back of her thighs, a freezing torso sought warmth from
her back. She reached out and grasped the cold hand
she knew would be there. Intertwining her fingers with
the others, she brought the hand round to her breast,
shivering involuntarily as the cold arm rested heavily
on her warm side. Wrapping her legs round Tim's, she

61

sighed softly in her sleep. She and Tim had a tacit agreement to warm one another after night calls, and she had kept to her side of the bargain. Not like the last time, when he had recoiled from her chilled body.

She snuggled down into her pillow, then quietly, surely, the fog drifted from her sleep-numbed brain. Tim! Tim was back. Here in the bed beside her. She opened her eyes, focused on the familiar outlines. The open door, the dressing-table, its mirror glinting grey reflected light from the bed, the huddled shape that lay behind her own.

Slowly she turned to face her husband, her fingers still clutching his cold hand to her breast. She ran her hands lightly along his naked body, looked into his face. It was then that she choked back a scream. There was no face. No face!

She could feel his body beneath the bedclothes, see his shape outlined under the duvet. Painfully, agonizingly, the scream continued to rise into her mouth, choking, strangling, silent until the full horror of what she saw hit her with all the force of a nightmare. Tim was there in the bed beside her. But his shoulders marked the end of his body. He had no head.

Chapter Three

Judy sat in the canteen pretending to read the article Alan had marked for her in the current issue of the *Lancet*. She had a table to herself. She'd rung Alan's consulting rooms earlier and tried to persuade him to bring Daisy and join her here for the tea break, but he'd refused. The hospital was buzzing with rumour and gossip. He'd ordered tea to be taken to his rooms; that way, he felt, he could at least shield Daisy from the prying eyes and questions for a little while longer.

She glanced up, and out of the corner of her eye spotted a collection of smirking housemen, Eric Hedley amongst them, huddled together round a canteen table that was far too small to hold them all. Determinedly she returned to her article, and tried to drum up interest in the revolutionary surgical techniques that the author had successfully employed in the treatment of Parkinson's disease.

She heard muffled laughter, and concentrated harder on the diagrams in front of her. Tim's disappearance accounted for only a small part of Hedley's glee. She knew only too well what he, and the majority of her male colleagues, thought of her. Realized they were wary of her feminist standpoint.

Her blunt, uncompromising outspokenness invariably put off even the most intrepid Don Juan. None of them ever flung a stray half-humorous pass at her the way they did, Tim notwithstanding, at Daisy. But then, she smiled secretively, none of them had ever seen her naked, had never guessed at the sensual passions that lurked beneath the starched exterior of her doctor's coat. And, most crucial of all, no one had guessed that she was the product of an ill-starred marriage that had not made her averse to men, only to formal, legalized marriage.

She had passed her formative years an unwilling witness to the deteriorating relationship between her parents. She'd watched what had begun as love twist and warp, until it had turned into an ugly, choking parasite that crippled and stunted both the people she loved. Her father and mother, transformed from the loving, witty, and talented people who'd overseen her babyhood, into the bickering, drunken fools who'd blighted and embarrassed her teenage years.

Her parents! Even now, she cringed at the bitter memories that grew more poisonous with the passage of time. They'd both been dead for some years, but still she found herself regretting the might-have-beens.

If only her mother had been more open . . . more honest. Left her father for one of her many lovers. Made her own life . . . built a career for herself. Any one of those 'ifs' might have been enough to diffuse her father's jealousy, make him realize that he couldn't own a woman, not even his wife. Might have prevented the mania from developing within him that finally led him to take a shotgun, first to her mother's head, then to his own.

She had learnt a lesson from her parents' example, and learnt it well. Marriage was a strait-jacket. A stifling strait-jacket that invariably killed the very passions and emotions it was supposed to foster. She had no intention of allowing her own life to be regulated by a man wielding the restrictions and traditions of a left-over medieval institution! Instead, she had sought, and found, another solution which amply fulfilled her sexual and emotional desires. A solution that didn't include juvenile housemen like Hedley.

'You look terrible.'

She woke from her reverie, half expecting to see Hedley or one of the other housemen, poised ready to pump her about Tim. Instead, Trevor Joseph stood before her, two glasses of orange juice in his hands.

'I could say the same of you,' she countered smartly, and with more justification. 'Tell me, is that what the police force calls plain clothes?'

Trevor Joseph shifted uncomfortably from one foot to the other. His frayed, black and white brushed cotton shirt had seen better days, but it wasn't by any means his worst shirt. Plain clothes in the Drug Squad rarely meant reasonable clothes, and today he'd dressed for what was for him normal duty. Black corduroy slacks, smooth and shiny at the knees and seat, trainers with the sole parting company from the uppers in more than one place. No belt. His thick, straight, dark brown hair hung heavily over his threadbare collar, and even his drooping moustache needed a good trim. He didn't need Judy Osbourne to remind him he looked like a slob. He was all too conscious of the fact. It was just his damned luck that Peter had been proved right and they had been assigned to the Sherringham case. And Peter, in a fit of righteous pique, had point-blank refused to stop off on the way to the hospital to allow either of them time to change. 'If upstairs sees fit to move the Drug Squad over to Missing Persons at a moment's notice, then they can bloody well take us the way we are.' That was Peter's attitude, but it sat uncomfortably on Trevor's sensitive nature.

'I'm sorry,' he apologized. 'I was trying to say you look whacked. I'd like to talk to you if I may. I saw your glass was empty, so . . .' He held up the orange juice.

'I was just leaving.' Judy stared irritably at him for a moment. He gave her a timid smile. Gradually her irritation faded in the face of his patient good humour. Trevor Joseph was tall, nearly six foot, but he was anything but intimidating. Slightly built, he was pain-fully thin, and there was a childish pleading expression in his eyes that brought out a maternal instinct she normally kept well in check. The man was pathetic, far too polite to be a policeman.

'I'll drink your orange juice,' she relented. 'But I warn you, I have only a few minutes left of my break.'

'That's all right,' he said diffidently, 'Our people telephoned your administration this morning. We've been given permission to talk to anyone we want to. And as long as we don't actually delay any life or death matters we can take all the time we need.'

'You mean I don't have to trail behind Miss Palmer-Smith on ward rounds for the rest of the morning?'

'Not if you talk to me.'

'Fire away.'

Trevor laid the two glasses down on her table. She looked around the room. All the housemen had left except Eric Hedley, who was deep in conversation with Peter Collins.

'You're here in force,' she commented.

'Peter and I got here an hour ago.'

'And you're questioning everyone?'

'Anyone and everyone we think can shed light on Tim Sherringham's disappearance.' Trevor rummaged in his pocket and brought out a notebook.

'Shouldn't we move to Sergeant Collins' table?' Judy suggested mischievously.

'I don't think that would be a good idea.'

'Have you any clues as to what's happened to Tim Sherringham?' Judy enquired bluntly as soon as Trevor had sat down.

'None, and to be perfectly honest, if any other doctor had disappeared from here we wouldn't even be asking questions.'

'Then you're here just because Tim's a Sherringham?'

66

He nodded in reply to her question. 'Have you any idea who would have been at that party Tim and Daisy Sherringham attended the night before he disappeared?'

'I can guess.' Judy sat back in her chair and looked up at him. 'I was Daisy's bridesmaid six months ago. The reception was held in Richard's house . . . mansion, whatever you want to call it,' she finished in exasperation. 'There were four cabinet ministers present, pop stars, actors, sportsmen, personalities – you name it, Richard and Joanna are friends with it.'

'And Tim?'

'Ah, you are a policeman after all. I was wondering when the real questions were going to start.'

'I don't like the idea of prying into other people's affairs any more than you do,' he emphasized, 'but under the circumstances . . .'

'The circumstances? The circumstances are a doctor who had everything going for him disappearing without rhyme or reason, while his poor wife is half out of her mind.'

'Where is Daisy Sherringham now?' he asked quickly, grasping the opportunity to talk about her.

'Here.'

'Here?' Trevor looked eagerly around the canteen.

'I meant here in the hospital,' Judy snapped, losing patience. 'She had a bad night. I couldn't leave her alone in her flat this morning. And with Tim missing, and Daisy unfit for any real work, I thought it might put too much of a strain on the hospital if I decided to take a day off as well. I persuaded Administration to allow Daisy and me to switch duties. She's working with Alan in the paediatric clinic, so he can keep an eye on her, while I'm stuck with the hospital dragon.'

'The dragon?' He looked at her in bewilderment.

'Miss Palmer-Smith, surgical consultant.' Judy finished her orange juice and glanced over to where Peter

Collins and Eric Hedley were still deep in discussion. 'Your colleague's taking notes. Shouldn't you be doing the same?'

'I've got a good memory,' he said, but he pulled a pencil out of his back pocket all the same. 'Would you say Daisy and Tim Sherringham have a good marriage?'

'Ecstatic.' Judy smiled at the look of confusion on his face. 'I'm not being sarcastic,' she insisted. 'I mean it. Those two are special people, really special, believe me.'

'You've known them a long time?'

'Since medical college.' She looked at him keenly. 'What is this?'

'Anything, any fragment of information you give me may help. At the moment we haven't a single clue. We don't even know what we're looking for. A kidnapping? A runaway? Please . . .'

'Daisy and I went to college together,' Judy continued. 'We arrived on the same day, green and fresh from comprehensive school, believing we'd made it. Little did we know, the real work hadn't even begun. Tim Sherringham was my father.'

'Your what?'

'My father,' she repeated. 'Second and third year students at our college were assigned to freshmen. They're supposed to teach newcomers the ropes, pass on second-hand textbooks, explain the pitfalls, you know the sort of thing?'

'I can imagine.'

'Well, Tim Sherringham was my college father, and Daisy was my room-mate. Being Tim, he took his responsibilities seriously. One day he came over with some notes he thought I'd find useful. That was it. Instant chemistry. They went out together that night, spent every holiday together ever after, and she moved in to his flat, or rather Richard Sherringham's London flat, that summer.'

'Neither of them had anyone else hovering in the background?'

'Not that I was aware of.' Judy found it hard to suppress her anger at the personal nature of the questions. The last thing she wanted was to be disloyal to Tim or Daisy in any way. Why the hell should she sit here discussing their private affairs with Trevor Joseph?

'No other girlfriends, boyfriends, fiancés?' he pressed.

'Daisy and Tim were popular. Of course they'd both been out with other people, they're normal. But it's obvious you've never been to medical college. The workload is horrendous. There's very little time left over for socializing. Once they'd met, they spent whatever little free time they had with one another. Neither of them ever went out with anyone else again, at least not to my knowledge. And although I can't speak for Tim, Daisy certainly didn't have any serious affairs before Tim came along.'

'After they met, were there any quarrels?'

'Nothing. Absolutely nothing. Look, Sergeant Joseph, I'm sorry I can't come up with any dirt for you . . .'

'Would you rather talk to Peter Collins?'

'You bastard.'

'It comes with the job. These questions have to be asked. How they're asked depends more on you than on me.'

'Fire away, policeman,' she gibed.

'Does Daisy get on well with Tim's family?'

'How on earth do you expect me to answer that one?' Judy rested her face on her hands.

'OK, let's put it another way. Do you know of any strain between Daisy and the Sherringhams?'

'What are you getting at?'

69

'The truth, I hope,' he answered shortly.

'All I can tell you is what everyone knows. Tim and Richard are close. Closer than most brothers. Richard brought Tim up. Their father died when Tim was ten or eleven and his mother died before that.'

'So Richard Sherringham is much older than Tim?'

'Fifteen years'

'Would you say Daisy and Richard resented one another in any way?'

'Not at all.'

'No relationship can be this perfect. Surely there must be something?'

'For heaven's sake!' Judy was tired not only physically, but mentally. This questioning was going on for ever. 'Daisy gets on well with Richard and his wife. It's just that . . .'

'What?' Trevor grasped eagerly.

'Richard and Joanna aren't quite like the rest of us.'

'In what way?'

'Blast you for being so bloody persistent.' She grappled with her thoughts for a moment, then she admitted, 'They're rich. Their lifestyle is different. To a new member of the family, or an outsider, they can be a bit intimidating. Distant. Maybe not because they intend it to be that way, but because we're all wary of their money. What they stand for.' She fiddled with her empty glass. 'I'm not putting this very well, am I? Ignore it. I'm probably making a mountain out of a molehill.'

'Not at all,' he said in a less aggressive tone. 'I get the general picture. Daisy said something yesterday about Richard wanting Tim to work in his clinic. Do you know anything about that?'

'The subject of Richard's clinic is guaranteed to start the nearest thing to an argument Tim and Daisy ever have.'

70

'Tim Sherringham wants to work in his brother's clinic?'

'I don't know, or at least I don't think so. I can only tell you what I've gleaned from Daisy. Richard wants Tim to work with him, but most of the time Tim's content to work here.'

'And the rest of the time?'

'We all get fed up occasionally. Tim's not a saint, but I'll say this much for him, he only gets fed up when he can't give his patients the treatment they need. The days when the essential equipment breaks down are the worst. Or when he comes across someone in a clinic who's been on a waiting-list too long, when what should have been a minor problem has turned into major surgery.'

'And Daisy's opinion on Richard Sherringham's clinic?'

'Daisy broadcasts her views to anyone who'll listen. She believes, really believes, in a National Health Service. Everyone getting free treatment whenever they need it.'

'An idealist?'

'An idealist whose dreams shatter every day in the face of the reality of this place,' Judy observed cuttingly. 'Most women would have loved Tim's connections, the family money. Personally, I think Daisy hates it. But that doesn't mean she hates Tim's brother.'

'That sounds too complicated for me.'

'Daisy has little respect for a system that gives the best medical care to the richest people. And that's Richard Sherringham's system. He's a good doctor, some say the best in his field, and Daisy feels his services should be available to anyone who needs them.'

Trevor Joseph laid his black notebook down on the table next to his untouched glass of orange juice.

'You're no nearer, are you?' Judy said. He looked at her. 'You're no nearer a solution,' she reiterated.

'If you mean you've given me no obvious clues as to why Tim Sherringham has disappeared, I'll agree.'

'I can't hand you what isn't there.'

'More's the pity.' He watched as she fiddled with her empty glass. She turned it upside-down on the table and studied the dregs as they slid down the sides of the tumbler on to the stained formica table-top.

'You've told me about the Sherringhams,' he said quietly. 'What about the hospital?'

'What about, what about the hospital?' she enquired flippantly.

'Does Tim Sherringham have any enemies amongst the staff? Does anyone resent him? His connections, his money?'

'Daisy'd be the first to tell you she and Tim have no money, only what they earn.'

'What about his flat, the Mercedes?'

'Gifts from a generous brother,' she stated flatly. 'And if you're talking about jealousy and resentment, the only person in the hospital who falls into that category is the one who's talking to your colleague.' She flicked an angry glance in the direction of Eric Hedley and Peter Collins. 'That particular houseman wanted to be a registrar. Tim was the better man and he got the job. Eric believes he should have been given the post on age and seniority.'

'I see.'

'The other thing you may as well know about Eric Hedley, is that he's a compulsive gossip and a snake.'

'Anything else?'

'I loathe the beast.'

'I'd never have guessed.'

'So, Sergeant, you have a sense of humour after all.'

Trevor smiled at her. 'I have a sense of humour,' he asserted quietly, 'but in my line of work I don't often have a chance to air it. Can I ask you one last question?'

'As long as it is the last one. Frankly, I've had as much of this as I can take.'

'Is there anyone hovering in the background of your life?'

'Is this a pass, or official business?' she demanded testily.

'I could make it official.'

She pressed her hands tightly around the upturned glass on the table. 'I fail to see what the hell my private life has to do with this.'

'Elimination.' Trevor Joseph kept his voice low, soft. 'You're the wife's best friend. Men often have affairs with the wife's best friend . . .'

'And you think . . . My God!'

'I did say elimination,' he reminded her.

'There was someone up until a few months back. A journalist.' She looked up at Trevor. 'He's disappeared too, but don't worry, Sergeant, you won't be asked to look into his case. He was kidnapped in Beirut seven months ago.'

'I'm sorry.'

'Thank you.' She cut him short. 'Now it's my turn to demand something of you.'

'If I can help, I'll try.'

'Go easy on Daisy.'

'I intend to. You said she had a bad night.'

'She did.'

'You're a doctor. Couldn't you have given her something to make her sleep?' There was a hint of reprimand in his voice.

'I did.'

'It didn't work?'

'No.' Judy rose from the table. 'If you don't need me any more . . .'

'Not for the moment, but I may have to come back to you.'

'You'll tell me . . .'

73

'The minute we find anything, I promise.' He walked to the door with her. 'What exactly do you mean by a bad night?' he asked casually as she pressed the lift button.

'You've had your last question, remember.' She turned to face him anyway. 'Daisy woke up screaming sometime around two-ish. She was convinced, absolutely convinced, that Tim had got into bed beside her. She said she felt him next to her.'

'But isn't that only natural? I mean, after yesterday.'

'That after a day like yesterday she'd dream about him? Yes, it's only natural.' The lift clanged open in front of them. 'Only he didn't have his head.'

'What?'

'The Tim Daisy saw, or rather thought she saw last night, was headless. He ended at the shoulders. I won't bore you with Daisy's description of the blood and torn muscles.' She stepped into the lift. 'Freud might have made something of it, Sergeant Joseph. I can't. Goodbye.'

The doors closed, leaving Trevor standing in the empty foyer. Headless! He shook his head in pity. My God! Poor, poor Daisy Sherringham.

The door to the canteen swung open, almost hitting him. Eric Hedley barged out and swaggered past. Time he and Peter pooled information. He walked back into the canteen, and noticed that Peter had brought two coffees to his table. His partner was getting thoughtful in his bachelorhood.

'Well, how did you fare with the lady?' was Peter's opening gambit.

'Nothing, absolutely nothing.'

'I did better.' Peter passed him a coffee complete with envelopes of sugar and tiny tub of milk.

'Judy warned me that Eric Hedley is the hospital gossip. He's universally disliked.'

'Of course he is, old man,' Peter agreed glibly. 'And

you can get more out of a disliked misfit in ten minutes than you can from a full day's conversation with an upright, clean-thinking, right-minded citizen. I thought you would have realized that by now.'

'Peter, there's no dirt in this case.'

'There's always dirt. You've just got to know where to look for it. For starters, self-righteous, blue-eyed, blonde Dr Osbourne is being serviced by your friend Alan Cummins.'

'I don't believe it,' Trevor said flatly. 'Alan and I go back years. He dotes on Carol and the kids. I'd know if there was anything going on.'

'We'll soon find out,' Peter said dismissively. 'According to Eric Hedley, more than one person has seen Alan climb the stairs to Judy's hospital apartment.'

'Even if they are having an affair, which I doubt, it's still got no bearing on the Sherringham case.'

'Now that's where you're wrong.' Peter leaned forward across the table. 'People follow people. Like doctor like doctor. Dr Cummins screws Judy Osbourne and Dr Sherringham screws . . .' He flicked back through the pages of his note book '. . . Dart, Amanda Dart. She's a student nurse in Maternity. It would appear that she and Tim Sherringham have been seen together, whispering, hiding in linen cupboards, leaving the hospital arm in arm when Daisy Sherringham's on night duty.'

'This,' Trevor flicked his index finger at Peter's note book, 'could be the rantings of a jealous man.'

'Could be, or it could be the end of the thread we're looking for. What's the matter with you, Joseph? You're uncommonly touchy on this one. Don't want to see the knight in shining armour or the damsel in distress knocked down to gutter level?'

'And if they don't deserve it?'

'We'll apologize,' Peter said flatly. He picked up his

notebook and drained his coffee cup. 'Are you coming down to the maternity ward with me, or not?'

Trevor finished his coffee and followed Peter out through the door. There was a bitter taste in his mouth that had its origins in more than just foul instant coffee. Peter had him taped for what he was. A romantic. But was it really so naïve of him to expect that most people only slept with their partners? That some women didn't sleep with any and every man who made a pass at them behind their husbands' backs? Peter's wife, his girlfriend, surely they were the exception, not the rule?

'Sergeant . . .'

'Collins, Peter Collins.'

'Sergeant Collins.' Sister Hemming gave him the full benefit of her most withering expression. It might have stood a chance on a lesser man.

'Sister Hemming, we're not here for the benefit of our health. We're engaged in police work. Now, if you'd like us to call Hospital Administration, we'd be only too delighted to do so.'

'That won't be necessary,' she replied curtly. 'I received their directive this morning. But I still fail to see what useful information Nurse Dart can possibly give you.'

'She works on this ward. Dr Sherringham . . .'

'Dr Sherringham is the registrar. Nurse Dart is a student nurse,' the sister stated firmly. 'I can assure you she knows nothing that could possibly be of any interest to you.'

'Perhaps we can be the judges of that,' Peter said evenly. 'Now, do you have a room that we can use to interview Nurse Dart?'

The sister knew when to give way. 'You may go into my office.' She thrust the door open grudgingly. 'I'll send Nurse Dart in immediately.'

'I'm glad I'm not about to have a baby.' Trevor closed the door behind him.

'Tartar of the old school.' Peter sat behind the sister's desk. Pushing a tray full of patients' notes to one side, he put his feet up.

'If there is anything between Tim Sherringham and this nurse, the sister certainly isn't in the know.' Trevor perched on the windowsill behind Peter.

'But then she's hardly the type of warm, loving human being that you'd want to confide in,' Peter muttered laconically.

There was a timid knock at the door.

'Come in,' Peter called out loudly.

'Sister said you wanted to see me.'

'Yes. Come in. Sit down.' Peter pointed to the only other chair in the room, a hard chair that faced the desk.

Any doubts Trevor might have had about Hedley's allegation disappeared the moment Amanda Dart walked into the room. His first impression was of spectacles. Huge, black, cheap frames holding deep pebbled lenses. The rest of her was insignificant. A peaky face balanced on top of an inadequate body. Scrawny arms and legs that reminded him of winter branches with the bark scraped off, protruded from a regulation yellow, short-sleeved uniform dress. She was tiny, no more than five foot tall. Her hair was straight, mousy, cut short in an unfashionable, institutional style. Orphan Annie would have looked like royalty in comparison. And Tim Sherringham, six foot six inches, one-hundred-and-ninety pounds, blue eyes, black curling hair, by all accounts possessing the kind of looks that attracted women like ants to sugar, and affluent and sophisticated to boot, was supposed to be having an affair with this girl. Never in a million years. This time Peter really had led them down the wrong alley.

Amanda sat down, her weak brown eyes peering

77

up anxiously at Peter, her hands twitching nervously, fiddling with a grubby handkerchief that she wrapped and unwrapped round her fingers.

'Don't be afraid, there's nothing to worry about.' Peter's gruff tones made her feel even more uncomfortable.

'You're policemen?' she faltered in a small voice.

'That's right. I'm Sergeant Peter Collins, and this,' he indicated Trevor, 'is Sergeant Trevor Joseph. We're here to ask everyone questions about Dr Tim Sherringham. You know Dr Sherringham?' She nodded, too afraid to speak. 'You know he's disappeared?' She nodded again, then bent her head and looked down at her lap, and for the first time Trevor noticed red rings around her eyes. She'd been crying. Tim Sherringham or the bloody-minded ward sister?

'Did you know Dr Sherringham, I mean Dr Tim Sherringham, very well?'

'Everyone knows Dr Sherringham,' she whispered. 'He's kind. Always got a word for everyone, no matter who they are or what they do. He treats everyone the same, whether they're a consultant surgeon, or a student nurse . . .' Her voice faltered and she blew her nose noisily into the handkerchief. Trevor's sixth sense needled irritatingly. There *was* something between Tim Sherringham and this girl after all. He could feel it. The question was what? Tim Sherringham couldn't possibly have any romantic interest in Amanda Dart. Not with Daisy waiting at home. He wouldn't believe it.

'What did Dr Sherringham say to you?' Peter demanded forcefully.

'Not a lot.' The girl made an effort to pull herself together. Trevor found it painful to watch as her hands knotted themselves in agonizing spasms. 'He said no more to me than he said to any of the other student nurses.'

78

'We've heard differently, Nurse Dart.'

Her eyes grew round behind the lenses. 'I don't understand,' she ventured.

'In that case, I'll spell it out for you.' Peter lifted his feet down and leant across the desk towards her. 'We have witnesses who have seen you and Dr Sherringham leaving the hospital together. These same witnesses have seen you and Tim Sherringham whispering in linen cupboards, sluice rooms. Do you understand me now?'

'I don't know what you're trying to say.' Her whole body was quivering. She was clearly terrified.

Trevor stepped in. 'We're trying to help Dr Sherringham. He could be hurt, lost somewhere, in trouble. We simply don't know. The only thing we do know for certain is that he disappeared while driving to this hospital. You've worked on this ward with him. You must know something of what goes on. He told his wife he was coming in to operate on a Mrs Hawkins. Was this person important to Dr Sherringham?'

'You'd better ask Sister,' she said humbly, sidestepping the question. 'I'm only a student nurse.'

'But you do know the patients on this ward?' he pressed. 'Mrs Hawkins, for instance?'

'Yes, I know Mrs Hawkins. She lost her baby.'

'You haven't answered Sergeant Joseph's question,' Peter broke in heavily. 'Was Mrs Hawkins important to Dr Sherringham?'

'She'd had a lot of miscarriages. Dr Sherringham tried to reassure her, tell her it would be all right this time. But she was no more important to him than any of the other patients. He treated . . .'

'I know, he treated everyone the same.' Peter stared coldly at her. 'What about the times you went off alone with Dr Sherringham?' he demanded. 'Where did you go?'

'I never went anywhere with Dr Sherringham,' she

insisted. The tears were back in her eyes. Trevor could see them welling up, misting her lenses.

'I could take you down to the police station,' Peter threatened.

'I'd still know nothing. Nothing, I tell you. I know nothing.' Her voice wavered in hysteria, then her sobs began, hoarse, low-pitched.

'Amanda,' Trevor jumped down from the windowsill and knelt before her. With his hands on her shoulders, he looked up into her face, 'I think you do know something. Why won't you tell us what it is? However trivial you believe it to be, it could help us. It could be more important than you think.'

'How many times have I got to tell you, I don't know anything, I can't tell you anything. I can't help.' She reached up and pulled her glasses roughly from her face. They were soaked in tears. There were angry red pressure marks at the sides of her nose where the frames had rested. She scrubbed at her eyes with her dirty handkerchief. Trevor felt as though he were holding a child. A grubby, crying child.

'You can lock me up if you want.' She turned her misted eyes blindly to where Peter sat. 'I don't care. You can do whatever you want to me. But you can't make me tell you any more than I've already said.'

'We'll see about that.' Peter leant back in his chair and rubbed the side of his nose lightly with his thumb. 'I think we'll start with your version of the last time you and Dr Tim Sherringham were on duty together.'

Twenty minutes later, Amanda Dart left the office. She sagged like a limp rag that had been wrung dry. Trevor didn't feel much better. Only Peter had survived the interview apparently unscathed. And they were still no further forward.

'I don't know about you, old man, but I want back

to the drug squad, and back now.' Peter returned his feet to the corner of the desk.

'There has to be something that we're missing.' Trevor turned away from the cluttered office and stared out of the window. Matchbox cars and miniature people moved in and out of the car park below. Neat ranks of cars glinted in the spring sunshine. His eyes shifted automatically along the rows, pausing at every blue car. He couldn't stop searching for a particular type of Fiat.

'Let's look at what we've got.' Peter reached inside his jacket and produced a pack of cigars. He offered one to Trevor. Trevor shook his head. 'We've got a doctor who gets called out at three-forty in the morning, only he isn't really, at least, not according to the records.' He struck a match on his boot and lit his cigar. 'We've got a hospital department and a telephonist who swear that Tim Sherringham wasn't paged until seven-thirty that morning, by which time he's disappeared off the face of the earth. We've got a clean stretch of motorway, a blue Fiat that's vanished along with the doctor, an apparently normal wife who's close to flipping her lid.' Trevor turned away from the window and gave Peter a hard look. 'Oh yes,' Peter grinned, 'you're not the only one who's heard Judy Osbourne's story. A clerk in Admin listened in on Judy and Alan Cummins' conversation early this morning. I know all about the headless husband.' He drew on his cigar. 'Where was I? Oh yes, we've also got a snide bastard who insists that Tim Sherringham was having a torrid affair with a girl who looks and acts like a child at the most pathetic end of adolescence. I admit it. I'm stumped. At this stage in the game I'd believe someone who told me that Tim Sherringham had run off with a circus strong man.'

'It doesn't make much sense,' Trevor agreed.

'It doesn't make *any* sense. On the other hand, we

could forget this nurse, discount the tales of happy marriage and accept that Tim Sherringham was leading a double life, and that he simply slipped into it with some dolly bird he picked up on the way.'

'There's just one thing wrong with that theory.' Trevor lifted the window catch and flung the casement open. 'A registrar in a busy general hospital doesn't have much time for a double life. Tim Sherringham has only had one weekend off in the last two months, and then he and Daisy sailed down to Cornwall. Apparently they never left their boat.'

'Tried the evenings?'

'Two nights out of three he and his wife leave the hospital together around six or seven. If one or the other is on duty, more often than not they both sleep in the duty flat.'

'Togetherness. Damn and blast their loving mediocrity.' Peter spat a curl of tobacco from his mouth. 'It leaves nothing for us to grab hold of.'

'Sergeant Collins.' The sister threw the door open. 'If you've quite finished browbeating my staff . . .'

'We have, Sister.'

'Then I'll thank you to put out that cigar. There's no smoking allowed in this office or on the wards.'

'In that case, we'll leave. Until next time.' Peter lifted his feet from the desk, and rose from the chair. 'Thank you for your hospitality.'

'Where to now?' Trevor asked, as soon as they were out in the main corridor. 'Ask more questions?'

'No point.' Peter walked decisively towards the lifts. 'We've done all we can. If upstairs want more, they can call in the heavy squad.'

'Alan, can I have a quick word?' Judy stuck her head around the door of Alan's consulting office.

'If you'll excuse me,' Alan apologized to his small patient and her anxious mother. 'I won't be a moment.'

82

Daisy left the chair she'd been sitting on all morning, and followed him out through the door.

'Daisy!' Judy protested.

'If you're going to talk about Tim, I'd rather hear the worst for myself,' Daisy said quietly. Alan looked at her keenly. She was calm. Too calm. Had been all morning. Sooner or later the façade would shatter. It was inevitable. He only hoped that someone would be able to pick up the pieces when it happened.

'Daisy, it's nothing more than a rumour. Gossip of the worst possible kind. It's just that I wanted to tell . . . warn Alan before he heard it from someone else.'

'If it's about Tim's disappearance, then I think I have the right to hear it too,' Daisy insisted.

A nurse walked past. 'Let's move out of this corridor.' Alan pushed Judy and Daisy into one of the examination cubicles, pulling the curtain behind them. 'Now, if we keep our voices low, maybe the rest of the hospital won't hear what you have to say, Judy.'

'Daisy, I'd be happier if you weren't here,' Judy pleaded.

'Tell me, Judy. Straight.'

'I said it was rubbish,' Judy warned as she paced up and down. 'Those two policemen, your friend and his sidekick,' she looked accusingly at Alan. 'They've been asking questions around the hospital all morning.'

'I saw them arrive.'

'They've talked to one person too many. I'd say it was Hedley.'

'And?' Daisy demanded.

'Whoever it was told them that Tim was having an affair with one of the nurses in maternity.'

The silence lasted only a few seconds. 'Which one?' Daisy might have been enquiring about a dress Judy had bought.

'The small mousy one with glasses.'

83

'Dark?'

'I think her name is Dart, Amanda Dart.' Judy laid her arm around Daisy's shoulders. 'I told you it was preposterous.'

'But it's being said.'

'You know what this place is like. There's always gossip. I wanted to talk it over with Alan. Discuss the best way of tackling it.'

'But shutting me out?'

'Daisy, you have enough to cope with as it is. Judy was thinking of you . . .'

'I realize that, Alan. Thank you for your consideration, but I am neither an invalid nor a child.' She sat on the edge of the examination couch. 'Have you heard anything else?'

'No. Nothing new. Daisy,' Judy caught hold of one of her friend's hands, 'wouldn't it be better if you went home, rested for a while. I could take some time off and come with you. We could . . .'

'We could what?' Daisy questioned coldly. 'Search for Tim's headless body, or sit and play patience until some stranger stumbles across what's left of him?'

'Daisy, it was a nightmare.' Alan felt a *frisson* of apprehension as he faced the strength of her conviction. 'Is it any wonder you had strange dreams last night? Under the circumstances . . .'

'If you'll excuse me,' Daisy interrupted, not even attempting to listen to what he was trying to say. 'I'm going to do what I should have done yesterday.' She took off her white coat. Folding it neatly, she laid it on the end of the examination couch.

'Daisy.' Judy grabbed at her sleeve, stopping her from walking out. 'Where are you going?'

'Don't worry, I shall be quite safe.' Daisy looked calmly from Alan to Judy. 'I'm going to Richard's. Hare will know how to contact my brother-in-law. Richard will know what to do.'

84

'Daisy, wait, I'll go with you.' Judy fumbled with the buttons on her coat.

'Thank you, but that won't be necessary, I'll go alone.'

'Shock,' Alan diagnosed, shaking his head as Daisy's heels clattered down the corridor towards the main entrance.

'She shouldn't drive, not in that condition,' Judy insisted.

'Run after her.' Alan picked up the internal phone from the wall. 'I'll get a taxi to meet you at the main entrance. Stay with her until she's in Richard's house.'

'I'll do that.'

'Once she's there she won't be our problem any more. The butler will take care of her, and Richard Sherringham will return as soon as he's told about Tim. She's not really our responsibility. She's one of them, a Sherringham.'

'Sherringham or not, she's my friend,' Judy called, as she ran after Daisy.

Amanda Dart shut herself into her minute cell in the nurses' hostel. The sister had made her leave the ward. She'd wanted to work, but the old bag had forced her to go. Told her she wasn't fit to be on duty. Fit! What did that old battleaxe know about fit, or feelings? She wasn't even human. She didn't know what went on inside people. How you could work day in, day out for weeks on end, thinking, worrying the whole time. Dr Sherringham had been the only one in the whole hospital to notice something was wrong. He'd been the only one to take the trouble to listen. And now he'd gone. Perhaps for good. Just like . . .

'No.' She threw herself on her bed and buried her face in the pillow. She'd wanted to tell the police. God, how she'd wanted to talk, to them, to anyone. But Dr Sherringham had said no. Tell no one, not until they knew more. If it had just been the one with the moustache . . . He seemed kind. Nicer than the other one. But Dr Sherringham had been so positive. No policemen. And she'd respected his decision. After all, what had the police done for her? Laughed at her. Told her waifs and strays were ten a penny. That they could go to the Shelter and pick up any number they wanted any night of the week. Who cared what happened to runaways. They come, they go. Drifters! The country's full of them.

'Full of them . . . full of them.' She could almost hear the desk sergeant's sneering voice. Then she slept. When she woke, her room, never bright, was shrouded in shadows. A door banged somewhere down the hall. She could hear voices, cutlery clattering in the distance. Supper time.

She pulled herself reluctantly from her bed. The cover was damp where her face had lain. She'd been crying in her sleep. She filled the sink with cold water and washed her hands and face. Then, wiping her glasses on a towel, she put them back on. She would go and see the priest. He'd promised her he'd help if he could, and perhaps he'd heard something new about Robin.

Her hair needed combing. She did it mechanically without looking at the result, then she reached for last year's sale bargain brown raincoat. She picked up her beige vinyl handbag and checked the contents. Her keys, her purse – there was four pounds and some odd silver in it – a pocket mirror, a comb. Everything she needed. She'd skip supper; she could always pick up some chips later if she was hungry. She had one last pang of conscience before she left the room. Dr Daisy, Dr Sherringham's wife.

Dr Daisy, as everyone in the hospital knew her, was beautiful. Tall, slim, long glossy dark hair, soft grey eyes, a sweet smile, lots of friends. She was always

86

talking or laughing with someone, calling out to the convalescent patients whenever she walked past their beds. Confident, self-assured, intelligent and beautiful, Dr Daisy was everything Amanda had ever wanted to be. What if Dr Daisy had heard the same story the sergeant had, and worse still, believed it? Shouldn't she go and see her? Tell her everything? After all, Dr Daisy had a right to know the truth. Tomorrow! That was it . . . she'd go into the hospital early tomorrow, find Dr Daisy, tell her what she knew. She opened the door and stepped out into the corridor.

'Amanda!' Emma Hasset, her arms full of paper plates and cups, bumped into her. 'Aren't you coming to Claire's hen party?' she asked, not unkindly.

'No. No, thank you,' Amanda stammered awkwardly. She still found it embarrassing to be invited to anything in the hostel. She didn't fit in, no one really liked her, so why did they bother?

'Come on, let your hair down for once. I've got some wine,' Emma waved a two-litre bottle under her nose, 'and Claire's bought tons of cake . . .'

'I'm sorry, I'm going to visit someone.'

'Well, call in when you get back?' Emma suggested persuasively. 'There's bound to be a crumb or two left over.'

'Thank you, I'll do that.' Amanda turned away from Emma and locked her door, then walked quickly down the corridor.

She knew, and Emma knew, that she wouldn't go anywhere near Claire's room. But they had kept up the pretence. Amanda was too sensitive, too conscious of her background to let anyone get near her. The upbringing that had singled her out as 'different' had remained with her, had become ingrained in her character until now she really was different from the rest of the student nurses. The dirt, the squalor she had struggled to cope with during a childhood that

87

was constantly miserable. The hand-me-down-clothes mentality she couldn't escape from, even now, had scarred her more than the beatings her drunken father had inflicted indiscriminately on the whole family. For the first time in her life she had a little money of her own, had done for nearly two years, but her monthly wage packet gave her no sense of security. Perversely she still bought the cheapest, never the best. She wasn't worth the best. And that sergeant, that ridiculous sergeant, how could he have repeated the gossip once he'd seen her? Her and Dr Sherringham. Was the man blind, or stupid?

Andy was stiff and cold. Had been all day. Ever since he'd woken up on the beach. But there wasn't going to be no beach for him tonight. He'd go to the pier. That's what he'd do. It was warm in the old theatre. Warmer than outside, and there was the sea to listen to. It made him feel good, and the clown might be there. The clown could make him believe he was a child again. All he needed was some change. Change for a bottle, and he'd be just fine.

He shuffled down the promenade, heading away from the pier towards the town. There'd be no change close to the pier. Too many looking for it around there. And no one dropping it. Too many like him. That was the problem. He screwed his eyes up tightly, then looked up at the sky. It was dark. Night already.

Bending double, he poked in the grassy, weed-choked verges, picking up anything that glittered. A milk bottle top, a sweet wrapper . . . a washer. He secreted the washer carefully in his greasy rags. It might be valuable. Someone might give him change for it. One of those in the Shelter who was too simple or too far gone to know the difference between change and washers.

The moon was rising over the bay when he reached the end of the promenade, and he'd found no change.

If he didn't find something soon it would be too late. The off-licences would be closed, and they never let him in the pubs. Threw him out before he'd even reached the bar. Just because they had change and he didn't. There was nothing for it but to walk back. The theatre was warm whether he had a bottle or not. He stared at the beach. The tide was in, washing close to the sea wall. Perhaps there'd be change down there.

He felt his way carefully down the steps to the beach. The wall and the steps were both crumbling, but that wasn't why he fingered the stone work. Once Blackie had found change in one of the cracks. He'd shown it to Andy. It was a gold one. A pound. They'd spent it on cider. Blackie was always one to treat you when he fell lucky. Fool! He, Andy, knew better than to treat anyone. A bottle didn't go far these days. Not as far as when he first started. Back then a bottle would last him all day.

He kicked his way along the shoreline, scuffing the sand with his shoes. Gravel and small shells poked their way into the gaping holes in his boots. Then a wave came and wet his feet. Soaked them. Next they'd be cold. And there was nothing worse than cold feet. His Mam always used to say, 'Keep your feet warm, Andy. Whatever you do, keep your feet warm.' How could he now they were wet?

He sat down and took off his shoes and socks. He would spread them out on the wooden boards of the theatre. They might dry by morning, and in the meantime he'd wrap his toes in a bag. He knew where there was a pile of good bags. On the pier, hidden under the stage in the far corner next to the machine that hummed. Thick, brown paper bags that kept you really warm, not like the black bags in the Shelter that stuck to your skin, glued tight by your own sweat. There was no warmth in black bags.

He found his prize in the shallows. Soft, squishy,

wet, it was bobbing up and down with the gentle movement of the incoming waves. He picked it up and unzipped it. A stream of water thickened with goodies poured out. He fished carefully in the water, closing his fingers around a comb, and a broken mirror. He tucked them away in his rags. You never knew. They could be worth change. There were girls in the Shelter now, young girls. They might give him change for a comb and a mirror. He thrust his hand through the open zip. He felt something. Keys. A small bunch of keys. He held them up for a moment, then threw them away in disgust. Keys weren't worth anything. He heard the plop as they landed on the surface of the water. They disappeared quickly. He'd throw the handbag too. Bags could catch you out, trip you up. He'd found that out a long time ago. Never keep anything that could be recognized. Someone would see it, and then there'd be trouble. They'd want the comb and the mirror back, and . . . A grin cracked through the grime on his face and framed his few broken, blackened teeth. He pulled out a purse. It was wet like the bag, but he could feel small, hard circles through the sodden cloth. Change. Lots of change. He'd have his bottle after all.

He emptied the coins swiftly into his hand, secreting them in the same folds of rag that concealed the comb and the mirror. Then he threw the purse and the handbag after the keys and walked away.

Lightened of its waterlogged load, the handbag floated on the surface of the waves, its pale colour standing out in sharp contrast to the inky streaks on the blue-black sea. Andy climbed on to the promenade, singing as he went. He was happy. He had his change, and soon he'd have his bottle. Wet feet didn't matter. Not when he'd be warm and dry tonight. With a drink inside him to keep him company.

'Dr Daisy.' Hare glided noiselessly before her chair, as

though he were moving on well-oiled wheels. 'I'm sorry it's taken so long to reach Dr Richard. He's on the telephone now. You can take it here.' He handed her a cordless phone on a silver salver. He didn't even trust her to walk to the telephone, she thought wryly.

'Daisy, I'll leave you to it.'

'No.' Daisy caught at Judy's hand. 'Stay, please.'

She picked up the receiver. 'Richard.'

'Daisy. What's wrong?' Terse and to the point, that was Richard. She swallowed hard.

'It's Tim.' She choked on the revelation. 'I don't know where he is.'

'What you mean, you don't know where he is?'

Daisy flinched as his impatience travelled across the Atlantic. 'He left to go to the hospital the night before last.' God, had it only been two days? 'No one's seen him since. Richard, the police say he has a woman, but I know . . . I know . . .'

'Daisy? Daisy? Are you there?'

Unable to speak, she nodded.

'Daisy? Daisy!'

Judy gently took the receiver into her own hands. 'Richard, it's Judy Osbourne.'

'What's happened?' he demanded.

'Tim's disappeared.'

'What do you mean, disappeared?'

'No one's seen him since he left to answer an emergency call the night before last.'

There was a brief silence at the other end. Judy could almost hear the cogs in Richard's mind moving, turning, weighing up the situation. 'I'll leave for the airport now,' he said briefly. 'Where are you telephoning from?'

'Your house.'

'Good. Tell Daisy to stay there. Put Hare on.'

'Hare,' she called out loudly.

He was standing behind her chair. 'Dr Osbourne?'

91

'Dr Sherringham would like to speak to you.'

The butler took the receiver. Judy looked helplessly at Daisy. She was sitting hunched in a massive green leather chair that dwarfed her slender figure, staring dry-eyed at the green and gold pattern on the Persian carpet. Judy would have felt better able to cope if Daisy had been ranting and raving. Alan had diagnosed shock. Well, sooner or later it was going to give way. But to what? Judy glanced down at her own feet, not knowing what else to do.

'Dr Daisy?' Hare handed Daisy the telephone. 'You don't have to say anything,' he suggested diffidently, 'just listen.'

'Daisy. I'm leaving for the airport now. I'll be with you tomorrow. Stay at the house until I arrive.' There was a click, then the line went dead.

'If you'll drink this, Dr Daisy.' Hare removed the receiver from Daisy's hand and pressed a glass into it. Judy watched impotently. Already, she had been relegated to the position of onlooker. The Sherringham machine had ground into action, manipulating, controlling. It was taking over, and it was nothing if not efficient. Tomorrow, Richard would be here, and she'd be superfluous. Alan was right. Daisy's pain, Tim's disappearance, they were none of her concern. Daisy was a Sherringham, and from a distance of three thousand miles, Richard had assumed command.

Chapter Four

Twenty years before Tim married Daisy, Dr Theodore Sherringham, an extraordinarily successful psychiatrist, even by California standards, introduced his eldest son, Richard, to his newest research assistant. Hand-picked from among his most brilliant students, she was blonde, beautiful and the daughter of an old friend, a rich, influential British politician. But none of those factors had swayed Theodore in making his choice.

Ability, and ability alone had secured Lady Joanna Holbourne the coveted post. Richard noticed Joanna's blatant and complete adoration of his father, and smiled at his father's indifference to her physical charms. Theodore Sherringham lived for his work, and Joanna would have been treated with the same polite indifference whether she'd been man, woman or trained ape.

Richard had extended his fleeting visit long enough to dine with his father and Joanna. He'd watched Joanna flutter her eyelashes, and had listened as she talked in impressive laboratory jargon in an attempt to gain Theo's attention, then he'd left the table and driven off to return to the Los Angeles hospital that had offered him an opportunity to develop his own budding surgical career.

Three weeks later, Theodore Sherringham's world fell apart, taking with it all Richard's hopes for his own future.

Theodore's professional demise was well documented by the media. He had paid twenty-five students to take part in an experiment. What the students hadn't been told, and the press never discovered, was that the experiment had been designed to test the power of a new hallucinogenic drug Theo was trying to perfect.

Joanna had hired the student bar on the fourteenth floor of the main campus building. She'd set up a buffet and created a party atmosphere. Quite what went wrong was never publicly divulged, but that didn't stop the television crews and the papers from wild speculation. Was it mass hysteria that led to fifteen of the students throwing themselves out of the windows to their deaths on the concrete below? Was it some kind of induced madness that led to the remaining ten students being carried out of the building in strait-jackets?

The resulting outcry forced Theodore to close his successful clinic, research laboratory and the medical school that he'd built out of nothing more than his own wits and ability. Broken by the scandal, he killed himself. And it was Richard who found him, slumped lifeless over his desk, a brain spattered bullet embedded in the wall behind his head.

Richard was devastated by the loss of the man who had been father, mentor and friend for as long as he could remember. But worse was to follow. An army of reporters camped outside his father's house for days on end. Tim, away at boarding-school, was harassed by the media. Richard's contract was terminated by the Los Angeles hospital.

By the day of his father's funeral he'd understood exactly why Theodore had committed suicide. A strong police presence ensured that the press were kept at a distance for the first time since Theo's death. He'd stood slightly separate from the tiny group of mourners, the few who, despite the scandal, had remained loyal enough to attend the interment. The quiet peace of the cemetery closed in around him until the promise of eternal rest presented an increasingly attractive alternative to life. Then Joanna stepped in and stood beside him.

Despite her own grief, she'd salvaged what she could of Theo's assets, had collected Tim from his school and had even arranged the funeral. He'd been grateful to her for that much, and genuinely sorry when she'd announced her imminent return to England after the ceremony. Then she'd extended an invitation to him to follow as soon as he could.

He took the lifeline she offered. He ordered his father's lawyers to convert all of Theodore's assets into cash. Then he left for England, taking Tim with him.

George, Lord Holbourne, Joanna's father, was waiting for him. Joanna had spoken highly of both Sherringhams, father and son, and discreet enquiries into the value of the Sherringham fortune, coupled with the six-thousand-mile distance from the scandal, enabled George to greet the son of his old friend with very good grace.

Holbourne influence and Sherringham money won Tim a place at one of England's best public schools, and secured Richard's membership of three exclusive London clubs. During Richard's inaugural dinner at one of these clubs, George casually mentioned the run-down clinic he owned. Richard was grateful for the suggestion. He'd already realized that England offered a new life, free from the destructive tentacles of the scandal that had ruined his father. He visited the Holbourne Clinic, and saw the raw, ready-licensed material he needed to open his own, private hospital. It also had the added advantage of an old, well-respected name to attract the right kind of custom.

The day after his visit, Richard bought a half share in the Holbourne Clinic, turning it into the Holbourne and Sherringham Clinic. Then he set to work on its transformation.

George watched from a distance, well satisfied with

the changes Richard intended to make, but Joanna visited the clinic regularly to offer suggestions which Richard, more often than not, acted upon. Their mutual grief brought them closer together. Lonely, a little lost in an unfamiliar land, Richard made tentative moves towards Joanna. And she responded. Somehow, almost without him knowing how it had happened, he found himself married to her. The wedding was splendid. One British magazine went so far as to call it 'the society wedding of the year'. It was left to the American press to hit a sourer note.

The exiled prince has married his princess. It remains to be seen whether he can find her a castle, or attract a court.

Even before the article had appeared, Joanna had scoured the area around the clinic for a suitable plot of land on which to build. Planning restrictions or vast modern estates plagued her schemes at every turn, until an optimistic estate agent sent her details of a white elephant that had been mouldering on his books for years.

Grenville Manor had stood empty since the end of the Great War. A barn of a house set in forty acres that bordered the sea, it had attracted occasional interest but no buyers. The foundations were undeniably Tudor, but any original architectural beauty the house may have once possessed had long since been sacrificed to the fashionable whims of successive generations.

The last owner, a Pre-Raphaelite-influenced bachelor, had neglected the house, but had lavished both wealth and affection on the grounds. He'd planted the seeds of a wood that swept from the back terrace down to the sea. Ignoring the smashed windowpanes and leaky roof of his home, he'd had a boathouse built on the beach. He'd paid out a small fortune to have a natural cave hollowed out into a most unnatural grotto, and had employed bemused locals to sweep away every vestige of formal garden, croquet and tennis lawn, turning them into the artificial wildernesses so beloved by Millais and Rossetti.

When Richard and Joanna first walked through the gap where the gates should have been, they viewed a house that was little more than an unstable shell and gardens that had become bramble-ridden rubbish tips. The woodlands alone had been treated kindly by the passage of time. They'd been transformed by the years into the wild fairyland envisaged but never seen by the eccentric bachelor years before.

Swayed by Joanna's enthusiastic ideas of what the place might become, Richard gave his seal of approval to the purchase. They bought the estate, and secured the services of a fêted architect. Then they proceeded to attack the problems arising from their new acquisition in the way they attacked every problem – with money.

Richard endorsed the architect's decision to rebuild the manor as the elegant Georgian residence it had never been. Then he turned his attention to the clinic, transferring all responsibility for the house to Joanna. She threw herself wholeheartedly into the project. New, old, interesting original or quality antique, if it was worthy of note she dovetailed it into the house, and as Richard had foreseen, the watchful eye of the architect ensured it was done tastefully. Sherringham agents toured stately homes and churches earmarked for demolition, salvaging ornate ceilings, panellings, staircases, and whole rooms which were carefully transferred to what was rapidly becoming known as 'the Sherringham Mansion'.

A Roman-style swimming-pool was sunk into the Victorian rose garden. A sauna and solarium were set into a newly-built folly-style classical temple. An antique fountain was imported from Italy as a centrepiece for the restored rear terrace. Whatever Joanna or the architect wanted, they bought, and when Richard protested at the mounting bills, Joanna cleared them with what she referred to as her 'nest egg'. Grateful to her for freeing him from responsibility for the house, Richard continued to expand on his grand plans for the clinic, never once realizing that he was re-creating Theo's empire in an English climate.

The Sherringhams moved into the manor the day the work was completed. Tim joined them for the school holidays, and the exterior work continued. The Victorian tennis and croquet lawns were re-laid. An indoor games complex fitted into the walls of the old kitchen garden. The stables were rebuilt, and Joanna bought hunters for herself, Tim and Richard, although only Tim rode with any regularity.

The woods, the beach and the early twentieth-century boathouse received the architect's seal of approval, so were left undisturbed. Those were the areas Daisy gravitated to during the early nightmarish days following Tim's disappearance. And it was on the beach that Judy Osbourne found her, sitting cold and alone at the break of dawn, on the second morning after Richard's return.

That night had been the worst one of all for Daisy. Richard had sent her to bed early, ordering her to rest, as if she could summon sleep on command. He made her feel helpless, like a small child, but, too exhausted to argue, she did as he ordered. She swallowed the pills and water he gave her, and after he closed the door she lay silent and unprotesting between the Japanese embroidered sheets and stared at the ceiling.

Then it happened. Just as it did every night. Slowly, imperceptibly, the numbing indifference that shackled her senses so mercifully during the day dissipated, leaving in its wake a tense, crawling fear. When she recognized the first darting arrows of pain that heralded the onset of awareness, she tried to draw comfort from the vaguely familiar trappings of childhood: the shaded nightlight next to the bed; the feel of starched, clean linen next to her skin; the faint sounds of music that told her waking life still went on somewhere in the house. Childhood! She would concentrate on childhood. The time before her twelfth birthday, when her mother was still alive. Soft words, and hands stroking her hair as she lay in bed. Light, quick footsteps, her parents walking round the house, clearing, tidying. Dishes clattering in the kitchen.

She almost succeeded. The door that led into the past opened slightly, allowing a pungent bouquet of memories to flood into her mind. But the past proved to be as fragile as a collection of summer flowers suddenly released from a winter press. The harder she tried to turn her memories into tangible, coherent thoughts, the more elusive they became. Reminders of what had been flared brilliantly, tantalizing, then just as quickly died, and always in the background was that other memory. All the nights since Tim had disappeared, merging into one ghastly experience that she longed to block from her consciousness.

It only happened when she was asleep. Or did it? Last night she could have sworn she was awake. It was real, so real that she could recall every detail, even now. She closed her eyes tightly, hoping, praying to any deity who would listen. 'Not tonight. Please God, not tonight.'

Her soft whispers tore into the silence of the room, until even the sound of her own voice terrified her. She clenched her fists, dug her nails into the palms of her hands. She was awake and in full control. She would remain that way. She would survive until dawn, and when dawn broke she would feel nothing again, just as she'd done yesterday and the day before. A sweet, blessed nothingness, tinged with the welcome prospect of future oblivion.

It crawled in on all fours. She didn't see the door opening. She didn't need to. First there was the knowledge, the absolute certainty, that something was *there* in the room with her. Then the swift, jerky, scurrying movements across the floor. Sideways, backwards, forwards, all the while moving inexorably towards her. It grappled awkwardly at the foot of the bed, pulling at the duvet, clambering, climbing. Then it was on the bed, still on all fours, poised like a bull about to charge.

She grabbed the pillow and stuffed it into her mouth in an effort to stifle her unborn screams. The thing waited, its chest heaving. She sat up, and as she shrank backwards, her eyes never leaving the grotesque figure for an instant, her back cracked against the headboard. Carved wooden mouldings bit painfully into her spine. She could retreat no further. She wanted to close her eyes, but she couldn't. Black evening trousers, white shirt, open at the neck. He was still dressed the way he'd been when he'd left the apartment.

The truncated neck, bloody and torn, was on a level with her own head. An enormous flap of skin flayed wide from shoulder to shoulder, quivering with her movements in the bed, alternately exposing and concealing the collar bones which were strangely clean and white in comparison with the mess between the rigid arms.

Then the other came. Just as it had every night since she had come to the mansion. Like Tim, it crawled in on all fours. Scuttling, creeping, but more timid than Tim, it took an eternity to join him on the bed. It was shoeless. Grimy toes poked through gaping holes in the wrinkled tights. A shabby, shapeless, mud stained raincoat was draped around it. The same gory mess where the head should be. Together, yet separate, they crouched as though they were about to spring. Fixed, immobile, like stuffed predators incarcerated in a glass case.

Without warning, Tim sat back on his haunches, held out his arms to her in a macabre mockery of a loving, welcoming pose. And she wanted to go to him. So help her God, she wanted him!

The pillow in her mouth choked her. She couldn't breathe. The room wavered before her eyes, but Tim remained within her sights. She needed him. How she needed him! To be in his arms, her head on his chest. Her lips turned to his . . . Lips . . . A tide of vomit rose in her throat at the thought. Suffocating, she wrenched the pillow from her face and threw it at him. She needed to breathe, but the air was tainted, foul with the stench of rotting flesh. She retched, drew breath, and tasted the indescribable slaughterhouse atmosphere they had brought to her bed. Then she heard a scream. Low, bestial, the cry of a creature in torment. She didn't even recognize the noise as her own.

The light snapped on. She recoiled from its glare as Richard strode into the room, dressed in the same grey suit he had worn all day. He sat beside her bed, took her wrist in his hand and counted her pulse. She looked from Richard to the foot of the bed. It was empty, the white lace counterpane smooth. No maggots, no rusty stains of old blood, no stench.

Richard released her wrist. He bent down and picked up her pillow from the floor and laid it next to her on the bed. 'Do you want to tell me about it?'

She looked at him. His voice was calm, controlled, but the grey streaks in his auburn hair seemed more pronounced then they had been even two days before. Drained of colour, his face was lined, hollow-cheeked. He loved Tim, but, like her, he remained locked in his own grief. Why couldn't they reach out, comfort one another? 'It was a nightmare.' Her voice sounded odd, pitched high by the recent terror.

101

'I heard Daisy scream.' Joanna stood in the open doorway, a blue silk négligé draped over her slim, boyish figure, her cropped blonde hair shining in the glare of the bedroom light.

'Another nightmare,' Richard diagnosed abruptly.

'I'm sorry I disturbed you,' Daisy apologized. 'It won't happen again.'

'If the journey from Italy hadn't knocked me for six, I'd offer to sit with you. But tonight I really need my beauty sleep. Perhaps I could get the housekeeper . . .'

'I'm fine,' Daisy interrupted unconvincingly.

'Well, if you're sure . . .' Too polite to argue, Joanna took the proffered cue. 'Richard,' she nodded to her husband.

'Good night, Joanna.'

They were both so formal, even with one another. Daisy looked up at Richard.

'If you're sure you've quite recovered . . .' There was resignation in his voice.

'I'm sure.'

'And you won't tell me what it was?'

She shook her head.

'It won't go away unless you talk about it,' he said, using the standard doctor–patient ploy in an attempt to gain more information than she was prepared to give.

She looked down the lace counterpane towards the foot of the bed. Nothing! 'It was a dream,' she repeated wearily, trying to convince herself as much as him. Richard leaned over and smoothed the damp hair from her forehead. A strangely paternal gesture for him. She looked up into his eyes, and for the first time she saw a resemblance to Tim. A fleeting expression that went beyond his slighter build, dark auburn hair, and green eyes. The obvious physical differences between the two brothers.

'If you need me, you'll call?'

'Yes,' she lied.

'Sleep well, Daisy.'

'And you, Richard.' She despised the polite exchange of words, the ridiculous pretence of normality that they both clung to.

He left the room, closing the door quietly behind him. She lay tense, frightened, watching the minutes tick by on the digital clock on her bedside-table. One . . . one-thirty . . . two . . . The grandfather clock in the hall tolled out twice, shattering the quiet of the house. Unable to stand the oppressive silence or the waiting a moment longer, she stole from her bed, and pulled on her thickest jeans and sweater. Carrying her shoes, she crept from the room, down the corridor and staircase and out through the kitchen door.

She sat on the cold stone balustrade of the terrace, staring into space, until the glow of the false dawn that precedes the real one lightened the sky. Then she walked down the rough track that cut through the woods to the beach. Nature held no terrors for her to match those that lurked in the recesses of her own mind.

She couldn't have said where she was going, or what she was doing. She only knew she wanted to run as far from the house and her nightmares as possible.

Judy slammed three coins into the vending machine, and stared at the selection on offer. Wishing they'd keep the canteen open during the night, she thumped the buttons for white coffee, one sugar. Her coffee came all right. Without the cup. Cursing, she lashed out, kicking the machine viciously.

'If you'd take the time and trouble to read the notice pinned to the wall, you would know you have to insert a cup before pressing the buttons,' Eric said smugly, taking a plastic cup from the stack on the floor.

'Can you change a pound?' Judy enquired, resisting the temptation to kick him, as well as the machine.

'I don't believe I can.' He didn't bother to put his hand into his pocket to look.

She crashed down on to one of the threadbare stained armchairs in the doctors' rest-room. The hour before dawn was the dog-end of the night shift. And it hadn't been an easy one. Two car accidents resulting in one fatality and five injured. One wife- and baby-battering, and a sleepwalking drunk who'd stepped off the balcony of his third-floor flat. And those were in addition to the cardiac arrest on Ward 9, and the still birth on the maternity ward.

Eric sat opposite her. 'I don't suppose there's any news of Tim Sherringham?'

'Are you asking out of concern, or because you're wondering when to apply for his job?'

'The hospital can't run efficiently without its full quota of registrars.'

'Have you already put in for it?' she demanded suspiciously.

'I've approached Bassett.'

'You bastard.'

'If it hadn't been me, it would have been someone else. The one thing I've learnt about the Health Service is that you have to take care of yourself. Perhaps you like being a houseman, Osbourne. I've set my sights on higher things.'

'That's easy to do when you're sitting in the sewer.'

'If you weren't a woman . . .'

'You'd what, Eric? It strikes me you don't know what to do with anyone. Man or woman.' She left her chair. 'There's just enough time for me to check the wards and Casualty before I finish duty. Afterwards, I'm going to get myself a real cup of coffee.' She stared at his plastic cup, bulging precariously from the hot liquid that had distorted it.

'You're afraid that one day you'll have to take orders from me,' he crowed.

'On the contrary. I'd never take orders from you, Eric. No matter what title you stick to your name.'

She left to tour the wards. But she couldn't stop thinking about Tim . . . and Daisy. She hadn't spoken to Daisy since Richard had returned, and all she got whenever she telephoned the mansion was Hare's voice, polite but firm, sidestepping all enquiries with a 'Dr Daisy is resting at the moment and cannot be disturbed.'

She decided to forego her coffee when her shift ended and drive out to the Sherringham mansion. She wasn't that tired. Daisy had to eat, they could breakfast together. And she'd be on hand if any news came through. Good, or bad.

Daisy was sitting so still that in the dull light of early morning Judy failed to differentiate between her and the large rocks that littered the beach. Despite the thick sweater she wore, Judy was half frozen, her brain dormant from the cold and lack of sleep. She walked out of the woods along the narrow path that skirted past the boathouse and onto the verandah that culminated in a small wooden quay. Stepping on to the quay, she shaded her eyes and looked out to sea, scanning the horizon for a small boat.

'Good morning.' Daisy's quiet greeting unnerved her.

She glanced around anxiously.

'I'm sorry, I didn't mean to startle you.'

She looked in the direction of the voice, and saw Daisy curled, small and forlorn, on the shingle.

'I've been on night duty. I wasn't tired so I decided to call in and see you on the way home.'

'Since when has this place been on your way home? You live in the hospital, remember.'

'Whatever.' Judy shrugged her shoulders, dismissing the effort she'd made to be with Daisy. 'Hare was up. He showed me to your room. When we found it empty we were quite worried. Then he said he'd seen you walking down this way quite a few times during the past couple of days. He thought you might have taken one of the boats out.'

'Tim and I used to spend a lot of time here before we were married,' Daisy said flatly, showing little interest in anything Judy said. She was loath to relinquish her warm, loving memories of Tim. *Tim laughing in a dreadful Italian restaurant Alan had insisted on taking them to after a full day's surgery. Tim winking at her over Palmer-Smith's head at a party. Tim shouting furiously at Eric Hedley in the hospital canteen. Tim at the helm of their yacht, the* Freedom. *Tim exploring the wooded creeks at Helford, catching crabs when the tide turned. Tim lying next to her in bed . . .*

'Are you all right?' Judy left the quay and crunched her way towards Daisy over the pebbles.

'Fine.'

Suspecting sarcasm, she studied Daisy closely, but she found only a peculiar detachment written in Daisy's red-veined eyes. If she hadn't known better, she would have put the remoteness down to drink or drugs. 'Are you trying to catch pneumonia?' she asked, braving Daisy's silence.

'I couldn't sleep.' Daisy turned and looked at Judy. 'It was good of you to come, to be concerned.'

'Don't be ridiculous. You're the closest thing to family I've got. If I can't be concerned about you, who can I be concerned about?'

'All the same, I know what it feels like after a night shift. Every muscle aching, exhausted. Too tired to think.'

'I had an easy time of it. Eric was there to do all the difficult bits. I just made the coffee, read the *Lancet* and slept between patients.'

'I'll believe that when I see it. Was he very bloody?'
Daisy asked, showing a slight spark of interest.

'Isn't he always?'

'He's after Tim's job.'

'You know perfectly well he's always been after that.'

'But now Tim's gone he's likely to get it. Isn't he?'
Daisy looked to Judy for confirmation.

'You know the hospital board. They move slowly on
everything. By the time they get around to even thinking about appointing a new registrar, Tim will be back.'

'Tim's not coming back. Not ever,' Daisy insisted
quietly. 'He's dead, Judy. I know he's dead.'

There was a moment's peace broken only by the
mewing of the gulls.

'Tim will be back,' Judy contradicted firmly. 'Daisy,
you're tired, you're not thinking straight.'

'I'm not as tired as you.'

'You're depressed because of what you've been
through in the past few days. Everything will sort itself
out. I promise you.' Judy laid a cold hand on top of
Daisy's even colder one. 'Is there anything I can do to
help?'

'Richard is doing everything that can be done.'

'There must be something I can do.' Judy drew
closer to her.

Dawn had burst over the sea in all its red-gold glory.
Soon, Daisy knew, she would be able to relegate the
nightmare images back into the coffers of her mind.
Day, bearable day, was just beginning. There'd be
things for her to do. Actions that would fill the gaping
holes of time, enabling her to carry on for just that bit
longer. Food would be placed in front of her. She'd
make a pretence of eating. Richard would offer her
sedatives, rest. She'd fight his demands . . .

'What can I do?' Judy repeated.

'Nothing.' She pulled her hand from under Judy's
and turned up the collar on her sweater. 'There's

107

nothing for either of us to do. As I said, Richard does whatever has to be done. He telephones the police. Gives the orders. All I do is sit and wait.'

'For news?'

'For anything.'

Daisy hunched her shoulders, huddling within her sweater, then suddenly without warning she shuddered uncontrollably. Judy tried to put her arm around her but Daisy shrank from the touch. The weight of Judy's arm lying across her shoulders irritated her. The warmth of Judy's leg permeating through the heavy canvas of her jeans revolted her. She didn't want Judy near her. She didn't want anyone except Tim, and she wanted him with an intensity that burned. She needed to hold her husband, to feel his breath on her cheek, the bulk of his torso locked safely in her arms. Moving away from Judy, she wrapped her arms tightly around her legs and rested her chin on her knees. Cold, small, self-contained, she resumed her blind study of the sea.

'Tim's not dead!' Judy murmured thickly.

Daisy stared blankly out to sea. She'd heard Judy, but she said nothing. How could she? How could she even begin to tell her about the night? How she'd crawled through the last few days in an unfeeling stupor, only to fall prey to awareness during the lonely hours. And how those hours bore agonies that gnawed into her, destroying her very being.

'What do the police think?' Judy asked when she'd summoned up enough courage to interrupt Daisy's reverie.

'They still think Tim's run off with another woman.'

'But that's ridiculous. Tim would never walk out on you, much less with another woman. Anyone who knows him knows at least that much. Surely the police have some idea, some clue that offers a better explanation than that?'

'No, there's nothing. When Tim left the flat to

answer that emergency call, it was the last time I, or anyone else, saw him. It's almost as if someone wiped him clean off the face of the earth. If it wasn't for his clothes, the photographs I have of him, I'd begin to doubt his existence myself.'

She rose stiffly from the beach and walked towards the shoreline, scuffing the sand with the toes of her trainers. 'Do you know, the police have made me relive every second of the last few days and nights Tim and I spent together a hundred times over, and every time I come to the same conclusion. Nothing out of the ordinary, nothing different happened during that time. That party Richard and Joanna gave, it might have been any one of a dozen parties they've given this year.' She turned and stood in front of Judy. 'You saw Tim that last day, you spoke to him. Did you notice anything strange, anything different?'

Judy stretched out her hand, and Daisy pulled her up from the ground. 'Tim was Tim. He's always the same. I had lunch with him, Mike Edmunds and Tony Pierce in the hospital canteen that day . . . the day before he disappeared.'

'What did you talk about?' Daisy asked.

'What doctors always talk about. The state of the Health Service. Lousy pay. Lousy chances of promotion. Eric Hedley, the patients, you know the sort of thing.'

'Did Tim say anything in particular?' Daisy pressed.

'He complained about the lack of funding and facilities in the hospital. How much he'd enjoyed that last weekend break with you. How little free time any of us had.'

'Richard asked Tim to work in the clinic the night of the party,' Daisy offered abruptly.

'Daisy, you know full well Richard's always asking Tim to work in his clinic. It's a standing joke between them. Tim wouldn't leave the General.'

109

'Richard struck home that night, I'm sure of it. When Tim was dressing he told me Richard had only got out of bed in the middle of the night once during the last ten years, and that was the night Joanna's father had a heart attack.'

'Every time I've seen Richard and Tim together, Richard's had a go at Tim for working for peanuts in a general hospital. Daisy, you know as well as I do, Tim would never consider private work.'

'Did you see Tim speak to anyone else that day? Did you hear him say anything out of the ordinary?' There was a demanding desperation in Daisy's voice that made Judy want to manufacture something, anything, to ease the pain.

'I didn't see him again after that lunch. When I left the canteen he was playing cards with Tony and Mike.'

'What was Tony doing in the General?'

'Saying goodbye. He's holidaying in Arabia, remember. Following in the great Lawrence's footsteps.'

'Tony was at the party.'

'He *is* Richard's anaesthetist.'

'I saw him but I didn't get a chance to talk to him.'

'Lucky you. All he could talk about when I saw him was how he'd had enough of anaesthetizing hysterical hysterectomies and old men's prostates, and that he simply couldn't wait for his holiday to start. Daisy, don't you think you're clutching at straws here?'

'I just feel so bloody helpless, so . . . so . . . outnumbered,' she said wearily.'Richard's taken over. Joanna pats my hand and assures me everything's going to be fine. And now you . . .'

'Hey, I'm your friend, not your in-laws.'

They began to walk up the beach towards the woods. 'Since Tim disappeared, everyone's been tiptoeing round me talking in whispers, hiding in corners, having earnest discussions behind my back.'

'That must be foul.'

110

'It is. Promise you'll treat me as normal, no matter what.'

'I promise.'

They left the beach and walked into the woods. 'God, this place is beautiful.' Judy paused for a moment and looked closely at Daisy. What she saw made her forget all her ideas about sleep, for that morning at least. 'What say you to going out for a couple of hours? We could buy breakfast somewhere.'

'Richard . . .'

'Why should we consider Richard?' Judy said blithely. 'What do *you* want to do?'

'Aren't you tired? Shouldn't you sleep?'

'This afternoon maybe.'

'I'd like to get away from here. If only for a couple of hours.'

'To do what?'

'Nothing in particular. Look in on the flat. Drive into town, perhaps visit the hospital.'

She didn't have to say any more. Judy read the silent plea mirrored in her eyes. It wasn't enough for Daisy to know that Richard was doing everything humanly possible. That the police were out beating the countryside for Tim. She needed to look for him herself.

'Lucky I brought my car. I'll give you five minutes to get out of those damp clothes, then we can go.'

'Thank you.'

Judy found her eagerness pathetic. She held out her hand. 'Race you to the top.'

Peter Collins spun the wheel of his car. It swerved violently off the inside lane of the motorway, screeching to a halt behind the ragged line of police vehicles and ambulances that were dotted at intervals along the hard shoulder.

'Did this have to happen just before my leave?' he moaned. 'I had it all planned out. Ten days in the

111

fleshpots of Paris. They'd never have found me to call me in,' he added wistfully.

Trevor scarcely heard a word Peter said. His attention was already fixed on the small groups of uniformed figures clustered around the grass verges and hedge-rows that grew below the level of the road.

'You two have come just in time.' Their superintendent, Bill Mulcahy, opened the passenger door of Peter's car and poked his head inside. 'An inch-by-inch search.' He grinned sadistically. 'Right up your street.'

'Is it Tim Sherringham?' Trevor asked, noting the ominous sheeted area below the bank.

'One of them might be,' Bill muttered laconically.

'One of them?' Peter slammed his door and walked round to where Bill was standing. 'How many have you got down there, for Christ's sake?'

'Two at the last count,' Bill answered baldly. 'And we've only been digging since first light. The last find was fox-chewed and a bit scattered, so we couldn't really be sure what we had until the forensic boys got here. A few minutes ago they confirmed it. It's a corpse all right.'

'Two.' Peter let out a low whistle.

'The atmosphere down there is pretty ripe,' Bill chuckled maliciously, pointing to a green young constable who was busily heaving up the contents of his stomach on to the hard shoulder.

'What the hell is this?' Peter looked quizzically at Bill. 'That's not for the likes of me and you to say, son.' Bill nodded towards a couple of imposing cars parked in the middle of the line. 'The big boys from London arrived ten minutes ago. We're strictly back-up material on this case, my boy. Important people are involved here. Take my advice. Do as you're asked, no more, no less, and be polite at all times. If you don't, you might find it's your head that's on the chopping block.'

'You want us to search?' Trevor stepped out of the car, blessing the urgency of the early morning call that had prevented him from eating. He couldn't stop his imagination playing around with the idea of the 'pretty ripe' atmosphere. What would five days of light rain and warm spring weather have done to Tim Sherringham? Pretty ripe. He wished Bill had used another adjective. He'd never had a very good stomach for this kind of police work. He set his back deliberately on the white-faced young constable and looked to Bill for his instructions.

'Take four men each and systematically comb the verges and hedgerows on the other side of the motorway,' Bill ordered.

'Any clues as to what we're looking for?' Peter queried.

'Nothing. Everything. You'll know it when you see it. You'd better believe that by the time this is over we'll have the cleanest motorway verges in Europe. Right, if you two get across the road and section it off, I'll send the men over to you as soon as they arrive.'

'How much do you want us to cover?' Peter looked at the thin lines of woodland that seemed to stretch endlessly on both sides of the road.

'Eventually the whole lot, from London to the sea,' Bill said humourlessly. 'But ten miles either side of this point will do for today.'

'Ten miles,' Peter groaned. 'We'll never do it before dark, and what about meal breaks?'

'Forget breaks for today. You're a policeman, and everyone knows policemen don't need to eat or sleep. Oh, and by the way, I want both of you down at the station the minute it gets too dark to search any more.'

'Why couldn't this have happened two days from now?' Peter grumbled as he stepped back into the car.

'Trevor, you've met Daisy Sherringham, haven't you?' Bill asked.

113

'Yes. Peter and I took down the missing person's report on her husband.'

'May I ask why you two went and not the duty constable?'

'Personal favour to one of the doctors at the hospital. He's been good to us, and we're . . .'

'I know, I know. We're good to him,' Bill finished dryly. 'How well do you know Daisy Sherringham?'

'I've been to her flat to pick up some photographs of her husband, tell her there was no news. You know the sort of thing.'

'Was she upset?'

'What the hell do you think? Of course she was upset.' Trevor's temper began to rise as it always did whenever Daisy Sherringham was talked about in the bland impersonal tone that Bill was using right now. 'Her husband's disappeared, for Christ's sake.'

'Fond of him, was she?'

'I'd say so. Yes. They'd only been married six months. What's this leading to, Bill?'

'Do you want to come with me to the Sherringham house if we have to tell her that's her husband down there?'

'If?' Trevor's bewilderment showed in his face. 'What's the problem? How ever many bodies you've got, you have a description, you've got photographs, surely to God you can tell whether or not one of them's Tim Sherringham. Five days out in the open can't have made that much difference?'

'Do you, or do you not want to be there if I have to ask one of the Sherringhams to identify the body?' Bill demanded in the hectoring tone he usually reserved for belligerent members of the public.

'Yes,' Trevor shouted irately. 'Yes, I want to be there.'

'Right, now that's clear, I'll call on you if we find

Tim Sherringham.' Bill turned his back and walked down the incline to the screened-off hedge.

'What the hell was that all about?' Peter enquired as Trevor opened the car door.

'Bill asked .if I wanted to go along with him to the Sherringhams.'

'And you agreed! Christ, I'd rather spend all day digging in dirt than take time out to do that. Weeping widows aren't my scene.'

Trevor remained silent. He couldn't justify his compliance with Bill's request even to himself. Was he egotistical enough to believe that he could make a better job of breaking bad news to Daisy Sherringham than anyone else? Or was it merely voyeurism? he wondered, disgusted by the thought. The instinct of curiosity that lies dormant within us all. A desire to cold-bloodedly watch the grief of others. To discover, albeit second-hand, the dreadful, empty finality of death. Just how shattering it can be when it happens to one of the few people you really care about. And all the while, the corner of detachment flapping in the mind, pushing conjecture beyond events, posing the question as to whether you'd behave as badly, or as well, when it was your turn to suffer.

And Daisy *was* suffering. He was certain of it. He'd taken a suicidal junkie into the hospital yesterday, and he'd seen Judy Osbourne in the casualty ward. He'd asked after Daisy and she'd brushed him aside with a terse noncommittal reply that had nothing to do with their dislike of one another. She hadn't needed to elaborate. Daisy was staying with Richard and Joanna Sherringham at the Sherringham mansion. Two days ago everyone in the station had been warned.

All communications and directives relevant to, and concerning the disappearance of Dr Timothy Sherringham are to go directly to Dr Richard Sherringham, *personally.*

The great man hadn't been back in the country ten minutes before rockets had begun to fly down from London. What was being done? Had they searched the town? The motorway? The hospital? Questioned all witnesses thoroughly? (What witnesses, at four in the morning, for pity's sake?) And still the pressure kept coming, tightening, building, until there wasn't an officer in the station who didn't react like a bear with a sore head at the mere mention of the Sherringham case. Did they need extra men? Specialist teams? Forensic assistance? Yesterday helicopters had flown down from London with heat-seeking cameras, presumably in response to Richard Sherringham's suggestion. And today . . .

'Ready to start?'

Trevor stared uncomprehendingly at Peter. Then he realized, they'd driven through the underpass. They were on the opposite side of the motorway.

'The search, remember,' Peter prompted irritably.

'Yes. Yes, of course, fine.' Trevor stepped out of the car and studied the terrain they had to cope with.

'You could hide a bloody elephant in those bushes over there,' Peter cursed, 'let alone the size of clue we're supposed to be looking for.'

'There may not be anything at all.'

'Bloody great. It's bad enough looking for something that's there, without wading through muck for something that isn't.'

'There's no pleasing you today, is there, Peter?' Trevor rubbed his hands and blew into them, warming himself against the early morning chill. He turned up the collar of his anorak and walked over to the verge of the hard shoulder. Looking across at the other side of the road, he mentally keyed in his position. Body bags were being unloaded from one of the waiting police ambulances. How long would it be before Bill

116

came for him? One hour, two? 'Damn and blast.' He turned and lashed out savagely, kicking a stone from his path. It tumbled through the thick swatches of unkempt grass and hit a tree.

'Destroying evidence,' Peter shouted back at him. 'I'll tell on you.'

'You do that, mate,' Trevor answered. 'You do just that.'

'Judy.' Richard walked out of his study on to the terrace.

'Richard.' Judy turned from the magnificent view that swept over the woods down to the sea, and looked at him. Richard was as immaculately turned out as ever, in a suitably sober suit and discreetly splendid tie, but the hand he offered her shook slightly, and there were deeply etched lines of pain and suffering drawn around his eyes and mouth.

'Would you like more coffee, madam?' Hare enquired, taking her cup and putting it on a tray.

'No, thank you.'

'Sir?'

'No, thank you,' Richard replied irritably. 'It's good of you to come,' he muttered to Judy in a tone only fractionally lighter than the one he'd used when speaking to Hare.

'I was worried about Daisy. Is there any news?'

'Nothing since last night.' He walked past the butler, and lowered himself into one of the Victorian wrought-iron chairs that were scattered along the terrace. 'But I'm hoping we'll hear something today. I saw the press and TV people yesterday. "Went public", as the police so quaintly put it.'

'Is there anything I can do?' Judy asked uneasily, drawing a chair close to his.

'Not unless you can enlighten us in any way.'

117

'I wish I could. Everyone who knows Tim knows he wouldn't leave Daisy . . .'

'I think we're all agreed on that point.'

'On what point?' Joanna, simply dressed in a white linen shift, a brilliant green scarf tied loosely around her slim throat, came out of the house and joined them.

'Tim wouldn't leave Daisy,' Richard replied shortly.

'Hello. Judy, isn't it? Judy Osbourne. I hardly recognized you without your bridesmaid's dress.' Joanna sat next to her. Judy noticed that even at this unearthly hour of the morning, Joanna was wearing the minimum of make-up and the maximum of perfume, her short blonde hair combed in a gentle, perfect sweep across her forehead. She looked closer to twenty-five than her actual forty-five years.

'We were talking about Tim,' Richard stressed.

'Richard, I'm as fond of Tim as anyone,' Joanna said calmly, 'but at this moment in time, there's nothing we can do to help him. We simply have to sit and wait. All this talking, mulling over of details that may or may not be significant isn't doing anyone any good. Least of all Daisy.'

'And speaking of Daisy,' Judy interrupted, anxious to escape from what she felt to be an impending argument, 'I'd like to take her into town this morning.'

'That's out of the question,' Richard snapped. 'She's under a great strain. She needs rest, and quiet.'

'Surely a short drive followed by breakfast out couldn't do her any harm,' Judy persisted.

'In her mental condition any undue exertion could cause serious damage to her health.'

'When I spoke to her this morning she seemed calm and coherent enough to me.'

'You've already seen Daisy?' Joanna raised one of her perfectly-arched eyebrows.

'I came here after my night shift. Daisy wasn't in

118

her room and Hare suggested I look for her on the beach. I found her sitting there.'

'That is exactly what I mean,' Richard broke in hotly. 'Do you mind telling me what time that was?'

'I'm not quite sure,' Judy lied.

'Dawn!' Richard exclaimed. 'Possibly before. And you're trying to tell me that Daisy is calm and rational. It's hardly calm, rational behaviour to go walking through the woods before dawn. And for all we know, she could have been wandering about for half the night.'

'Isn't it possible her restlessness could be no more than a normal reaction to the stress she's under?'

'I had no idea you were an amateur psychiatrist,' Richard mocked.

'I agree with Judy,' Joanna drawled lightly. 'A short trip to town couldn't possibly harm Daisy. You admitted last night that none of the sedatives you've been giving her appear to be working. Perhaps if she made an effort, went out for a short while, it might tire her. She may well rest later.'

'And if your theory falls flat on its face and Daisy becomes hysterical?'

'I'd bring her back immediately,' Judy promised. 'Please, Richard. We'd be gone an hour or two at the most. I'm tired myself.'

'Isn't that all the more reason for you to sleep now instead of going into town with Daisy?' Richard glared at her coldly.

'We'll be back before lunch.' Judy rose. 'It's not as if I'm whisking Daisy away to the Bahamas. Besides,' she threw in her trump card, 'Daisy's looking forward to it.'

'You've already discussed this with Daisy?' Richard's face darkened in anger.

'We talked on the way up from the beach. I asked her what she'd like to do today. Breakfast out seemed a good idea. I think she just wants to get away for a while.'

'Richard, Judy could have taken Daisy out to breakfast and been back in the time you've taken to argue about it. A drive to town, a meal . . .' Joanna shrugged her shoulders. 'What possible harm could there be in that?'

Embarrassed by Joanna's open disagreement with Richard, Judy looked purposefully towards the house. She caught a glimpse through the open French windows of Daisy moving about in the living-room. No wonder Daisy wanted to go out, if this had been the atmosphere in the Sherringham household since Tim had disappeared. Her mind made up, she pushed her chair under the table. The metal legs screeched painfully over the glazed veranda tiles. 'I think I'll go and see if Daisy's ready.'

'Town, breakfast and back.' Richard stared at Judy frostily. 'Don't forget for a second that Daisy's suffered a traumatic shock. No stops along the way. No newspapers, and no other people.'

'Whatever you say.'

'And you'll be back by midday.'

'Of course. I'll find Daisy, then we'll go.' She walked swiftly into the living-room before Richard had time to formulate any further arguments. A telephone began ringing somewhere in the house.

'Have a good time,' Joanna called after her.

'Thank you.'

Judy smiled at Daisy and pointed towards the front door. They passed Hare in the main hall.

'You'll take me to the flat?' Daisy asked.

'Wherever you want to go,' Judy answered, humouring her. If she'd had to decide at that moment between Daisy's sanity and Richard's, she would have opted for Daisy's without hesitation.

*

120

'There's nothing for me to do here,' Joanna said decisively, rising from her chair. 'On the other hand, there's a great deal that I could be doing in the lab.'

'I thought there was nothing pressing, that's why you decided to take a holiday.'

'There isn't anything pressing, but there is work. I need something to take my mind off . . .'

'Off Tim?'

'If you must know, off you and your bloody awful mood, Richard. I'll see you later.'

'As you wish.'

As Joanna walked swiftly into the house, Hare appeared on the patio. 'The police on your private line, sir.' Hare laid a telephone on the table in front of Richard.

'Thank you, Hare.' Richard picked up the receiver, keeping his hand firmly over the mouthpiece. 'Have all the other incoming calls rerouted to my office at the clinic,' he ordered brusquely.

'I've already arranged it, sir.' The butler looked at him oddly. 'You asked me to do it last night.'

'I'd forgotten,' Richard countered irritably. 'That will be all.'

Richard put the receiver to his ear. 'Richard Sherringham,' he barked abruptly.

'Dr Sherringham, this is Superintendent Mulcahy.'

'Yes,' Richard growled impatiently. Why wasn't the man getting on with whatever it was he had to say?

'I don't have any definite news for you, sir. Not at the moment, that is.' For the first time in his career Bill Mulcahy found himself struggling for words. If this had been an ordinary case, he wouldn't have concerned himself with informing relatives at this stage. But then this was no ordinary case, and Richard Sherringham no ordinary public.

'But you have something,' Richard suggested tersely.

'Two bodies.' Bill Mulcahy's hesitance disappeared

as his innate professionalism took over. 'The heat-seeking cameras picked up one, and the other was close by. They were hidden in the hedgerow at the side of the motorway. Part of the route your brother would have taken in travelling between his flat and the hospital.'

'Is one of them Tim?' Richard's knuckles whitened as he tightened his grip on the receiver.

'Identification's impossible at this stage, sir.'

'My brother's only been missing for five days, Mulcahy.'

'One of the bodies has been dismembered and badly mutilated.'

'And the other?' Richard demanded.

'The other has no hands, or . . .' Bill Mulcahy took a deep breath, '. . . head, sir.'

'It's not Tim. It can't be Tim . . . not Tim . . .' Richard's voice was weak, wavering, but his words were loud enough to be heard by Bill Mulcahy sitting miles away in his police car parked alongside the motorway. The line went dead. Bill looked across at Trevor in the passenger seat.

'What do you think? Possible kidnapping?' he asked, visibly brightening at the thought of a theory he could actually work on.

'And the other body?' Trevor questioned logically. 'Another kidnapping? Or a hit-and-run thrown there by chance to make a nice tidy pile for us to find?'

'Don't jam my wheel, Joseph,' Mulcahy ordered briskly. 'Not when I'm barely into first gear. And by the time I get into second, we'll have this one sorted, you mark my words.'

Chapter Five

Alan Cummins hadn't taken a coffee break since Daisy had left the hospital for Richard's house. Instead he'd taken to spending his free time in the chilly, formaldehyde-ridden atmosphere of the mortuary. Patrick O'Kelly, the pathologist who ran the unit efficiently, if somewhat eccentrically, had come to expect Alan's visits, and in his own peculiar way, looked forward to them. Most of the staff, doctors and nurses alike, tended to avoid the place unless they had definite business there such as post-mortem reports to pick up or study. He found it gratifying to think that a colleague was actually seeking the mortuary out for reasons that had nothing to do with professional interest or expertise.

At ten o'clock in the morning, Patrick had just finished a post-mortem on an unexpected sudden death. The audio tape had gone to the typing pool, and he and his assistant were enjoying the sandwiches and coffee they'd laid out on a spare slab. Then, punctual to the minute, Alan walked through the door.

'Before you ask, the only new one in today is a death on the surgical ward. Female, twenty-three-year-old, car accident,' Patrick mumbled through a mouthful of wholemeal and Camembert.

'Nothing else?' Alan sat alongside Patrick on the stainless steel slab. Patrick and his assistant Paul were sitting happily, but Alan found the temperature of their improvised seat uncomfortably low.

'We may have something for you later,' Patrick continued, swallowing his bread. 'Had a call from the police about an hour ago. They've found something on the motorway.'

'Something?' Alan's heart began to pound erratically.

'I asked about Tim Sherringham. Hope it's not him. Nice fellow. They wouldn't say much more. You know the police. But whatever it is they've found, it's big. A Home Office pathologist is already on the scene. They asked if I'd co-operate with any work he had to do here. Do you want to see the notes on your last battering case?' he asked, jumping topics in the same breath.

'Yes. OK,' Alan agreed, preoccupied with thoughts of Tim, not the battering case Patrick had referred to. He wondered how long it would take for the police to turn up with the 'something' they'd found on the motorway. Would it be this morning or afternoon? Someone, perhaps it had been Patrick, had once given him a long lecture on the amount of work that had to be done 'on site' when a body was found. It must have been at a party, because he'd been rather drunk at the time, and full of rich food. It hadn't taken much to make him feel squeamish.

'I'll get that report for you.' Patrick drank the last of the coffee from his paper cup and screwed his sandwich wrappings into a ball, before jumping down from the slab. 'Bring out 347,' he called to Paul over his shoulder. 'We'll do that one next.'

'The old man with the suspected secondary tumour?'

'That's the one.' Patrick led the way into his cluttered office. He opened a drawer in the massive filing cabinet and flicked through the files. 'Here it is.' He handed a folder to Alan. 'And in my opinion not one of those injuries is accidental.'

'Thanks, Patrick. I really appreciate this.'

'It's a bit late for that poor mite.'

'But it might save his brothers.'

'I hope so. I don't like seeing them that young.'

'Next one ready,' Paul called out from the post-mortem room.

124

'Do you mind if I stay here a while and read through this?' Alan asked. 'No one will think of looking for me in here.'

'You want to be around when the police arrive with the body they've found.' Patrick pulled a pair of rubber gloves over his enormous hands. 'You know, you could always read that report in the comfort of your own office. I'll give you a call as soon as they arrive.'

'I'll hang on for a couple more minutes, if you don't mind.'

'I don't mind. Make yourself at home,' Patrick offered expansively, pointing to one of the vacant slabs. 'I understand how you feel. I didn't know Tim Sherringham well, but as I said, he always struck me as being a nice chap.'

Alan followed Patrick back to the main post-mortem area. An elderly corpse was laid out on one of the shallow sinks that were used for dissection. Paul had already turned the tap on. Thin trickles of water coursed around the skeletal body and ran out through the drain. Patrick picked up his scalpel, and with one swift, practised, downward turn of his wrist made the routine throat to pubis incision, standard to most post-mortems. Paul clipped back the skin flaps while Patrick turned on and tested the bone cutter. The whirring of the blades drowned out the sounds of the police ambulance arriving. By the time Patrick had finished sawing through the ribcage, the main doors were open and the first of the trolleys was being wheeled in.

A white cotton sheet covered whatever was lying on the stretcher. Two uniformed policemen were pushing the trolley, its castors clattering noisily over the tiled floor. They stuck in a gully, then a sharp shove from one of the policemen freed the offending wheel. It drew closer, finally grinding to a halt a few feet from where Alan was standing.

'Where do you want it, Doctor?' The policeman

125

behind the trolley looked to Alan, assuming he was the one in charge.

'You can put it over there.' Patrick looked up from the lung he'd just begun to dissect, and pointed a bloody finger at the far wall.

'There's another one in the ambulance,' the policeman informed him casually. 'And the Home Office doctor told me to tell you he'd be along as soon as he's finished the site work.'

'How many are there?' Patrick asked, digging his fingers back into the lung.

'Two at the last count. This one is still recognizable as human. The other is a limb collection.' The policeman nodded to Alan, then pushed past, wheeling his load to the far wall as Patrick had instructed. Two more policemen arrived with the second trolley. After an indication from their colleague they also pushed their load against the far wall. 'That's it for now, Doctor.'

'Thank you. I expect I'll be seeing you later.'

'Looks like it.' They left the room.

Patrick glanced at Alan. He lifted his hands up and away from the body he was delving into, and shook them briskly free of excess fluids. 'Do you want to take a closer look?' he asked Alan bluntly.

'Yes,' Alan breathed hoarsely. The abstract concept of Tim dead was one thing. The reality of Tim lying on this mortuary trolley was quite another. But he had to see for himself whatever was lying there. He simply had to.

Holding his hands at shoulder height, Patrick walked over to the parked trolley. Alan followed.

'Paul,' Patrick called. 'Come and pull these sheets back for me, will you please?'

'Right away.' Paul dropped the instrument he'd been holding and walked over to the trolley closest to him.

126

He pulled back the sheet quickly, folding it neatly and hanging it over the end bar.

'And the other one, please,' Patrick said quietly. Paul did as he asked.

Alan stared down at the two heavy-duty, clear plastic body bags that were laid out end to end on the trolleys. It took him some time to become accustomed to the distorting layers of plastic. Then he noticed the feet of the one closest to him. Wrapped in secondary bags, they were blurred to the point of indistinction, but he could make out the dirt. Great clumps of it, clinging to the bodies and lying loose inside the bags. A sudden soft thud of something live rattling against the interior of the thick plastic played on his shattered nerves. He shuddered violently.

'Maggots,' Patrick said coolly, noting a wriggling mass spiralling out of the raw end of one of the arms. 'This one's obviously been left in the open for a couple of days, and the insects have homed in. Corpses make excellent egg incubators and maggot nurseries. If I were a blowfly I'd look no further. Better prepare two Lysol baths, Paul.'

'Yes, sir.'

Alan heard Patrick and Paul talking, but he understood nothing of their conversation. It registered only as a jumble of words. He continued to stare blankly at the two bags. The ends of both were neatly gathered into frills, bound tightly with thick black tape. They reminded him of oversized giftwrapped boxes of bonbons. A sudden image of a French confectionery shop flooded into his mind, bringing with it all the sights, sounds and smells of a Parisian summer. It was one of those instant flashes of calm, totally disconnected thought that often precedes severe shock. Slowly his mind began to clear, and as it did so, grim actuality dawned. He saw the reality of the bagged body closest to him, and sensed something was wrong. There was

127

something odd, peculiar . . . 'Dear God, there's no head,' he exclaimed.

'No head, and no hands,' Patrick agreed, reading the mutilated corpse as if it were a book. 'Pity I can't open the bags and take a closer look. I have to wait for the Home Office chap to do that.'

'Daisy. Poor, poor Daisy.'

As if she were responding to Alan's cry, the main door opened, and Daisy ran in, Judy Osbourne close on her heels. She paused for a moment, looking around wildly.

'Daisy.' Patrick moved swiftly, blocking her view of the trolleys. Paul moved even faster. He replaced the covering sheets deftly, leaving no corner bare.

'I want to see him,' Daisy demanded, trying to side-step Patrick. 'For heaven's sake, I'm his wife,' she protested. Judy caught at her hand, but she jerked herself free. 'I'm not hysterical,' she screamed unconvincingly. 'And I know what he looks like. He hasn't got a head, has he, nor has the other one?'

A stunned silence, punctuated only by the sound of dripping water from the dissection slab, descended on the mortuary.

Daisy looked hard at Patrick. 'He's wearing black evening trousers and a white evening shirt,' she continued. She closed her eyes tightly, conjuring up the ghoulish nightmarish images that had prevented her from sleeping. 'The woman has torn stockings, and a raincoat . . . a brown one,' she finished hesitantly.

Patrick looked at her uneasily. 'You've been on the motorway. You've spoken to the police?'

'We haven't been anywhere near the motorway,' Judy interrupted. 'I brought Daisy to the hospital to see Alan. Before that we were in town. We couldn't even drive on the motorway. It was closed. We didn't know why until we got here and heard the rumours.'

'I don't need to see what's on those trolleys,' Daisy

said. 'I've seen Tim every night since he disappeared. Ask her.' She turned to Judy. 'You tell them. Go on, tell them.' Her voice rose hysterically. 'Tell them how I saw Tim that first night. And I've seen him every damned night since he disappeared, without . . . without . . .' She choked on the words until they became rasping, guttural sobs.

Alan put his arm awkwardly around her shoulders. He looked mutely at Patrick.

'Patrick, please,' Judy begged.

'Uncover the bags, Paul,' Patrick ordered quietly, tearing off his gloves. He reached out and took hold of Daisy's elbow. She allowed him to propel her towards the trolleys. Her knees were trembling, her hands shaking. Patrick tightened his grip on her. 'I can't open the bags. Not until the Home Office pathologist arrives. You understand?' Daisy nodded, desperately trying to keep her emotions in check. She looked down at the trolleys. The plastic bags were thick, giving the encased corpses an estranged, specimen-like appearance. Still, immobilized, they held none of the terrors of the night-time visitations that had begun to haunt even her waking moments.

'That could be a woman.' Patrick pointed to the trolley nearest him. 'The limbs have been severed from the torso, but there's a brown raincoat, and one of the legs is encased in a stocking. The head and hands appear to be missing. I can't say any more than that for the present.' Sickened by the sight of the mutilated corpses, Alan stepped back. 'And the other one . . .' Patrick replaced the sheet on the first trolley and turned to the second. He'd known Tim, liked him, but in the mortuary he was pathologist first, man second. 'White evening shirt, black evening trousers . . .'

Daisy heard Patrick's voice droning on. She looked down, but she saw nothing. Blinding tears fell thick

129

and fast from her eyes, raining down on to the hard, unyielding surface of the bag below.

'The body is dressed as a male, is probably male. Five foot six inches tall . . .' Patrick paused as he realized the significance of what he'd said. He ran his forefinger along the length of the trolley where the body lay. 'How tall was Tim?' He asked quickly.

'Six foot six inches,' Daisy whispered. It was the first time she'd heard anyone other than herself speak of Tim in the past tense.

'I thought so. This corpse can't possibly be Tim's.' Patrick replaced the covering sheet.

'It hasn't got a head!' Alan exclaimed. 'How in hell's name can you tell the height without a head?'

'Very simply,' Patrick replied confidently. 'By using tables related to the length of the long bone. I've worked out heights, approximate to one or two inches, on a lot less corpse than this.'

'Tim was always getting into trouble over his height,' Alan rambled. 'If anyone asked him, he would always say he was about six foot. It used to make short men mad.'

Patrick turned to Daisy. 'The police have found no other bodies.'

'Then Tim's still alive!' Judy interrupted eagerly.

'All it means is that wherever Tim Sherringham is, he's not part of this little consignment,' Patrick replied logically. 'I'm sorry, Daisy. It doesn't make it any easier for you. You're back where you started. Not knowing. Sometimes I think that's far worse than the certainty of death.'

'At least there's a chance Tim's alive,' Judy insisted.

'No.' Daisy shook her head. 'He's dead. I know he's dead. It can only be a matter of time before he's found. And when he is, he'll look like these.'

Alan opened the door. Judy wrapped her arm gently around Daisy's waist and led her out of the mortuary.

When Daisy was out of earshot, Alan turned to Patrick. 'You'll telephone?'

'The minute I see anything remotely resembling Tim Sherringham,' Patrick agreed, snapping on a fresh pair of rubber gloves.

Peter Collins slumped wearily on to one of the hard wooden chairs in the soulless room Bill Mulcahy grandly referred to as his 'office'. It was just across the corridor from the largest hall in the station. Usually echoing and empty, the hall now bustled with uniformed and plain-clothes officers, and an abundance of telephones, switchboards and computers. It had been designated as Incident Room for what the press had already christened the 'Motorway Murders Pile-up'.

Peter had just left the late-night briefing, and he hadn't liked it. In fact he hadn't liked anything about his entire day. The way his and every other local's noses had been pushed out by the London 'boys'. The way he'd been working for what seemed liked forever, without a break. And above all, he didn't like feeling empty. He was hungry. So damned hungry, he wondered if he was still capable of eating.

Bill Mulcahy and Trevor Joseph joined him. Both looked as exhausted as he felt.

'It's so long since I've eaten, my stomach thinks my throat's cut,' Bill complained.

'Don't worry. Peter will buy us all a steak in the Beachcomber on the way home.'

'It's your turn,' Peter growled. 'I was the one grafting in the dirt all day while you two swanned around in the car comforting grieving widows. Remember!'

'Grieving brother, actually,' Bill corrected. 'The widow was out with Judy Osbourne, and she's not a widow yet. You were at the briefing.'

' "Yet" being the operative word. If some nut's prowling the motorway looking to chop unsuspecting

131

souls into little pieces, and a man goes missing while travelling along that motorway, it doesn't take a genius to put two and two together. We didn't dig in the right spot today, that's all. And don't take that as an admission that I want to go digging in the dirt again tomorrow.'

'You won't have to.' Bill sat behind his desk.

'Back to the drug squad?' Peter brightened visibly.

'Not exactly,' Bill hedged.

'Oh, come on, the news is out. The pushers aren't stupid. They'll figure that we're tied up on this, and organize themselves a bloody field day.'

'What have you got in mind?' Trevor asked.

'There are some things that need checking out. Might be something . . .'

'Might be nothing. But knowing the force, it'll all be bloody legwork!'

'Knock it off, will you, Peter,' Bill ordered. 'We're all tired. We've all had enough. What makes you so damned special that you have the right to complain?'

'Let's get on with it, Peter,' Trevor suggested. 'Otherwise we could be here all night.'

'And then we'll never eat.' Peter resigned himself to the inevitable.

'If this is going to take long, Bill, perhaps we should send out for a take-away,' Trevor suggested.

'Good idea. You order for all of us.'

Trevor opened the door and called one of the duty officers. By the time he'd closed the office door and sat back down, both Bill and Peter were in a calmer frame of mind.

'It would be a right feather in our caps if we could outsmart the London boys on this one.' There was a ghost of a smile playing around Bill's mouth.

'Are you suggesting we run our own investigation?' Trevor asked warily. The last thing he needed was to get caught between two factions of superior officers playing the dubious game of one-upmanship. Experience had taught him that the only possible outcome in that situation was trouble for the poor blighter jammed in the middle.

'Not separate investigations. Work in isolation during the day, but exchange of information, complete information,' Bill flashed a warning glance at Peter, 'every night. I've talked this over with the man in charge, and he agrees with me. So much information has flooded in, and is still flooding in, after the six o'clock news, that it's become practically impossible for any of us to evaluate the worth of what we've got. It could take months to sift through it all, and in the meantime two locals prodding and poking in the right places might, just might, hit the jackpot.'

'And that's us?' Peter swung his legs on to the only spare chair in the room.

'That's you.'

'Where do we start?' Trevor asked.

'By going over what we've got.'

'That's easy enough, at any rate.' Peter settled back as comfortably as he could. 'We haven't got much to go over. A missing doctor, two unidentified bodies, neither of which tallies with the said doctor's description, and an ongoing search.'

'And I thought you two were coppers. We've got a killer, or killers, who know their motorway.' Bill pulled his notebook out of his pocket and referred to its well-thumbed pages. 'Whoever it was carried the victims there after they'd been murdered elsewhere. There was very little blood or staining on site, and the pathologist was sure the last one wasn't killed where she was found – what was left of her was dragged under that hedge after death. From the knife marks in the ground there's also a strong possibility that the first victim was decapitated after death close to where we uncovered him. The forensic boys have given us reason to believe that the murderer, or at least one of them if there was more than one, may have walked down alongside that hedge to the river bank to wash before leaving the scene. There was no blood, but marks were found in the mud to indicate some activity took place. And then apart from what we've gleaned from the site evidence, we've got a well-heeled important brother who's married to a peer's daughter, and a peer who happens to be a cabinet minister, no less, who might be regarded as a soft touch by a possible kidnapper. So, given nothing firmer to go on, we could consider the possibility that Tim Sherringham was kidnapped.'

'That hedge could be a disposal area for one of the London mobs,' Peter murmured. 'You know that could well tie in.'

'Might even explain the missing heads and hands,' Trevor chipped in. 'No fingerprints, no easy identification from mug shots.'

'But still take away the "ifs" "maybes" and suppositions, and you're left with precious little hard evidence.'

'Sooner or later someone's going to identify one of those bodies, head or no head,' Bill persisted. 'And then there's the missing appendages. They have to be somewhere. And if they're maggot-infested and rotting, they're generating heat, and sooner or later the heat-seeking cameras will pick them up, just as surely as they picked up that corpse today.'

'And if they're burned, or buried miles away? Weighted and dumped out to sea for the fishes to feed on? Dissolved in acid? Walled up in a kitchen cupboard, next to a stove?' Peter was beginning to enjoy himself.

'As I said, even without heads we have colouring, hair and skin. Height, approximate weight. We can check the files.'

'Have you seen the size of the missing persons files, Bill?' Trevor asked. 'Just in this station alone.'

'There has to be blood-stained vehicle.' Bill side-stepped the issues they were raising. 'You can't carry bits of mutilated corpses without some staining. Checks have gone out on all the garages and cleaners. We may well get leads in from those.'

'If the body was well wrapped and the wrappers have since been disposed of?' Peter continued to play devil's advocate.

'There's the timing. One of those bodies has only been in that hedge for two to three days. Someone, somewhere along the route the murderer took, could have seen something suspicious. And someone – family, friends, workmates – must be missing her.'

'The pathologist was careful to point out that all he could say for certain was that the body had been in the hedge for a couple of days. All he had to go on to determine time of death was the level of growth of bluebottle maggot infestation, and the maturity of the larvae. The victims could have been killed some time ago, kept in cold storage, and dumped at a later date,' Trevor mused.

'Then evidence may turn up to suggest where they were kept in the mean time.' Bill's patience, brittle at the best of times, was rapidly reaching breaking point. 'Look, all I can say is tread carefully with what we have got, and make the most of it.'

'Like Daisy Sherringham's headless body nightmare?' Peter had to get it in. The one oddity none of them had even tried to explain.

'Could be she knows more about her husband's disappearance than she's letting on.' Bill cracked his knuckles. 'Perhaps we don't have to look any further than the family for the solution to Tim Sherringham's disappearance?'

'You're a mile out on that one. Apart from the fact

it wouldn't explain away the headless corpses in the hedge, Daisy would never in a million years . . .'

Trevor was halted in mid-sentence by a knock on the door. A keen young constable opened it and stuck his head round.

'Supper at last!' Peter lifted his feet from the chair.

'Afraid not, sir, but the duty officer thought Superintendent Mulcahy might like to see this.' He handed Bill a piece of paper. 'The telephone numbers of the witnesses are on it, sir. This makes two sightings.'

'Thank you, Constable . . . Harries, isn't it?'

'Yes, sir.'

'Don't forget the food,' Peter reminded.

'I'll bring it as soon as it arrives, sir.'

'You mind you do.'

Bill looked carefully at the paper the constable had brought. He stroked his chin thoughtfully for a few moments, then, making a quick decision, he handed it over to Trevor. 'This could be something for you to start with. On the surface it looks weird, but then two sightings of the same thing could be significant. Must be truth of a sort in there somewhere. And then there's the timing. It couldn't be more perfect.'

'What is it?' Peter asked from behind closed eyes.

'A clown,' Trevor read. 'A clown dressed in a black and white suit with black and white make-up. A pierrot?' he looked questioningly across at Bill.

'We've got enough bloody clowns on this case already, if you ask me.' Peter settled back as comfortably as he could on his two hard chairs.

'This one was seen on the motorway,' Bill said. 'Two people on two different nights saw a clown close to the spot where the bodies were discovered.'

'Had they been drinking?'

'That's for you to find out.'

'These descriptions don't make much sense.' Trevor studied the scribbled report. 'A lorry driver saw what looked like a pierrot hitchhiking at around four in the morning five days ago. When he stopped, the man disappeared. Melted into thin air. He even left the cab of his lorry to look. What do you make of that?'

'That the lorry driver's a screwball.' Peter yawned. 'Would you stop to pick up a clown at four in the morning?'

'I don't know. If I saw a car broken down next to him, maybe I would.'

'Then you're a screwball too.'

'There's no mention of broken-down cars, and if you look at the physical descriptions they don't tally,' Bill pointed out to Trevor. 'The first sighting goes back two weeks. You'd better see the witness and try to pin him down closer.'

'According to this, that clown was short and plump.'

'And the second sighting goes back only five days and reports a tall thin man.'

Trevor tossed the paper on to the desk. 'Why do the nuts crawl out of the woodwork every time there's a murder?'

'They've made it easy for us. All we want is a tall, thin, short, plump clown. There can't be many of those about. Once we've caught it, we've got our man.'

'Snap out of it, Peter,' Bill grumbled. 'Clown or no clown, you're not helping.'

'A clown, a clown.' Peter emerged from his stupor.

'That's enough.'

'I'm serious.' Peter sat up and rubbed his eyes with his knuckles. 'I've heard someone talking about a clown recently. The clown's back . . . he's back.' He looked at Trevor. 'Does that ring a bell with you?'

'No.'

The door opened and the same constable as before entered the room carrying three large, pleasantly odorous cardboard boxes. 'They didn't have steak, sir, so I

137

took the liberty of choosing three double portions of pork chops and chips.'

'Young man, you will go far.' Bill snatched the top box.

'I know where I heard it.' Peter opened his box. 'Andy.'

'Andy?' Trevor bit at his plastic sachets of salt and vinegar and emptied them over his chips. 'Andy's a right clown himself. The man's addled. You can't believe a word he says.'

'I found him on the beach a couple of nights back when I was walking home from the pub. I asked him why he wasn't sleeping in the Shelter. He told me the clown was back, on the pier.'

'Sounds like scintillating conversation.' Bill stuffed a whole chop 'eye' into his mouth. 'It really makes sense,' he mumbled.

'There was a lot more. I only wish I could remember some of it. It ran along the lines of the pier being open, and the clown hanging out there. He said he could sleep in the old theatre on the pier.'

'Do you think it's worth checking out?' Bill looked from Peter to Trevor.

'Isn't the pier wired off?'

'It is,' Peter confirmed. 'Who owns it, Bill, the council?'

'Don't know. You'll have to look into it.'

'We could call in there and take a look on the way home?' Trevor suggested.

'You out to get medals?'

'No, another hour's sleep tomorrow morning.'

'Eight o'clock sharp,' Bill emphasized. 'And be grateful for it. If you were still on motorway detail it would be dawn.'

'My back is grateful, believe you me. Another day bent double peering into thick undergrowth and I'd be crippled for life.'

138

'There isn't a copper on the force who hasn't had his fair share of backache at one time or another.' Bill wolfed down the remainder of his chips. He sat back in his chair, swung his feet on top of the mess on his desk and let out a large satisfied burp. 'While you're checking out the pier, you may as well check out the shelter for down and outs. Sam Mayberry may have picked up on something. This clown of Andy's, for instance.'

'Will do.' Peter followed suit and belched.

'And Trevor.'

'Mm.' Trevor concentrated on the chop bone he was gnawing.

'Daisy. Daisy Sherringham. You get too involved there, my boy, and you'll find yourself back on the beat quicker than you can whistle "Rule Britannia". Do you understand?'

'Yes.'

'But while you're at it you may as well go and visit the Sherringhams. Take Peter with you. That's an order.'

'Yes, sir.' Trevor only just managed to keep the sarcasm from his voice.

'Sit on them a bit. The London boys are going through the guest list for the dinner party, but that doesn't mean you can't talk to the relatives. The brother and his wife, for instance. What's her name?'

'Joanna, née Lady Joanna Holbourne,' Trevor answered.

'That's the one. And one final word while we're on the topic. Bear that headless dream in mind. I'm not keen on this psychic nonsense, and I do believe that villains come from every class. High as well as low.'

'I won't forget.'

'I guess that just about wraps it up for today.' Bill stretched his hands above his head. 'I don't know about you boys, but I'm for one last check in the incident room and bed.'

'We're for the pier, then home.'

'The pier?' Peter raised his eyebrows at Trevor.

'The pier.'

'In that case, the pier it is.' Peter formed a rough funnel out of his cardboard box and used it to tip the small hard remnants of chips into his mouth. Then he screwed up the greasy packaging and flicked it expertly into Bill's overflowing wastepaper basket.

'Well, what are we waiting for, Joseph?' He got up and rubbed his sticky fingers roughly in his short brown hair. 'Let's go.'

Andy could hear them talking and scrabbling outside. Avoiding the holes, he sat carefully on the rough wooden boards of the theatre floor, and laughed. He laughed and laughed, rolling around from side to side. They wouldn't get in. They'd never get in. The only ones who knew the secret beside himself were the clowns. He could see one of them on stage now, silent and alone. Lying like a limp puppet waiting for the master to pull the strings and give him life.

He stopped laughing and stared, but the clowns remained still, staring back at him. Perhaps soon the clown would sing. Tell some jokes. He hoped so. Those were the best times. It was so easy then, so easy to pretend. He'd take a chair to where the back row used to be, put his feet on another chair, close his eyes. Then he'd go back.

The sands would be crowded, like they had been when he was little, just after the last war. The women with their big patterned dresses tucked up into their knickers, holding hands with small children, jumping them high over the waves that splashed on to the beach. The men lying in deck chairs, knotted handkerchiefs on the tops of their heads, glass bottles of beer buried to the neck in the sand within arm's reach. The Punch and Judy show set up in front of the steps that led to the promenade. A big, noisy, restless half-circle of children sitting around it. The grown-ups standing on the edge, moving slyly away just before the clown came with his rattling jar. And heavy over everything, the salt sea tang that carried on its breeze so many other smells. Stewed tea, vinegary fish and chips, the sweet sickly smell of lollies and rock melting under the hot sun.

And there'd be clowns. Always clowns, more ragged and not as good as the ones his mother remembered from her own early days, or so she'd tell him. He used to sit on the edge of the moth-eaten grey blanket his mother took to the beach, watching the clowns move among the crowds, singing, smiling, joking, handing out bits of paper telling people the times of their shows on the pier. He'd beg, and his mother would look at him, a frown creasing her worn face. 'Perhaps later, Andy. At the end of the week, if there's money left over.'

Money! Change! It had always been a problem. There'd never been enough, not until he was in the army, and even then he'd lost most of his pay. Cards. The others had always beaten him at cards, and that left him short for beer. Water poured into his mouth at the thought of beer. He wanted a drink so badly he could almost taste it. Beer, gritty, warm and flat as it had been when he'd scrabbled under the deck chairs as a child and stolen sneaky sips from the buried bottles. Beer, cool and frothing as they'd served it in the German pubs when he'd been in the army.

Dazed by remembering, he looked around. There was no beer here. Only the clown, sitting in the darkness of the empty theatre. The moonlight shining through smashed windows. The sole light that brightened the stage now. Then he heard a humming, and

141

remembered the box under the stage, at the back. It would be cold in the box. There'd be no drink there. There never was. And he'd found no change that day to buy a bottle. But he could suck at the ice bars that formed on the inside of the box. It wouldn't be good, not like a bottle, but it would be cold. And wet.

He crawled under the stage boards. Had to be careful. The floor had lots of holes. Once his leg had fallen through and he'd hurt himself trying to get it out. He heard the humming. The machine buzzed all the time. It was hot and stinking. He could see the outline of the box, grey in the darkness, then the moonlight poured in through the broken window at the back. He was over the sea now, in the big room at the end of the pier. He could hear the waves swishing beneath him. He looked before he crept out from under the boards. Had to be careful in this room because of the clowns. There might be one or two lurking around and they didn't always leave him alone. One was especially bad, the one who came in sometimes late at night. The thin one. Last winter that clown had seen him, and hissed and stamped. That was when he'd run away and hurt his leg.

He couldn't see anyone. He crept low to the box. Then, crouching by its side, he lifted the lid and put his hand inside. It was hairy. Cold, weedy hairs, he could feel them. Pushing the hair aside he scrabbled at the sides of the box and ran his fingers over the ice, trying to pull a piece off. He dug the tips of his fingers in, brought them out and licked them. They were cold, and they tasted of metal, of iron.

He put his hand back in and touched the hairs again without wanting to. He reached past. There was something. Something loose, thin, cold that came away in his hand. He pulled it out, snapping it with a loud crack. A piece fell off and brushed past his hand as it fell to the bottom of the box. But he held on to what he had. He pulled it out and looked at it. Two circles of glass. Glasses. You could see better with glasses. He put them on the end of his nose. But there was only one arm. They fell off. He picked them up from the floor and pushed them into his rags. He might get change for them. Blackie might give him something for glasses. Blackie was daft.

He forgot about the glasses and put his hand back into the box for more ice. He licked his fingers. It was good. Not like a bottle. But good.

'The only way Andy could possibly have slept on this pier is if he flew in.' Trevor faced the barricade of rolled barbed wire and planks that stretched across the opening where the turnstiles had once operated.

'I only repeated what the man said. I didn't guarantee it as true.'

Trevor studied the crumbling steps that led down to the sands. 'Do you think there could be another way in?'

'I think we should come back in the morning when we can see what we're doing. Besides which, it's drinking time we're wasting. I'll buy you a pint at the White Hart.'

'It's after twelve.'

'That's when the White Hart livens up.'

'It's illegal to drink after hours.'

'Only when there isn't a policeman present. Look, I'll tell you what, we'll drive round to the White Hart and have a chat with the landlord. He's been in the place for years. He'll know who owns this pile of crap. And that could save us a lot of leg-work in the morning when we're knocking on doors, trying to find who has the key.'

'Key? Axe, more like it.' Trevor surveyed the barricades. He took one last look down the steps. Much as he hated to admit it, Peter was right. It would be stupid to try to do more by moonlight. 'You buy.' He turned his back reluctantly to the pier.

'The first pint, at any rate,' Peter agreed, leading the way back to the car.

'Daisy, are you sure that's what you want to do?' Judy asked.

'I'm sure.' Daisy was sitting in an uncomfortably small armchair in the middle of Judy's minute living-room. Judy and Alan were sharing the matching utility settee.

'You shouldn't be alone,' Alan insisted. 'Not now. Why don't you take a break? You can always stay with Carol and the kids.'

'No. I want to get back to work, the sooner the better. And I want to move into a hospital flat.'

'You want this?' Judy waved her hand at the spartan surroundings.

'I don't think I could cope with living alone in the flat, and I simply can't spend another day in Richard's mausoleum . . .' Daisy's voice faltered as she remembered. She'd used the term mausoleum before. The last time she'd spoken to Tim. She'd been angry with him because he'd talked about working in Richard's clinic, and she'd retaliated by calling the place a mausoleum. God, was there nothing that didn't carry a reminder of that night!

'Daisy.' Judy came and crouched beside her chair. 'You can't know for certain that Tim is dead.'

'Do you think I want Tim dead? I've thought of nothing but Tim alive since we walked out of the mortuary. But I know.' She looked into Judy's eyes. 'I know, Judy. He's dead. I don't need more proof or to have anyone tell me what I'm certain of now. I've lost Tim. I'm alone, and it's so damned . . . hard.' Cold, numb nothingness had been replaced by anger. And for the moment it was sufficient to sustain her.

She looked around the room, the furniture, the over-bright curtains that didn't match the carpet, the atmosphere of transience that was a part of rented accommodation. The feeling of not really belonging, just passing through. Using the cupboards to store belongings that were on their way to somewhere else, somewhere more permanent. Was this going to be her life from now on? A solitary, single flat with no one waiting for her to come home?

But even this flat of Judy's held memories. Tim had been here. He'd sat next to her, a sandwich in the hand he'd rested on her shoulder, a whisky glass in the other, his head thrown back as he'd laughed raucously at one of Alan's or Judy's jokes. Were all the flats the same? Would she ever find a place where she could think peacefully of Tim, without reminders staring her painfully in the face?

'You're not alone.' Judy reached out and tried to touch her hand.

'Oh yes I am.' She turned a bleak, dry-eyed face to Judy. 'I'm not looking for pity or sympathy,' she warned harshly, forestalling sentimentality. 'I'm not sure how to explain what I feel. There was us, and now there's me. And I don't even know who I am any more.' She read the look of embarrassed anguish on Alan's face, and softened her voice. 'I know what *we* like. I can tell you what Tim and I do in our spare time, what food we eat, how we'd furnish a room, what our taste is. But *me*,' she smiled wryly, 'that's quite another matter. Tim became a part of my life, a part of me, from the first moment we met. I can't really remember what I did, where I went, or even who my friends were before he was there. Now I have to start again. And to be honest I can't find a reason for doing so. I don't mean it in a morbid sense,' she looked from Judy to Alan, 'but tell me, what do I do? Do I continue to work here, walk the corridors, go to the canteen, drop in on the staff parties? Tim won't be there. I'll never turn a corner again and see him unexpectedly, but the reminders will be there. And they'll hurt,' she said bitterly. 'And then what happens after work's over? There'll be no one to wait for, no one to cook for, no joint plans to be made. I could leave the hospital, of course, but to go where? I can't think straight, let alone act decisively. I know that I have to start again,' she said finally, 'but I simply don't have the will, or the strength left to do it.'

'For what it's worth, you have our friendship,' Alan offered humbly, breaking the silence that had fallen over the room. 'And before you say anything, I'm not offering pity. Judy and I think a lot of you, and Tim,' he added gravely. 'And we'd be honoured if you saw fit to lean on us until you find your own strength again. And you will find it, Daisy,' he promised. 'Sooner than you think.'

'I hope so, if only for your sake. I'm leaning rather heavily on both of you at the moment.'

'Lean away, that's what friends are for.' Judy turned her mind to the immediate and the practical. 'We'll help you move from your flat into one of the hospital flats tomorrow. If that's what you really want to do.'

'It is.'

'And I'll do what I can to persuade Administration to put you back on the rota,' Alan offered.

'Thank you. I'd like to stay here, in town . . .' Daisy locked her fingers together and stared down at them, '. . . until . . . until Tim is found.' Her voice cracked under the strain of formulating her nightmares in blunt uncompromising words. 'I'll begin where I left off. The longer I delay, the worse it's going to be. And the flat.' She took a deep breath. 'I don't think I'll ever be able to face living there without Tim. I'm going to hand the keys back to Richard.'

Tomorrow stretched out in front of her. She'd be

146

busy, there'd be things to do. And the day after, if she was lucky, Administration would allow her to return to work. Life would move on, one day at a time. That's how it would be from now on. Nothing to look forward to. No elaborate plans for the future. Just the moment, and that's all any of us really have, she reflected grimly, allowing herself one brief moment of self-pity.

'It would be better if you lived in a hospital flat close to Judy, rather than alone in the your own flat,' Alan agreed. 'But will you be able to get a flat tomorrow?'

'I should think so,' Judy said purposefully. 'Apart from being very basic and utility, as you can see, hospital flats are far too close to work for comfort. Anyone who takes one has to accept that for practical purposes they're on call virtually twenty-four hours a day, three-hundred-and-sixty-five days a year. There are two empty on this floor at the moment.'

'Then, hopefully, Daisy can move into one of those.' He leant forward and grasped Daisy's hand. 'Promise me one thing. Don't give Richard the keys to the flat. At least, not yet.' He took his courage in both hands. 'Not until Tim's found, one way or another,' he blurted out quickly.

'I promise.'

'And now, I'm going to drive you to Richard's,' Alan announced, rising stiffly from his seat.

'Can't I stay here, just for tonight?' Daisy pleaded.

'You know you're more than welcome.' Judy sat on the arm of the settee. 'But we promised Richard.'

'Of course.'

'Daisy, there's nothing wrong at Richard's, is there?' Alan asked, sensing her reluctance to leave.

'No. No, of course not. It's just that I'm comfortable here,' she hedged unconvincingly.

'I'll come with you if you like,' Judy offered. 'I'm sure that butler of Richard's could find a spare mattress.'

147

'No.' Daisy found the courage to put on a brave face. She kissed Judy on the cheek. 'It's only for one night. I'll see you tomorrow.'

'First thing.' Judy opened the door. 'And we'll move you out of both the flat and Richard's. If there's any problem getting a flat, we'll sort out a put-you-up here.'

'Where's it going?' Alan enquired dryly. 'In the bath?'

'These flats have hidden spaces and delights.' Judy forced a smile. 'I'll enlighten you about them tomorrow, Daisy.'

'Thank you.' Daisy walked into the outside corridor. Night closed in around her. She felt herself slipping away from Judy and Alan, even as they spoke.

'They'll find Tim soon, Daisy. I promise you. This can't go on much longer. It can't.'

'Do you really believe that?'

Alan took her arm and led her towards the lifts.

Trevor felt sick as well as tired. The back room of the White Hart was not only stuffy, it was filled with the most incredibly overpowering smells of sweat and decay. It was also decorated in the most horrible begrimed, nicotine-stained shade of puce he'd ever seen. And to add insult to injury, the beer was warm and flat. Peter had assured him it was a fine pint of real ale, but in his opinion the cloudy depths looked and tasted more like the dregs of a forensic specimen. Even the landlord, obese, with piggy eyes and slicked-back, greasy black hair, parodied the essential conception of what 'mine host' should be.

Ben Gummer had been a fairground wrestler, in his time a good one, according to Peter, but sitting in Peter's idea of a good pub, Trevor was seriously beginning to question his partner's judgement. And then again, whatever Ben Gummer had been, he'd long since gone to seed. The torn trousers, tied at what passed for a waist with string, and the filthy ripped vest left nothing of the bulky, sagging figure to the realms of imagination. Trevor sat opposite the landlord at the small round table Peter had commandeered, and watched, repulsed, yet at the same time strangely fascinated, by the sight of the fat man's dirty white flesh wobbling in and out of the holes in his clothes.

'Don't allow any down-and-outs in here, you should know that, Peter.' Ben took a long draught of his beer. 'My customers,' he looked at the group of seedy men collected around the bar, 'aren't exactly the upper crust, but none of them are at the chewed end of a rope either.'

'So you don't know anything about the down-and-outs who sleep on the pier?' Trevor wanted to get the police business over and done with quickly so he could go home. He was beginning to look on his poky flat with a new fondness; the present surroundings were enough to make him look fondly on almost anywhere, even the station.

'I don't know about the pier as it is now.' Ben spat beer as he talked. 'It's years since I've set foot on the boards, but the pier as it was, well, that's a different story.'

'When was that, Ben?' Peter settled back in his broken chair. He was clearly at home, happy at the prospect of a full night's drinking. Damn him, Trevor thought, remembering that they'd come in Peter's car. Peter had the keys, and it was too far for him to walk back to his flat.

'Just before the war. I came out of the army, thought I'd finished with King and Country for good.' He winked slyly at Peter. 'Little did I know I'd be back and fighting for real a couple of years later. Well, I got myself a pitch on the pier, good one, too. Two of the stalls at the far end next to the theatre. Knocked them into one and set up a wrestling booth. Really raked it

149

in. Like scraping flies off honey. Those were the days. I lived well. Best suits, best food, best drink and,' he leered at Trevor, 'best women.'

'The pier, Ben.' Peter lifted his glass.'You'd still know your way round it?'

'Like the back of my own hand,' Ben boasted. 'Just like the back of my hand.' His words began to run into one another. 'Pier wasn't new, not even then.' He set down his glass. 'According to the old pros it was run down. But then I didn't work it when it was new. That was long before my time. My father's too.'

'Who did you pay your rent to, Ben?' Trevor pushed. 'Council?'

'Council! Not the council. Toffs owned it then. Still do, if I remember right. They tried to hand it over to the town back in the fifties, but the council wouldn't have it. Place is falling apart, cost too much to put it right. But then isn't that just like the bloody toffs. Bleed something dry, take the money, run like hell and leave someone else with the mess.'

'Can you remember the name of the toffs?' Trevor asked impatiently, ignoring the warning look Peter was giving him.

'Of course I can.' Ben leaned conspiratorially over the table. 'Called themselves lords. All airs and bloody graces, but those of us who worked the pier knew the truth. Lords or no lords they married dirt. A showgirl who started off by showing more than women used to in those days. Now, of course, it's all different. You can open the paper and see it spread out in front of you . . .'

'Who was this woman?' Even Peter's concentration was flagging.

'She danced for the pierrot troop who worked the pier theatre back in the twenties. My father's time,' Ben divulged patronizingly. 'Old George who watched the turnstile told me it was common knowledge that she'd give out a lot more back-stage after the show,

150

but only if you had sixpence to spare.' He licked his wet lips. 'If you had money, she'd dish out whatever tickled your fancy, if you take my meaning. But if you ask me, she got what she wanted all right. Caught her lord, lock, stock, title, money, the lot. Like a dog after a bitch on heat, he couldn't leave her alone. Kept on coming back for more. And in the end, she wouldn't take money. Marriage was what she was after, and that was what she got. Her Ladyship. Lady! Common prostitute, that's all she ever was.'

'Who?' Trevor demanded wearily. 'Who did she marry?'

'The same lot that owns that flash clinic on the headland now,' Ben revealed triumphantly.

'The Sherringhams?' Peter almost choked on his beer.

'No, the Holbournes. Lord Holbourne, that's what he called himself. Her son's still on top. High-class bastards. And the likes of me and you, the workers,' he emphasized, 'where are we, that's what I'd like to know? As badly off as our fathers ever were. It's not right. We should have a share of what they've got. Liars, thieves and prostitutes, that's what that bloody toff family were, and still are for all their fancy clinic.'

He continued rambling, but Trevor and Peter stopped listening. They looked at one another, the same thought in both their minds. Joanna, Richard Sherringham's wife, was a Holbourne. Her father had built the clinic that bore his name as well as Richard's. And the Holbournes owned the pier that Andy slept on, and more to the point saw clowns on. There had to be a connection.

'Where?' Trevor asked. 'Where's the tie-in?'

'Probably up another blind alley. The same one our short, fat, tall, thin clown's sitting in.' Peter drained his glass and handed it to Trevor. 'Your round, I believe.'

Chapter Six

Richard Sherringham woke early the next morning. He opened his curtains to a sky barely flushed by the first rays of dawn. He showered, shaved, dressed and still the hand on his watch hovered before six. He closed the door quietly on his bedroom and walked down the gallery. The house was silent, but a strip of artificial light shone beneath the door of Joanna's room. He hesitated for a moment, debating whether to knock. He'd scarcely spoken to her since her return, and even when he had, their exchanges had been anything but civil.

He was realistic enough to recognize their estrangement was more his fault than hers. He knew she was fond of Tim. She was coping with the stress of his disappearance the only way she knew how; by immersing herself in her ridiculous programme of research for the cosmetic company. She'd done much the same thing after his father's death and her miscarriage. It really wasn't such a bad reaction. Better to immerse oneself in work than to snarl and snap at everyone, as he'd been doing for the past few days.

Perhaps if he made the first move . . . he tapped lightly on the door, and waited. When there was no response, he walked away quickly. Later . . . he'd try to talk to her later.

He paused outside Daisy's door and listened. He heard nothing. Assuming she was still peacefully asleep he walked down the staircase. The full-length oil painting that had been his wedding present to Joanna dominated the impressive entrance hall. Her slim figure stood outlined against a background of summer greenery. She was wearing a plain white dress, her blue eyes as free and untroubled then as they appeared now. He couldn't deny Joanna's beauty, nor her strengths. She was the perfect wife, the perfect hostess, intelligent, witty, charming. For years she'd stage-managed the cocktail and dinner parties that had proved so conducive to his financial and business dealings. But . . . there had always been that 'but'.

Joanna's even temper and placidity had never excited any strong passions within him, not like . . . A rare smile lit his face as another image floated into his mind. The image of the woman who for many years had been his mistress. She remained as loving, undemanding, and raunchy as ever. She understood him without having to ask any questions. She could match her mood to his, merely by sensing the atmosphere he carried with him. His life would be so different if he could be with her permanently.

Plagued by a sudden, demeaning feeling of guilt, he turned away from the portrait and wrenched open the front door. Perhaps he should consider divorcing Joanna, and not only for selfish reasons. She couldn't be happy. She must know, sense, that he didn't love her as completely and wholeheartedly as a husband should.

And Tim? No matter how he tried to stop thinking about his brother, there was the pain of knowing that something had happened to him. He loved Tim. Loved him for his own sake. After their father had died, Tim had meant more to him than anyone else, much, much more than Joanna. It wasn't simply because Tim was the only family he had left. Tim had become friend, brother, and to a certain extent the son he'd never had. Once this was all over, he would make plans for himself and his mistress – and for Tim. But they wouldn't include Joanna.

He'd take care of her, of course. He owed her that

much. And now that his social and financial position was unassailable, that side of things would prove easy to manage. There was such a thing as civilized divorce. George might prove difficult. On paper the Holbournes owned forty per cent of the shares in the clinic, but they had no real interest in the day-to-day running of the place. He could buy them out. If he made an offer soon, while he was still with Joanna, they'd have no reason not to take it.

He closed the door and walked down the path that led to the garage. Yesterday... He shut his eyes tightly. He preferred to forget yesterday. The body in the evening shirt and trousers. He'd been so certain it was Tim. But it hadn't been. And that meant Tim was alive. He had to keep believing that much. He had no reason not to. He'd paid the money. Done all they asked him to do. Sooner or later there'd be a call. And Tim.

When he reached his office he'd make some enquiries, put out discreet feelers. He'd tread slowly, carefully. Eventually he'd find people who could track down whoever had made those demands. They'd find Tim. And once they'd found him, he and Tim could plan together, for their future.

Cautiously, he mulled over the problems which his plans might throw up. Despite the obvious drawbacks, the idea of divorcing Joanna appealed to him. He played with the concept, building clean new castles in the air, but once he opened the garage doors and stepped into his car, he forced himself to think of work. Perhaps he'd try Joanna's therapy. She was probably right; sitting around the house, sniping at her, quarrelling with everyone, none of it would do Tim any good, wherever he was. Work was what he needed. It would fill both his time and his thoughts.

And if... no, God damn it... *when* Tim returned, he'd insist, he'd demand, that his brother join the staff at the clinic. No more shilly-shallying, playing with pretty socialist ideals and publicly-funded general hospitals. He hadn't schemed for twenty years to stand by and watch his brother, his only brother, for Christ's sake, work himself to shreds for pocket money in a National Health hospital. Daisy . . . well, Daisy would have to learn. Tim was destined for greater things, and she could either keep up or be left behind.

His Bentley started at the first turn of the key. Quietly, it purred its way out of the garage and down the driveway. He activated the gates with the remote-controlled switch in the car, then he turned out on to the secondary road that skirted around the headland.

He flicked the switch on the dictaphone that he'd had built into the car, then, thinking better of the idea, he closed it and turned on the radio. Ringing, disgustingly cheerful Bach flooded from the speakers. He turned it off abruptly. He needed to think, to plan out his next few days. He'd abandoned his lecture tour of the States, but that was no reason to waste the next four weeks. He'd call London, arrange an immediate theatre list for the clinic. Tony Pierce might be somewhere in the depths of Arabia, but he'd soon replace him with another anaesthetist. There was that chap Tim had insisted on inviting to the last party. The one who worked at the General. Edmunds. Mike Edmunds, that was it. Once a decent salary was waved under his nose, he'd leave the General just as Tony had. And when Tony returned, he could rent out the second theatre complete with anaesthetist. Run the two at full capacity. Keep Edmunds on purely to serve the Harley Street surgeons who paid dearly for the privilege of using the clinic's facilities.

Expansion, that was the answer. Particularly after Tim came in with him. Tim was a first-class surgeon, and once Tim was in, Daisy'd follow. Alice Palmer-Smith said she had the makings of a reasonable doctor.

155

He drove on, turning up the broad, cherry-tree bordered driveway to the clinic. He stopped half-way and turned off his engine. The towers of the clinic rose before him. Tall, gleaming with the reflected light of the sunrise, the bronze-tinted windows glinting blankly, and as he'd hoped at the planning stage, secretively. It was a fine building, and it housed one of the best-equipped medical complexes in Europe. He had every right to be proud of it. It was his. His brainchild.

If the place had been left to the care of the Holbournes, it would still be housed in the Victorian villa that now served as a staff hostel. George's ideas of medicine were hidebound by traditions that were forty years out of date. The Holbourne Clinic, as opposed to the Holbourne and Sherringham Clinic, had consisted of private rooms, sympathetically-trained nurses and a sedative-laden drugs trolley. No more.

The new buildings, the modern equipment, the annexes for specialized therapy, facilities that top doctors queued to use, were all the result of *his* planning, *his* vision. But since his hopes for the clinic had been realized, he'd allowed himself to grow complacent. He'd thought there was nothing more to strive for. But now he had Tim to find and persuade into partnership. He had no intention of losing his brother a second time.

He'd build another theatre for Tim. A new wing to house the additional patients, and a suite of consulting rooms adjoining his own. Possibly even a home for Tim and Daisy on the lower cliff-face. A Canadian split-level house. Far enough away to ensure privacy, but close enough to be counted an advantage to the clinic. If his divorce worked out, he might even consider one for himself. There was more than enough land.

He restarted the Bentley and drove on, the pain generated by Tim's disappearance momentarily anaesthetized by the image of the medical utopia that rose clearly and magnificently in his mind's eye. He had the land, the money. The political climate had generated unlimited work and people who could well afford his fees. Why shouldn't he expand? Create a luxurious present and secure future for Tim, as he had done for himself?

'It's eight-thirty.' Trevor peered through the half-open door into the gloomy recesses of Peter's flat.

'I won't tell if you won't.' Peter opened the door wide enough for Trevor to walk through, then slammed it noisily.

'So this is home.' Trevor stared at the basic utility furniture and cord carpet universal to cheap rented accommodation. The flat was clean, uncluttered and meticulously neat, which was more than could be said for his own place. But it also had about as much personality as a second-hand furniture showroom.

'The only things I'll answer for are in the wardrobe and the food cupboard.' Peter rubbed his hands vigorously in his short hair, spiking it up even further. 'And that's the way I like it,' he snarled defensively, opening his sleep-ridden eyes wide enough to glare at Trevor.

'That's fine by me, but something you won't like is Mulcahy's reaction when he finds out we've been slacking.'

'Hell, we didn't leave the White Hart until four . . .'

'That wasn't all work.'

'We got a couple of leads, didn't we. In my book that's work.' Peter stared at Trevor for a moment, then realizing he was fully awake and further sleep, though desirable, was a day away, he conceded. Untying the belt on his dressing gown, he walked into the bedroom to dress. 'Make us some coffee, will you,' he shouted over his shoulder. 'You'll find everything you need in the kitchen.'

'All right.' Trevor looked around. A door to his left

led into a tiny, spotless galley kitchen. The only items on the work surface were a small electric grinder and a coffee machine. Both obviously new. He opened the cupboard above them and found a jar labelled 'coffee beans'. If it had been his own place, the jar would have contained coupons and elastic bands. As it wasn't, it held rich, dark shiny beans.

He set about his task reflecting how little he really knew Peter. He'd worked with him for years, on occasion twenty or more hours a day. They ate together, and generally worked well together, in spite of the more glaring differences between them, but they rarely met outside working hours. And if anyone had asked him what Peter was like, the last words he would have included in his list of adjectives were 'organized', and 'domesticated'. Yet clearly both applied.

'You found everything?' Peter walked in. Barefoot, trousers on, shirt flapping, he was rubbing a towel over his shorn scalp.

'Couldn't fail. Tidy place you have here.'

'It's the way a kitchen should be.' Peter pulled two cups and saucers out of one of the cupboards. 'No clutter. Nothing that isn't absolutely essential. You wouldn't believe the junk Wendy used to dot around the house. No need for any of it. Stuff standing around, just waiting to be dusted.'

'Do your own cleaning?' Trevor wanted to get off the topic of Wendy before Peter went into one of his tirades.

'I keep it tidy, but I pay a woman down the hall to come in a couple of times a week to give the place a real going-over.' He poured out two coffees. 'Milk and sugar?' Trevor nodded, and Peter handed down some dried milk and sugar from the top cupboard.

'Well, what's new?'

'Not much.' Trevor heaped sugar into his cup.

'No hangover after last night?'

'I couldn't drink that muck.'

'No taste, that's your problem.'

'Possibly. I went to the Shelter early this morning.'

'It's before nine now. What do you call morning?'

'Seven.'

'Did you see Sam Mayberry?'

'Yes.'

'Well, do I have to drag every word out of you?'

'He hasn't seen Andy in weeks. He doesn't know anything about the pier, but he's heard rumours of it being used by down-and-outs, and he does know a clown. An old chap known as Gramps. Apparently, the fellow claims he was once a professional singer-comedian. He was with the last troupe of pierrots who worked the pier, back in the fifties, or so he says.'

'And now he haunts motorways.' Peter began to button his shirt.

'Limps along them, more like it. He's frail, over seventy and has a wooden leg.'

'An ideal murder suspect. Did you see him?'

'For what it was worth. He was in one of the dormitories at the shelter, his leg hanging on the post at the end of the bed. Out for the count. Too far gone to remember who he was, let alone talk. Sam said he'd keep him there until this afternoon.'

'So we start with the Sherringhams.'

'You start with the Sherringhams.' Trevor finished his coffee and rinsed his cup under the running tap. 'I've already started, remember.'

Hare, the epitome of the well-trained, well-bred English butler, from the tips of his gleaming black shoes to the top of his well-brushed, slightly balding head, opened the door, and listened politely as Peter spoke.

'Dr Richard Sherringham is out. Her Ladyship is breakfasting on the terrace with Dr Edmunds, and Dr Daisy is still asleep,' he informed them, in reply to

159

Peter's enquiry. 'If it's absolutely necessary I could wake Dr Daisy . . .'

'Please don't,' Trevor interrupted.

'Perhaps we could speak to her Ladyship.' Peter almost choked on the title.

'If you'd like to come this way, Mr . . .'

'Sergeant. Sergeant Collins. And this is Sergeant Joseph.'

They followed Hare through the galleried hall, into the drawing-room and out on to the back terrace.

'These gentlemen are with the police, Lady Joanna,' Hare announced. 'Sergeants Collins and Joseph.'

'Is there any news of Tim?' Joanna was pale, but perfectly in control of herself and her voice.

'None, but we'd like to ask you a few questions, if we may,' Trevor replied.

'Of course. Sit down.' She indicated the vacant chairs at the table. 'Bring some more coffee and two extra cups, please, Hare.'

'Some place you've got here.' Peter sat down and stared at the stone cupids on the fountain that splashed tranquilly in the centre of the terrace.

'We like it, and it suits us,' Joanna replied dismissively. 'Have you met Dr Edmunds? He's thinking of joining the staff at my husband's clinic. I'm sorry, I didn't catch your names.'

'Sergeant Collins, Peter Collins, and this is Sergeant Trevor Joseph.'

'Pleased to meet you.' Joanna rose to the occasion and offered her hand to the two policemen.

'Dr Edmunds.' Trevor extended his hand.

'Please call me Mike.' He wiped the marmalade from his fingers in a napkin before shaking Trevor's hand.

'How can we help you?' Joanna asked.

'As you've probably guessed, we're investigating the disappearance of Tim Sherringham.' Trevor took the

160

seat Joanna offered. 'And we'd like to ask you about the last party you and your husband gave here.'

'I know Tim disappeared that night, but nothing out of the ordinary happened at that party, Sergeant.'

'If you'd let us be the judge of that.' Peter slipped easily into his professional manner.

'Where would you like me to begin?' Joanna moved slightly in order to allow Hare to put down the tray of coffee he'd brought.

'At the beginning.' Trevor smiled in an attempt to lighten the heavy atmosphere Peter had imposed with his ham-fisted formal method of questioning. 'What time did the party begin?'

'The usual time. Seven-thirty for eight. Most of the guests arrived during that half-hour. Except Tim and Daisy, of course. They're invariably late for everything. They work such long hours at the General.'

'I can vouch for that,' Mike chipped in.

Peter took the coffee-cup Joanna handed him. 'Would I be right in saying that you often give dinner parties here?'

'You would. But we entertain no more frequently than my husband's position demands. We constantly receive invitations to dinners, balls, official openings – you know the sort of thing – and etiquette demands that we reciprocate.'

'Reciprocate, or provide a platform from which to do business?'

'My husband frequently mixes business with pleasure, Sergeant Collins. If one must discuss work, then it is obviously more civilized to do so over coffee and brandy after a fine meal.'

'From what I can see, and what I've heard, your husband doesn't need to bring his work home.'

'What you can see, Sergeant Collins, is a substantial proportion of my husband's assets, and as to what you've heard, I surely don't need to tell someone in your profession that people in general, and the press in particular, are prone to exaggeration.'

'What did Tim and Daisy Sherringham do when they arrived here?' Trevor steered the conversation back on course.

'They drank champagne, circulated and talked. That is the general purpose of a dinner party.'

'Who did they talk to?'

'Not many people at that point in the evening. As I've already explained, they didn't arrive until just before dinner was served.'

'What time was that?'

'Eight, eight-fifteen.'

'Did you talk to either Tim or Daisy that evening?'

'Of course. I was the hostess. Tim sat opposite me, Daisy was a little lower down the table.'

'Who decided the placings?'

'I did. Richard often uses Tim as an extra host at our parties. He converses well with all kinds of people.'

'Was Daisy annoyed by their separation?'

'I wouldn't have thought so. It isn't usual for husbands and wives to sit next to one another.'

'Did anything happen during the meal?' Peter pressed.

'We ate.'

'Could you tell me what?'

'Sergeant, do you really expect to find clues to Tim's disappearance in the menu?'

'May I remind you of the seriousness . . .'

'You don't have to remind me of anything, Sergeant Collins,' Joanna interrupted coolly. 'I'm close to Tim. I want to find him. But I fail to see what possible connection there could be between Tim's sudden disappearance and the menu for the evening.'

'Lady Joanna,' Trevor flashed a quick warning glance at Peter as he sat forward on his chair, 'I'll be honest with you. At this moment we're searching in

162

the dark. We have no firm evidence of any kind, and the little we do know doesn't make any sense. We're not in a position to even hazard a guess as to what might have happened to Tim Sherringham. A detailed account of that party would be a start. A point we can work from. We need to know who saw Tim that night, who spoke to him, made plans with him. Please? Tell us what you know. It may seem trivial to you, but it could give us the break we're looking for.'

'Snails caviar canapés, broiled salmon, pigeons *chaudfroid*, roast capon, potatoes *à la duchesse*, bread sauce, puff potatoes, asparagus *au gratin*, French lettuce salad, strawberry mousse, cheese soufflé, and coffee.' Mike looked at Peter. 'The menu,' he offered. 'You wanted it.'

'You were at the party?'

'Of course. I was invited.'

'Do you make a habit of memorizing the menus of dinner parties you've attended?'

'Not always. Most are forgettable. This I remembered because Richard mentioned that Joanna had found it in an old Edwardian cookery book. I believe the snails caviar to be the only concession to modernity.'

'It was.' Joanna smiled.

'But still, to memorize a whole menu.' Peter was uncertain whether or not he was being taken for a fool.

'What did Tim talk about over dinner?' Trevor directed the question at Joanna, but Mike answered.

'The last trip he and Daisy had taken to Cornwall. They'd sailed down to Falmouth, and anchored in Helford Creek. Tim loved the place. He said if he had enough money he'd buy a cottage down there. One that overlooked the river.'

'But surely Tim Sherringham could have bought any house he wanted!' Peter exclaimed.

'Apart from a modest inheritance from his father,

163

Tim and Daisy only have their salaries, and doctors who work for the National Health Service don't exactly earn fortunes,' Joanna informed Peter caustically.

'I'll say they don't,' Mike murmured in support.

'But Tim Sherringham has a Mercedes, he owns an expensive flat . . .'

'Wedding gifts from Richard, but he gave Tim no money, at least not to my knowledge. And just before the wedding, Tim told me he and Daisy had taken out a bank loan to buy their yacht, the *Freedom*. If they were as well off as you'd like to believe, I rather think they would have bought the yacht outright.'

'So in your opinion, apart from the expensive gifts your husband gave him, Tim Sherringham lived the life of a working doctor?'

'Yes.'

'Most certainly,' Mike added emphatically.

'How come one brother has all this,' Peter nodded at the house behind Joanna, 'and the other has to exist on his salary?'

'My husband owns his own clinic, Sergeant Collins. Tim works for the NHS.'

'It's as simple as that?' Peter raised his eyebrows.

'As simple as that,' Joanna reiterated.

'Nothing to do with your husband inheriting the Sherringham family wealth, and Tim inheriting nothing?'

'Richard's father's will stipulated that his assets be split equally between them. Tim's half was placed in gilt-edged securities until he came of age. Richard spent every penny of his, and more, buying this place. At the time no one could have foreseen that property prices would escalate beyond all reasoning.'

'Did your husband buy this house before you married?'

'No, we bought it the year after, and before you ask, it didn't look like this when we acquired it. It was a shell. We renovated it, using whatever money we could lay our hands on, including a small inheritance from my aunt.' Joanna was clearly becoming increasingly irritated by Peter's blatant, bulldozing methods.

'So where did Richard Sherringham live when he met you?'

'In a house,' Joanna paused just long enough to annoy Peter, 'in California. He and Tim came here for a holiday after his father's death. Did you know that his father and mine were old friends?'

'No, I didn't.'

'To cut a long story short, he decided to stay in England, and my father offered him a half share in the clinic.'

'Offered?' Peter looked inquisitively at her.

'Sold,' she corrected. 'And, knowing my father, he made sure that Richard paid the top market price.'

'And Richard Sherringham had the means to pay and enough left over to buy this place?'

'If you're looking for financial motives, Sergeant, look elsewhere. My husband was a practising doctor in America and a wealthy man in his own right when I met him. He had more than just his father's inheritance. I, on the other hand, was anything but well heeled.'

'You've just said that your father sold Richard a half share in the clinic.'

'My father isn't me, Sergeant, and he has old-fashioned ideas on bringing up children. I received everything I asked for until the day my education finished. After that I found myself on my own. I'm not saying he threw me out, but he didn't give me any money either. I was expected to go out and earn my keep.'

'Why did your husband buy his way into the Holbourne Clinic? Surely a doctor of his standing could have opened his own place?'

'I've no idea.' Joanna poured herself another cup of coffee.

'Was it your influence, perhaps?' Trevor ventured.

'I doubt it. He bought a share in the clinic long before we got engaged. Perhaps you'd like to ask him yourself?'

'Can we go back to the night of the party?' Trevor pulled out his notebook and laid it on the table. 'Did Tim Sherringham talk about anything other than his holiday in Cornwall, and wanting to buy a house down there?'

'Of course he did.' Mike scratched his nose thoughtfully. 'He talked about nuclear threats and disasters, the state of the National Health Service, Tony Pierce's forthcoming trip to Arabia . . .'

'Who's Tony Pierce?'

'Richard's anaesthetist. He used to work in the General with Tim and Daisy before my husband enticed him into working at his clinic.'

'He's a damned good anaesthetist, too,' Mike commented enthusiastically.

'And Tim Sherringham talked to him?' Trevor looked at Mike.

'After dinner a few of us, including Tony, escaped into the billiards room.'

'And now he's in Arabia?'

'The party that night was something of a *bon voyage* affair.' Joanna pushed her coffee-cup to the centre of the table and leant back in her chair. 'Richard was leaving the next morning for a lecture tour of the States. My father and I were going to Italy to holiday in the family villa . . .'

'And Tony Pierce?'

'Richard intended to stay in the States for at least six weeks. Possibly longer, if things went well. It was the perfect time for Tony to take a holiday. An anaesthetist has no work without a surgeon, and Tony's

166

always had a thing about Lawrence of Arabia. He'd only taken the job in the clinic to earn enough for his dream holiday, if you can call it that. He intended to retrace Lawrence's footsteps across Arabia. I only hope he's succeeding and the trip's living up to his expectations.'

'What about Tim Sherringham?'

'Tim and Daisy took four weeks out for their honeymoon six months ago. I invited them to stay in the villa in Italy, but they had very little holiday entitlement left.'

'You ate dinner, talked about various trivia, then what?' Peter sat back in his chair and eyed Mike suspiciously.

'We left the dinner-table and mingled for a while.' Mike frowned slightly with the effort it took to recall what, until now, had been an insignificant event. 'Tim mislaid Daisy, he looked for her without success, then we broke away from the main party and hid in the billiards room.'

' "We" being Tim Sherringham, you, and this Tony Pierce?' Trevor's pencil hovered over his notebook.

'That's right.'

'Did you find out what happened to Daisy Sherringham?' Peter ferreted after the loose ends like a fox following the scent of rabbits.

'Not really. We left the billiards room around one o'clock. By then Daisy was none too happy. Apparently she'd been conned into spending the greater part of the evening with one of Richard's less sensitive Conservative guests. Daisy's politics are left-wing Socialist to Communist, so, as you can imagine, she had a fun time.'

'She was furious when you came out of the billiards room?'

'I'd say she was more relieved than angry. If Daisy and Tim quarrel, I've never seen any evidence of it.'

167

'Who did Tim talk to before you went into the billiards room?'

'Anybody. Everybody.' Mike shrugged his shoulders to hide his growing impatience with Peter's endless, and to him, seemingly pointless, questions. 'No one in particular comes to mind, and as far as I can remember the standard of conversation I got involved in was anything but scintillating. It ran along the lines of "how nice to see you again", "wasn't the dinner simply perfection", "and do you work in the clinic with Richard?" Do you want me to continue my recollections of the chitchat?'

'That won't be necessary,' Peter barked gruffly.

'What happened in the billiards room?' Trevor asked.

'We played billiards.' Much to Peter's annoyance, Mike, like Joanna, punctuated his reply with a slight, yet perceptible pause. 'Tim was on form, beat us all hollow, but there's nothing unusual in that. If I remember correctly he even had the gall to complain of a headache while he was doing it. I had to get another bottle of whisky to help cure the one he gave me.'

'Did Tim Sherringham leave the billiards room at all after you started playing?' Trevor looked up from the notes he was making.

'No.'

'And while you played, you talked about Tony Pierce's trip to Arabia, and the state of the NHS. Anything else?'

'A lot of inane jokes, general chitchat.'

'What exactly was said about the Health Service?'

'What is there to say? The whole system's disintegrating. Tim and I admitted as much to Tony, and Richard, when he called in briefly to escape from his duties as host. There are waiting-lists that people can, and do, die on. Poor equipment that's not repaired or replaced when it breaks down. Cut backs . . .'

'Don't you read the papers, Sergeant Joseph?' Joanna interrupted cuttingly.

'Nothing on a more personal basis. About Tim or his job?' Trevor smiled at Joanna, but tactfully ignored her remark.

'Not really. Tony grumbled about his patients. As I said, Richard came in, but he only stayed a few minutes. He asked Tim to leave the hospital and work in his clinic . . .'

'And they quarrelled.' Peter grasped at the revelation.

'No, they didn't quarrel, Sergeant.'

'My husband and his brother have never "quarrelled", as you like to put it.' Joanna stacked Peter's and Trevor's cups on the tray without offering them more coffee. 'They're too polite and well bred. In order to understand the significance of Richard's offer of a job to Tim, you have to understand the situation between them. Richard's been trying to get Tim to work in his clinic since the day Tim qualified. It's a family joke.'

'Tim's a good doctor, but he's perfectly happy where he is,' Mike emphasized. 'Not many get to be a registrar at his age.'

'Daisy wouldn't dream of leaving the Health Service to work in private practice, no matter what the incentives in pay or conditions. And where Daisy goes, Tim goes. My husband knows full well he's casting the proverbial pearls before swine whenever he offers Tim a job, but if you ask me, he can't help getting a dig in now and again. Good-natured brotherly love, and all that.'

'Is there anything else you can recall about that evening? Any other person who spoke to Tim? Any piece of information?' Trevor asked.

'Not really. Tim and Daisy left around one or one-thirty. Tony Pierce, Richard and I played billiards

169

until about three or four o'clock.' Mike hazarded a guess.

'I wouldn't know. Richard was still up, but I went to bed around two,' Joanna added.

'You said Daisy Sherringham disappeared during the early part of the evening. Could she have spent that time with another man?'

'That's ludicrous.' Joanna dismissed the comment with a wave of her well-manicured hand.

'Daisy and Tim have only been married for six months. They're incredibly happy. Or rather they were until this happened. Have you quite finished looking for things that aren't there, Sergeant Collins?' Mike glared furiously at him.

'Just one or two things more, if you don't mind, and then we'll leave you in peace.' Trevor pocketed his notebook. 'As I said earlier, we have a few leads, but they don't make much sense as yet. If you bear with us for a while longer we might be able to make some headway. I apologize if my questions seem strange.'

'Strange I can cope with, slanderous I find objectionable,' Joanna replied.

'These won't be slanderous.' Trevor fiddled with his pencil. 'The pier . . .'

'The pier?'

'Does your father still own it?'

'I believe so,' Joanna concurred.

'I know it might seem an odd thing to ask, but would you mind explaining how your father came to own the pier?'

'My father's mother was a Mudesly, Maud Mudesly. My grandfather fell in love with her after seeing her in a show at the pier theatre. She worked as a pierrette in her father's concert party – Mudesly's Merry Moppets, would you believe. It was her grandfather, Michael Mudesly, who built the pier. Her father, Malcolm, followed his father into show business. When Malcolm

Mudesly died in the twenties, he left the pier to my grandmother. It wasn't surprising, as she was his only child. She had no hankering to go back to her old life, so she rented the pier out to one of her father's friends. And there ends the family connection with the pier. My father is very disparaging of that part of his inheritance. He tried to pull the place down a few years back, but a preservation order was slapped on it as a result of campaigning by some Victorian architecture society or other. So, too costly to repair, and too valuable to pull down, it was, as you can see, left to rot.'

'Your grandmother. Can you remember her?'

'I'm afraid not. She died before I was born. My father and my aunts have told me stories about her. She must have been quite a girl in her day. Family history,' she looked Trevor in the eye, 'is all very interesting, but do you mind telling me where this is leading to?'

'I'm afraid I can't tell you very much. Only that a down-and-out thinks he's seen a clown on the pier.'

'Brave man to go near the place. From what I've seen, it looks as though it's likely to fall into the sea at any moment.'

'Does anyone here have a key to the pier?' Peter asked.

'Key? Are you being serious, Sergeant? My father called in army advisors when he erected those barricades. The last thing a cabinet minister needs is an action for damages over dangerous property. If you want to look around the pier you'd better take a bulldozer, not a key.'

'Then there's no easy way in to the place?'

'None that I'm aware of.'

'You never use the pier?'

'No.'

'And your family?'

'Really, Sergeant Collins, how many times do I have

171

to tell you, the place is nothing more than a derelict, dangerous, encumbrance.'

'There's just one other thing.' Peter looked hard at Joanna. 'A pierrot was also seen flagging cars down on the motorway on the night Tim disappeared.'

'I see.'

'What do you see, Lady Joanna?' Peter demanded.

'The connection you've drawn between the pier and Tim's disappearance . . .'

A bloodcurdling scream silenced her mid-sentence. Joanna and Mike were out of their chairs and half-way through the drawing-room before Peter and Trevor could move. Trevor left his seat and rushed into the hall in time to see Joanna leading the way along the gallery. She burst open the door of one of the bedrooms, Mike close on her heels. Taking the stairs two at a time, Trevor and Peter went after them. When they reached the bedroom door, they saw Joanna and Mike standing in the room and Judy Osbourne sitting on Daisy's bed, Hare at her side. Judy was smoothing Daisy's hair, whispering soft words of comfort that had little effect on the violent spasms that jerked through Daisy's body.

'A nightmare,' Judy explained quietly to Joanna and Mike, as Trevor and Peter ran panting into the room. 'I'm afraid I disturbed her when Hare let me in.'

'The same headless dream as before?' Peter enquired brutally.

'Would it be possible for you to give Daisy a few minutes of privacy before you begin interrogating her?' Judy demanded.

Daisy stared blankly at the men in the doorway, then, slowly, recognition dawned. She closed her eyes, tensed her muscles, and made a supreme effort to regain control of herself. Trevor found the performance unbearably painful to watch.

'I'm sorry, I didn't mean to frighten you,' she whispered to Judy in a small remote voice.

'What did you see?' Peter pushed past Mike to get into the room.

'It was a nightmare. Nothing more,' she continued in the same distant vein.

'Describe it!'

Peter's authoritative insistence cut through Daisy's disorientation.

'The same headless bodies as before. The man in the evening suit. The woman in the brown raincoat. She's thin. So thin. Her arms and legs are like sticks. There were glasses, thick-lensed glasses. They were lying on the floor . . .'

Her voice trembled, her lips continued to move, but no sound issued from them. Her eyes were wide open, but it was obvious that she wasn't focusing on anything in the room. She was looking inwards down the dark tunnel leading to the nightmare world that had so recently held possession of her.

Trevor stepped forward and laid his hand on Peter's shoulder. 'It's time for us to go.' He turned, took one last look at Daisy. Tears were falling from her eyes and streaming down her thin white cheeks. No sobs. Just pathetic, silent tears.

Joanna held open the door. 'If you'd like to wait downstairs,' she said icily. Embarrassed, Trevor walked out into the gallery. Peter followed him, but not before he'd given the bedroom a good once-over. His mind worked feverishly, assimilating the information he had gleaned. The closed suitcases standing in a neat square at the foot of the bed. The open wardrobe doors, revealing empty shelves and rails. The black tailored suit draped over the chair next to the bed.

'If you'll excuse me, Sergeant, I must get Judy's bag

out of her car.' Mike overtook Peter and Trevor on the staircase.

'I think we've just about covered everything,' Trevor answered politely. 'If there's anything we can do for Dr Sherringham . . .'

'I don't think so. But thank you, Sergeant Joseph.'

'Just one more thing.'

'As you can see, Sergeant Collins . . .'

'Why were you here with Joanna Sherringham this morning?'

'Tony helps her with her research work when he isn't assisting Richard. She wanted to ask me if I'd do the same. Now if you'll excuse me, I'm sure Hare will show you out.'

'We'll find our own way.' Peter walked swiftly down the stairs. 'I expect we'll be seeing you again sometime.'

'I expect so,' Mike answered automatically.

Hare overtook them on the stairs. 'Gentlemen.' He opened the front door for them.

As the door closed on them, Trevor started towards the car, but Peter stood on the step for a moment and surveyed the immaculately-manicured lawns and gardens. He looked left towards the stables, then right to where the swimming pool was only just visible through the open stonework and trees. Some place.

He stepped down and turned his head to look up at the house. 'Tell you what, Joseph, despite what the lady says, you don't come by these sort of goodies by honest graft, that's for certain. I think digging's called for here. Deep digging. And what's the betting we'll find something rotten at the core?'

Alan Cummins responded swiftly to Mike's call. He delayed only as long as it took him to dump his morning's work-load into Eric Hedley's unwilling lap. Then he left. He'd been gone about an hour when the call came through. Eric excused himself to the mother and toddler sitting in Alan's consulting room and picked up the receiver.

'Eric Hedley,' he said briefly, willing it to be the voice of officialdom enquiring after Alan.

'It's Patrick O'Kelly here. Can I talk to Alan?'

Eric swivelled his chair away from the patient and lowered his voice. 'He's not available at the moment. Can I take a message?'

'Get him to call me as soon as he comes in.'

'Does it concern Tim Sherringham?'

'Not really.'

'Is it . . .'

'Just pass on the message. I have to go.' The line went dead.

Eric bit his lip thoughtfully, then turned to face the woman and child. 'Now, about this heart murmur . . .'

'She'll sleep for a couple of hours.' Alan crumpled the syringe he'd used on Daisy and threw it into his case. Judy slid from the side of Daisy's bed on to the floor. She covered her face with her hands. She was drained, mentally as well as physically. Less than an hour had passed between Mike's call and Alan's arrival, but each minute had seemed to last an eternity. She'd tried to deal coolly and calmly with Daisy's disorientation and incoherence, but eventually the ramblings became lunatic ravings, and the intensity of emotion had terrified her. Despite Mike's presence and support, she'd begun to be drawn into Daisy's nightmare world of headless bodies and walking corpses.

'You could have given her that shot.' There was a hint of accusation in Alan's voice.

'I was waiting for the Valium to take effect.'

'In a situation like that, Valium's useless.'

'For God's sake. I'm only a houseman. Daisy's my friend.'

'You can't blame Judy for not thinking straight.'

175

Mike's voice sounded loud, odd in the silence that had fallen over the room now that Daisy was finally quiet. 'Daisy's ravings were enough to terrify anyone.'

'She needs expert help,' Alan diagnosed. 'And not from a paediatrician either. If it was up to me, she'd be on her way to the General right now.'

'To the psychiatric ward?' Joanna sneered.

'No, to one of the single rooms that are kept for staff emergencies. Working for the Health Service doesn't have many perks, but reasonable medical care is one. If Daisy was capable of making a rational decision, I know she'd agree with what I've just said. Would Richard allow her to go to the General?' he asked.

'No, he'd want her in his clinic.'

'She'd hate that.' Alan snapped his case shut. 'Why did you allow Mike to call me and not Richard?' he demanded bluntly.

'Because Richard's not thinking straight. He's not like this,' Joanna pointed to Daisy, 'but he's irrational, aggressive. Totally unlike his normal self.'

'Well, someone's got to take responsibility for Daisy,' Alan said forcefully. 'And I'd be only too happy to.'

'I'd be only too happy to let you.'

'The question is, will Richard let me?'

'If you move Daisy to the General, I'll tell Richard about her relapse this evening when he comes home. By then her condition should have stabilized, one way or the other.' Joanna rose from the chair she'd been sitting in.

'Are you sure that will be all right?'

'As you said, it would be what Daisy would want for herself.'

'And Richard?' Judy asked.

'I can handle Richard,' Joanna said confidently.

'Then let's move her, right now.' Judy picked up the telephone and dialled the number for the ambulance service.

Mike looked at Alan. 'What state is Daisy going to be in when she comes round?'

'I don't know. From what I saw before I sedated her I can say she's totally exhausted, but I don't know enough to diagnose whether this outburst is the onset of a full breakdown or just the result of strain, coupled with lack of sleep. Obviously, these damned nightmares don't help. But you've spent the last few days with her, Joanna. You know more than me. Is this the first outburst?'

'The first like this.'

'Have there been signs she's been building up to this?'

'Nothing obvious. But I'm rusty. It's years since I've practised.'

'They're on their way.' Judy replaced the receiver. 'This wasn't quite what Daisy had planned for today. She wanted to go back to work, move into a hospital flat.'

'Work's out of the question for the moment,' Alan decreed. He glanced at his watch. 'I'm sorry, much as I might want to, I daren't stay any longer. Eric Hedley's taken over my clinic, and he'd be only too delighted to drop me in it. If anyone in Administration finds out that I left the hospital, my head will be on the block . . .' He squirmed with embarrassment when he realized what he'd said. 'You know what I mean,' he finished awkwardly.

'We do.' Judy handed him one of Daisy's suitcases. 'Here, take this and leave it in the hall on your way out.'

'I hate mortuaries.'

'I know you do,' Peter said flatly.

'Then why did I have to come here?' Trevor squirmed uncomfortably as a whiff of formaldehyde-ridden air wafted towards him.

'Because Bill asked us to.'

'You could have come by yourself.'

'Quit moaning.' Peter pushed Trevor through the double doors ahead of him.

The headless corpse was laid out on the dissecting slab. Patrick O'Kelly, under the Home Office pathologist's eagle eye, made the throat to pubis incision. He struck just as Trevor and Peter walked through the door. It was well timed. Too well timed, Peter decided, recalling another pathologist of his acquaintance, who had a weird and wonderful sense of humour. The minute he heard the footsteps of a new recruit on the stone staircase that led to his mortuary, he'd shelve the body he was working on, whip out a new one, and stand, scalpel poised, ready to make the initial incision the moment the rookie walked through the door.

Trevor stopped in his tracks and stared down at the headless, handless corpse. He watched, mesmerized, as Patrick carefully pulled back the fragile, decaying flaps of skin, fat, and muscle. Delving deep, Patrick continued to probe, pushing aside a selection of slimy rubbery intestines. Trevor coped with the sight. Better than he had expected. It was the smell that finished him. Once the warm, heady, meaty stink of corpse hit his nostrils, he vomited, barely managing to turn his face to the wall.

'Sorry about my colleague,' Peter apologized, as Trevor, still retching, ran for the door.

'We're used to it.' Patrick O'Kelly looked up and grinned in amusement.

'You've come to check out the identification?' the Home Office pathologist enquired briskly.

'Identification?'

'Haven't you heard?' Patrick demanded. 'One of the nurses from the hospital went missing a couple of days ago. Dart ... Amanda Dart. One of your lot came round and made some enquiries. She was last seen wearing a brown raincoat. Just like that one.' He indicated the array of clothes and limb segments laid out on the slab behind him. 'Your man added up two and two, and came up with the right answer. As long as you don't touch, you can help yourself to the details.'

'Thank you, sir.' Peter turned to the mutilated body. Damn it all, he could kick himself for not seeing it before! Thin, small frame. He'd questioned the girl. Probably on the day she'd been murdered.

A white-faced Trevor was back, standing at the head of the slab, staring down at the neatly-ranged bundles. Brown raincoat, stick-thin limbs laid out in a semblance of body shape.

'She saw the body bag,' Trevor whispered. 'We know Daisy Sherringham came here. She saw the coat, she saw the thin arms and legs through the body bag.'

'And the glasses?' Peter demanded. 'Just tell me. Where in hell did she see the glasses? Because I can't.'

'They could have been here.'

'Did you find a pair of spectacles close to this body?' Peter asked Patrick.

'Sorry, no spectacles.'

'There has to be a logical explanation. There has to be.'

'Then tell me what it is,' Peter answered coldly. 'You just tell me what it is.'

Chapter Seven

'I still think we should be grilling Daisy Sherringham, not prancing around down here,' Peter grunted, as he swerved his car into the cul-de-sac of decaying Edwardian houses that hid, among other obscenities, the fetid shelter for the homeless.

'Give over, will you, Peter,' Trevor snapped with uncharacteristic vigour. His bout of nausea had left him more than a little irritable. 'Daisy Sherringham was in one hell of a state this morning. What makes you think she'll have recovered by now?'

'She may have. And before you start mollycoddling the lady of your dreams, you should remember what Bill said about villains coming from every class, high as well as low.'

'We know she saw those body bags.'

'Saw the body bags. But she must have X-Ray vision to spot details like stick-thin limbs through that thick plastic. You know damned well how difficult it is to see anything clearly once it's been bagged. And that body was chopped. Badly chopped. Can you imagine what it looked like in a bag?'

'The raincoat would be recognizable,' Trevor protested.

'All right, I'll give you the raincoat, she may have spotted that. But not the glasses. Where are they? Where did she see them? In her nightmares? I'm sorry, I don't buy it, Joseph. She bloody well knew before we did that the body was Amanda Dart's.'

'How? How did she know?'

"If I knew the answer to that one, I wouldn't be here, I'd be arresting her now. Dr Daisy Sherringham hysterical and raving, and amongst her ravings she gives an accurate description of an article belonging to the victim – an article that is now missing. That doesn't spell coincidence in my book. That spells complicity.' Giving vent to his frustration, Peter braked hard. The car screamed to a halt in the turning bay of the cul-de-sac.

'For Christ's sake, the girl's at the end of her tether. Anyone with eyes in their head can see that!' Trevor exclaimed. 'Damn it all, she's no more capable of murder than a . . .'

'Than a what? Have you considered the possibility that the murders might be why she's cracking? She doesn't like what she's done, or seen, in her spare time, and going barmy is the result.'

'You're insane!'

'When you try, you can be a good copper, Joseph, but you're not thinking straight on this one.' Peter jerked the keys out of the ignition and turned to face his partner. 'Just answer me one question. Why did Daisy Sherringham come up with clear descriptions of the murder victims before the full details were known to us, let alone the press?'

'I didn't hear . . .' Trevor began heatedly.

'That's your problem. You didn't hear, because you're bloody well not listening. Well I am, and unlike you, I'm not carrying a torch for the lady. I haven't a clue, yet,' he emphasized his last word, 'what we've got here. All I know is that the deeper I dig, the more Sherringhams I come up with, and they're not smelling all that sweet either. And now, when everything I know tells me I ought to be arresting Daisy Sherringham and taking her in for questioning, I find myself sitting outside this dump to see, of all things, a geriatric with a wooden leg who worked as a clown on the pier forty years ago. You've gone soft in the head if you think this is going to lead to anything. You're not making

181

sense. And believe you me, Joseph, if you go down for the chop on this case, you go alone. You're not taking me with you.'

'What charge would you arrest Daisy Sherringham on? Come on? What concrete evidence have you got that will stand up in court?'

'I've got the descriptions. She gave them in front of witnesses. If that isn't complicity . . .'

'Complicity!' Trevor spat out the word. 'Don't give me complicity. Complicity with who? Did anyone see her dump those bodies on the motorway? Was she seen threatening either of the victims? Christ! We don't even know the name of one of the victims, let alone who he associated with. Peter, it's you who's cracking. We haven't enough for suspicion, let alone complicity.'

'We'll see what Bill thinks about it.' Peter opened the car door and stepped on to the rubbish-strewn road. Seething, Trevor followed suit.

Sam Mayberry, the small, greying, gnome-like priest who ran the hostel for the homeless was sitting on the front doorstep talking to a filthy, wild-looking creature whose most noticeable feature was his long black hair.

'I expected you two to turn up earlier than this,' Sam lilted in his soft Irish brogue.

'Sorry Sam, got held up.' Trevor sidestepped past Peter, who was glowering at Sam's companion.

'This is Blackie,' Sam said gently. 'Blackie, these two gentlemen are with the police, but they've not come to hurt you.' Blackie stared at them warily from beneath his thatch of matted hair and overgrown eyebrows.

'Is the chap we want still asleep?' Trevor asked.

'No, he's eating in the kitchen.' Sam rose stiffly to his feet. 'Come in. I'll make you tea.'

'Thanks, but I've just had one,' Peter replied quickly.

'Me too,' Trevor added. He'd been in the hostel before. Often. Despite Sam's efforts, the place was

182

invariably splattered with the most obnoxious filth and after his experience in the mortuary the last thing his stomach needed was a dubiously grimy cup filled with greasy tea.

'Gramps.' Sam smiled at Peter. 'He's the one who used to work as a clown.'

'So Trevor tells me.'

'Well, he can be a bit strange at times,' Sam warned gently. When Peter didn't reply, Sam, with Blackie following like a faithful dog, led the way through the high-walled, central passage to the back of the house.

'Gramps lives mostly in the past,' Sam ventured as they reached the kitchen doorway.

'I get the message.'

'Gramps,' Sam called out loudly to an old man who was sitting at a battered formica-topped table in the ill-lit kitchen. 'Gramps?' The old man huddled over his bowl and grunted. 'These two gentlemen would like to talk to you.' Another grunt. 'About the pier.'

'The pier. Things I could tell you about the pier.' The old man remained hunched over his bowl of cereal, but his grey, pinched face lit up at the mention of the pier. For an instant, Trevor caught a glimpse of the young man hidden in the depths of the human wreckage seated before him.

'Pier used to be crowded in the old days,' the old man recited in a singsong voice. It may even have been the same stage accent he'd used to deliver his scripts. 'People dressed in their Sunday best. Women with skirts on, sometimes gloves and hats as well.' He looked up, his mind jerking uncomfortably back into the present. 'None of your shabby dress like today,' he exclaimed loudly, and ironically, considering the rags he was dressed in.

'Do you ever go to the pier now?' Peter demanded impatiently.

183

'Eh. Go to the pier now? No point, young man. No point. Pier's closed.'

'We all know the pier's closed.' Peter's voice increased in volume with his temper. 'But we've heard that some people have been using the pier. Sleeping on it, even.'

'Sleeping on it? You can't sleep on the pier.' The old man shook his head. 'Couldn't even sleep on the pier in the old days. The sea's dangerous, and the pier's old. Not safe.' He continued to shake his head vigorously from side to side. 'Not safe,' he repeated. 'And there's wire around it, barbed wire, like they used in the war. A man could cut himself to ribbons on it and still get nowhere. It's not like it was in the old days when people wore their best clothes . . .'

'To hell with the old days.'

'Peter, give him time,' Sam admonished.

Furious with Peter, Trevor was about to intervene. Then his attention was drawn to Blackie. The man was crouched on his heels, swaying backwards and forwards at Sam's feet. He was playing with something. Fondling it, placing it to his lips, licking at it. When it was covered with spittle, he began to polish it in the folds of his greasy rags. Trevor sensed that Blackie knew he was being watched, but the continued scrutiny didn't deter the tramp. He carried on licking and polishing whatever it was he was holding. Then, as Blackie held it up to the small square of murky light that struggled in through the high window, Trevor saw for the first time what Blackie was treasuring so fondly. Spectacles! A pair of thick-lensed, black plastic spectacles.

Continuing with the elaborate farce, Blackie held up the glasses and pushed them on to his nose. They swung wide on their one arm and fell on the cracked linoleum. Trevor stared down at them. The thick lenses reminded him of leaded glass. He hadn't seen lenses like those since . . . since . . .

184

'Not then, Gramps. *Now*.' Peter's harsh insistence was crumbling in the face of Gramps' obduracy.

'Don't go near the pier, not now. Can't. I tell you, it's wired. And now without my leg . . .'

Peter ran his hands through his hair and glanced at Trevor. But Trevor's attention was still fixed on Blackie and the glasses. He watched Trevor move closer to the old man, crouch down and hold out his hand.

'Blackie.' Trevor spoke softly. 'Can I take a look at those? I won't hurt them, I promise.'

'They're mine.' Blackie hid them quickly in his rags.

'Where did you get them?'

'Bought them. Bought them fair and square.' He scuttled sideways, scurrying away from Trevor like a crab.

'I'll pay you twice what you paid for them.' Trevor fumbled in his pocket and pulled out a handful of coins. 'Here you are.' He opened his hand and showed Blackie what he held. 'Take what you want. Go on. Take it all.'

Blackie saw the glint of gold and silver. He thrust his hand into his clothes, and fingered the spectacles. They were no good. They wouldn't stay on, not like Father Mayberry's. It was Andy's fault. Andy was always getting change out of him for things that were no good.

Trevor waited patiently while Blackie hesitated. Putting Blackie's reluctance down to wariness, he piled the coins on the floor between them. 'Take them, Blackie,' he offered. 'They're yours. Just give me the glasses and tell me where you bought them.'

'It's all right, Blackie,' Sam smiled. 'No one's going to harm you. It's all right.'

Gramps was more agile, and quicker witted than either Peter or Trevor had given him credit for. Forgotten in the new interest evoked by Blackie, he suddenly

185

swooped down from the table, scooped up the money and hopped out through the door.

'Gramps!' Sam shouted after the limping figure. 'That's stealing. Come back!'

'Leave him, Sam, it doesn't matter.' Ill humour forgotten in the interest generated by the new lead, Peter walked over to where Trevor was still crouched on the floor. He dug into his own pocket and laid out a selection of coins that bettered the ones appropriated by Gramps.

'They're yours, Blackie.' Without taking his eyes off Blackie, Trevor pushed the pile of money towards the old man. 'Just give us the glasses, and tell us where you found them. It's very important.'

Muscles tensed at the ready, Peter remained standing equidistant between the two doors. There was no way he'd allow Blackie to do a bunk like Gramps had.

Blackie stared at Trevor for a moment, then, without warning, he pulled the glasses from his clothes and threw them down next to the money. 'Andy sold them to me.' He grabbed the money greedily. 'He never sells me anything that's good. Never. Cheat. That's what Andy is. Cheat.'

'Did Andy tell you where he got them?'

'No. Andy never tells me nothing. Never.'

'Where's Andy, Sam?' Peter asked.

'As I told Trevor this morning, Andy hasn't been in here for weeks. As a matter of fact, I've been quite worried about him. I spoke to Father Roberts down at the day-centre, and he said Andy still goes there occasionally. It's my guess he's sleeping rough. I only pray he's not going to get hurt, wherever he is.'

'The pier. Andy sleeps on the pier. The clown looks after him. I know.' Blackie nodded wisely as he pushed the coins Peter had given him deep into his pocket.

'Have you seen the clown, Blackie?' Trevor asked.

186

'Of course I have. Once. Singing and dancing on stage.'

'Was it Gramps?' Peter demanded.

'Don't be stupid.' Blackie spat contemptuously on the floor. 'Gramps can't dance no more. Not since they chopped his leg off.'

'Who chopped his leg off?'

'Hospital. That's what happens if you go into hospital. They chop your leg off.'

'Blackie, I explained it all to you,' Sam said patiently. 'Gramps had gangrene. He would have died . . .'

'Have you ever slept on the pier?'

'No. Only been there once. Don't know no more. Not going to talk no more.' To emphasize his words, Blackie clamped his toothless gums firmly shut.

'How did you get on the pier?'

Peter's question was met by obstinate silence.

'Do I have to take you in? Perhaps you'll feel like talking after you've sat for a while in one of our colder cells.'

'Don't take me away. Father, don't let them put me away.' Blackie flung himself along the floor and locked his hands tightly around Sam Mayberry's ankles. 'Please don't let them shut me up,' he cried, as large fat tears cleared streaks of dirt from his face.

'Tell the gentlemen what they want to know, Blackie.' Sam gave Peter a hard look as he stroked Blackie's wild, greasy mane. 'Answer their questions as honestly as you can, and no one will take you away, I promise.'

'How did you get on the pier?' Peter repeated.

'Andy took me,' Blackie sulked. 'That's all I know. Honest, Mister. We went there in the dark. I didn't see nothing until we were inside. We went in so quick I couldn't show you how. Really quick. The clown was there. He was funny. There was lights, and singing. It was warm. Andy had a bottle. We drank the bottle

187

and listened to the singing, then we went. That's all, Mister. We didn't break nothing, I didn't do nothing. Honest. Don't put me away. Please don't put me away.'

Trevor moved closer to Blackie, his stomach churning at the rancid smell of rotting cloth and stale sweat that emanated from Blackie's unwashed body. 'If we took you to the pier now, Blackie, could you show us how you got in?' he asked gently.

'Couldn't.' Blackie's eyes glinted black and cunning from beneath the tangle of hair. 'It's wired up now. Can't get on the pier. No one can, not since the wire's been put there.'

'Blackie, were you on the pier recently?' Peter's temper escaped its temporary check, and continued to rise.

'Not since the wires.' Blackie's eyes darted nervously around the room. 'Can't say no more. Can I go?' His hand closed over the money in his clothes. 'I don't know no more. Honest. I'll swear on the Bible. Ask the Father. It's the truth. I want to buy food, Father. I'm hungry. Can I go?'

Sam looked to Trevor and Peter.

'Let him go. He'll be easy enough to find should we want him again.'

Blackie needed no second bidding. He scurried out of the door as though ants were biting his heels.

'I hope you're right about finding him again.' Trevor laid his handkerchief carefully over the spectacles on the floor and wrapped them in it. 'Andy isn't proving too easy to find at the moment.'

'We'll put a description out on him,' Peter said shortly, as he headed out of the door. He needed fresh air, and he needed it now! He didn't want Trevor to realize it had been his disgust with Blackie, the room, the whole decrepit decaying shelter, that had made him cut the interview short. He simply couldn't stand the kitchen another moment. 'If every copper on the beat

188

looks for Andy, he won't last long on the streets,' he predicted as they reached the front door.

'Is all this necessary?' Sam asked. 'If all that Andy's done is break into the pier . . .'

'There's a bit more to it than that, Sam. I'm afraid I can't tell you very much, but take my word for it, it's important.' Trevor tucked the wrapped spectacles into his shirt pocket, as he gulped in great mouthfuls of fresh air. Peter wasn't the only one who'd been sickened by the close, mixed odours of the mouldering house.

'I understand,' Sam said tactfully. 'It's difficult work you two'll be doing.'

'If you hear of anyone, anyone at all using the pier, will you phone the station?' Peter asked.

'Of course. Are you afraid that the drug pushers have taken over the place?'

'Drug pushers?' Peter looked at Sam in bewilderment, then his mind cleared. 'We've been taken off the Drug Squad, Sam.'

'I'm sorry to hear it.'

'They haven't sacked us.' Trevor grinned, amused by the expression on Sam's face. He leaned against Peter's car and looked up at the clean blue sky. 'Like everyone else down the station, our usual work is taking second place to the motorway murders.'

'Murders. Not here in town, surely?'

'Sam, where do you live? The television and newspapers have been full of nothing else for days.'

'You know me, Peter. We've no television in the hostel. And there's never enough time to read the papers. The only ones I see are days old, and generally wrapped around something.'

'Two bodies have been found at the side of the motorway that runs into town. The heads, and the hands, have been removed,' Trevor explained succinctly. 'As you can imagine, they're proving to be difficult to identify. These,' he tapped the glasses in his pocket, 'just might clinch our first identification.'

'Two bodies. And no one's claimed the poor souls. How dreadful. I'll say a prayer for them.'

'You can say a prayer for a missing doctor while you're at it, Sam. The one pressing missing person report we do have doesn't fit the description of either of the bodies.'

'A doctor. I don't know what the world's coming to. Two bodies and no families to claim them. It's so sad.'

'Has anyone gone missing from the hostel lately, Sam?' Peter tried a long shot.

'You know what the hostel's like, Peter. People come, people go. Youngsters are the worst. Some stay a few nights, a week or two at most, then move on. We have our regulars like Blackie and Gramps, but they make up less than a quarter of the people who sleep here on any one night. And the young girls . . .' The priest shook his head in despair. 'There are so many of them, and more arrive on the doorstep every day. They shouldn't be here. Not mixed in with the old men, the drunkards, the drug addicts. They should have a hostel of their own. A new and cleaner one.'

'So you couldn't say if anyone's gone missing?'

'Andy's the only regular that's staying away at the moment. I try to talk to the drifters, but I couldn't tell you very much about them. Who they are, where they're going – it's their business. If I tried to make it mine, I'd never get them in here.'

'That doesn't help us very much.' Peter unlocked the car door.

'It's society,' Sam pronounced wearily. 'No one cares, really cares for their fellow man. Not any more. None of this,' he pointed at the festering building behind him, 'would have happened in the old days. In village communities there were families and friends willing to help people through a crisis. Now the youngsters believe everyone's against them. They trust no one, and they run. From authority, the police, even their own families and friends. Only the other day I had a couple in here asking after a young man. I couldn't help them. The boy they were looking for had slept here for a week, and moved on. It was a pity. They were obviously worried about him. Made me wonder why he'd run away in the first place.'

'Can you remember the name of the lad the couple were looking for, Sam?'

'No. No, I'm sorry, I can't. I'm absolutely hopeless with names,' he apologized.

'Try, Sam,' Peter insisted. 'It could be more important than you know.'

'I think the others called him Robin, but I couldn't be certain of it. Dark-haired, good-looking boy. I remember one of the girls teasing him, telling him he should be a pop star.'

'The couple who came looking for him. Were they his parents?'

'No. They were too young to be his parents. I think the girl was his sister, the man probably her boyfriend. Nice young fellow. They came about ten at night when the place was crowded. He watched me turning people away. I think he noticed how much I hated having to do it. Before he left he gave me a donation for the hostel fund. There's not many do that.'

'Do you remember their names, Sam?' Peter pressed.

'I told you I'm not very good with names.' Sam pushed his glasses further up his nose. 'He gave me his card, though. In case the boy came back.' He dug into the pocket of his cassock and pulled out a folded conglomeration of bits of paper. He thumbed through them awkwardly. 'Here it is,' he announced gleefully, separating a stiff card from the rest. 'I wrote the boy's name on the back. Robin, Robin Dart, that's his name.' He flipped the card over and read the name and address engraved on the back. 'Dr Tim Sherringham, Grantley Mews.'

'I don't believe it.' Peter let out a long slow whistle. 'I simply don't believe it.'

'Here.' Trevor reached for his wallet and pulled out copies of the photographs he'd taken from Daisy. 'Is this the man?'

'Yes. Yes, that's him,' Sam agreed. 'Fine young fellow. He's not in any trouble, is he?'

'Not with us.' Trevor pushed the photograph back into his wallet. 'But he's the doctor who's been missing from home for five days.'

'Sam,' Peter pleaded. 'Think hard. Can you remember the name of the girl Tim Sherringham was with, and what night they came here?'

'The girl said she was Robin's sister, so it follows her name was Dart, too, but her first name . . .' He shook his head doubtfully.

'Was it Amanda?' Trevor asked.

'Could be. I just can't remember.'

'Can you describe her?'

'Small, thin, large glasses, not a bit like Robin. I remember thinking they were nothing alike.' Comprehension suddenly dawned on Sam. 'Do you think those could be her glasses? That something's happened to her?'

'That's what we're trying to find out.' Peter sat on the low wall that fronted the hostel. 'You still haven't told us exactly when Tim Sherringham and Amanda Dart came here.'

'Working here as I do, all my days are the same. Sometimes I feel as if they've all merged into one long day. They may have come a week or two ago, but I really can't be any more precise than that. I really can't.'

'Please, Sam,' Trevor pleaded. 'You said the hostel was full, that you were turning people away. Something

192

else must have happened that day. You must have heard some news, seen someone. Come on, think. This is the first break we've had.'

'I'm sorry, Trevor. I turn people away from here every night. I remember them coming. I remember him giving me . . .' A smile lit Sam's face. 'He gave me a cheque. I paid it into the bank, but they'd keep it, wouldn't they? And it would have the date on it.'

'Can you come to the bank with us now?' Peter opened the back door of the car.

'But the hostel . . .'

'There must be someone who can take over from you for a couple of hours.'

'A couple of hours.'

'Sam, this is a murder enquiry. You're the first definite lead we've had.'

'If it's that important, perhaps you can stop off at St Mary's. I'll ask one of the curates there to cover for me.'

'Bless you.' Peter rubbed his hands together. For the first time since Tim Sherringham had vanished and the mess had been uncovered on the motorway, they had a lead. Somewhere to go, and someone to see. Bill's theory had proved right. A couple of locals digging in unlikely places had come up with more than the whole of the London squad, for all their fancy equipment and bright ideas.

'Welcome back to the land of the living.'

Daisy opened her eyes slowly. She was in a strange room. The light was shaded, muted, and there were metallic noises in the background.

'Hospital from the inside.' Judy smiled down at her. 'You had us all worried for a while.'

'I can't remember . . .'

'Believe me, you don't want to.'

'I was at Richard's . . .'

193

'And now you're here in the General. And as soon as you feel strong enough, we'll move you up into my flat.'

'What's the time?'

'Seven in the evening.'

'Damn! I've slept the entire day away, and I wanted to do so much.'

'It can all wait until tomorrow.'

'But you took a day off, especially . . .'

'Lucky I did.' Judy moved from the chair at the side of Daisy's bed and walked to the window. She opened the blinds. Twilight was gathering, and the streetlights encircling the bay were beginning to flicker with the red glow that preceded amber.

'You've been here all day?' Daisy propped herself up on one elbow. Her mouth was parched. Her head swam crazily, and every time she moved, the room around her wavered in and out of focus.

'I enjoyed the rest. Sitting next to a sickbed all day with feet propped up and a store of magazines to read is heavenly.'

'Busman's holiday?'

'You should know better than that. When does a houseman ever get time to sit next to a patient?' She picked up Daisy's wrist and took her pulse. Then she bent over the bed and studied Daisy's eyes.

'I'm fine,' Daisy announced irritably.

'So I see.'

There was a gentle knock at the door, followed by a whispered, 'It's me. Are you decent?'

'What the hell do you think we're doing in here?' Judy asked as Alan walked in through the door.

'I had no idea, that's why I knocked. Glad to see the patient alive and scowling. You must be feeling better.' He picked up Daisy's wrist.

'You can put that back. Judy's just taken it.'

'And?' He looked questioningly at Judy.

194

'She'll live.'

He sat on the bed. 'Can you remember what happened?'

'Judy told me I don't want to.'

'You had a nightmare.'

'All I can remember is going to bed in Richard's house. Then . . . then . . .'

'Waking up here?'

'Yes.'

'I went to Richard's this morning to collect you, as arranged.' Judy opened Daisy's case and brought out her dressing gown. 'You weren't up, so Hare took me to your room. When I walked in you went crazy. You appeared to be still asleep, but when I tried to wake you, you screamed all the louder. Unfortunately, you made enough noise to bring up Joanna and Mike who were breakfasting on the terrace.'

'Joanna and Mike?' Daisy's eyes grew round in amazement.

'Joanna and Mike,' Judy repeated. 'Mutt and Jeff were there too, and true to their flat-footed profession they insisted on barging in as well.'

'How did I get here?'

'After we sent the police off with a flea in their ear, Mike called Alan. Between us, we decided the best place for you was here.' Judy draped the dressing gown around Daisy's shoulders.

'And Richard agreed?'

'He wasn't consulted.'

'But he's found out now,' Alan announced wryly. 'That's why I'm here. To tell you he's on his way.'

'Oh God!'

'Oh God nothing.' Daisy swung her legs over the side of the bed. 'What can he say? I'm fine. I'm over twenty-one. And I've decided to move in with Judy, if she'll have me.'

'How many times do I have to offer?'

'Are you sure you're feeling up to moving anywhere?' Alan asked, steadying Daisy as she slumped forward.

'I'm sure.' She gripped the edge of the bed for support.

'That was a pretty hefty dose I . . .'

'Of what?' She glared at Alan.

'You don't want to know.'

'Oh, but I do.'

'Wouldn't it be better if Richard finds you in my flat when he arrives here?' Judy intervened tactfully. 'If he sees you in here, like this, he might try to get you into his clinic.'

'Good idea. He can hardly pick me up and carry me out once I'm settled into your place,' Daisy agreed.

'You'll have to move quickly. As I said, he's already on his way.'

'Someone needs to go downstairs and redirect him to my flat. Very slowly.'

'You have womanly charms and wiles I lack.' Alan sank into the only chair in the room.

'Thank you for volunteering me. See you upstairs in a few minutes, Daisy.'

Daisy reached for the suitcase that Judy had left on the bed. She pulled out the black suit and underclothes she had laid out the previous night in Richard's house. Then she stood up.

'Careful.' Alan supported her by her elbows. 'How about if I walk you to the bathroom, one step at a time. You can dress in there with the door slightly open. I promise not to come in unless I hear a crash.'

'Thanks.'

'I really did knock you out, didn't I?'

'Looks like it.'

Alan left her sitting on the edge of the bath. Then he went back for her clothes. He handed them modestly through the gap in the open doorway.

'This nightmare of yours, can you remember any of it?' he asked cautiously, returning to his chair.

'Yes,' she called back weakly.

'Has it happened every night since Tim disappeared?'

'I think so. I go to bed, sometimes I could swear I'm still wide awake, then . . . then they come.' Her voice quivered with suppressed emotion.

'The woman in the raincoat and the man in the evening suit?'

'Yes.'

The plastic upholstery screeched protestingly as Alan shifted his solid bulk over its shiny surface.

'As Judy said, Trevor Joseph and Peter Collins were in Richard's house this morning. They followed Joanna and Mike upstairs when you screamed, a natural enough reaction, I suppose. When you spoke about your nightmare, they heard. All of it. And, from what I can gather, you mentioned something that wasn't even found until later.'

'What?'

'Trevor wouldn't, or couldn't tell me.'

'And now I'm a suspect.' It was a statement, not a question.

'I'd like to be able to contradict you.'

Daisy reappeared from the bathroom. Her black suit and crisp white cotton blouse showed little sign of the packing they'd been subjected to, but her face was alarmingly white. Her eyes were set in dark circles that accentuated their unnatural brightness.

Alan tried to smile at her, but his usually cherubic face was grimly serious. 'I spoke to Trevor this afternoon. I'm afraid the police aren't very imaginative. They see only what's laid out in front of them.'

'Headless corpses. An over-emotional female who describes them perfectly, if a little prematurely. It's a logical progression of thought. Tell me. Have the police

197

interrogated anyone close to me yet? Asked my friends if I could be the killer?'

'Not as far as I know. But I've no doubt that they will.'

She staggered to the bed and took a hairbrush from her suitcase, then unplaited her hair and began to brush it out. Alan watched. She didn't have full control over her movements. Once or twice the hairbrush banged awkwardly against her head. He lacked the courage to offer to brush it for her, or to tell her about the rest of Trevor's conversation. How Trevor had hinted at new evidence and leads. Leads which implicated 'certain people'. Then there was the promise that Trevor had wrung out of him. A promise to watch Daisy until the morning, when the police would come for her. He'd given his word. If he hadn't, Daisy would be in custody now, her privacy violated by police presence in this room, or at best outside the door. He'd begged Trevor for a breathing space for Daisy. And one night was all Trevor would offer. Tomorrow, she'd have to face questions he didn't want to think about. And they'd be flung at her from the mouth of a more brutal interrogator than Trevor Joseph. He had no doubt of that. The only solace he could offer was the pathetic comfort of short-lived ignorance, and he despised himself for not being able to do more.

'It'll work out all right in the end, Daisy.' He wrapped a thick, clumsy arm round her thin shoulders. 'Sooner or later something in this mess will make sense. It has to.'

'You really think so?'

She turned to him, resting her head on his shoulder. His physical presence was warm, comforting, but it wasn't enough to dispel the fears that crowded in on her. Not so much the claustrophobic, paralyzing terrors of the mutilated corpses that peopled her nightmares. More the insidious, durable fear of loneliness. Of being left hanging precariously in midair. Of having her familiar world wrenched away and replaced by a hostile alien land. Nothing real, nothing recognizable remained for her to grasp at. Tim, the backbone of her life, was no longer with her. She was waiting for, actually wanted to see, the final public proof and display of his death. She needed to see his corpse, mourn him. And as long as he was found, she didn't care what state he was in. Certainty, any certainty, would be better than this.

She concentrated on a vision of Tim, dead. Not his body. That would have been too much. But his gravestone standing somewhere peaceful, like one of the sleepy churchyards they'd visited in Cornwall.

Beloved husband of Daisy.

She'd be left with her work in the hospital, with an empty flat that would never resound with Tim's laughter again. She forced herself to dwell on the practicalities of her new existence. Shopping baskets holding only a few items. Not enough washing to warrant switching the machine on. Evenings spent sitting in front of the TV. Endless cups of coffee and biscuits because it was too much trouble to cook for one. And at the end of the day, a quick interchange of words with Alan and Judy, who had their own lives to lead. No one to gloat over triumphs with, no one to sympathize with the failures. Letters addressed to *Mrs* Sherringham. Not Mr and Mrs. A bleak, empty meaningless life.

She'd cope with it. She was coping now, wasn't she? And when the vision became reality her nightmares would cease. She believed that much. She had to. The alternative was too horrendous for her to contemplate.

'The key to the doctor's disappearance is in the phone call, Bill. It has to be.' Peter swung back on his chair and lifted his coffee cup to his lips.

'What do you think, Trevor?' Bill Mulcahy turned

to Trevor, who'd been sitting quietly, too damned quietly for his liking, by the door ever since he'd come back from telephoning the hospital.

'I agree with Peter. The key to Sherringham's disappearance has to lie in that call. Daisy Sherringham says she answered it, but she only spoke briefly to whoever was at the other end. It was Tim Sherringham who told her he'd been called out on the Hawkins case. And that means one of two things: either whoever was at the other end of that line knew Tim Sherringham's workload and patients, or . . .'

'Or?' Bill pressed impatiently.

'Or Tim Sherringham wanted to disappear and used the Hawkins case as an alibi.'

'Funny time to choose to disappear, four o'clock in the morning. And that still doesn't solve the problem of who made the phone call.'

'Suppose Tim Sherringham had a lady friend,' Peter suggested. 'Not Amanda Dart, that's pushing it too far, but someone else. Another nurse, perhaps. What better time to run off with her than four in the morning? The man worked all day in the hospital in full view of staff and patients. He travelled to and from the General with his wife. Everyone agrees Daisy Sherringham practically lived in his pocket.'

'So when did he fit the girlfriend in?' Trevor queried.

'He found time to spend a couple of hours with Amanda Dart in the hostel for the homeless,' Peter retorted. 'Doctors work shifts; we know Tim and Daisy occasionally worked different hours. It's conceivable he could have taken time off from Daisy before, booked into a hotel with a glamorous dolly bird. Need I say more?'

'I don't buy it. Daisy . . .'

'Grow up, Joseph. There's no such thing as the perfect marriage, or the perfect woman. Besides,' Peter raised a mocking eyebrow, 'this theory accommodates your lust for the lady quite nicely. Who better to console the slighted wife than the strong handsome bachelor policeman.'

'Let's drop the suppositions for a moment and consider the facts,' Bill ordered. 'Shall we start with the bodies, and then move on to the missing doctor?'

'By all means,' Trevor concurred.

'Thanks to routine police work, we've got our first firm identification. And thanks to you two, we've got her glasses, if not her head.' Trevor winced at the sick joke. Bill looked to Peter. 'Still nothing on Andy?'

'We've got every copper on the beat plus Sam and the Salvation Army looking out for him. He'll turn up in his own good time.'

'I just hope his good time proves to be ours.'

'Any news on the second victim?' Trevor asked.

'We've had the PM report in. Not much in it we didn't already know.' Bill picked up a paper from his desk and scanned it. 'Appendix scar, not recent. Old fracture of the lower left arm. Undigested salted peanuts in his stomach.'

'On his way back from the pub?'

'Club, more like it, given his evening dress, or private party. But we're into guesswork, not facts, now, Collins. Unlike Amanda Dart. With her, blood tests, height, weight, skin colour, vaccinations all check out. One of her brothers is flying out from Northern Ireland tonight. He's an army private. I've arranged for him to be interviewed after he's identified what's left of Amanda. I'm not hopeful, but there's a possibility that he might be able to shed some light on this Robin Dart mystery. Unfortunately for us, the Darts weren't exactly what you'd call a close family. More a textbook case for the social services: drunken father serving time for beating his wife to death; kids in and out of care from the day they were born.'

'Amanda and Robin must have been close for

Amanda to go looking for him in the hostel,' Trevor chipped in.

'With Tim Sherringham, exactly one week to the day before Sherringham disappeared.' Bill threw the pencil he was holding on to his desk. 'Any theories on that one?'

'None.'

'Trevor?'

'Sam Mayberry and Luke Roberts down at the day-centre agree that Robin Dart could have been no more than a youngster down on his luck. On the other hand, they both recall signs of nervous illness, or, given his lifestyle, symptoms of drug abuse.'

'Any hard evidence? Hypodermics? Association with known pushers?'

'None.'

'Did they come up with the names of friends, places he hung out?'

'Nothing.'

'No ideas on where he went?'

'No. Without knowing more, it's difficult to say why he went missing, that's if he really is missing, or why Amanda and Sherringham went looking for him in the hostel.'

'And you call yourself a detective? Try looking for more, boy. Try looking.' Bill pulled a paper out of a bulging file on his desk. 'Helpful social worker went through the records for me. When Robin Dart left care at eighteen, he was found a living-in job as a skivvy in a London hotel. But he wasn't happy with his lot in life. He auditioned for drama school, and, all credit to him, he was accepted. Then, for some reason that's not recorded, he left. I rang the principal. He puts Robin's disappearance down to lack of money. The next time he was heard of, was when he rang the social services here. They'd sent him to London, but as he'd passed the age of eighteen, he was, officially at least, an adult.

They couldn't, or wouldn't, help. The entry that recorded the phone call closed his file. I can only surmise he packed his bags and came back to this town because his roots and his sister were here. And we all know it's a short trip from the railway station to Jubilee Street, particularly when you're low on friends and money.'

'An everyday story of our country's folk,' Peter muttered laconically. 'But nothing you've said sheds any light on the Sherringham connection. Or throws any light on my theory of Tim Sherringham running off with another woman.'

'Aren't both of you forgetting Tim Sherringham in all of this?' Trevor said calmly. 'Nearly a week of investigation hasn't turned up one breath of scandal to implicate the man.'

'Eric Hedley . . .'

'You marked Hedley down as a misfit, not me. And even Hedley had no evidence against Sherringham. Only half-cocked malicious gossip. Wasn't he the source for your story about Tim Sherringham and Amanda Dart?'

'Point taken,' Peter conceded grudgingly.

'Could be we're missing the obvious. That Tim Sherringham only felt sorry for Amanda Dart. Pity, pure and simple. You saw the girl, Peter.'

'She was pathetic by any standard, but I've never said Amanda Dart was Tim Sherringham's bit on the side. There has to be someone else.'

'Who?'

'Now there you have me, but we do know Daisy tried to live in his pocket,' Peter said keenly, reluctant to let his theory go. 'Supposing Sherringham was worried about her finding out about his affair. Wives ask questions, particularly when it comes to cash. I know!'

'The cheque he gave Sam was drawn on a personal account. No other signatory,' Bill said baldly.

'The man who gave Sam a hundred pounds was

worried about change for his dolly bird?' Trevor's voice was heavy with sarcasm. For the first time since the Sherringham case had landed in his and Peter's laps, his reasoning was devoid of emotion, calmly based on logical thought, and he intended to press his advantage to the limit.

'No one knows for certain when Robin Dart went missing,' Trevor continued evenly. 'Sam and Luke can't remember, but they both agree he hasn't been seen in months, rather than weeks. The one person who could have helped us there is Amanda Dart, and she's one of our victims. Supposing she was upset by her brother's disappearance and the upset began to affect her work. Sherringham worked on the same ward as Amanda. Perhaps he found her crying, say after a run-in with your friend Sister Hemming, Peter. We know from Judy Osbourne that Sherringham had a social conscience, and the cheque he gave Sam proves he was a soft touch. Perhaps he offered Amanda the use of his shoulder, and listened to the story of her missing brother. The Tim Sherringham I've heard about would try to help.'

'There you go again, Joseph, expounding your great belief in the milk of human kindness. How many times do I have to tell you that no one does something for nothing in this life?'

'The man was a doctor, Collins, not a policeman. Perhaps, unlike you, he still had some humanity left.' Bill turned to Trevor. 'OK, Joseph, I'll buy your story as far as Amanda Dart and Sherringham go, but where does it fit in with the motorway bodies, apart from the obvious connection of Amanda being one of the victims?'

'Perhaps Robin Dart and Sherringham have been murdered too.'

'Dear God, we've got enough bodies without looking for more!'

'Trevor's not the first copper around here to suggest there might be a second body-dump.' Bill silenced Peter for the second time and looked at Trevor. 'Have you checked out the clown sightings?'

'They check out.'

'That's not what I asked.'

'If you must know, we delegated,' Peter admitted. 'And while we're on the topic of clowns, Joanna Holbourne had a pierrette for a grandmother. Richard Sherringham's father-in-law still owns the pier. Trevor and I went over it personally,' he emphasized the last word. 'The fortifications appear to be impregnable, but we have a couple of unverifiable clown sightings on it, or rather in it, by down-and-outs.'

'Want a search warrant?'

'May as well. By the way, Trevor,' Peter smiled disarmingly, 'You haven't told us when Daisy Sherringham's coming in for questioning.'

'She's in severe shock. Alan asked if she could remain in the hospital just for tonight.'

'And you agreed?'

'The woman's ill!'

'The woman gave accurate descriptions of murder victims before they were released to the press. Explain that if you can.'

'I can't, but I do know Daisy . . .'

'Excuse me, sir.' Constable Harries knocked and opened the door in one quick movement.

'Yes?' Bill snapped.

'We've had a response to the "have you seen them?" photographs of Amanda Dart that we put out to the press. Also, someone's rung up with a sighting of Sherringham's blue Fiat.'

'And?'

'A Mr . . .' Harries consulted a slip of paper that he held in his hand, '. . . Douglas says he walks his dog every day on the cliffs above Hunter's Cove.'

'Are those the cliffs that border the Sherringham estate?' Peter interrupted.

'Hunter's Cove and the woods behind it are part of the Sherringham estate,' Harries agreed.

'And?' Bill repeated.

'He says he saw Sherringham's blue Fiat parked off the road, on the grassed area of the cliff itself. Apparently it was parked in the same spot for three days. Four days ago he checked round it, looked through the windows and took the number. He said he was thinking of reporting it to us. It's such an out-of-the-way place.'

'Get on with it, Harries.'

'It wasn't there on the fourth morning, sir.'

'Exactly when, and for how long was the car parked there?'

'Mr Douglas saw it the morning after Dr Sherringham disappeared. It was on the clifftop for two days after that, then it went.'

'And he comes forward when it's too damned late for us to see for ourselves. Great. Bloody great! Have it checked out, Harries,' Bill ordered.

'Call was made direct to the incident room. London squad's already sent men out to the cliff, and to interview Mr Douglas.'

'Forget it, then. Anything else?'

'Yes, sir. Two people have come in. They're both prepared to swear they saw Dr Sherringham and Amanda Dart boarding a yacht in the marina five nights ago. That's the night after the doctor disappeared and the evening of the day Amanda Dart last worked at the hospital.'

'I'm aware of the timetable of this case, Harries.' Bill narrowed his eyes. 'Are they nuts?' he enquired suspiciously.

'Not obviously so, Sir. And as far as I can make out they're not connected. One's a retired Colonel. Intelligence.'

'Where are they now?'

'Outside, sir. I thought you might like to interview them before the London squad.'

'Show them in. One at a time.'

'Yes, sir.' Harries opened the door. 'There's just one more thing, sir.'

'Spit it out, Harries.'

'Richard Sherringham's solicitor is here, sir. He wants to make an official complaint. Something about Dr Sherringham's wife being harassed.'

'I'll deal with that one.' Peter was out of his chair and through the door before Bill and Trevor had time to stop him.

'Harries?'

'Sir?'

'Wheel the Colonel in. And Harries . . .'

'Sir?'

'No need to tell the London boys anything about this just yet.'

'Yes, sir.'

Chapter Eight

Robin Dart crouched down, spine straight, arms out-stretched in front of a battered cabin trunk.

'One, two, three, then lift,' he murmured under his breath, steeling himself for the back-breaking load. He lifted, groaned, then staggered to the rust-spotted van parked alongside the open door of the community centre.

'That the last of the costumes?' a fair-haired girl called as he off-loaded the trunk on to the floor of the transit.

'I sincerely hope so.'

'I'll check round,' she offered. 'You want to drive?'

'Fine.' He gave the trunk one last valedictory shove, before slamming the van doors.

'Don't lock up. I've promised Alex and Damian a lift.' Jock, the Scottish member of the Community Theatre Group, stuck his head round the side of the van.

'Fine,' Robin repeated absent-mindedly as he climbed into the driver's seat. The fair-haired girl reappeared.

'Nothing forgotten,' she said brightly, moving along the bench seat to make room for Jock.

'Then let's go.'

'To the Builder's Arms?' No one objected, so Robin headed that way.

Jock leaned over the girl and fiddled with the radio. '*Arts Review* will be starting on the local station in a couple of minutes. We should get a crit.'

'It had better be good,' the girl shouted in an effort

to make herself heard above the noise of the engine. 'I've worked my arse off for this production.'

'Haven't we all?' Robin was a trifle sour. He was the newest member of the theatre group, but he'd been with them long enough for the glitter of getting his equity card to have worn off. He was also tired of getting the worst parts, the biggest loads to carry, and most of the stick when things went wrong. Now if Jock should leave . . .

'Local news.' Jock glanced at his watch. 'Good. We haven't missed any of the reviews.'

'Quiet,' Robin hissed.

'Robin Dart, five foot ten inches tall, brown eyes, straight dark hair. Robin's last known address is the hostel for the homeless in Jubilee Street. If anyone has seen Robin Dart during the past six months, or knows his present whereabouts, would they please contact their local police station. I repeat, Robin is not wanted in connection with any crime. Police and relatives are concerned for his safety. So if you've seen anyone resembling Robin, or if you know where he is, please ring . . .'

Abruptly, Robin reached out and silenced the radio. He swung the van round a corner. 'If you don't mind, I'll drop you at the Builders and catch up with you later.'

'Are you going to the fuzz?' Jock pulled a face. 'Hey, listen everyone, Robin's going to the fuzz.'

'I won't tell if you won't,' Damian or Alex, or perhaps both, sang out from the back as Robin screeched to a halt in the pub car park.

Two people, one a lonely widow, the other a crusty old bachelor, had been taking their separate evening walks along the marina when they'd seen a man and a woman board a boat. From the shore, a distance of perhaps a quarter of a mile from the moorings, they'd both

209

watched them enter the cabin. And now each was prepared to swear that the people they'd seen had been Tim Sherringham and Amanda Dart.

The twig-thin widow had chirped, 'I saw her photograph on the front page of the *Herald* tonight, and I said to myself, that's her. That's the one. How many other women wear glasses that thick?'

'Not many men stand that tall,' the Colonel had barked. 'It was him, I tell you. I saw him plain as I see you now.'

'And what was the name of the boat they boarded?' Bill had asked.

'Couldn't see that far,' the Colonel bellowed. 'When you get to my age the eyes go.'

'And yet you can be sure you saw Tim Sherringham and Amanda Dart?' Trevor hadn't been able to resist the gibe. That was when Bill gave him a hard look and he decided to leave the room.

'Sergeant Collins, I wish to make a formal complaint.'

'Of course, sir.' Peter pulled a chair close to his desk, and offered it to the solicitor. 'If you'd care to sit down, perhaps we could discuss the matter.'

'There's nothing to discuss.' The solicitor summoned every inch of superiority that his exclusive schooling had instilled into him. 'Dr Richard Sherringham spoke to Dr Cummins at the General this evening, and he informed . . .'

'He informed Dr Richard Sherringham that we wish to interview Dr Daisy Sherringham as a matter of urgency.'

'Dr Daisy Sherringham is very ill.'

'We *are* trying to find her husband.'

'By harassing her?'

'By trying to establish the facts. This morning, Sherringham described an article belonging to a murder victim, before the article was found. We would like to know how she knew about this article, and we would also like to discuss her movements during the past two weeks. Where she went. What she did. Who she spoke to.'

'I'm confident that Dr Richard Sherringham or I can furnish you with the facts you require, Sergeant Collins.'

Peter pulled a cigar out of his pocket and rolled it between his fingertips. He wouldn't get anywhere with this one, and he knew it.

'My card, Sergeant Collins. Dr Richard Sherringham isn't denying you access to his sister-in-law. Merely suggesting that it would be better for you to wait until she is well enough to receive you.'

'And you wish to be present?'

'Myself and her medical adviser.'

'Richard Sherringham?'

The solicitor inclined his head. Peter drummed his fingers impatiently on the tabletop, while he worked out his next move.

'My complaint, Sergeant?' The solicitor's carefully modulated tones intruded into Peter's thoughts. Peter stood up and opened the door of the interview room.

'Constable Harries will take it. If you'd care to come this way.'

Alan Cummins pushed his way reluctantly into the crowded pub. He trod on the foot of a cook, sidestepped past a group of porters downing pints, and reached the bar.

'Full tonight.' Mike Edmunds pocketed his change and turned to greet him.

'Damned place is always the same after the day shift,' Alan grumbled. 'Anyone would think that hospital staff have no homes to go to.'

'What will it be, Doctor?' The barmaid who'd served Mike hung about waiting for his order, oblivious to the bangs and shouts coming from the other end of the bar.

'Pint and a curry, Mavis.'

'Wife at the mother-in-law's again?' She winked at Mike. 'We only ever see him in here when he's a grass widower.'

'She'll be back tomorrow.' Alan took his pint and felt in his pocket for change.

'Beef or chicken?' She pointed to the bar menu. 'Beef or chicken curry?' she repeated.

'Is there a difference?'

'Not so you'd notice.'

'Make it beef.'

She took his money. 'Where will you be sitting?'

'There's a stool free at my table,' Mike offered. 'In the corner.'

'I'll bring it to you when it's ready, Doctor,' Mavis smiled.

'You never do that for me, Mavis,' Mike complained.

'You didn't set my son's hernia to rights.'

Alan watched Mike cross the room as he waited for his change. The place was literally bursting at the seams; some of the drinkers had spilled out into the car park and were half sitting, half leaning against the cars. Then he saw the stool Mike had offered him, sandwiched between Mike and Eric Hedley.

'Oh well, beggars can't be choosers,' he muttered under his breath.

'Pardon, Doctor?'

'Nothing, Mavis.' He pocketed his change, reflecting that he'd only come to the pub anyway because he couldn't stand his own company. It was always the same when Carol and the kids went away for a night or two. Not that she did it that often. He would have preferred to have spent the evening at Judy's, but Richard Sherringham's arrival had put him off that idea. Tim he'd liked on first acquaintance, but on the few occasions he'd met Richard Sherringham he'd found the man arrogant and self-important.

He wondered, not for the first time, if that were really the case, or if it was sheer prejudice on his part. Perhaps he was merely suffering from the effects of an outsize inferiority complex because the man's professional talents were undoubtedly superior to his own. Or possibly it was simply a little of Daisy's antipathy to private medicine rubbing off on him.

But then again, if he was truthful, it wasn't really Richard who'd pushed him out. It was the girls themselves. Judy had everything so well organized. The dinner she was preparing was enough for two, no more, he's seen that at a glance. And Judy was right to organize things that way. She was closer to Daisy than the Sherringhams. She, better than anyone, knew what Daisy needed, what Daisy was feeling right now. After all, she'd known Daisy for longer than anyone else in the hospital. Even Tim.

He fought his way to Mike's table, carrying his pint awkwardly, slopping the froth over the side of the glass and down the neckline of a rather buxom auxiliary nurse who worked in Casualty. He braced himself for a telling-off, but she merely smiled weakly at him.

'I don't know why I come here after a hard day.'

'To see people standing up instead of lying down?' he suggested.

Mike pulled the stool out from under the table for him. 'So, Carol's at her mother's?'

'Yes, it's half-term. She's taken the kids over there.'

'And when the cat's away, the mice will play.' Eric Hedley grinned snidely.

'In here?' Alan raised his eyebrows as he sank his beer. 'You've got to be joking.'

'Oh, I don't know, there's that blonde nurse from the surgical ward standing over there. Now I wouldn't mind her ministering to my needs on a dark night.'

'You wouldn't,' Mike retorted.

'We can't all have our lady loves on tap.'

'Lay off, Eric.'

Alan put his pint down on the table. 'How are things with Amy?'

'We hope to get married when she's done her finals.'

'Good for you.' Alan clapped him on the back. 'That's what the world needs. More married men.'

'That's why I was at the Sherringham house this morning.'

'I didn't ask,' Alan pointed out.

'I know. You wouldn't. But Richard Sherringham's offered me a three-week stint working as his anaesthetist in the clinic. I'll just be standing in for Tony until he gets back.'

'And you're taking it?'

'I've four weeks leave coming to me. If I work through, it'll give me just about enough cash to put a deposit on a house.'

'Then you don't intend to stay in private practice.'

'Tony'll be back at the end of the month. There's no way a surgeon needs two anaesthetists. But I might carry on with the odd bit of freelance work for Joanna Sherringham. Medical tests and examinations on volunteers who've been trying out the cosmetics manufactured by the company she works for.'

'And very lucrative it is too, old boy.'

Glasses in hands, Alan and Mike stared at Eric Hedley.

'Don't look so surprised. Married men aren't the only ones who need cash, you know,' Eric gloated. 'I've been working for her for months. She's expanding. It was my suggestion that she sub-contract more of her work out. I simply can't cope with it all.' He finished his whisky and soda and handed Mike the glass. 'So in a way you've got me to thank for your good fortune. I'm drinking old malt.'

*

214

Unlike Jock, Robin Dart didn't detest the police. He was wary of them, went out of his way to avoid them, which hadn't always been easy when he'd lived in Jubilee Street, but that evening he was prepared to trade his distrust for outright hatred. He would have enjoyed throttling the duty officer at the town's main station. He could have watched quite impassively as the man's large, fat face turned purple.

'Now, if you'll fill in this form . . .'

'I came to help,' Robin protested, not for the first time.

'I appreciate that, sir.' The slight pause before and after 'sir', just to let him know he didn't quite warrant the title. 'Now, if you'll just give me your name and address. Your profession . . .'

'What the hell has my name and address to do with anything? I came because I heard Robin Dart . . .'

'Robin Dart?' Trevor stopped in his tracks, sloshing coffee over the edge of the plastic cups he was holding. 'Did you say Robin Dart?'

'I did.' Robin stared suspiciously at the tall, thin, scruffy individual who'd halted in front of him. The man would look more at home in the back of the theatre van than in the police station, he reflected warily. If this character was one of today's coppers, he'd better take a closer look around the pubs he patronized in future.

'How would you like a cup of coffee and a chat in a quiet room down the corridor?' Trevor offered.

Robin sidestepped a constable who was half carrying, half dragging a drunk along the route that led to the cells. 'Do I have to sign anything first?'

'You want it unofficial, you've got it unofficial.'

Robin forgot the duty officer and remembered the 'family' who were worried about him. 'Family' could only mean Amanda, and he'd got no sense out of the hostel when he had tried to phone them on the way here.

'All right,' he assented wearily.

'Time of death. Time of death . . .' Bill Mulcahy flicked through the reports. 'Here you are . . . Take your pick . . . Bloody pathologists. The Home Office variety are no better than the locals.'

'Coffee, sir?' Harries offered, carrying a tray into Bill's office.

Bill looked up quizzically. 'I thought Sergeant Joseph was doing that.'

'He's interviewing someone who's volunteered infor-mation on Robin Dart.'

'I hope that someone is a more likely case than the two who volunteered information on Amanda Dart and Tim Sherringham.' Peter reached for the coffee.

'Difficult to say, sir.'

'Problems with the solicitor, Collins?' Bill enquired bluntly.

'Nothing I can't handle.'

'Glad to hear it.' Bill spooned sugar into his coffee.

Peter lifted his eyes to the hapless Harries. 'How would you like to do a bit of research?' he asked patronizingly.

'Can I, sir?' Harries asked Bill.

'If you want to volunteer for legwork, boy, that's your look-out.'

'I need to know Daisy Sherringham's movements over the past couple of weeks. What shifts she worked, what she did and who she saw in her spare time.'

'That sounds easy enough, Sergeant.'

'Not when you have to do it discreetly, it isn't.' Peter looked at him. More than ever, Harries' clean-cut, clean-shaven face and eager expression reminded him of a faithful and trusting puppy dog. 'Think you can handle it?'

'Yes, sir.'

'You want it, you got it.'

'I'll start work on it right away.' Harries picked up Peter's empty cup and left the room.

'I can't remember you being that obliging when you were in his shoes,' Bill commented, taking a biscuit from the tray.

'Can't recall you being as sweet to me as you are to him.'

'We all mellow as we get older, Collins. One day it'll even happen to you.'

'That'll be the day.'

'Right.' Bill handed him a sheaf of papers. 'Potential witnesses who've phoned in. Back to work, lad. This is a murder enquiry, not a bloody picnic.'

It took some time for Trevor to locate the only free interview room, so he had ample time to size up his volunteer witness. The man was under six foot, but he carried the impression of more height. Thick set, well built, he had the slant-eyed, high-cheekboned features of the Eastern European. His thick blue-black hair hung straight and greasy to his collar, and his arms, bulging with well-developed muscles, swung easily by his sides. He reminded Trevor of a slightly better-looking, young version of Charles Bronson, but for all the outward show of hard physique there was something soft about the man – the mark of the artist, the dreamer. Trevor wondered idly, as he finally ushered him into an empty room.

'So this is comfort, police style.' The man pulled one of the hard chairs out from under the table and sat on it. Trevor had been in this interview room and the others like it many times, but the remark prompted him to look around, and for the first time he saw the place as it really was. Blank beige walls, parquet floor-ing, utility metal-legged table, uncomfortable polypropylene chairs – hardly what you'd call inspiring, or even pleasant decor. But despite the disparaging comment, his witness was more relaxed here than he had been in the corridor outside.

'You know Robin Dart?' Trevor pushed one of the coffees he'd carried into the room across the table towards him.

'More than know him.' Robin rested his elbows on the table, and ran his hands over his face. When he looked up, his eyes were wary, probing, as if he were the one searching for clues in Trevor's demeanour, not the other way round.

'You are him?' Trevor asked intuitively.

'Yes, Constable.'

'Trevor. Trevor Joseph.' Trevor consciously dropped the 'Sergeant'. 'Thank you for coming in.'

'The radio message said "family" was worried. Family can only mean one person.'

'Do you mind telling me who that is?'

'I don't like games, Trevor Joseph.'

'Your sister's been worried about you. She went looking for you in Jubilee Street.'

'I thought she was well rid of me.'

Trevor leaned back in his chair and reached for his coffee. Self-pity was something he wanted to discourage. Particularly when he remembered what he had to tell this man before they left the room.

'Supposing you start with why you left drama school?'

'I came here to tell Amanda I was fine. Why the interrogation?'

'No interrogation. Just a couple of questions. They may help us, and Amanda,' Trevor added as an afterthought.

'Amanda. She's not in any trouble is she?'

Was it his imagination, or had the colour drained from Robin's face? It was difficult to tell under the

218

neon light. Robin's hands were certainly shaking. He saw Trevor looking at them and hid them under the table.

'Supposing you answer my question first. Then I'll tell you about Amanda.'

Robin sank his face into his hands. 'It's all my fault.' His voice sounded strained, muffled by his fingers. 'She didn't want to do any of it. I forced her.'

'Try telling me about it.' Trevor didn't understand what Robin was telling him. But he was experienced enough not to press a reluctant witness with too many questions.

'I couldn't give a damn about me. Only Amanda. She's worth ten of me. And you're a bloody fool if you can't see that it's my fault she did what she did.' Robin moved one of his hands and took a cigarette from a crushed pack in his shirt pocket. He pulled a box of matches out of his frayed denim jacket and lit the cigarette, drawing in and exhaling the smoke sharply. Then he began to talk.

'A couple of years ago I got a place at drama college in London. Thought I'd made it. Michael Caine watch out, here I come.' He gave a short, bitter laugh. 'I didn't learn much in college except how to drink, swear and talk a lot of bullshit. In the end I got fed up of being short of money, so I started busking. Playing the guitar in the underground. To say the least, I was naïve. I didn't realize there were pitches and pitches. I moved in on someone else's and they beat me up pretty bad. College found out about it, they weren't too pleased either. That coming on top of a load of other things you already know about, was enough to get me the boot. I had no money, nowhere to go, I was hurt. I'd only just come out of hospital. I tried ringing the social services – they'd sent me to London in the first place – but they wouldn't help, so I thought of Amanda, and hitched my way here. It wasn't really fair of me, I know. She lives in the nurses' hostel. She couldn't have put me up even if she'd wanted to. She offered me money, but when I arrived here it was late, and she didn't have enough on her for me to rent a room or anything. The banks were closed, so,' he shrugged his shoulders, 'I ended up in Jubilee Street.'

Trevor took a gulp of coffee. It was a story. Truthful? Or carefully phrased to hide the shady incidents that lurked in Robin's past? And what was it that he was supposed to already know about?

'There was this guy in Jubilee Street . . .' He looked at Trevor. 'You ever been in Jubilee Street?' he demanded. Trevor nodded. 'Then you know what the place is like. This guy, Lee, he wasn't like the others. He wasn't a loser. Just a bloke down on his luck. He couldn't stand the muck, the filth, and the old drunkards either. And he was getting out. Told me about it. Asked if I wanted to go along with him. Of course I said yes.'

'Did you have any joy?' Trevor had seen just how short the slide between the respectable end of town and Jubilee Street could be when someone was on the way down. He'd also noticed how steep it was when that someone tried to drag themselves back up.

'Oh, *he* had joy all right. I didn't. That was the bloody problem. He'd seen a notice on the board at the day-centre. "Young people without family ties wanted to work abroad." Nothing more specific than that. He'd taken the notice down so there'd be less competition for the job, whatever it was. When he read it again he decided that there might be room for more than one. So he asked me if I'd like to go along for an interview.'

'And you went?'

'Yes, I went. It was hotel work, in Saudi Arabia. He had experience and he was offered a job. Good money, good prospects, free food, accommodation – the works. He grabbed at the chance.'

'And you?'

'Oh, I was offered a job too. Only there was a medical. He passed, and I didn't.'

Trevor let his curiosity ride. It wasn't the time to ask what Robin took. The shaking hands, the nervousness – heroin, cocaine, crack – the man certainly had the grey, pinched look of long-term sickness about him. But then again, there was nothing in his symptoms that couldn't be put down to Jubilee Street – that's if he still lived there.

'So this mate of yours took the job and left you behind?'

'Wouldn't you have?'

'Probably.'

'I saw Amanda the next day. She gave me money. Enough to pay a month's advance rent on a place, but I spent it. When she found out what I'd spent it on, she wouldn't give me any more. I begged her to help me. She gave me the address of a place. I went there once, but I didn't go again . . . and then . . .' Robin's voice tailed off as he squashed the butt end of his cigarette in the tin ashtray on the table.

'And then?'

'That's why I'm here, isn't it? To tell you about the stuff Amanda took from the hospital and gave to me. It wasn't the money. She would have given me every penny she had if I'd wanted it for anything else. But she was afraid for me. Afraid I'd use infected needles. Afraid of what the pushers use to cut the drugs. So she raided the drugs cabinet on the ward she worked on. She got me needles and . . .'

'Morphine,' Trevor murmured, remembering the ward Amanda had worked on.

'Morphine and pethidine. She told me it was the

221

same, but it wasn't. And some small round pills . . .
omnapon . . . I think they were called.'

'I know the ones.'

'They weren't much use unless you took a few at a
time.'

'You're lucky to be alive, mate.'

Robin pulled out another cigarette, and sat there,
staring at it, not attempting to light it. 'She hated
doing it. But I made her. In the end we had a terrible
argument.' He shuddered at the memory. 'She told me
she wouldn't get me any more morphine or needles.
That I was a hopeless case. That I didn't even want
to help myself.'

'What happened then?' Trevor pushed gently.

'I threatened to telephone the hospital. Shop her for
stealing drugs from the ward. I warned her that she'd
lose her job, that she'd never make a nurse. I knew
how much she wanted to be a nurse.' He pushed his
greasy hair away from his face. His forehead was damp
with sweat. 'I begged. I pleaded for her to help me.
Just one last time.'

'And did she?'

'No.'

Trevor finished his coffee. He pushed his cup to the
edge of the table.

'Did you shop her?' he asked softly.

'No.' Robin finally lit his cigarette. 'I went back to
Jubilee Street that night. I had nowhere else to go. I
was ill, shaking all over. I'd hit bottom and I knew it.
No money for a fix. Amanda had turned her back on
me. Then a guy came up to me. He'd noticed me
shaking. He gave me a couple of pills. They helped, a
bit. He also gave me the address of a place I could go
to. He'd been there. It hadn't worked for him, but he
told me that it had worked for some of the guys there.
But he warned me that no one could really help. That

if I was going to do anything I'd have to do it by myself.'

'And you went?'

'I went. I've been clean now for a while. It's not been easy, but I've got a job with a theatre group. Not much, but it's a start.'

He played with the box of matches on the table. 'I've been meaning to go and see Amanda. Tell her I'm fine, but you know how it is? I was afraid to face her. That last row we had, the things I said to her – I didn't know if she'd forgiven me. But that doesn't mean I don't care for her.' He looked at Trevor fiercely. 'She's all I've really got. I've never bothered much with the others.'

'Your other brothers and sisters?'

'Brothers. Amanda's my only sister. You won't be too hard on her, will you? It was all my fault. None of it's hers. I made her do it. And she's worked so hard. The last thing I want is for her to lose her job.'

'Was Amanda ever with anyone when you saw her?'

'No.'

'Think hard. Did you ever meet any of her friends? Anyone who worked with her at the hospital?'

'No. Say, what is this?'

Robin ground his second cigarette to powder in the ashtray on the table, then reached into his crushed pack for another. He saw Trevor watching him and kicked his chair backwards and turned away. Trevor noticed the way Robin's hands shook as they carried a fresh cigarette to his mouth. He witnessed the small pantomime in silence. He didn't know whether Robin had any problems besides the ones he'd told him about, but what he did know was that Robin Dart was a man close to breaking point. And that was enough to make him want to tread softly, not push any harder than he had to. Experience had taught him that gentle methods usually reaped more benefits with the Robins of this

223

world than the heavy-handed tactics Peter habitually employed. He played with his empty coffee cup for a moment, considering his next move carefully.

'Tell me about your friend. Did Amanda ever meet him?'

'My friend?' Robin looked at him blankly.

'The one who got the job in Saudi Arabia.'

'Amanda never met him, and I never saw him again. I told you, he got the job.'

'And he left for Saudi Arabia, there and then?' Trevor tried, unsuccessfully, to keep the surprise from his voice.

'They gave him money. A room for the night. He was going to go up to London the next day. To begin his training.'

'Where did they put him up?'

'The hotel where they interviewed us.'

'Which is?'

'The Grand. On the front. Know the one I mean?'

Trevor nodded. He knew it. It had seen better days, but it was a palace compared to Jubilee Street.

'What was the name of the people who interviewed you?'

'The man was called Jones. I've no idea of the name of the firm.'

'The medicals. Where were they held?'

'In the hotel, after the interview.'

'Did you get the name of the doctor who examined you?'

'Neither he, nor the nurse, volunteered the information, and I didn't ask.'

'What did he look like?'

'Middle height, short brown hair, not exactly fat, but chubby, brown glasses. I remember thinking he was . . .'

'What?'

'Well, not exactly gay, but . . .'

'Effeminate?'

'Neuter, more like it.'

'Colour of eyes?'

'Sorry, I can't remember.'

'And the nurse?'

'She was a looker. Good figure. Black glasses, but you could imagine her taking them, and a lot of other things off, if you know what I mean.'

'Hair, eyes?'

'Brown hair, I think her eyes were blue, but I'm not sure.'

'The examination, what did it consist of?'

Robin squirmed uneasily in his seat. Trevor looked him squarely in the eye. 'Robin, I'm not going to bust you for what you took. If I'd wanted to do that I would have done it by now. You've helped me to answer some questions, and I'm grateful. If you ever need me to help you, I'll return the favour, I promise.'

'The examination was pretty general.' Robin's words tumbled out in a sudden torrent. 'Blood tests, urine, chest X-ray, heart, lungs, vaccination test.' Robin pulled up his sleeve and showed Trevor a small scar on the inside of his arm.

'That was it?'

'That was it.'

'Do you think you failed because you were an addict?'

Robin took a deep breath, and raised his eyes slowly to Trevor's. 'The doctor checked the veins at the back of my knees.'

'Mainlining heroin?'

'I told you, I'm clean now.'

Trevor noted the crushed pack of cigarettes that Robin had left on the table, his nicotine-stained fingers, the jerky hand movements that escalated every time he spoke. He was off it all right.

'If it's any help, I believe you.'

'It's a help,' Robin muttered dejectedly, fingering the empty cigarette pack. 'It all helps.' Trevor said nothing. He'd seen junkies who'd climbed out of the pit before. He'd also seen some of them afterwards. When they'd slid back into the gutter.

'What happened then?'

'The doctor asked, I told him the truth. Then I left.'

'Your friend?'

'I went. He stayed. We said goodbye. I'd only met him the night before.'

'And you never saw him again?'

'No.'

'You said his name was Lee. Lee what?'

'I don't know. He didn't say.'

'He never said where he was from?'

'No.' Robin shifted uncomfortably on his seat. He persisted in playing with his empty cigarette pack.

'Would you like me to get you another packet of cigarettes?'

'Yes. Yes, that would be good.'

Trevor opened the door and called to the duty officer, then he sat back down. 'Tell me more about Amanda. Did she ever talk about the hospital?'

'Of course she did. She told me about her patients, the babies she'd helped deliver.'

'Did she mention any of the doctors?'

'She talked about one who worked on her ward. I think there was more than a touch of hero worship there. Apparently he'd got her out of a jam with the ward sister. I wondered if I'd caused the jam, but Amanda never said what it was. However she did say the sister was a right bitch.'

'Can you remember the name of the doctor?' Trevor asked.

'Amanda never said.'

'Was Amanda going out with him?'

226

'I tried that tack, but Amanda said he was married. Happily married.'

Trevor fiddled with his pen for a moment, then threw it on to the table. Robin Dart was telling the truth. He had no reason not to. After all, the man had walked in here of his own accord, no one had forced him through the door. He was scared, but his fear was for his sister, and what she'd done because of him. Not for himself. And for the first time, some light had been shed on Amanda Dart's connection with Tim Sherringham. If Tim Sherringham had caught her stealing needles and morphine capsules, he may well have prised the truth out of her. And that would have given him reason enough to visit Jubilee Street in her company, to look for the brother who had made her risk what little she had – her training, and her career. But where in hell did all this tie in with the murder of Amanda Dart and the disappearance of Tim Sherringham?

'Look, can I see Amanda? Is she all right?' Robin's voice was shrill with concern.

'I need to talk to you some more.'

'I'd like to see Amanda and then, if it's all right with you, I'll have to go. I'll come back later if you need me. Stay as long as you like. All night. I don't mind.' Robin rose awkwardly from his chair. 'I promised some people I'd meet them in a pub. I'm their transport,' he added. The truth was he'd just realized where he was, what he'd said, and who he was talking to.

'Did you know that Amanda went to the hostel in Jubilee Street to look for you?' Trevor tossed off the question with a carelessness belied by the watchful expression in his eyes.

'You told me.' Robin stopped half-way to the door. 'Did anything happen to her down there?'

'We don't know. Robin,' Trevor steeled himself, 'there's no easy way to tell you this . . .'

'What is it?' Robin asked suspiciously.

227

'Amanda's been murdered.'

'Murdered.' Robin stared at Trevor in total bewilderment. If he was acting, Trevor decided, it was a convincing performance.

'We have no clear idea of how, or why. Her body was found at the side of the motorway.'

'One of those headless bodies everyone's talking about?'

'Yes. That's why we put that call out on the radio for you. We've contacted your brother in Northern Ireland. But we wanted to find you to tell you . . .'

Robin had stopped listening. He fumbled his way back to the table. Head bowed, he leant heavily on the tabletop, but even the pressure of his body weight wasn't enough to stop his hands from shaking. 'I should have stayed away from her. I should never have come here.'

'What makes you think that your seeing her had anything to do with her death?'

Robin clenched his fists, pushed himself away from the table and walked towards the door.

'If you remember anything else, anything at all, no matter how trivial . . .' Trevor was reluctant to let Robin go. There was always more. Every witness left something out, it was a policeman's job to find out what. The sergeant who'd trained him had drilled that saying into every recruit. What the sergeant hadn't told him, or any of the rookies, was how, short of using brute force, to detain a witness who wanted to run out through the door.

'You'll come back? Tomorrow?'

'If you want me to.'

'Would you like me to get you some more tea?'

'No. No, I'm fine.'

Trevor watched him walk down the corridor. The man was anything but fine. He'd look him up tomorrow

228

if he didn't come in. There might be something more. That one omission the sergeant used to talk about.

Thick swirls of grey shadowy darkness enveloped the stage where the pierrot sat, patient, immobile, blindly staring. The setting sun had long since traced its dying patterns of light over the broken chairs and lumps of feathery dust that littered the auditorium, and the moon had not yet risen high enough to cast its small light through the broken window set close to the roof.

The worst thing about the darkness was the cold it brought. If it hadn't been for the drop in temperature, the pierrot would have welcomed the deepening shadows for their merciful kindness. Dense, intangible, they hung heavily around the stage, curtaining off the worst obscenities of dereliction and decay, but the one thing they couldn't soften was the harsh, incessant droning of the sea as it crashed hollowly against the rusting legs that held the rotting pier boards above water.

Life was this. The stage, the sea, the cold, the emptiness inside. The pierrot had no memory, no past, no future, only this bleak existence. But without a past to compare it with, it didn't matter. Nothing mattered except hunger. The deep gnawing hunger that tormented mind as well as body.

The clown wanted to move. To breathe in the outside air, to walk, to exercise, to get warm. To search for food and drink. But there was no point. There was no memory of checking, only the certain knowledge that the stage exits were bolted and barred. The low apron that separated stage from auditorium, once used by leading pierrots as a platform from which to entertain the audience during scenery changes, had caved in. Ragged-edged holes splashed across the width of the theatre like ink drops. Impenetrably black, they led straight down into the depths of the swaying sea.

229

Trapped! But not forever. Not forever. There was always cunning and . . . the pierrot's gloved hand reached up inside his sleeve.

A rat scurried across the far corner of the stage. One swift movement, a flash of cold steel, and it lay, squealing, pinned to the splintering boards. The pierrot watched unmoved, impassive.

Hunger and hunger alone occupied the thoughts that travelled across consciousness. Echoes sounded along the metal substructure. A boat moored beneath the pier. A bundle was coming. There must have been bundles before, because he knew about them. Bread! He could almost feel its soft, springy texture. Smell the warm, comforting aroma of freshly-roasted meat, the hard, crisp exterior of green apples. And after food, the trap door would close. He would be alone again.

Had to think, to concentrate, to remember! Head hurt with the effort. Other images pushed in, dancing, crowding, never still. Colours, bright colours. Streaks of purple, red, orange, green. Vivid, lime green. Smells, textures. Worlds where gross pink-lined shells walked on spindly legs. Music, above all, music, crying, wailing, sweet, yet more bitter than any cry of torment. Of stringed instruments. Dancing – music – dancing. Crowds. A scream, loud, long, drawn out, the pierrot's scream.

From somewhere below, another echo. The pierrot swallowed the tinny vibrations, digested them. The vibrations meant change, food. A way to get out? Had to get out. But not by sitting here. Had to move. Banish the paralyzing cramp in arms and legs. Out there was a road. A boat. A river.

Images, no more, no less distinct than the ones that had come before, flooded in. A red car, a road, hard, its surface glittering with the distant lights of the car. The moon, full, golden, set like a primary jewel in a star-dusted, midnight-blue sky. A ragged moon playing peek-a-boo with grey rain clouds, the air damp with the promise of rain. A man sitting in the car. A knife sinking to the hilt in soft pliant flesh. A head wrapped in a coat. A head with eyes that stared, a mouth that lolled open displaying rows of teeth spattered with fillings, and a tongue, fat, pink, white-coated.

The sound of a foot striking metal. A scraping, a scrabbling. Now! Not much time. Had to move. Get out. Slowly, painfully, the pierrot's freezing, silk-clad limbs extended forwards, crawling awkwardly towards the rat. Its squeals were quieter, less frantic than they had been. It still lived. One steady hand on the knife handle. A sharp twist. A scurry of small furry feet hitting grey-black air, then quiet stillness.

The hand that opened the door and pushed in the bundle was close to the stage. It would be easy to reach out, greet it. Easy to slash downwards. Easy to gain freedom. To take the boat that clanked dully against the pier's skeleton, to row upriver. Anchor under the bridge that carried the road. To leave the boat. Walk through the bushes, the smell of wet decaying earth and pungent greenery strong, yet tainted. Mixed with the deeper, poisonous smells of car exhaust. Wait . . . wait for what? Cars? Creeping, secretive, avoiding people, all people except one. But it could be done, the pierrot had done it all before. Or had it been a dream? Waking, dreaming, it was the same.

The pierrot lifted the knife. It left the splintered wood, the rat skewered half-way up the blade, a furred piece of meat on a kebab, fleas dropping from the small carcass like gobs of fat falling from the joint on a roasting spit. Pressing the blade to the floor, the pierrot laid a silk-slippered foot against the pulsating body and pushed. The blade was suddenly bare. Kicking the rat into the off-stage depths, the pierrot cleaned the blade between his white-gloved fingers, adding stains to the old, encrusted ones that already stiffened the white silk.

231

The door at the back. Knife at the ready. It was easy. So easy.

Chapter Nine

'To hell with it. I'm not going to stand by and do nothing while Daisy Sherringham walks free.'

'Do you mind telling me what you are going to do, Collins?'

'She gave us an accurate description of those glasses . . .'

'You're beginning to sound like a scratched record.'

'Daisy Sherringham worked all her shifts at the hospital during the past two weeks, sir. I called someone I know up there. A nurse. She checked for me.' Harries beamed at Peter from the doorway.

Trevor concealed his amusement behind a hastily contrived yawn. Harries was either a hero, or what was more likely, an idiot. Even he had more sense to break into an ongoing argument between Bill Mulcahy and Peter.

'Damn Daisy Sherringham.' Peter crashed his fist down on Bill's desk.

'But we can't damn her, Sergeant.' Bill's voice was ominously restrained as he reassembled his scattered papers. 'May I remind you who we're dealing with here. Lord Holbourne is a cabinet minister. His daughter, Lady Joanna Holbourne, is married to Richard Sherringham.'

'And Daisy Sherringham is . . .'

'A doctor and connected through marriage to the Holbourne family.' Bill's voice didn't rise one decibel, but Trevor noticed the tale-tale pulse throbbing at the side of his temple. Time to duck. 'We have no hard evidence that links Daisy Sherringham, or indeed anyone, to the motorway murders.' Bill shuffled the last of his papers back into place.

'And Daisy Sherringham's nightmares?' Peter pressed. 'Go on, explain those away if you can.'

'Perhaps you'd like to spend the next few years investigating the possibilities and probabilities of clairvoyance, Collins?'

Bill had pulled out his trump card. Rank. Peter had lost, but anger unabated, he looked for, and found another target.

'And you,' he turned to Trevor. 'You let this prime witness . . . this . . .'

'Robin Dart,' Trevor supplied the name Peter was searching for.

'Whatever. Presumably he isn't related to anyone important so he could still be helping us with our enquiries.'

'He told me all he knew about his sister and her relationship with a doctor we can only assume to be Sherringham.'

'How in hell do you know that he told us everything?'

'The bloke had no reason to lie. I promised him an off-the-record interview. If we offer discretion and don't come up with the goods, word will soon get out. And where will that leave us with our narks?' Trevor stared obstinately at Peter. 'Besides, I had to tell him that his sister was dead. He was upset, he needed a break . . .'

'So do I.'

'We've had enough information in tonight to keep even you busy for the next few days, Collins. Do you want to work with us, or plod the beat with our constable friends?'

'I'm tired . . .'

'Apology accepted,' Bill muttered quickly, halting Peter mid-torrent. 'I wouldn't say any more if I were you,' he warned. 'We're all tired, Sergeant Collins, and just this once I'm likely to carry out my threats.'

'Where do you want us to start?' Trevor asked.
'Harries?'
'Sir?' Harries bounded forward eagerly.
'Search warrants. See to them.'
'Yes, sir.' Harries pulled out his notebook and pencil.
'Daisy and Tim Sherringham's boat . . . better make
that a general sweep of the whole marina. If you contact
the port authorities and the yacht clubs they're gener-
ally co-operative. Say we've reason to believe down-
and-outs are sleeping on some of the boats.'
'Yes, sir.'
'Note on the warrant that the team are to look for
anything that might tie in with Tim Sherringham or
Amanda Dart. Search for any unexplained signs of
occupancy.'
'Yes, sir.'
'Tim Sherringham's flat . . .'
'Apartment,' Peter corrected snidely.
'I could probably get in there tonight. Daisy . . . Dr
Sherringham's never blocked us before.'
'That was before the solicitor made his complaint,'
Peter griped.
'The solicitor isn't Daisy Sherringham.'
'Fine, you try the lady, Joseph, but go ahead with
the warrant, Harries. We're looking for papers, diaries,
covering prescriptions for morphine, anything that
backs up Robin Dart's story.'
'Yes, sir.'
'The pier.'
'You'll need a bloody tank to get in there,' Peter
grumbled.
'Whatever it takes, Collins, whatever it takes. We'll
do that one as soon as we can.'
'May I suggest we take Peter's friend Ben Gummer
on to the pier with us.'
'Why?' Bill enquired.
'He used to work there, knows his way around it.'

'Travel with a guide. Good thinking,' Bill agreed flatly..'We can always do with extra help. We're looking for traces of occupancy . . .'

'And clowns,' Peter added.

'Flippancy, Collins.'

'I'm deadly serious.'

'I'm glad to hear it. And while you're at it, Harries, warrants for the hospital.'

'The hospital, sir?'

'The hospital,' Bill repeated. 'In particular, Tim Sherringham's consulting rooms and office. Amanda Dart's room at the hostel, and the maternity ward. Check on anyone there who remembers Tim Sherringham and Amanda Dart talking together. And check every morphine prescription against a phial number, and the number of reported breakages, and doses given to individual patients. If Amanda Dart stole drugs for her brother and Sherringham covered up for her, there's got to be evidence of it.'

'Hospitals can be tricky, Bill. Particularly when it comes to staff nicking drugs.'

'Who said anything about drugs? With reference to the disappearance of Dr Timothy Sherringham and the murder of Student Nurse Amanda Dart. From the available evidence, which I'm not at liberty to divulge at present, I have reason to believe that person, or persons unknown, are endangering the lives and property of the General Hospital and its staff. I wish to search the environs of the hospital and the nurses' homes for signs of breaking and entering, concealed weapons . . .'

'I get the message,' Trevor conceded.

'See if you can pick up any more information from his colleagues on Tim Sherringham's movements. That friend of yours, Trevor, Alan Cummins, and Judy Osbourne. But don't forget to keep pressing his brother

236

while you're at it. That man knows something we don't.'

'Does that mean the hospital searches and the Sherringham interviews fall on us?'

'It does. Any complaints?' Bill glared at Peter.

'Not at all. I love the Sherringham mansion. It's so wonderful to see the English aristocrat at home. Even if he is American.'

'Nice to see you happy with your assignment, Collins, because if I have my way you're going to see a lot more of him.'

'Anything in particular you want us to get out of Sherringham?' Trevor breached the atmosphere building up between Peter and Bill.

'You'll know it when you see it.'

'What fun we're going to have.'

'Aren't you, Collins,' Bill replied dryly.

'Right, Trevor, shall we take a look at what you've gleaned from this junkie friend of yours?'

'He says he's off drugs, and I believe him.'

'Do you, now?' Bill looked at Harries who was hovering awkwardly next to the door. 'The warrants, Harries.'

'Yes, sir.' Harries scuttled out of the door.

'First I think we should try to track down Andy, or whoever gave Blackie those glasses. Agreed?'

'Agreed,' Trevor concurred absently.

'What do you think?' Bill beamed. 'We'll find out more if we put someone in undercover?'

'My hair's too short,' Peter excused himself sharply. 'I'm too well known among the dossers. Besides, as last year's experience proves, I'm allergic to body lice.'

'I wasn't thinking of you, Collins.'

'If I must, I must.' Trevor resigned himself to the inevitable.

'See what you get for letting your hair grow,' Peter crowed.

'I hate to admit it, but you're getting too well known for undercover.'

'A wig, make-up?'

'This could take more than a one-night stand. If you're going to track Andy down and persuade him to show you how he gets on to the pier, always provided he does, of course, then it could take as long as a week, maybe two. Dossing in Jubilee Street, recreation in the day-centre. And then again, I'm not forgetting that Tim Sherringham disappeared and Amanda Dart was murdered after visiting Jubilee Street. It could be coincidence, or it could be they talked to the wrong people. If something nasty is going on down there, I want to know about it.'

'If you're talking long term, you're talking about putting in someone new, someone clean,' Trevor observed.

'Harries?' Peter suggested.

'And you said *your* hair was too short.' Trevor snorted.

'He could be ex-army. Thrown out for . . .' Peter looked heavenwards for inspiration, '. . . stealing?'

'You want to manufacture the cover story? You've got it. He's all yours.' Bill grinned sadistically. 'Provide Harries with background, wardrobe, briefing, the works, but whatever you do, don't forget the contact points and times. We don't want Harries following Tim Sherringham into oblivion.'

'I suppose not,' Peter grunted, wincing at the work load Bill was dumping on him.

'If we're talking about oblivion, Robin Dart told me something odd,' Trevor said thoughtfully. 'He mentioned that he and a kid called Lee went for interviews in the Grand Hotel. They were both offered jobs as hotel workers in Saudi Arabia. Then they were given medicals. He failed, but this kid Lee was taken on.'

238

'Nothing odd about that. Would you employ a junkie?' Peter asked.

'It's not that. He said this Lee was taken on straight away and began his training in London the next day.'

'Perhaps they're short of hotel workers in Saudi Arabia.'

'What kind of a hotel owner, particularly a foreign one who has to pay fares, does his recruiting in Jubilee Street?'

'You holding something back?' Bill asked.

'No. It just didn't smell right, that's all. Robin never saw the boy again.'

'Check it out.'

'It's not going to be easy. I only have Lee, no surname. Robin never knew or couldn't remember the name of the firm. Only that he was interviewed by a man called Jones.'

'Check if the Grand has any record, and brief Harries to be doubly careful. Sort it out tonight,' Bill ordered briskly. 'You'd better find another dogsbody for the station, Collins, and inform Harries he's been drafted into the plain clothes squad.'

'Will do.'

'You going to the hospital to see Daisy Sherringham?' Bill asked Trevor.

'I am.'

'You know what to ask her?'

'I've taken it all down.' Trevor patted the pocket that held his notebook. 'The Dart girl. Possible existence of diary. And permission to search the flat and the yacht.'

'Don't forget to mention the sighting of Tim Sherringham and Amanda Dart at the marina, two days after Sherringham's disappearance.'

'The retired colonel and the mad lady. Bill . . .'

'Did I say push it? It's worth a word or two. Watch her reaction carefully, that's all I'm asking. And if you come up with anything weird and wonderful in the Sherringham apartment?'

'I'll phone you.'

'At home. Come hell or high water I intend to be in my bed by midnight.'

'Afraid you'll turn into a pumpkin?' Peter smiled.

'I'll get more sleep than you tonight, Collins, and that's a fact. The transformation of Harries is going to take you hours,' Bill gloated.

'And hours.' Trevor kicked his chair under Bill's desk.

'That's the happiest I've seen you all day, Joseph. Is it Peter's workload or the thought of seeing the lady that's made your star shine?'

'Neither,' Trevor answered cautiously.

'Well, enjoy yourself, but don't forget, the lady's business.'

Trevor noticed the frosty smile on Bill's face. 'I won't,' he said quietly as he walked out of the door.

Andy saw it fall. He was hiding under the pier, curled up tight, almost under the boards. He always tried to hide when the second clown came. The thin one.

He hated the thin one. Wriggling snakes of fear crawled over his skin every time he caught sight of the stick-like limbs clad in flimsy silk. He'd crept up high under the pier where he could watch the tethered boat rock against the rusting supports. Sooner or later the thin clown would climb back down, sit in the boat, row away, and he would be free. Free to creep into the theatre ... sit in the back row ... But then it happened. While he was watching and waiting for the clown to leave.

It fell right past him. If he'd stretched out his arm, he could have touched it. It was that close. It jerked forwards and glanced off a protruding bar. Doubled up, it hit the water with a resounding splash that

240

sprayed the rocking boat with dark droplets of water. Then it sank. He looked down, it rose again, a small ball of white bobbing on the black surface of the sea, struggling towards the boat.

He shrank backwards until his back strained against the creaking boards. He was afraid. Afraid of the clowns, of being seen – of death. Wrapping his fingers tightly around the freezing ironwork, he remained still, silently watching and waiting. If he moved he might be caught. Forced to follow the neck-breaking plunge of the rag doll figure that struggled in the water beneath him.

The other clown was climbing down. Andy saw the dark shape make for the boat. The thin clown moved away, back into the water. Into the shadows. A few minutes more. If he could hold on for a few minutes more, he'd be all right. He tried to forget the cramp that numbed his fingers, the fear that crawled along his veins. If the clowns went, he'd be safe again. He would crawl along the top of the iron framework, and up through the hole in the floor. Then he could sit in the back row. Put his feet up, and live like a lord.

He moved his leg slightly, seeking reassurance. It was still there. The half bottle. Tied tightly with the rags he had wound around his left thigh, under his trousers. It wouldn't slip out. He'd be all right tonight. His spirits rose in anticipation. Life was perfect. He had a bottle, somewhere quiet to drink it where he wouldn't be disturbed, where he wouldn't have to share. Tomorrow . . . But then who wanted to think about tomorrow? Tonight he had a bottle. He was king!

'I'm sorry, I didn't mean to disturb you.'

'If you're embarrassed because you've walked in on an argument, why don't you say so and stop pussyfooting around with half-baked euphemisms.' Judy strolled

241

back into her tiny flat, leaving Trevor standing awkwardly, and superfluously, in the doorway.

'Have you any news of Tim?' Daisy looked up anxiously from the sofa and the magazine she was pretending to read.

'No.' Trevor moved his weight from one foot to the other, hunching his shoulders into the padded anorak that was too thick for the time of year. 'No, nothing,' he repeated, sticking rigidly to the small square of living-room that acted as hallway.

'Are you coming in?' Judy demanded from the open-plan kitchen area that she'd retreated to.

'Yes, just for a minute. Thank you.' Trevor closed the door behind him and walked into the room. He sat stiffly on one of the hard upright chairs that were meant to be grouped around the small pine-veneered dining-table. He cleared his throat, reluctant to break into the heavy atmosphere that lay between Daisy and Judy.

'Are you going to tell us why you've come here at this time of night, or do we have to drag it out of you?' Judy snapped.

'There've been a couple of developments. It's difficult to know whether they're important or not. I thought Dr Sherringham,' he smiled weakly at Daisy, 'might be able to shed some light on the evidence that's come in.'

'If I can, I'd be glad to help.' Daisy stretched out her feet, feeling for the shoes she'd kicked off earlier. She found them and rose from the sofa. 'Are you doing anything now, Sergeant Joseph?'

'No.' Trevor looked wonderingly from Daisy to Judy.

'In that case perhaps you'd like to take me out for a meal. I'm starved,' Daisy said with forced heartiness.

'I'd be delighted to,' Trevor stammered.

'Daisy, it's eleven o'clock at night.'

'There are always the Indian and Chinese places. They never close.' She slipped on her shoes, picked up her handbag and lifted her coat down from the stand. 'You really should go and see your friend, Judy. I mean it. It's crazy for everyone to disrupt the flow of their lives because of Tim's disappearance. You're not helping me, or Tim, by sitting around here in the depths of despair,' she added cruelly. 'Besides,' she smiled a bright artificial smile, 'Sergeant Joseph will look after me, won't you, Sergeant?'

'Of course,' Trevor replied gravely, more shaken by Daisy's brittle energy than he had been by her distraught ravings earlier that day.

'So it's all settled, Judy. See you later.'

'You'd better take a key.' Judy rummaged in her cavernous handbag that stood on the kitchen sink.

'I can always get the porter to let me in.' Daisy headed for the door.

'I won't be late,' Judy shouted after her. 'I'll make it a quick visit. I'll be back in an hour or two.'

'Don't hurry, take all the time you want.' Trevor left his seat.

'You'll stay with her until I get back?' If Trevor hadn't known Judy better he might have accused her of pleading.

'I promise I won't leave Daisy alone.'

'In that case, shouldn't you be going after her?'

Trevor walked through the door, reflecting that there were some people you simply couldn't reach out to. No matter how hard you tried.

'Indian, Chinese, or Italian?' Trevor asked when he caught up with Daisy on the stairs.

'Whatever you like.' The flare of nervous vitality that had sustained her in the flat had burned itself out.

'Chinese?' he suggested gently.

'Anywhere, as long as there's bright lights and people,' she replied irritably.

'Can't promise we'll find either at this time of night, but we can try.'

243

Blessing the impulse that had made him take his own car into work that morning, he steered Daisy out of the building, into the car park and the front seat of his car. He started the engine and drove steadily out on to the main road that led into town.

'You said there'd been developments,' Daisy prompted accusingly.

'There have, but before we start I want to warn you about something. And I want you to listen to me very carefully.'

'That sounds serious.'

'It is.'

He stopped at traffic lights and glanced across at her. Her face was pale under the reflected glow of the streetlamps, the strain she was being subjected to evident in every taut muscle in her face and hands. She saw him looking at her, and turned away, burying her hands deep in the pockets of her three-quarter-length coat.

'Every media appeal connected with unexplained disappearances, or murders, especially a bizzare case like this, attracts what we refer to down at the station as "the nuts".'

'And you think that some of the new developments don't mean anything because they've been provided by these nuts?' The lights changed and he started the car.

'I don't know,' he said gravely. 'That's the problem. You never know until the end of a case whether the evidence you've collected is accurate or, to put it bluntly, a load of rubbish. Do you remember that woman who disappeared in February?'

'Yes.'

'Over a two-week period we were provided with fourteen definite sightings of that woman in her green sports car, some of them corroborated by people who didn't know one another from Adam. Then we found her, still in her car, at the bottom of the East Dock. She'd driven herself over the edge exactly one hour after she'd quarrelled with her husband. The car clock bore that out. Most of the people who said they'd seen her were genuinely mistaken, or at least I like to think they were. They simply wanted to be of some help, and there's no doubt that without the assistance of Joe Public's eyewitness accounts we wouldn't solve half the crimes we do. That means, like it or not, we have to treat everyone who walks into the station and offers information the same, be they nut or sensible being. And believe you me, it's not always that easy to tell the difference between the two.'

'And just what have you heard about Tim that's so terrible?' Daisy enquired tersely.

Trevor turned down a side-street and parked outside the neon-lit façade of a Chinese restaurant. He turned off the car ignition before facing her.

'Does the name Amanda Dart mean anything to you?'

'So that's it! Judy told me there was a rumour going around the hospital that Tim was having an affair with a nurse called Dart who worked on the maternity ward. And no doubt, now that Tim isn't here to deny it, you believe every word of the sordid little tale.'

'It's what *you* believe that's important.'

'Tim wasn't having an affair. I would have known about it if he was.' Her voice was steady, but it took all the self-control she could muster to keep it that way.

'That's the conclusion I've come to. But there is a tie-in between your husband and Amanda Dart. Piecing together what little we've discovered, I think Amanda Dart may have stolen drugs from the hospital for her brother. He was a junkie, and he admitted to me tonight that he put pressure on her. He also said there was a doctor who got Amanda out of a jam with the ward sister.'

'And you think the doctor was Tim?'

'Does it sound like the sort of thing he'd do?'

'I don't know. Tim would help anyone if he could. But stealing drugs is enough to get anyone instant dismissal. Doctor, nurse, consultant, it makes no difference, the hospital will give them their marching orders if they're caught doing that. I can't see Tim condoning it.'

'What if he felt sorry for the girl, felt it wasn't her fault?'

Daisy shook her head. 'I doubt it.'

'We know Tim went to the hostel for the homeless in Jubilee Street with Amanda Dart. Does the mention of the hostel ring a bell?'

'No.'

'They went to look for her brother, Robin, the junkie who was pressurizing her,' he explained. 'Exactly one week to the day before he disappeared. There's no doubt about the visit or the timing. Tim gave the priest who runs the place a donation. A cheque drawn on his personal account for one hundred pounds.'

'That sounds like the sort of thing Tim would do,' Daisy said thoughtfully. 'But I can't imagine why he didn't mention it to me.'

'I hate asking this. But were you and Tim close? I mean did you discuss everything?'

'Everything,' Daisy insisted. 'Absolutely everything that was important. We've lived together for years. We've never kept secrets from one another.'

'Were you particularly busy the week before Tim disappeared?'

'No more than usual.'

'Did Tim often go off by himself?'

'Are you suggesting that Tim sneaked away from me whenever he could to sleep with other women?' Daisy's voice was pitched alarmingly high.

'I'm trying to find out what he did in his spare time.' Trevor kept his voice low, patient. 'Anything. Any clue, any hint as to what he did when he wasn't at the hospital or with you might help us find him.'

'Tim is dead.'

'Your husband and Amanda Dart were seen standing together on a berthed yacht down at the marina two days after he disappeared.' Trevor hadn't meant to fling the report at Daisy in that way. He just couldn't help himself.

Daisy took a deep breath. 'Does that come from one of your nuts?'

'It comes from a retired army intelligence officer, and a middle-aged woman. Two totally unconnected people.'

'Have you searched the marina?'

'Not yet. We're in the process of getting a warrant.'

'But you think they were standing on board the *Freedom*?'

'The *Freedom*?'

'You saw a photograph of it,' she snapped irritably. 'Our yacht.'

'The boat wasn't identified.'

'Suppose I want to go and take a look at the *Freedom* now?'

'I thought you were hungry?'

'Not any more.'

'I'll drive you.' He didn't try to argue with her. Instead, he turned the ignition key and slid the car into gear. Quickly, he ran through a mental check-list of the equipment he kept in the boot of his car. Torch, ropes, basic first-aid kit, blanket, pickaxe . . . that wouldn't be much use on a boat, unless you wanted to sink it in a hurry.

He headed for the centre of town, and the marina. Then realization hit him with the bracing force of a jet of cold water. What in hell's name was he doing? He could almost hear the deep tones of Bill Mulcahy's broad northern accent. 'What do you think this is, lad, a bloody picnic? It's a murder enquiry. There's dead bodies cluttering up the morgue.' Dead bodies, and he was driving off to a deserted marina in the middle of the night with a hysterical woman in tow. Much as he liked Daisy, he couldn't really call her anything else at that moment. But if Tim Sherringham was alive, and they found him, it would be worth it. Wouldn't it? He could sit and watch someone else's happiness even if he hadn't quite managed to engineer his own.

Judy Osbourne glanced in the mirror of her car more from habit than from any real fear of being followed. Jealous wives didn't have the other woman followed. Not in this day and age. There'd be little point in indulging in such a wasteful exercise. A quick visit to a solicitor, a petition for divorce, a waiting period – 'irretrievable breakdown of marriage'. That was it. A short and sweet road to freedom, for the partners concerned, at least. Not for the other woman. Other women could, if they weren't careful, find themselves offered the vacant position of wife. And that was the last thing she wanted, or needed. Her life suited her perfectly just the way it was.

She enjoyed the fringe benefits, the lack of responsibility that went with the role of mistress. The excitement of the private assignations, the constant struggle for time that made her wring dry every moment she spent with her lover. The pleasure of the unexpected presents he lavished on her whenever he had a pang of conscience. Swift, silent, lovemaking, all the more passionate for its urgency. Whispered endearments in the dark, furtive pressing of hands, the exchange of fleeting knowing smiles on the rare occasions when their public lives overlapped.

It amused her to have a secret life. To love another completely, wholeheartedly, without having to subjugate career, ambition or personality to the mind-numbingly tedious daily grind of domesticity. When she woke in the morning there was always delicious anticipation. Would today be one of 'their days'? Would they be able to snatch an hour or two together? Any day could, by a flicker of chance, become a combination of birthday and Christmas. And the best part of all was not knowing when it would happen.

The stunted apple tree that hung low over the old stone wall signalled her to slow down the car. She dropped her speed, made a sharp left turn and bumped her car gently along the twisting path. Ahead, just to the right, a tiny cottage clung precariously to the cliff face. No doubt one stormy night the sea would enfold it, batter away its fabric with swollen waves. But not tonight. Tonight the sea below lay calm, glittering back the reflected glow of the moon with a placidity that belied its occasional deadly strength.

She parked the car between two high, dry-stone walls that conveniently shielded both parking area and cottage from view of the rare passer-by. Unless you knew the exact location of the retreat you could walk the path for hours and still miss it, which was precisely why she'd asked him to buy the place for her.

She locked the car and walked down the rough-hewn steps that had been cut into the cliff. When she turned the corner she saw a light shining ahead. He'd arrived before her. That didn't surprise her. He lived closer to the cottage than she did, and he'd seemed impatient when he'd telephoned, as though he couldn't wait to see her. If she hadn't known him better, she might have even said he'd sounded upset when she had told him she couldn't make it, and semi-hysterical when she'd phoned later to say she could meet him after all. But she must have been mistaken. He was never upset. Always the epitome of enviable calm, self-possession. Daisy's presence in the room probably unnerved her.

That was it. The last thing she wanted was anyone, least of all Daisy, finding out the identity of her lover.

She hummed a tune softly as she approached the front door, her thoughts centred around the soft, deep, double bed in the cosy bedroom. They had a couple of hours. That peculiar sergeant would take care of Daisy. The idiot was besotted with her. He had the type of crush on Daisy that twelve-year-old schoolgirls usually get on actors and pop stars.

'Judy!'

The door opened. Richard stood in a yellow pool of light, his auburn hair tousled, obviously uncombed since he'd been at her flat earlier. She stepped back and stared in disbelief. He looked like a man at the end of his resources. His suit was rumpled, as if he'd slept in it. His shirt front was stained, his collar twisted.

'God, how I need you. Seeing you earlier and not being able to touch you only made it worse.' The hands that reached out to her trembled uncontrollably. The bearded cheek pressed against her face was damp with tears. 'They're no nearer finding Tim,' he breathed shallowly, quickly.

She looked up at him. 'I know,' she answered, inwardly shrinking from the wreckage of the man she thought she knew so well.

'Tim's not dead,' he insisted with a maniacal intensity that terrified her. 'He's not. He's alive. I know he's alive. He'll come back.' He grasped at her shoulders and shook her savagely, oblivious to the pain he was causing. 'Joanna doesn't think Tim's alive.' His voice quietened to a wheedling, rambling tone. 'But then she wouldn't. She doesn't give a damn for anyone other than herself. Never has. She doesn't love Tim. She doesn't love anyone. We had the most dreadful argument.' His eyes, blank, demented, stared unblinkingly into Judy's. 'Joanna and I have done nothing but quarrel since Tim disappeared. She hates Tim, she hates him because I love him. He's the only family I have left. You know I don't love Joanna. I never have. Judy, I've decided. I'm going to divorce her. I'm going to marry you. Darling . . .' He buried his head in her arms. His whole body shuddered against hers, as he surrendered to a bout of uncontrolled sobbing.

Judy stood silent, her body meshed tight to his in the open doorway. Unable to move, she returned his embrace simply because she was there, and there was nothing else for her to do. Finally, when he became a little quieter, she wrapped her arm around his waist and led him into the living-room of the cottage. He was on the verge of a breakdown. He had to be tranquillized, put to bed. Gentle, but firm handling. And she wasn't going to botch it as she had done with Daisy earlier that day. Damn Tim for getting himself lost, murdered, whatever!

Reluctantly she relinquished all thoughts of the double bed and concentrated on the drugs that were locked in her bag in the boot of the car. She'd manage Richard for tonight. She'd stay with him, do whatever she could.

Tomorrow – tomorrow, if he was no better, she'd get help. If Richard was capable of any understanding, she'd put him straight. Her life was her own. If Joanna had really left him, then no doubt he'd want another wife, another crutch to prop up his ego. but she wasn't volunteering for that post. Love was one thing, nurse-maiding and housekeeping quite another. He'd have to look elsewhere for a replacement chattel.

'It looks clear enough.' Trevor swept the port side of the boat with his torch beam one last time before leaving the boarding ladder and stepping on to the deck of the *Freedom*. He turned and extended a hand to Daisy, who climbed up after him. 'Is this how you left it?' he

251

asked, illuminating the neatly-coiled ropes and folded sails.

'It looks untouched.'

He flashed a light on the closed doors that led below. 'How do we get into the cabin?'

'We always leave a key taped to one of the life-jackets.'

'Not very wise,' Trevor, the policeman, commented.

'Tim always said, that if anyone really wanted to get in, all they'd have to do is take an axe to the door.'

'Most break-ins are the work of amateurs, and amateurs are notorious for taking advantage of the opportunities kind people hand them. Like keys taped to life-jackets.'

He walked around the bulge of the cabin and shone his torch over the starboard side of the boat. 'Looks just the same,' he called softly back to her. 'Here, if you hold this,' he handed her the torch, directing the beam towards the door handle, 'I'll take a quick look at the door.' He stood under the portico that shielded the cabin entrance from the weather, and turned the knob. The door swung open.

'Are you sure you always lock it?'

'I'm sure. The last thing Tim and I check every time we leave the boat is the door. We couldn't possibly have . . .'

'Ssh!' Trevor ordered abruptly. He pushed her hand, the torch beam fell to the floor.

'Can you hear anything?' she whispered.

'No. But that doesn't mean there's no one there.' He fumbled in his pocket, brought out a handkerchief, and wrapped it around his fingers. For the first time in his professional life he, who usually balked at carrying firearms, actually wished he'd booked out a gun. He had a sudden vision of the mutilated body he'd seen stretched out in the mortuary that morning. The other body! The mind that conceived those horrors was sick

252

enough to be capable of any bestiality. And if the geriatric colonel was right, God alone knew what he'd find inside.

'You stay here until I call you,' he murmured softly. 'When you go in don't touch anything. Is there a light in the cabin?'

'Switch is to the right of the door.'

He entered the cabin cautiously, forcing himself to put one foot in front of the other and move forward. The first thing that struck him was the smell. A foul stench filled his nostrils. It was more, much more, than just the closed-in musty smell of damp upholstery and wet floor that he normally associated with boats. He reached to the right and fumbled with his shrouded hand for the switch. He flicked it on.

'Christ!' He stepped back smartly, treading on Daisy's toes. He turned, groped past her blindly, and rushed to the rails, heaving his head over the side. He only just made it in time.

'Don't go in there!' he shouted, as soon as he'd stopped retching. 'In God's name, don't go in there.'

The plea came too late. With the torch still switched on, hanging limply at her side, he saw Daisy's slight figure standing in front of the illuminated doorway. The cabin beyond her silhouette was a charnel house. Red blotches, heavily shaded with darker clots, were spattered over floor, walls and ceiling, a random decoration of gore. To the left of Daisy he could see the formica table-top. A severed hand lay there, its end cut clean, the fingers and palm upturned, a bizarre parody of an art deco table centre.

'Daisy, please, come back,' he whispered hoarsely, dragging himself forward. He reached out, intending to pull her to him. Then the light cut abruptly and all went black. He made a grab for the torch that hung limply in Daisy's hand, the one remaining source of light.

Disorientated by the sudden blackout, Daisy extended her hands, feeling for a wall, anything solid she could grasp hold of. The torch beam swung precariously from side to side as she searched. Trevor followed the wavering beam of light, but at the very moment he closed his hand over Daisy's, something gripped his left shoulder from behind.

He screamed, agonized, as an excruciating pain shot into his arm, paralyzing it. Iron fingers possessed of superhuman strength closed around his right wrist, wrenching his arm behind him and upwards. Forced back, away from Daisy, he tried to call out to her. He wanted to tell her to run, to get away. But no sound issued from his pain-numbed lips. Helpless, floundering, his mouth opening and closing like a beached fish's, his legs were kicked out from under him. The vice-like grip intensified. A sharp crack rent the air. He knew with a certainty that penetrated the grey waves of pain, shock and sheer terror that were sweeping over him that he'd heard the sound of his own bones breaking.

'Daisy! Run! Get away! Go!' The screams and shouts he'd conceived in his mind were translated into muted whimperings that fell on deaf ears. Daisy still stood transfixed before him, her shadowy figure outlined behind the glow of the torch. It was the last thing he saw before he was thrown aside on to the deck.

His mind wavered faintly on the indistinct borders of consciousness. He tried to look up. He had to know if Daisy was safe. A white-painted face flitted in and out of the torch light. The make-up was streaky, the black outlines around the eyes ran down into greasy pools that merged with the red of the mouth. A clown's face! It was a clown's face! The clown, the damned murdering clown. And it was close to Daisy! He had to move. Protect her. There was no one else. He had to do it for her. He tried to move his arms. He couldn't.

His feet . . . He pushed the soles of his shoes hard against the deck, and arched his back high. He struggled to rise, and collapsed, a useless heap. Forcing himself to try again, he rolled his weight unwittingly against his right arm. Then he fell into a deeper blackness, one that didn't even have the small comfort of a flickering torch-beam to lighten its gloom.

Robin Dart hadn't been cheered by the two drinks he'd managed to down before closing time. In fact, if anything, they'd had the opposite effect. A deep depression had settled over him and he'd done something he hadn't done since he'd left London. He'd withdrawn into himself. Allowed himself to become preoccupied with his own guilty thoughts.

Dead! Amanda was dead. She'd led such a pathetic, miserable life. He should have done something for her. Instead, all he'd ever brought her was trouble.

'Mate, what do you think you're doing?'

'What?'

'You've driven past my stable,' Jock shouted.

'I'm sorry.' Robin skidded the van to a halt at the end of the street.

'Snap out of it, mate,' Jock advised as he stepped down from the van. 'Rehearsals for the new play first thing tomorrow morning. Eight sharp.'

'I won't forget.' Robin drove away before Jock could say any more. Jock was a reasonable actor, and occasionally an all right bloke. But he didn't want to talk to anyone, not now. He wanted to think. To remember. It was going to be damned hard to live with himself after this. And tomorrow, he hadn't told Jock, but he'd skive off. Go back to the police station. He wanted to see Amanda . . . or what was left of her. He'd have to talk to his brother – he should have asked that copper where he was staying. They'd have to arrange Amanda's funeral.

255

He jerked the van to a halt outside his bedsit, and looked across at the blank, dark window. The place that had pleased him that morning seemed seedy, shabby. He had nothing to tie him to this town any more. He could leave any time he wanted. Go elsewhere. Find another job. His rent was due next week. Another month – he wouldn't pay it. He'd move out, find someplace else. One that would be totally impersonal. Where he wouldn't have to walk past the General and see other girls in the uniform Amanda had worn.

He slid back the rusty door and stepped down on to the road. He locked the van, walking once around it to check the other doors. He was closing the back door when he heard the voice.

'Want to buy a fix?' A plump, bespectacled, youngish-looking man tapped him on the shoulder. Robin thought he'd seen him before. The pub? Jubilee Street?

'Don't use it,' Robin replied automatically, using the standard rejection that had been drummed into him in the rehabilitation centre. As he paused to let the man pass by, a small voice cried out from the back of his mind. What difference would it make if he took it, just this once? Amanda was dead. He had nothing going for him. One fix. A small dose to give him a good night's sleep. He could handle one fix, and be bright-eyed and breezy for whatever tomorrow threw at him.

'Now!' The voice was low, urgent. It came from the street at his back. Before he had time to turn, or cry for help, a hand covered his mouth and forced a handkerchief between his teeth. He gagged on the cloth. He tried to struggle, look to the pusher for help, but he was swept off his feet. The streetlights moved past his eyes at a crazy angle. Then he was thrust into darkness. Black, fetid air, heavy with the smell of petrol, closed around his eyes and cloyed his nostrils. The handkerchief was foul with his own spittle. He needed to throw up. Choking, he gasped for air, drawing the cloth further into his mouth.

'Steady with him.' The warning was whispered. A man's voice? Then he couldn't even be certain he'd heard it at all. He was thrust, face downwards, on to a soft mattress. The hands that held him were firm. But they didn't hurt. The more he struggled against their grip the more cushioned pressure was exerted between his shoulder blades. Someone was tugging at his sleeve. Rolling it up. He felt the prick of a needle. They were giving him a free shot. Nothing like a cheap fix. He should thank them for it. Thank them . . . Thank them . . .

His head was spinning. Spinning round and round on his neck. His thoughts whirled, merging into one with centrifugal force. There was a single confusion of noise. Voices. An engine starting. Driving off. Music coming from the street. Quiet music. Background music. From a television film? The back of a van. He saw it driving off down the street. What was he doing sitting in the road?

Had to get up. Go to bed. Jesus, he felt sick. Had he drunk that much? Couldn't remember. Had to lie down. That would stop him puking his insides up. Had to lie down. He reached out for the gatepost, missed it and fell. It took him a long time to fall. Such a long, long time. He couldn't breathe. Black spots in front of his eyes. Had to get to bed . . . had to . . .

The path to the house rose up to meet him. The concrete was as soft and downy as a feather bed. It enveloped him. He was warm. Warm, happy, comfortable. He would rest. Sleep. No worries. Worries would come tomorrow. Slip softly into sleep. His arm burned. The inferno spread to his shoulder. Scalding tentacles of fire, travelling fast, reaching out. He would go to sleep before the pain travelled to the rest of his body. Close his eyes. Sleep.

*

257

'Your name is?'

'Stacko.'

'Which is it short for?'

'Stephen Harries.'

'Good.' Peter reached for his coffee. 'The rest of the cover is?'

'My own background, sir.'

'I trust you can remember your life until the day you left school, Harries?'

'Yes, sir.'

'Followed by – come on, Harries, from the top, one more time.'

'After I left school I joined up.'

'For?'

'Three years.'

'Which regiment?'

'What do you want to know for?'

'Just right. I like the suspicion, Harries,' Peter finished his coffee and put his cup back on the tray. 'And if you're pressed?'

'Regiment's irrelevant . . .'

'Doesn't matter, not irrelevant. Big words mean education in Jubilee Street. And the junkies have a monopoly on that. We don't want to be mistaken for a junkie, do we, Harries?'

'No, sir,' Harries replied wearily, sick of being the butt of Peter's ham-fisted sarcasm.

'Right. Where did you spend most of your service life?'

'Germany.'

'Doing what?'

'None of your damned business.'

'Good. And if you're pressed.'

'Bit of this, bit of that. Marketeering in stolen service goods.'

'For which?'

'I was put in military prison.'

258

'And that explains the present haircut. But from now on, you grow it. Understood?'

'Yes, sir.'

'And then we may give you more little jobs. Just like this one.'

'Does that mean I'll be permanently attached to the plain clothes unit from now on, sir?'

'One thing at a time, Harries. One thing at a time,' Peter reiterated, unconsciously aping Bill's accent. 'How come a big-timer like you has ended up in Jubilee Street?'

'Came directly from prison to see a girlfriend. She'd moved without telling me, so I had nowhere to stay. Social services messed up my records. I'll only be in Jubilee Street for a short time. I'll soon be on to something better.'

'Fine, just the right hint of cockiness. And with a story like that, you don't have to turn up in completely filthy clothes. They wash them in prison. Lucky, lucky you. The times Sergeant Joseph and myself have crawled.'

The telephone at Peter's elbow buzzed.

'Mulcahy's office,' he shouted into the receiver, annoyed at the disturbance.

'Call for you, Sergeant Collins. General Hospital.'

'Put it through.'

'Yes, sir.'

'Is that Sergeant Collins? Sergeant Peter Collins?'

'Speaking. Who is this?'

'John Adams, Sergeant Collins. Porter at the General.'

'Yes?'

'Dr Sherringham asked me to phone you. Wants you to come over to Casualty right away.'

'Which Dr Sherringham?'

'Dr Daisy. Dr Tim's missing.'

259

'I know. This *is* the bloody police station! Why does Daisy Sherringham want to see me?'

'A policeman's been hurt. Sergeant . . . Sergeant . . .'

'Joseph?'

'That's him.'

'What's happened to him?' Peter's heart began a drum beat that thundered the blood around his arteries. His mouth went dry. Joseph! The fool was too damned soft. He'd been telling him that for years.

'He was attacked, sir. All I can tell you is that it's bad. Dr Daisy . . .'

'How bad is bad?'

'That's what Dr Daisy's trying to find out right now. If you could get here . . .'

'I'm on my way.' He slammed down the receiver. Damn and blast Joseph! Damn him to hell. He was supposed to be having a quiet chat with his lady love. A quick check round her flat. A scrabble in Tim Sherringham's desk. How in the hell's name did that turn into a rough house?

'Bad news, sir?'

'What?' Peter turned to Harries. He'd forgotten his existence.

'I asked if it was bad news, sir,' Harries repeated, stunned by the shock that had registered on Peter's face. Harries, like everyone else at the station, had always assumed Peter Collins incapable of feeling any human emotions.

'Yes, Harries,' Peter replied quickly, patting his pockets for his car keys. 'It's bad news.'

'Sir, about the briefing.' Harries leaped from his chair and followed Peter out of the door.

'You'll be fine, Harries. Just fine.'

'Do I come into town on the ten-thirty train tomorrow, sir?'

'Whatever you like. You're on your own.' Peter quickened his pace.

260

Harries walked back into Bill Mulcahy's office and sat down. He remembered the bodies in the mortuary. The vicious knife fights he'd helped break up in the dock area of the town. The junkies he'd locked up in the cells who'd given their address as Jubilee Street. Peter Collins was right. He was on his own. For the first time in his life. Totally alone.

Chapter Ten

'Trevor Joseph, where is he?' Peter demanded, as he stormed into Casualty.

'Are you Sergeant Collins?' the porter asked from behind the reception desk.

'Yes.'

'He's in the small emergency theatre . . . Hey! You can't go in there,' John shouted after Peter's retreating figure.

'It's all right, John. I'll see to Sergeant Collins.' Daisy pushed through the swing doors, holding them open with her elbows. She stood, gowned, masked, gloved, waiting for Peter to reach her.

'How is he?' he gasped, running towards her.

'There's no damage that six to eight weeks' rest won't cure,' Daisy said quietly. 'Dislocated right shoulder. A rather nasty bone break just above the right wrist. Severe bruising on left shoulder, cuts, scrapes, black eye, that's about it.' Beckoning to Peter, she stepped back into a small ante-room. She peeled off the rubber gloves and mask and tossed them into a bin. She washed her hands at the sink, then, pulling off her green hat, she turned to face him. Her face was white with exhaustion, but her eyes were bright, glittering.

In that brief instant Peter saw the Daisy who had caused Trevor to lose his head. If the moment and the place had been different, he reflected, he might even have taken time out to cast an eye over her himself.

'Can I see him?' he asked, suddenly realizing that he was breathing easier than he had done since he'd received the telephone call. Hurt! Trevor was only hurt.

262

Every copper expects to get beaten up from time to time. Part of the job.

'In a couple of minutes. The anaesthetist's bringing him round. I heard you shouting, so I thought I'd better get out here before John called in the heavy squad.'

'What happened?' Peter's sense of relief was rapidly dissipating into anger. He wanted to lash out, arrest whoever had put Trevor in hospital.

'Trevor drove me to the Marina. He said someone had seen Tim and Amanda Dart standing on a boat.'

'They were a couple of nuts.'

'Whatever,' Daisy interrupted. 'Anyway, I thought perhaps they might have been watching our boat, the *Freedom*.'

'And you and Trevor went out in the middle of the night to take a look?'

'Wasn't very bright of us, was it? But we only wanted to see if there were any signs of the boat being used.'

'And were there?'

'It had been used all right,' she said grimly, gripping the sink tightly behind her back. 'The cabin looked like a battlefield. Blood everywhere. And a hand. A single white hand lying in the middle of the table. There might have been more, I only had a moment or two to look. Someone cut the lights.'

'Someone was on the boat with you?'

'Obviously.'

'What happened then?'

'I was left holding the torch. Trevor, at least I think it was Trevor, reached out to take it off me. It was then the clown jumped him.'

'A clown? You're sure it was a clown?'

'I saw the face quite clearly in the torchlight. The make-up was streaked, cracked. It looked like days-old greasepaint, but it was meant to be a clown.'

'Go on.'

Daisy screwed here fists into tight little balls. She strained to stay calm, rational. Peter Collins wanted the facts from her, no more. No hysteria, no emotion, no embellishments. She'd put him down as a cold bastard the first time they'd met, now she was certain of her diagnosis. She didn't want to embarrass him, or herself, by showing any signs of weakness. Firmly suppressing her tears, she struggled to continue.

'After the lights went out, there was a lot of banging and scuffling. I tried to shine the torch, see what was happening. Trevor was fighting with the clown. I wanted to help, but everything moved so fast. Then there was a loud crack.' She bit her lip. 'I thought at first it was a gun shot, now of course I realise it must have been Trevor's arm breaking. It was then I shone the torch on to the clown's face. He was holding Trevor in front of him. He saw me, or at least the dazzle of the torchlight, then he tossed Trevor aside, like a . . . I've never seen such strength.' She shook her head. 'It was incredible.'

'And?' Peter prompted, forcing the pace.

'I shone the torch over the deck. All I could think of was Trevor. He'd screamed, I'd heard the thud of him landing somewhere. I knew he was hurt, but I didn't know where he'd been thrown. When I found him he was lying unconscious in front of the cabin door. I knelt on the floor beside him. Then . . .' She reeled at the memory, 'Then I realized the clown was standing in front of me.'

'An idiot dressed like a clown runs wild, breaks Trevor's arm, throws him on to the deck and you check on Trevor instead of running like a bat out of hell?' Peter stared at her in disbelief.

'I wasn't thinking straight,' she explained indignantly. 'I'm a doctor. Trevor had been hurt. I wanted to see if I could help.'

'Did the clown attack you?'

'That's the peculiar part, he didn't. I laid the torch down on the deck, and directed its light towards Trevor's face. As I knelt next to Trevor, I saw the clown in front of me. The light was shining on his black silk trousers. He was standing over both of us.' She looked up at Peter, her grey eyes wide in delayed terror. 'I stayed where I was, crouched above Trevor. I carried on, going through the motions of checking on Trevor's breathing. At that stage I wasn't even sure whether he was alive or not. The clown's legs stayed put for what seemed forever. But for the life of me I couldn't have moved away. I was simply petrified. I think I resorted to that ridiculous childish ploy, that if you shut your eyes and ignore it, the evil will go away. Whatever it was, miraculously it worked. One minute the silk slippers with their preposterous white pompoms were in front of me, the next they weren't.'

'You didn't see him again?'

'No. I heard the sound of a small-engined boat moving away from the *Freedom*. I panicked at first because I thought it was the one Trevor and I had used. I knew by then that Trevor was alive, but injured. The power was off, and presumably the radio. Trevor was rapidly going into shock. I remembered the emergency flares, and I knew if it came to the worst I could always set them off. But that would have meant going into the cabin to look for them.' She wrinkled her nose at the all too vivid memory. 'If I'd had to, I suppose I could have managed it.'

'After what you've told me, I don't doubt it.'

'In the event, I didn't have to. Trevor chose that moment to come round. With my help, he just about managed to crawl up off the deck. Our boat was still tied to the *Freedom*, where we'd left it, so I brought him here as quickly as I could.'

'And patched him up.'

'The duty doctor was dealing with the casualties of

a pub glassing,' she explained. 'But this theatre was free. John called an anaesthetist, then, at Trevor's insistence, you. As soon as Mike arrived I went ahead and set Trevor's arm. He needed a general anaesthetic. The bones had broken through the skin. They were badly splintered, but as I said, I think it's nothing that rest and time can't cure.'

'You're quite a woman.' Peter leaned back against the wall and stared at her. 'You remained cool enough . . .'

'Cool nothing,' she said abruptly. 'On the boat I was too scared to do anything that required movement, like run.'

'Still, not many people . . .'

'Please.' She recalled the first time they'd met, and gave him an icy glare. 'Compliments from you I cannot take.'

'He's coming round, Daisy,' Mike Edmunds called from the theatre.

'Can I go in?' Peter asked.

'As long as you don't upset him in any way.'

Trevor was stretched flat out on a trolley. The parts of his body that weren't covered with lurid red hospital blankets were swathed in bandages. He grinned weakly when he saw Peter follow Daisy into the room.

'You're going to be fine,' Daisy reassured him quietly. 'Your right arm's fractured just above the wrist, but that's the only war wound, the rest is trivial.'

'I wish it felt trivial,' Trevor moaned thickly. 'My shoulders hurt like hell.'

'Cursing already. You must be recovering,' Peter quipped in his usual sardonic manner. Trevor's face, pale, bloodless above the blanket, had shaken him more than he would have cared to admit. He loathed hospitals, sickness of any kind. It was as if Trevor's condition reminded him of his own weakness and mortality.

'Your right shoulder was dislocated.' Daisy folded

266

the blanket back, exposing a neatly-tied support bandage. 'It's not any longer, which is probably why it hurts. We,' she glanced across at Mike, 'had fun putting it back.'

'I'll take your word for it,' Trevor mumbled.

'And I think Sergeant Collins ought to take a look at your left shoulder.'

'Not likely, his idea of doctoring goes as far as the whisky bottle, no further,' Trevor protested.

'This shoulder comes under the category of police evidence.' Daisy looked at Peter. 'Here. Help me prop him up.' Peter obediently slid his arm behind Trevor's back. 'Not too far,' Daisy warned. 'There, look at the back of his shoulder.'

'Some bruising,' Peter agreed. 'What did you fall on?'

'Trevor fell on nothing,' Daisy answered. 'The deck was flat. If you look in front there's one more bruise. They're finger marks. That's where the clown grabbed him.'

'Come on.' Peter looked from Daisy to Trevor in disbelief. 'No one can grip with that kind of force.'

'That clown could,' Trevor insisted, wincing in pain. 'And if you two have quite finished poking me about, would you mind letting me lie down.'

'Not at all.' Daisy pulled a pillow off a shelf behind her and pushed it under Trevor's head. Peter lowered him back on to the trolley.

'Comfortable?' Daisy asked.

'Wonderfully. My whole body aches as if it has gone twenty rounds with a big ape. I can't feel my arms. And I'd be happier if my shoulders weren't part of me.'

'Aren't we being brave,' Peter mocked out of sheer relief. 'Stiff upper lip, old man, or were you napping when we were given that training lecture?'

'Did Daisy tell you all of it?' Trevor asked, forcing himself to remain conscious.

'She told me enough. I should knock your head off. What in hell possessed you to go tearing off, unarmed, in the middle of the night?'

'You were the one who called the Marina witnesses nuts. Besides, how was I to know there was a gorilla on board that boat? I'm telling you, Peter, whatever it was, it was strong. Unarmed combat skills were useless. Before I knew where I was he'd swept me off my feet, snapped my arm, and thrown me on to the deck.'

'So what have we got?' Peter asked. 'King Kong on the loose?'

'Sounds about right.' Trevor glumly surveyed his bandages. The anaesthetic was beginning to wear off. He was coming round to a fuzzy, and extremely painful awareness.

'Time the patient had a painkiller,' Daisy decided briskly.

'Want me to give it to him?' Mike asked.

'No thanks, Mike. I'll manage.'

'In that case, I'll love you and leave you. I've got a theatre date at nine tomorrow, or rather, today,' he said, glancing at his watch.

'Thanks a lot for coming out.' Daisy pulled a syringe off the trolley.

'For you, Daisy, any time.' He looked down at Trevor. 'This time tomorrow you'll feel more human, Sergeant, I promise you.'

'Thanks for the gas and the thought,' Trevor replied.

'Yes, thanks a lot,' Peter chipped in gruffly.

'All you have to do is roll over on to your . . .' Daisy looked at Trevor and screwed her face into a grimace. 'Left side?' she suggested.

'Must I go through this indignity?'

'If you want it to stop hurting, you must.' She pulled back the blankets, swabbed his bare thigh and slid in the needle.

'Admit it,' Peter joked. 'You only did this to get out of the workload Bill dumped on us.'

'From where I'm lying that workload looks good.' He shifted on to his back. 'I know my arms aren't much good, but if I took it easy tomorrow, I could come in the day after . . .'

'Like hell you could.' Peter looked to Daisy for confirmation. 'What say you, Doctor?'

'I say a couple of weeks complete rest, if not more.'

'No one's indispensable, Joseph, least of all you. Tomorrow, I'll organize that search of the pier.'

'Why the pier?' Daisy folded the blankets back over Trevor's legs.

'Because a drunken down-and-out thinks, only thinks, mark you, that he saw a clown there. And after tonight's little episode we can't afford to laugh at any clown sightings that come our way.'

'There've been clown sightings on the motorway, too,' Trevor added. 'Close to the spot where the bodies were found.'

'Then that clown we saw tonight murdered Tim.' Daisy's hand shook as she disposed of the syringe.

'Your husband is missing,' Peter interposed flatly, wanting to dampen the hysteria he sensed building in Daisy. He disliked emotional scenes almost as much as he disliked hospitals and sickness.

'Tim's dead.' Daisy turned her back on both Trevor and Peter. 'The cabin,' she began. 'The cabin . . .' Unable to control herself further, she buried her face in her hands.

Trevor stared at her back uneasily, wanting to help, not knowing how to. Peter barely managed to suppress his mounting irritation. Women! They were all the same. Give them half a chance and they cry, make a scene, embarrass everyone with their over-emotional play-acting. Why couldn't they keep it cool, under wraps, until they were alone somewhere?

269

'We didn't see Tim in that cabin,' Trevor ventured. 'That hand . . . it was small, Daisy. Those people at the marina, they could be mistaken. Perhaps the tall man wasn't him.'

'I'll get a forensic team together. We'll go over the boat at day-break,' Peter said abruptly.

'And if you find Tim?' she asked unsteadily.

'You'll be the first to know.'

Keeping her back turned to them, Daisy walked over to the sink in the far corner of the room. She washed her hands and then ran a perfunctory check over the instruments laid out on the trolley. She knew the nurse would have replaced everything as it should be. But going through the motions of a small, everyday task gave her the time she needed to get a grip on herself. Peter watched her closely. She was trying, he admitted grudgingly. And at least she'd held herself together long enough to patch Trevor up. Some women wouldn't have done that much. If he could keep things low-key, she'd last without breaking down again in front of him.

'First things first,' he said purposefully. 'I take it Trevor's going to be here for a few days?'

'This is the NHS,' Daisy pointed out. 'Not a rich man's clinic. We're stretched to the limit. A broken arm rates overnight, no more.'

'It's four now,' Peter said, glancing at his watch. 'What time do I come back to pick him up?'

'He'll need looking after,' Daisy warned.

'I'll stick him in my flat. The woman who cleans for me . . .'

'No.' Trevor woke from his drug-induced stupor. '*Him*, as you so kindly put it, is going back to his own place.'

'Stubborn, bad-tempered creature, isn't he?' Peter's joke fell leadenly on Daisy's ears. She jerked her head in the direction of the door. Peter followed her out.

'Look,' she began awkwardly. 'I could pull a few

strings, stick him in one of the cubicles that we set aside for staff. Or I could get him admitted to Richard's clinic.'

'The hospital would be better.'

'I'll do what I can.'

'I have to get back to the station. I've a million-and-one things to arrange.'

'Of course. Don't worry about Trevor. I'll get him moved to a ward.'

'I'll call in at Trevor's flat later,' Peter promised. 'Pick up his toothbrush.'

'Thank you. You'd better go in and say goodbye. Tell him I'll be back with a porter.'

'I will.' Peter watched until she turned the corner of the corridor, then he began to mull over the day ahead. That bloody clown had to be caught for a start. The boat? The pier? Where did they go if the lunatic wasn't on either? He'd check with Bill. Find out if they had enough men to stake out the marina and the motorway. The clown could be planning another murder. Might be as well to check all the mental hospitals in case a psychopath had escaped recently. Whoever or whatever the clown was, from Trevor and Daisy's description it was mad. That much was certain. And Harries. Poor Harries. He'd left him hanging in midair. He'd try and find him now and arrange contact times and places. If Trevor was still shouting for a piece of the action in a couple of days, he could take over that job.

He rubbed his eyes vigorously with his fingertips. So much to do and he was on his knees. What was it Bill had said? 'You're a policeman, and everyone knows they don't need to eat or sleep.' Well, this one would sleep. Just as soon as the forensic searches had been organized and he'd talked to Harries. If he tried to keep this pace up for much longer, Daisy Sherringham would have another patient to doctor.

*

271

For the past thirty years Ben Gummer had stuck to an unvarying routine. Winter, summer, day, night, it differed only on those rare occasions when major outside events, such as family death, intruded into his tight little circle.

He always kept the pub open until the last customer struggled out. Sometimes it was three, sometimes it was four in the morning. He saw the last of them through the doors, locked up behind them, then rubbed his hands in anticipation of what lay ahead. His favourite time of the day.

He cleared the spilt beer and glasses from a single table – the one nearest the bar. He gave it a quick wipe over with a filthy bar rag, then his bare arm, before emptying the tills out on to its scarred and chipped surface. Then he cashed up, bagged the takings and locked them in the safe, hidden behind the massive Edwardian mirror that hung over the bar. The closing of the safe door marked the end of his work for the day. The remainder of the dirty glasses and tables and the floor would be seen to later, when the cleaning woman came in at eight.

Generally, in the spring and summer, he was through by the time dawn broke. But whether it was light or dark, that was the hour he poured out his only stiff drink of the day. A tumbler full of brandy, laced with a raw egg. He never drank spirits while the pub was open. He'd seen too many landlords come a cropper by going down that road. Beer he could take in vast quantities, and he did, matching his customers glass for glass, talking, socializing, but never incapacitated. Brandy was different. It was for serious drinking. Which was why he kept it for first thing in the morning, or rather last thing at night.

He generally took his time over the drink. When it was finished, he plonked his dirty glass amongst the others, called his dogs and let them out through the back door. He'd bred German shepherds for years. Ever since he'd smuggled his first dog out of Germany, after the war. While the dogs ran over the beach he cooked and ate his breakfast. That, too, never varied. A large slab of steak accompanied by a mound of fried, left-over lunch potatoes, the lot smothered in brown sauce. He wolfed it down sitting on a stool in the pub kitchen.

Leaving his grease-laden plate and frying pan where they lay, he whistled the dogs in. Once they returned to his living quarters, he locked the back door and went to bed, staying there until the pub reopened at ten thirty. Any sleep he missed out on, he caught up with when the pub closed for the afternoon. Publican's hours didn't suit everyone, but they suited him. They certainly hadn't been to the liking of the women he'd married – both had left him within a very short time, and for years now, he'd clung obstinately to the fallacy that they'd deserted him because of the hours he'd kept, rather than the more likely cause of his own shortcomings.

Ben had never mourned the loss of his wives, only the vacancy they'd left in his bed. He missed his afternoon 'sessions', as he mentally referred to them, but as the years passed, and ever-thickening layers of fat settled over his pallid body, he'd come to accept the unpalatable fact that it was becoming harder and harder to find a woman to share his bed for even one night, let alone on a more permanent basis.

When he'd been young and had worked the pier – strange how often he'd thought about the pier since Peter Collins and that other policeman had brought it up a few nights ago – women had been easy to find. The only problem he'd had to cope with then was how to fit the maximum number into any one day. They'd buzzed round his booth like flies on a dead fish. At times he couldn't move out on to the boards for them.

Women of all shapes and sizes, with their thick red lipstick, heavy perfume, slim legs and sheer nylons . . . each and every one of them came to his mind in lustfully graphic detail.

He pushed his sauce-smeared plate aside and lit a cigarette. The images of women blurred, and were supplanted by a sudden, all too realistic vision of the unmade bed that waited for him upstairs. There was nothing quite as lonely as a double bed when you needed a woman, he reflected baldly. Some memories were definitely best left in the past.

He left the kitchen and walked to the back door. It wouldn't hurt him to take a careful look in the bar later on. There might be a likely woman or two lurking among the customers. Men were always walking out on women, couples separated, divorced, at all stages of life. It would be good if he could find a fairly reliable and grateful woman to share his bed. Someone not too pernickety, who knew how, and when to laugh.

He whistled to the dogs through the open door. Stupid brutes. He could hear them barking down on the beach. Should have come back by now. They knew the routine as well as he did. They could stay out for as long as it took him to eat his meal. No more. If they pushed their luck, he'd chain them up outside for the rest of the day. That would soon cure them of any mutinous ideas.

He whistled again. Shorter and more irate this time, but the barking continued unabated. Furious, he stepped outside, gasping and wincing as the raw, salt-laden air seared into his lungs and bit through the holes in his vest. He called out angrily. He could see the blasted animals. Down alongside the pier, pulling and playing with something that had been washed up on the tide. Damn it, the thing was still bobbing in the water. He'd have to dry the stupid mutts.

'Myrtle! Cyril!' He'd named the dogs after his least

favourite set of in-laws. He got a kick of telling his ex-wife that he enjoyed bullying anything with those names. Even stupid dogs. He whistled again. Still they ignored him.

With the cold spurring him on, he moved speedily through the beer garden to the gate. Myrtle was pulling at something with her teeth. A long dark streak against the white crest of the waves . . . Was it a rag? He squinted through the pale misty dawn light.

He scuffed his way across the soft sand. The dogs wouldn't leave whatever it was alone. It had to be meat, a carcass of some kind. Perhaps a sheep fallen over the cliffs lower down the coast? He moved closer. Myrtle was fighting with Cyril, between them they had a bone, a long bone. He shouted furiously. This time Cyril recognized the anger in his master's voice and sloped to heel. But Ben had to wade knee-deep into the sea to get Myrtle. He caught her roughly by the collar and pulled her away. Then he saw the parcel; sodden bread billowing out into the water, and a leg of roasted meat. He picked it up to make sure. It was a leg of lamb, or rather what had been roasted lamb before the dogs had got at it. Then he saw the knife, long, slim, sunk to the hilt between the bones. And pinioned to the leg by the knife blade was a black sleeve ornamented by a single white pompom. Just like the ones the pierrots used to wear.

Trevor edged his way warily out of sleep into consciousness. Around him, a cacophony of unfamiliar noises buzzed lightly. The ring of a telephone in the distance. The rattle of a trolley over hard floors. The clink of glasses and water jugs. Muffled voices speaking in low whispers.

He wasn't alone, he was sure of it. A radio was playing softly in the background. Classical music. A piece he didn't recognize. Cautiously, he opened his eyes, and looked directly at Daisy. She was sitting in an armchair that had been pulled close to his bed.

'So you've decided to join the land of the living,' she said brightly. 'How do you feel?'

'I don't know yet.' He moved slightly, tried to turn towards her and grimaced in pain.

'Your right arm's broken, your left shoulder's been dislocated,' she reminded him. 'So if I were you, I'd start slowly. Leave the breakdancing and weightlifting until next week.'

'I might do just that.'

He lay quietly for a moment, remembering the night before. The clown . . . the boat . . . Daisy . . . Peter . . . Daisy? What was Daisy doing here? Next to his bed?

'Have you been sitting there all night?' he asked, embarrassed by the thought of her here, witness to his sleep.

'No. We didn't bring you up until five this morning. Then I left you in the care of the ward sister. I've just called back to see how you're getting on.'

'What time is it now?'

'Two.'

He groaned. 'I'm sorry. I shouldn't have slept so long and you shouldn't have gone to all this trouble. I'll get up . . .'

'Perhaps later.' She used the brisk bedside manner he recognized from the time he'd broken his legs. 'And you're not putting me to any trouble. Sergeant Collins and I agreed last night that by far and away the best solution to the problem of what to do with you was to move you in here where you could be nursed properly. Fortunately, they're not that pushed for beds on this ward at the moment, so you can stay put. At least for today.'

'Peter suggested I stay here?'

'He did.'

276

'I'll kill him,' he muttered, worrying about what else Peter had said.

'You'll have a chance to kill him later.'

'He's coming here?'

'He rang about an hour ago. He told me to tell you that both the boat and the pier have been searched. There have been more developments – I love that phrase, by the way. It sounds as if the police have moved into the property market – and he'll call in as soon as he's free.'

'Great.'

'Important things first. What do you want for breakfast?'

'I have to eat?'

'You're not hungry?'

He shook his head.

'In that case, I'll get a nurse to wash you.'

'Oh no you don't.'

'It is their job.'

'And I'm fit enough to stagger to the bathroom,' he insisted. 'That is a bathroom door over there?'

'It is. This room is usually used by VIPs and staff.'

'I'm not used to preferential treatment.'

'Injuries received in the line of duty. You are trying to find Tim.'

'All I seem to have done is get myself into a right mess.' He lifted his head off the pillow and looked around for a dressing gown.

'Will you at least allow me to help you up?' she left her chair and reached for the striped hospital robe that hung on the back of the door.

'I don't think I could lift either arm high enough to stop you doing whatever you wanted.' He gritted his teeth, then, using his left elbow, he propped himself up in the bed.

Daisy sat next to him. 'If I slide my arm round your back, it'll give you the leverage you need to get up.'

277

'This is ridiculous,' he protested as she leaned over him.

'No more so than the performance we had to get you into bed in the first place. And before you look, I made sure the nurses left enough of your underwear on to spare your blushes.'

'Thank you.' His embarrassment mounted with each revelation she made.

With Daisy's help he managed to swing his legs over the side of the bed. She draped the dressing gown over his shoulders. He clutched the edge of the mattress tightly with his left hand. His head was swimming, he felt faint and nauseous. It would have been bliss just to fall back and lie still.

'Are you all right there for a moment?' Daisy relaxed her hold on him.

'I think so,' he said weakly. She disappeared and came back with a black plastic sack and a roll of white insulation tape.

'You're putting me out with the rubbish?'

'Not yet. That will come later if you give us any trouble.'

She lifted his right arm gently and slid the plastic bag over the plaster cast, taping the ends firmly against his bare skin. 'If you're careful not the soak this arm, the bag will protect against any accidental splashes. Keep it slow and steady and you'll cope. Ready for the great trek?'

'As ready as I'll ever be.' The bathroom door suddenly seemed very far away from his bed.

'Lean on me,' she ordered, rising with him.

'I rather think I have already.' As he stepped forward, the room began to go round. 'More than I should have.'

'Don't talk nonsense.' She guided him to the bathroom chair. 'There's no lock on the door, but I promise not to send the nurses in unless there's a crash.'

278

'OK.'

When he finally emerged, wrapped in towels, twenty minutes later, the bed had been remade with clean sheets, and a cold meal of pâté, French bread and salad lay waiting for him on a tray set out on the bedside-table.

'Thank you,' he said humbly.

'Don't thank me, thank the nurses.'

'Daisy, I may call you Daisy, mayn't I?' he asked as he walked slowly towards the bed.

'You may.' There was a touch of irony in her voice. 'Though it does seem a little late in the day to ask. And unless you want to catch pneumonia, you'd better let me put that dressing gown on you.'

'That's what I was going to ask you to do.' He handed it meekly over to her. 'With you being a doctor, I thought you'd have more idea than me how to dress an invalid.'

'It's quite simple.' She unwound the plastic sack from his right arm, slid his left arm through the left sleeve of the gown, and draped the right shoulder over his. 'The right sleeve hangs empty,' she said, pulling it through to the inside. 'You can now pretend to be Nelson. Just watch your eye, that's all.'

'I will.'

'Would you like to eat off the bedside-table, or shall I lift the tray on to the bed?'

He cast an appreciative eye over the food. 'I never realised hospital diet was so varied. And I'll sit up to eat, if I may. That shower's made me feel reasonably human again.'

'Just don't overdo it.'

'Yes, Mother.'

He sat in the only armchair. She draped a blanket over his legs and pulled the flap up on the table, manoeuvring the tray as close to him as she could. Then she poured out two coffees.

'This is marvellous.'

'I've heard hospital food called many things, but never marvellous.'

'I eat out a lot, generally in cheap places. So I'm afraid I'm not used to your standards.'

'And just what do you think my standards are?'

'The Sherringham mansion?' He parried her angry frown with a good-natured smile. 'I've been there,' he said lightly. 'The cat looking at the king, his servants, his palace – and all that.'

'The Sherringham mansion is Richard's house, not Tim's. I'm just one of the workers. With the simple, uncomplicated working-girl tastes my pocket dictates.'

'I believe you. Honest.' He reached over and helped himself to a piece of bread. The sight of him struggling to spread pâté on it one-handed amused her. She smiled, and the atmosphere warmed, became friendlier, more relaxed.

'I'm a country boy myself.' He didn't even attempt to cut the bread, but bit into it whole. 'From Devon.'

'I love Devon. Tim preferred Cornwall. But my first love was always Devon. My parents used to take me to Torquay every summer. After London it seemed like heaven.'

'Then you're from London.'

'As much as I'm from anywhere. I haven't exactly got what you might call roots. I'm an only child. My mother died when I was thirteen. My father remarried six years ago. He lives in Australia with my stepmother now, but I must admit I haven't gone out of my way to keep in touch. Of course we invited him to our wedding, but . . .' Her voice trailed off and her eyes clouded over with pain.

Trevor knew she was thinking not so much of her wedding, but of Tim. The knowledge made him angry. Not with her, or Tim, but with Tim's mysterious disappearance and the torment it was causing her. He didn't

280

want her to be miserable or upset. He wanted her whole life, and in particular this small part of the day they were sharing, to be happy. Perfect.

'My mother's still alive.' He continued the conversation, as if he hadn't noticed the pain in her eyes. 'She lives with my brother and his wife on the family farm. Runs it too, if I know her. Colin, he's my younger brother, he wanted to stay on. I couldn't wait to get away.'

'Do you ever go back?'

'Occasionally, when I get leave. But the idea of going back is always better than the reality, if you know what I mean.'

'I've never had the opportunity to go back, anywhere.'

'You expect it to be like it was when you were a child. It never is. I only wish someone had told me when I was young that I'd only be cherished and cosseted during my childhood. If they had, I might have made more of it.'

'Is that a broad hint?'

'Good God, no.' His face reddened.

'Did anyone ever tell you you're far too sensitive?'

'Not recently.' He finished his coffee and poured orange juice into his glass.

'Where in Devon is your farm?'

'Near Axminster. You know Axminster?'

She shook her head.

'There isn't very much to know. It's a very small town. And the farm is even worse. Remote isn't the word. If you take the narrow road west out of town, and travel endless miles, you eventually come to a cart track. The cart track winds down and around, over the hills and through woods until you think there's nothing left in the world but trees, and the track's going to go on for ever. Then suddenly you hit this hidden wooded valley. Deep in the hidden wooded valley . . .'

'You find a haunted house?'

He looked across at her and was pleasantly surprised to see her grey eyes shining in amusement. He was elated to think that in some small way he'd helped her lose sight of the greater traumas of her life, if only for a moment.

'Might be haunted.' He inflected mock gravity into his voice. 'The Joseph ancestral home is Elizabethan.'

'Genuine Elizabethan?'

'Genuine Elizabethan. And what's more, lived in by Josephs and only Josephs since the house was built during the reign of the Virgin Queen. However, I fear I must shatter your illusions. The men and women who lived out their lives within our beautiful, but now decrepit walls were far too slow-witted and content to do anything dynamic, like return to this world as spectres.'

'How disappointing.'

'For you, not for me. If I'd been brought up with ghosts around the house, it might have altered my way of thinking, and, who knows, my entire life.'

'Made you think more of the spiritual side of life than the material?'

'Are you telling me I'm suitable for the police force and nothing else?'

'You said it, not me.'

He poured himself another coffee. 'I hope there's more to me than just the force.'

She picked up an underlying hint of seriousness that he hadn't intended her to hear.

'What about the rest of your life?'

'What rest of my life?'

'The rest of your life outside the force.'

'When I was first posted here, I lived amongst civilized people. On the east side of town, no less. My flat was not quite up to Grantley Mews standards, but it was better than were I live now.'

282

'You moved down in the world?'

'When I had my first flat I had the trimmings to go with it. A mortgage, a cat, new furniture, fitted kitchen, a girl – in short, I lived the advertising man's idea of a normal life. When the girl moved out – ' he tried, and failed, to keep the bitterness from his voice ' – the flat, the trappings . . . it seemed pointless to keep them on.'

His mind flicked back to Mags. She'd been his girl, or had she? He'd thought so at the time. They'd lived together for six years. Longer than some marriages. He'd wanted to marry her. Nagged her the whole time. It was she who wouldn't make the commitment. And in the end he'd found out why. Peter had told him. Peter knew. Damn it all, everyone knew, except him. She'd lived with him, let him pay the bills, climbed into bed with him every night, just so she could carry on with the married man she loved.

Now, with hindsight, it was all so obvious, and so convenient, at least from Mags' point of view. What better sucker could there be than one who worked shifts for the police? He'd given her security and the flat as a base to work from. Because of his blindness the married man's wife had been as blissfully unaware of the whole affair as he'd been. Mags had used him, and the married man had used his wife. His girl? He couldn't say Mags had been his girl, not knowing what he knew now. Mags had been someone else's girl. Not like Daisy. If he could get someone to care for him the way Daisy cared for Tim Sherringham . . .

'I'm sorry, I didn't mean to pry.'

'You're not. I know all about you, so why shouldn't you know what little there is to know about me? Anyway,' he finished off his bread and took another piece, 'to cut a long story short, I moved out, rented my upmarket flat to an upmarket copper and his wife. Then I met Frank.'

283

'Frank?'

'He's an ex-copper. He was invalided out of the force after he got hurt in a fracas on the football ground. He owns a shop in a run-down area on the west side of town. He was having trouble with vandals, nothing serious, just kids on the loose. So I volunteered to rent the flat above his shop in an effort to keep trouble at bay. Arrangement suited us both – he was looking for a reliable tenant, and I was looking for somewhere different to live.'

'You rented out your upmarket flat . . .'

'Furnished,' he interrupted, his mouth full of bread and pâté. 'Don't forget, it's fully furnished, which is more than can be said for my present place.'

'You're a funny chap.'

'The move made sense at the time. Besides, living over a shop has definite advantages.'

'Such as?'

'I don't go hungry. Frank lets me forage at any time of the day or night. I keep a tally and pay him at the end of the month.'

'I thought you said you eat out a lot.'

'We have take-aways in the station sometimes. When we work late.'

'And that's eating out?'

'In my book it is.'

She looked out of the window. Her silence wasn't a condemnation of anything Trevor had said. Rather, it was a result of what he'd left unsaid. She visualized the life he led, right down to the last lonely detail. Impersonal, hectic working hours spent in the company of petty criminals, junkies and Peter Collins. And if she was faced with the choice of whiling away an hour or two with a junkie or Peter Collins, the junkie would come out on top every time.

After the bustle of the police station, the grim solitude of the flat he lived in. It was so different from

284

what her own life had been. Was that why fate had struck at her and Tim? She'd been happy with him. Too happy, perhaps. Had she tempted evil by taking their life together for granted? Had they been singled out for destruction because she'd forgotten to be grateful for their very special blessings?'

'Is this a long visit?' Trevor asked timidly, believing her silence to be rooted in her grief for Tim.

'No, because you need to rest.'

'I could smash you at noughts and crosses if you have a pen and paper.'

'If Tim and I hadn't been together, I would have taken you up on that offer of an evening out.' She felt the need to respond in some small way to his tact, his kindness. 'Do you remember the night you asked me? In Casualty?'

'I remember, but I didn't think you did.'

'Joseph! Joseph! Where the hell are you?'

'I hear the light step and dulcet tones of Peter.' Trevor resented the intrusion even more than he thought he would. 'Here,' he called back.

'Good God, the invalid's up.'

'And out of bed,' Daisy replied, determined to be polite and nothing else.

'Good, because we haven't much time.'

'Much time for what?' Trevor asked.

'I have a wheelchair on order. Have to get you to the mortuary as soon as possible.'

'Tim!' The colour drained from Daisy's face.

'You idiot,' Trevor snapped.

'Damn it, I didn't think.' Peter sat on the bed. 'It's not Tim,' he said quickly. 'It's someone quite different.'

'It might help if you started at the beginning,' Trevor suggested heavily. 'For instance, did you find anything on the boat or the pier?'

'The pier was a wash-out,' Peter complained, trying hard to ignore Daisy's pale face and tormented eyes.

'It took us two-and-a-half hours to cut our way in there. Then when we finally stepped on to the boards, we found whole bands of planks torn up. We couldn't go forward more than three or four feet at a time, and it took us another two hours to bring up the material we needed to bridge those damned gaps.'

'But did you reach the theatre?' Trevor asked impatiently.

'Eventually. It's in one hell of a state. The floor's treacherous. It wouldn't hold a sparrow in places, let alone a man. If Andy really sleeps there, he must hang from the rafters like a bat.'

'So you found nothing?'

'Nothing at all. We looked round the theatre. The planks in front of the stage were missing, there seemed little point in bridging that space. There were no curtains to speak of, so we could see all there was to be seen from the auditorium. Dust, broken windows, smashed chairs. That was about it. It's being boarded back up now.'

'And the boat?' Daisy wound her fingers tensely in the folds of her long black skirt.

'The boat was different.' Peter gripped his chair tightly. 'You didn't exaggerate at all last night,' he said grimly. 'Forensic spent all morning in the cabin. I've never seen anything like it. They went over it with a toothcomb, filled enough specimen bottles to keep the lab going for a month.'

'And?' Trevor demanded impatiently.

'You know as well as I do, it takes time for the reports to be made.'

'Come off it, Peter. It's me you're talking to, Trevor. By now you've got a fair idea of what happened in that cabin.'

'Was Tim murdered there?' Daisy pleaded.

'No. None of the blood or tissue samples that were taken matched your husband's group. I checked.'

'Then who was murdered on that boat?' Trevor pressed.

'Probably Amanda Dart. The stains match her grouping. We also found shoes that fit the size and description of those she was wearing when she was last seen at the hostel. Unfortunately, there was still part of a foot in one of them. And although the hand on the table wasn't in absolutely pristine condition, the pathologist's fairly certain it's hers.'

'Were there any stains from any other blood group?'

'None that I know anything about. Daisy, we're going to have to go over your flat,' Peter warned. 'There were five sets of prints in that cabin. If we can eliminate Amanda Dart's, yours and Tim's, we might be able to make a start on drawing up a list of suspects.'

'Was there anything to prove that Tim had been there recently?' She didn't want to believe that yet another blank had been drawn.

Peter shook his head. 'We found nothing in that cabin that connects with your husband's disappearance. And, believe me, it wasn't for the want of looking.'

'You said something about going to the mortuary,' Trevor reminded him.

'Call came in late last night. A junkie, fatal overdose. Right outside the house he was renting a room in. He was found by one of the people who lived in the house with him. There doesn't seem to be much doubt about the identification, but I thought you ought to take a look, just in case. His name is Robin Dart.'

Chapter Eleven

'Where do you want it, sir?'

Patrick O'Kelly waved the forceps he was holding in the direction of the wall. 'Over there.'

'This one's not likely to give you too much trouble, sir.' The porter pushed the trolley against the far wall.

'How do you know?' Patrick continued his foray with the forceps and the knife. 'Taken a medical degree in your spare time?'

'Not really, sir. But this junkie overdosed on heroin. He has fresh needle marks in his arm.'

'Thank you for your diagnosis. I only wish the coroner would accept it. Save us pathologists a lot of work if porters were allowed to give their opinions as PM reports.'

'Sir?'

'You may go.'

'Thank you, sir.'

'Shall I put it away?' Paul asked.

'Stay where you are,' Patrick ordered. 'Let's finish this first. Ah! Just as I thought.' He cut gleefully through a section of tissue. 'The serrations on this knife match the cuts on the neck and arm. This could be the knife the murderer used to decapitate the bodies that were found on the motorway. I can't say any more than that. If we had a stab wound to compare with the blade, it might be different. Sergeant . . . Collins, isn't it? No doubt you've come to see the results of the tests on the knife.' Patrick greeted Peter who had walked in pushing a reluctant Trevor in a wheelchair.

'Knife?' Trevor asked Peter.

'Ben Gummer found a knife washed up under the

pier early this morning. It was fixed in, of all things, a leg of lamb. He probably would have thrown it away if it hadn't been stuck through a black silk sleeve with a pompom attached to it.'

'A pierrot's sleeve?'

'Could be.'

'And this knife could be the one that carved up your bodies. But then again, the murderer could have used a different one with a similar cutting edge. The serrations match. I'm afraid I can't be more specific than that.' Patrick held the handle, blade uppermost, between his rubber-gloved fingers. 'It's a fairly common kind of knife. You can buy one just like it in the hardware department of any number of stores. Made in England, good quality, advertised as being able to cut its way through anything, including frozen meat. Sold as part of a set or singly. There are no deep wounds on your motorway bodies, so I can't compare the length of the blade.'

'But the killer used a knife?' Peter interrupted.

'To cut off the heads and hands. But there were no deep stabbing thrusts. And without actual wounds, it's impossible to attempt any sort of a detailed weapon comparison,' Patrick lectured.

'Any chance of seeing that sleeve?' Peter turned to Trevor. 'I know it's a long shot, but you might recognize something.'

'Like a pompom? For pity's sake, Peter, talk about clutching at straws.'

'Here it is.' Patrick passed Peter the plastic bag. 'Incidentally, there was an inch or two of thick brown paper sandwiched between the knife and the meat, suggesting that it was wrapped up.'

'In a food parcel, before Ben's dogs got at it.' Peter passed the bag to Trevor.

'It was dark, I didn't even see the face clearly, let alone the pompoms,' Trevor complained as he stared at the bag. 'Whoever attacked me was dressed in black and there were white balls or buttons on his clothes. I can't say any more than that.'

'But this could be his sleeve?'

'His, or any other pierrot's. I told you last night, the only thing I can say for certain is that whatever grabbed me was strong. Unbelievably so.'

'Perhaps Daisy'll remember more. She said she saw the clown face to face in the torchlight.'

'Daisy Sherringham?' Patrick looked up enquiringly from the comparisons he was making between the knife and sections of mutilated flesh.

'She was with Sergeant Joseph last night. They were both attacked by someone dressed as a clown,' Peter explained briefly. 'I thought this might jog Trevor's memory.'

'Difficult,' Patrick commented. 'As the Sergeant said, one sleeve is very like another.'

'Did your clown have two sleeves to his jacket?' Peter persisted.

'Yes . . . yes, I think so,' Trevor murmured, struggling to remember. 'If he'd had a bare arm I probably would have noticed.'

'Then either there are two clowns, or else your clown lost his sleeve after he attacked you. You didn't tear his clothes, by any chance?'

'No, I didn't,' Trevor answered irritably. He felt ill. His arm was beginning to throb. He wanted to leave the blinding whiteness and the cold Lysol-ridden atmosphere of the mortuary, and return to the soft, cushioned comfort of his hospital bed.

'Supposing there's only one clown,' Peter ventured thoughtfully. 'And he . . .'

'Beat me up, terrified Daisy Sherringham, then went along to lose his sleeve and his dinner in the sea?' Trevor suggested scathingly.

'Flippancy, Joseph?' Despite the disparaging note in

his voice, Peter suddenly realized how ridiculous his hypothesis sounded. He walked over to Patrick and handed him back the bag containing the sleeve. 'We really came here to see the junkie who was brought in last night.'

'This morning. You lot kept the body overnight.'

'Probably so the brother could identify him. He should be tagged as Robin Dart.'

'Help yourself. He's over there.'

'Thank you, I'll do that.' Knowing Trevor's reluctance to inspect corpses, Peter walked over to the trolley and pulled back the covering sheet.

'You can unzip the bag,' Patrick offered. 'But take care. Don't disturb anything. According to the porter it's an open-and-shut case, but we still have to make sure,' he commented sarcastically.

Peter tugged at the zipper delicately with his thumb and forefinger. He uncovered the face, no more. 'Is this him?' he asked Trevor.

Trevor turned his head and looked across at the trolley. His arm had gone past the throbbing stage and was now burning as if jets of scalding water played beneath the plaster cast. His legs had turned to jelly. If it wasn't for the wheelchair he would have sunk to the floor.

'Is this Robin Dart?' Peter repeated, reading the expression on Trevor's face.

'Yes.' Trevor shuddered. Last evening he'd sat with the man, drunk coffee with him. Talked to him. 'That's Robin Dart.'

'He could have picked a better time to kill himself.'

'That's if he did.'

'Joseph, a junkie turns up dead and you're suspicious? We've got enough of your actual murder victims here without looking for them under the bed. The man was a junkie. Junkies kill themselves all the time. Accidentally. Deliberately. What's the difference?'

291

'I'm not convinced.'

'Let's see if I can shed a little light.' Patrick left the slab he'd been working on and walked over to the trolley. He discarded his gloves before unzipping the bag, opening it fully. He looked at the cadaver for a moment, then he lifted Robin's left arm, pulling back the loose-fitting sleeve of the black sweater he wore. He placed his hands tightly around the fleshy part of the upper arm and squeezed. A spot of blood appeared in the crook of the elbow.

'There you have it, gentlemen.' He lowered the arm back on to the trolley. 'Fresh mark. Mainlining, and knowing what I do about the drug situation in this town, I'd say it was heroin.'

'Robin Dart didn't do that,' Trevor insisted.

'It's there, in front of you,' Peter countered. 'The man clearly overdosed . . .'

'Robin Dart was clean.'

'You'd just told him his sister was dead. That's more than enough reason for anyone to regress.'

'He was an actor.' Trevor was shouting and he didn't even realize it. He was in pain, tired of the mortuary, corpses, death.

'So?' Peter snapped truculently.

'Actors have to wear all sorts of strange costumes. Some of which leave the arms bare. He went to drama school. He started out with ambitions. He couldn't risk being found out. He was a junkie all right, but he used the veins at the back of his knees. And *only* the veins at the back of his knees. Told me so himself.'

'Are you sure?'

'Of course I'm sure.'

'How soon can we get a detailed PM on this chap?' Peter asked Patrick.

'I'll make a start after lunch. Sorry it can't be sooner, but one pair of hands and all that. There's no one else to take over. The Home Office chap is tied up with the specimens from the boat.'

Patrick turned over Robin's arms, ready to fold them back into the bag. Then he paused for a moment. 'Strange,' he commented thoughtfully.

'What's strange?'

'This.' He indicated a mark high up on Robin's right forearm.

'Vaccination. test,' Trevor muttered. 'He showed it to me last night. He had it done as part of a medical for a job.'

'That's no vaccination test, Sergeant.' Patrick fingered the mark as though he were making sure. 'That's a tissue-typing test. It's generally carried out on donors and recipients to match them prior to transplant operations.'

Harries wasn't happy. His initial elation at being picked out for undercover work had long since gone. In fact, it had faded into oblivion the moment he'd set foot in the crumbling, mould-spattered building that housed the day-centre for the homeless. It wasn't as if Peter Collins hadn't tried to warn him. He'd been regaled with the full police complement of unsubtle jokes concerning filth, lice and putrid smells, but none of it had struck a chord whilst he'd been sitting in the warmth and comparative comfort of the station. Then, he'd been far too concerned with the clothes he was going to wear and the manufacture of his cover story, to listen to Peter's unfunny warnings. He'd even been naïve enough to cast himself in a similar romantic light to an actor about to take the lead in a major production.

But each and every one of his misconceptions and heroic images had melted in the unwashed face of the human flotsam that bobbed around in the pungent atmosphere of the cafeteria at the day-centre. He forced himself to tag on to the end of the motley queue that waited, anything but patiently, for the stewed tea and thick slices of bread and butter that were on offer as lunch. He subdued his natural revulsion and noted the indescribable filth that was smeared over the rags of the time-hardened derelicts. He listened to the conversations of the younger people who still bothered to talk. Unintelligible, occasionally aggressive mumblings from the more obvious tramps. Obscene, noisy ravings from a couple of female junkies who'd clearly managed to finance their fixes for the day.

'I'll give you whatever you fancy for a fiver.'

He turned his head. The speaker had the flat-chested, spindly-legged, gawky look of a twelve-year-old. Except for the face. There was nothing underdeveloped or childish about that. The cold eyes and the grim set of the mouth lent her the same hard-bitten, calculating image that the fifty-year-old whores in the dockside pubs projected.

'Push off,' he growled abruptly. He barely managed to stop himself from adding the automatic, 'or I'll run you in'.

'Suit yourself.' The girl flounced off, as much as anyone could flounce in a tight, short denim skirt and laddered tights. 'It's you that's missing out, not me,' she mocked from a distance.

He bought his tea and bread and butter from the harassed woman who was too busy to talk, then he looked around for somewhere to sit. He decided against joining anyone. Friendliness wasn't part of his cover. He picked out a small table in the centre of the room. He laid out his meal on its mutilated surface, noting the dark brown stains on the plate, and the greasy film that floated on the surface of the tea. As soon as he reasonably could, he'd leave this parody of food and study the notice-board on the wall at the far end of the room. He knew what to look for. Peter Collins had drummed it into him.

He killed a few minutes by stirring his tea with the lollipop stick that had been provided, and tearing the bread into small pieces with his fingers. There weren't any knives.

'New here?'

'Yes.' Harries glanced up at the man who had spoken to him. Just his luck, he was looking for Andy, or at the very least a villain, and he'd ended up with a dog collar.

'Thought so. Haven't seen you around before.'

'Haven't been around,' Harries mumbled, quelling his desire to talk. He remembered his cover. Hardened ex-prisoner. Had to stick to it at all costs. With everyone. No matter how innocuous they looked.

'My name's David. What's yours?'

'Stephen . . . Stacko.'

'Down on your luck?'

'Isn't that bloody obvious?' Collins would be proud of him.

'The only way you can go now is up.'

'So they tell me.'

'Would you like to talk about it?'

'There's nothing to talk about.' Conscientiously, Harries gave his well-rehearsed impression of a hard case. He pushed back his chair and stared at David. There was something odd about the man, perverted even. Greasy brown hair, peculiar beady eyes that didn't blink, peering at him through thick-lensed glasses. The eyes of a maniac? Harries shuddered. He was being childish. Allowing the atmosphere to get to him.

'Have you anywhere to sleep tonight?'

'No.' Was that it? Was the vicar trying to pick him up?

'I could give you some addresses. Names of people who can help.'

Hastily, Harries revised his harsh judgement of the

man. He was being too cynical. After all, what would anyone get out of coming down here, to a place like this. Talking to down-and-outs. Trying to help them?

'Social services gave me the address of a place in Jubilee Street,' Harries snarled, still playing the ex-con.

''Ere, Father. Father, over 'ere.' The girl who'd tried to proposition him earlier was waving crazily at the priest.

'I hope we can continue our little chat later, Stacko.' The vicar smiled at him, as though they were in the middle of a mutually interesting and intimate conversation.

'Yeh, sure.' Harries went back to playing with his food. He messed it about, carried morsels to his mouth whenever he thought anyone was watching, but he was careful not to actually swallow anything. There were some things that went beyond the call of duty.

He waited twenty minutes or so. No one else came near him. Eventually, he pushed his chair back and stood up. He shoved his way through the mass of tables and went to the notice-board. There were Bible tracts posted there along the lines of, 'Jesus forgave the sinner and blessed the prostitute.' And one that, cover notwithstanding, brought a smile to his face, 'The meek shall inherit the earth.' There were also several postcards bearing block-printed announcements. 'St Mary's Church needs casual labour to clean up churchyard. Small remuneration.' Under the heading of 'beds for the night', the address of the hostel in Jubilee Street, and of the Salvation Army hostel in the next town. 'Run away from home? Phone this number now. We won't tell anyone where you are, but we can put your relatives' and friends' minds at rest.' 'Are you hooked on drugs or solvents? If you are, we can help. We listen, we don't judge.'

That was it. He glanced around the hall surreptitiously while he pretended to read. Nothing. No one-legged men, no wild men with black hair. He hadn't needed a description for Andy. The derelict was known to every copper on the beat. He was devastated. He knew it had been optimistic of him to hope for a result the first day out. Peter Collins had warned him that he could be kicking around for weeks, but – he breathed in the stench of the place – he didn't know how long he could stick it out. The shorter, the better.

'Looking for a job? A way out of your troubles?' David, the vicar, again.

'Yeh. Yeh, sure.'

'Perhaps I could assist you. I know someone who is looking to employ strong young men. It's heavy work, but well paid. Abroad.'

Harries tried to look interested. Collins had mentioned something about someone supposedly recruiting staff among the down-and-outs. Could be a racket. Though God alone knew what kind. Oh well, if he didn't succeed in one thing, he might succeed in another. He'd tell Collins about it. Five-thirty. He had to report in at the tobacconist's on the corner of Balaclava Street.

'If you'd like to come along with me, I'll introduce you to the recruiting manager.'

'What, now?'

'Unless you've something better to do.'

'No. Nothing pressing.' Harries thrust his hands deep into his pockets and followed the clergyman out of the centre. If he didn't make it to the tobacconist's on time it wouldn't matter. There was a bug in the heel of his left shoe that would enable the station to track him down any time they wanted. It was broad daylight. There were plenty of people around. And there was only him, and one middle-aged clergyman. Nothing he couldn't handle himself. One lucky break, just one, and he'd be joining Peter Collins in the plain clothes squad. Off the beat for good.

After Peter took Trevor to the mortuary, Daisy sat in the empty room for a while. She leaned back in the armchair Trevor had vacated, and closed her eyes. The ward was peaceful, but not silent. The thousand-and-one small noises that make up the daily life of a hospital came softly to her ears. The squeak of the nurses' rubber-soled shoes as they travelled over the vinyl floors. Buzzers clicking on and off, alerting staff to the patients' needs. A daytime television quiz programme vying with a radio sports commentary. The strident voice of the WVS volunteer who manned the library trolley.

Her whole body cried out for sleep, and for the first time in days she knew that she could have slept. No spectres would rise to haunt her dreams in a crowded ward during the daytime, she was sure of it. And she was tired. So damned tired.

She'd been up for most of the night, and the couple of hours she hadn't, she'd tossed fitfully on Judy's bed. Judy had taken the inflatable mattress herself, and had been sound asleep when she'd crept in after operating on Trevor Joseph in the early hours.

She knew if she didn't move soon she would probably doze off, and that would only create more problems for her tonight. Particularly if she managed to get the flat Administration had promised to find her one by the evening, and she was alone. But where could she move to? She couldn't bear the thought of sitting around Judy's flat without Judy, and the last thing she wanted to do was return to Richard's house. She really ought to motivate herself. Go down to Administration and demand a key. Then she could fill the empty hours until Judy's shift finished by moving her things out of one flat into the other, and preparing dinner for her and Judy.

She opened her eyes to see Alan backing out through the doorway.

'Sorry, didn't mean to wake you,' he apologized.

'I wasn't asleep.'

'You were certainly giving a good imitation of it. I'm on late lunch, so I thought I'd call up and see Trevor. Judy said you'd admitted him last night.'

'His charming partner has just wheeled him off to the mortuary to look at a body.'

Alan screwed his lips together, ballooning his plump cheeks out even further.

'I thought the same thing that you're thinking, but the body belonged to a junkie. Trevor knew him.'

'Dr Daisy?'

'Yes, Sister.'

The ward sister was standing in the doorway, sympathy written all over her motherly face.

'Sorry to disturb you, but there's a telephone call for you. I think it's Dr Richard Sherringham's house. You can take it in my office.'

'Thank you, Sister.'

'The man won't let up, will he?' Alan said once the sister had left.

'I think he understands now that I intend to stay here.' Daisy rose from her chair, and Alan gave her a bear hug.

'I have to go. I'll catch up with you later.'

'Thanks, Alan.'

'For what?'

'For being here, and helping.'

'I only wish I could,' he muttered under his breath as he walked away from her.

Five minutes after taking the telephone call, Daisy left the ward and walked purposefully towards the lift.

Pausing to allow a stretcher case, complete with drips and attendant nurse and porter, to pass her, she glanced up at the clock on the wall. Three-fifteen. Coffee break time. Everyone would be in the doctors' lounge. She walked to the elevator, pressed the button for the second floor and waited for the doors to close. Her hands began to shake, so she pushed them into the pockets of her white coat. Why did this have to come now of all times, on top of everything else?

Mike Edmunds saw Daisy discarding her white coat as he entered the lounge. He knew she'd been taken off the duty roster, but he also knew she'd been sitting with Trevor Joseph. He'd seen her there himself when he'd called into Trevor's room during his lunch break. Trevor had been sleeping, and Daisy'd had her eyes closed, so he'd crept away without disturbing either of them.

Daisy looked around the crowded room, a thin, pale figure in a calf-length, high-necked plain black dress. She acknowledged the expressions of embarrassed sympathy that greeted her from all sides, and edged her way towards Mike through the group of junior doctors milling around the coffee machine.

'Have you seen Judy?' she asked quietly as soon as she reached him.

'I think she's in paediatrics with Alan. You know what the patient lists are like down there. Not much chance of taking a coffee break.'

'Thanks.' She made for the door.

'Daisy.' He went after her. 'There's nothing wrong, is there? Nothing I can do?'

'No, and no.' She tried to smile, and failed, then left abruptly without another word. He looked after her retreating figure debating whether to follow her or not.

'Don't you think so, Mike?' Eric Hedley was standing next to him, eyebrows raised.

'Don't I think what?' Mike asked.

'Don't you think there's more future in private practice than within the NHS?'

'Definitely,' Mike concurred, with an air of gravity. 'From the Health Service's point of view, there's more future if you go into private practice.' Mike clapped Eric soundly on the back.

Eric stood boiling in the centre of the room. He knew Mike had made him the butt of the joke, but he didn't know how to retaliate. As the laughter died away, people began to glance at the clock and leave the room. Jealousy! Eric decided angrily, joining the crush in the doorway. Mike was jealous of his success and wanted it for himself. After all, Mike had only been offered a temporary post at the Holbourne and Sherringham Clinic, while he . . . Eric built marble towers in his imagination, basing them on the shaky foundations of the three afternoons he'd spent working for Joanna Sherringham.

Mike looked his watch. There was less than five minutes of the break left to go. He decided to look for Daisy when his shift finished. If there was anything wrong, or anything he could do to help her, Alan or Judy would know about it. He'd ask them then.

Daisy perched nervously on the edge of Alan's chair in his office. When Judy had finally finished with her patient, she came in and Daisy motioned to her to close the door.

'Do you know where Richard is?' she asked urgently.

'No, why should I?'

'Please Judy, don't lie to me. Not now. I know you're having an affair with him.'

'How did you find out?'

'Does it matter?'

'It does to me.'

Daisy took a deep breath and crossed her arms over her chest. She'd been dreading this moment for a very

301

long time. 'Tim found out when we were in our first year in college. He saw you and Richard walking arm in arm into that small hotel near the tube station. It was only a couple of days after he'd introduced us to Richard. Do you remember, that time Richard came to the college as guest lecturer?'

'How could I forget?' Judy turned away from Daisy and sat on Alan's desk. She picked up a stapler and began to fiddle with it. 'Why didn't either of you say something at the time?'

'It was none of our business. You were both over the age of consent. You knew what you were doing.'

'And now we don't. Is that it?'

'I had a telephone call from Hare a few minutes ago. He's been trying to raise Richard all day, without success. Richard's not at the house, and he hasn't been to the clinic today. Hare thought perhaps I'd seen him.'

'Richard's trying to cope with Tim's disappearance as best he can. He needs some time to himself,' Judy said defensively, thinking of the tranquillizers he was probably sleeping off.

'Joanna took the boat out last night by herself. She had an accident, slipped and fell against the edge of the cabin door, and cracked her collarbone. She's had it X-rayed and dressed at the clinic. She's resting at home right now, and although she insists she's fine, Hare thought Richard should be told about it. I hoped you'd be able to tell me where he is.'

'You're beginning to sound like that damned police-man you spend all your time with.'

'Please, Judy, don't make this any harder for me than it already is. Don't you see I had no choice but to talk to you and find out if you'd seen him? Aside from Hare and Joanna, I can't bear the thought of him missing. Even for a short while. There's Tim . . .' Daisy tried to ignore the stony expression on Judy's face and gazed out wretchedly through the wired-glass window.

Through a haze of tears she saw a cloudy sky, the silhouettes of thin-twigged treetops . . .

'Richard's in an old clifftop coastguard's cottage, about a mile from Hunter's Cove. I can't telephone, because there isn't one.'

'Thank you,' Daisy murmured gratefully.

'The cottage is mine. Richard gave it to me. We use it whenever we can get away.'

'Do you want to come with me?'

'Not until my shift finishes. It's going to be as much as Alan and I can do to clear the waiting room by five-thirty.'

'I'd be glad of the company, and I'm sure Richard . . .'

'There's one thing you – and Richard – should understand. Much as I might want to, I'm not in a position to offer any long-term help where Richard is concerned,' Judy asserted. 'I've got my job. My days are full.'

'Judy, surely if you love Richard, you'll want to be with him if he needs you. I don't know what the position is with Joanna, but . . .'

'I had, am having,' Judy corrected, 'an affair with Richard that his wife doesn't know about. That's all. There's never been any question of anything else between us. I can't bear men who lean too hard,' she said vehemently.

'And women?' Daisy asked quietly.

'You're different,' Judy said in a softer tone. 'You're probably the closest thing I'll ever have to a perfect friend.'

Embarrassed because, for once, she'd allowed her feelings to show through her usual tough, wisecracking exterior, she switched moods abruptly.

'Duty calls.' She jumped off the desk. 'Pick me up here at five-thirty.'

'Thanks. I'll telephone Hare and tell him that Richard is with me. Hopefully, he and Joanna will believe it.'

Daisy tried to put what she sensed to be a slightly sceptical tone in Hare's voice down to guilt on her part. Hanging up the phone, she looked round Alan's office. He was having a late lunch. Poor him, there'd be nothing on offer in the canteen except stale rolls, dried-up ham and warm lettuce.

Then she remembered the look on his face when she'd told him about the body in the mortuary. It worried her. That damned policeman could be lying. The body could be Tim's and they could be trying to keep it from her.

'Hello, Patrick.'

'Don't you trust the rest of us to tell you the truth?' Alan asked perceptively, looking up at Daisy from the mark on Robin Dart's arm that he was examining at Patrick's invitation.

'I know you come here at least twice a day, if that's what you mean. I just wanted a word with Patrick.'

'It's good to see you,' Patrick answered genially. 'And I'm sorry to hear there's still been no news of Tim.'

'Thank you. Sergeant Collins said a new corpse had come in.'

'I told you it wasn't your husband,' Peter said briefly.

'I know.' Daisy shrugged her shoulders. 'Thought I'd call in, just in case.'

'As you're here, you might be able to help us.' Ever the opportunist, Peter picked up the bag from the slab behind him. 'A clown's sleeve and a knife were washed up on the beach this morning. Can you remember any of the details from last night?'

'Such as?'

'Did the clown have two sleeves on his jacket?'

'Yes. Yes, he did.'

'You seem pretty definite on that point.'

'I am, just as I'm sure that the clown was taller than Trevor,' she said thoughtfully. 'It lifted him up, and its head was still above Trevor's, but . . .' She shook her head. 'Then again, the clown could have been standing on something. The deck of the *Freedom* is uneven. It all happened so quickly, I can remember nothing more than a loose collection of impressions, the running make-up, the satin slippers with their ridiculous white pompoms, the wide bottoms of the black silk trousers.'

'No knife?'

'I didn't see a knife, or at least I don't remember one.'

'Were the pompoms like these?' He handed her the bag.

'Could have been. I'm not sure.' She gave him back the bag and looked around. 'Where's Trevor?' she asked, realizing he wasn't in the mortuary.

'I took one look at him when I came in and sent for a porter to take him back to his room,' Alan answered.

'I suppose you overtaxed him?' Daisy accused Peter.

'Police business frequently can't wait. We *are* looking for your husband,' he added nastily.

Daisy's curtness vexed him. He'd deliberately gone easy on her, treated her gently since she'd patched up Trevor, and in return she'd done nothing but snap at him. He was the one who usually kept it short, brusque, and to the point. Damn it all, she'd taken on his role, and it was a new and unpleasant experience to be on the receiving end of ill manners.

'Daisy, can you spare a minute?' Patrick called.

'If I can be of any help.'

'We'd like a third opinion on this.' Patrick held up Robin's arm.

'Of course.' She looked down at the corpse. He was

so young. She struggled to hold back the tears that pricked at the back of her eyes.

'What do you think?'

'Skin test of some kind?' she suggested, still fighting to control her emotions.

'Tissue-typing?'

'Could be,' she said slowly, trying to recall a typical scar of that particular test.

'Slow down a minute,' Peter demanded. 'You said earlier that it has something to do with transplants, but what exactly do you mean by tissue-typing?'

'Tissue-typing is a necessary preliminary that has to be carried out before any organ transplant operation can be considered,' Daisy informed him coldly. 'It's standard procedure for every patient who's suffering from organ failure of any kind.'

'Whenever a transplant is being considered as a possible method of treatment, the tissue of both recipient and donor has to be examined closely in order to make the best possible match between the two. Kidneys, heart, lungs, liver, whatever the organ, the tissue-typing test applies,' Alan explained more fully. 'For example, people who want to donate one of their kidneys to a sick relative would have it done, or brain dead or dying patients who've already expressed a wish to donate their organs after death. Timing is crucial in transplant operations. The quicker an organ can be removed from a donor body into a recipient, the better the chance of success. And it helps if donor and recipient have been matched beforehand to cut down on the amount of time needed for theatre preparation.'

'Are you saying Robin Dart had this test to categorize his organs ready for a transplant operation?' Peter asked carefully.

'Either that, or he was being considered as a possible case for a transplant,' Patrick replied. 'Do you know if he was suffering from a heart defect, kidney failure, liver failure?'

'No. The only thing Trevor mentioned after interviewing him was his drug addiction, but even then, Trevor insisted he'd kicked the habit. He did tell Trevor he'd had some tests done recently during a medical for a job. Could this test have been carried out for any other purpose?'

'Such as?' Patrick examined the marks one last time.

'To find out if he was an addict?'

'Wrong test. Blood or urine would determine drug type and quantity.'

'The bodies that were brought in from the motorway,' Peter asked quickly. 'Were there any organs missing from those?'

'None. And I would have noticed. The heads and hands were gone, of course, but then you already know about those.'

'Could any part of the heads or hands be used in transplant operations?' Peter persisted.

'Possibly the cornea of the eye,' Daisy replied. She'd only just grasped the significance of Peter's line of questioning. 'Nothing else in the head has any use at all,' she couldn't resist adding. 'Brain transplants, Sergeant Collins, are still in the realms of fiction.'

'What I still can't understand is why tissue-type a junkie?' Patrick interposed. 'Drugs damage the usual organs used in transplants. Kidneys, liver . . .'

'Robin Dart's medical examination apparently came to an abrupt end once the doctor discovered he was an addict. Or at least that's what he told Trevor. Could you find out if he was suffering from organ failure of any kind?'

'I could if everyone left me in peace for five minutes,' Patrick agreed.

Peter took the hint. 'One last question. What do you need to carry out a tissue-typing test?'

'Such as?' Daisy enquired.

'Place, equipment. Do you need a laboratory? A hospital?'

'You need clean facilities and a small instrument to pick up a layer of skin.' Patrick laid down Robin's arm, and signalled to Paul to take over. 'The test itself can be carried out almost anywhere. The street, if you want to. Pathological side needs a reasonably-equipped laboratory, of course. But if you take your line of thought one step further, the organs used in transplants are a very dicey commodity indeed. They should be removed in sterile theatre conditions. Treated very carefully until they're placed in the recipient in an operating theatre. This is the only hospital for fifty miles capable of meeting those conditions. If anyone's carrying out illicit, undocumented transplants, it's not in this town.'

'But they could be done outside the town.' Peter's mind worked overtime. The Holbourne and Sherringham Clinic? Had Richard Sherringham built an operating theatre within his clinic capable of meeting the criteria necessary to carry out transplants? It could be done, given sufficient money. And Sherringham had money, connections and easy access to the rich who would be only too willing to pay, and pay handsomely, for an opportunity to improve their health, or extend their lives. There was a shortage of donor organs – the media were constantly appealing for more people to carry donor cards. Where better to find a supply of organs than among the homeless drifters who had no one to care whether they lived, died, or moved to the next town? But where in hell did that tie in with the bodies on the motorway, Tim Sherringham's disappearance, or someone giving the brother of one of the victims a deadly fix? That's if he was given it and didn't do it himself.

Had any down-and-outs really gone missing? Sam

had said it was impossible to put a figure on the homeless in this town or any other. They come, they go,
they drift. No one kept any records apart from the
social services, and they'd be only too happy to close
down a claim, which could be very convenient if what
he was thinking was even remotely close to the truth.

'I've got to get back to the station.' He turned to
Daisy. 'Is it all right for Trevor to stay here until
tomorrow?'

'In view of the way you treated him, I'd say he needs
at least one more overnight stay, if not more.'

The mortuary fell strangely silent after Peter had
left. Alan opened the door for Daisy, then looked back
at Patrick. 'You'll let us know . . .'

'The minute, God forbid, anything remotely resembling Tim Sherringham comes in. I promise you.'

The phone shrieked sharply, slicing into their conversation.

'Get that for me, will you, Paul?' Patrick clipped to
his coat the microphone and tape recorder he used to
dictate his post mortem notes. 'And if it's someone
asking us to accept a new client, we can't keep up with
what we've got.'

'Come in.'_

'You wanted to see me, Bill?'

'I did.' Bill motioned Peter into the only uncluttered
chair in his tiny office. 'How's Trevor?'

'Mashed about. Cut, bruised, nursing a badly-
broken arm, but he'll live.'

'Glad to hear it. Is he in hospital?'

'Yes.'

'For a broken arm?'

'Daisy Sherringham arranged his admission, after
she patched him up. I thought it best to go along with
the idea. Between his arm and the battered state of the
rest of him, he's not fit for anything useful.'

'I waylaid the tape you made.' Bill pulled a mini-cassette out of his dictaphone. 'Have you telephoned the pathologist yet to find out if Robin Dart was suffering from organ failure?'

'This afternoon. And the answer's no. He wasn't suffering from organ failure. And there wasn't much in the way of serious organ damage as a result of drug abuse. If he hadn't taken that last poisoned fix he could have lived to a ripe and satisfactory old age.'

'Poisoned?'

'Pathologist found enough cyanide in him to kill seven men.'

'That doesn't sound like a refined killer to me. That sounds like the work of a mob. Check with London. See if they've got any records of a Robin Dart working as a pusher or a carrier for anyone.'

'Will do.'

'Had some interesting visitors earlier.' Bill swung his feet up on the desk.

Peter said nothing, he knew Bill would tell him everything in his own good time.

'Daisy and Richard Sherringham came in with Judy Osbourne. Appears the man is beginning to show signs of cracking.'

'Richard Sherringham?'

Bill nodded. 'He admitted that he's had a ransom demand for his brother,' Bill crowed with a told-you-so grin on his face. 'Telephone call to the clinic two days ago, which is why we didn't pick it up.'

'Was it for much?'

'By my standards, a bloody fortune. By Richard Sherringham's standards I suppose it could have been far more.'

'And he paid up?'

'He paid up. In used notes, wrapped in brown paper. He jammed it into the wire under the pier at three this morning.'

'Then he walked away?'

'He did.'

'Bloody idiot. Was there a second call?'

'That's why he's cracking. It never came.'

'We could have told him as much. What made him come to us now?'

'Daisy Sherringham wormed it out of him tonight. I told you, he's very close to the edge.'

'Didn't you ask him what he was playing at? If there was a ransom demand he should have come to us.'

'Usual story. "You go to the police and you'll never see your brother alive again." '

'If Tim Sherringham's still alive, I'm a monkey's uncle. All he's succeeded in doing is pouring a pile of money down the drain. The ransom gone?'

'Did you doubt it? I've put men inside and outside the Sherringham house. Arranged taps on the clinic's phones, and put men into the clinic and the Sherringham apartment, but if you want my opinion, it's a bit like shutting the stable door after the proverbial. I've also organized another search of the area around the pier for tomorrow, but I don't expect to find anything.'

'The bloody pier again. We really went over it today, Bill. There was nothing. I swear it. Bloody nothing. Something doesn't smell quite right here.'

'Kidnapping never does.'

'I think we should search the Sherringham clinic. Thoroughly, and as soon as possible.'

'What for?'

'If you listened to my tape, you know about the junkie with the skin test.'

'You want to search Sherringham's clinic because a dead junkie has a skin test mark on his arm?'

'That's right.'

'There's no way anyone will issue a warrant for the Sherringham clinic on that evidence.'

311

'But . . .'

'Sherringham's clean, and his clinic's clean. The London boys have checked it out,' Bill insisted firmly.

'And because they say they've checked the place out, we have to back off.'

'You're not listening. Perhaps I should spell it out for you. At this very moment the Holbourne and Sherringham Clinic is crammed to the eaves with VIPs. They're there because they're sick. All of them are waiting for Sherringham, or some other specialist, to operate. The last thing those very important people want, or we want,' he frowned at Peter, 'is for anyone at the clinic to get upset by us clumping through the place with our hobnailed boots. People who are ill, especially *important* people, need rest, peace and quiet.'

'In other words, we've been nobbled by the brass,' Peter commented tartly, his temper rising.

'Not quite, Collins.' Bill's temper threatened to outdistance Peter's. 'What the London boys think, and . . .' He struck a match, and lit his pipe, sucking hard and puffing clouds of brown smoke into the room. '. . . I agree with them, is that some envious bastard, or what's more likely, bastards, wanted a slice of what Sherringham's got. They laid their hands on Tim Sherringham, got some information out of him that only the family knew, or at least enough information to convince Richard Sherringham they were holding him. Then they made a few phone calls either before or after they killed him.'

'And the bodies on the motorway?'

'Witnesses, or accomplices they wanted to silence.'

'And the Dart girl? The clown that attacked Trevor and Daisy Sherringham last night?'

'Whoever attacked Trevor last night kidnapped Tim Sherringham. The Dart girl could have been part of it, or what's more likely, she simply saw something she shouldn't have. We know that she went with Sherringham to Jubilee Street. We also know some of the characters who hang around down there. As I've been saying all along, Sherringham and the girl probably talked to the wrong people. Anyone could have seen him give Sam that cheque. Known who he was, or whose brother he was. As the saying goes, people with nothing have nothing to lose. Someone got greedy and dreamed up the kidnapping idea.'

'Someone from Jubilee Street?'

'Think about it. If Amanda went to Jubilee Street to look for her brother on the night she disappeared, she would have had to pass the marina. She'd have recognized Sherringham. The kidnappers could have been hiding him on his boat in the marina. Perhaps she passed by and . . .'

'I don't buy it. I . . .'

'Will you let me finish one bloody sentence!' Bill shouted. 'I didn't say it happened that way. Only that it could have. It's late, I'm tired, and I'm running out of theories. We'll start on this again tomorrow morning. Seven sharp. I'll expect you at the pier.'

'And in the meantime we have a lunatic clown running loose around the marina?'

'I've six men patrolling down there right now. Six men I've laid off normal duties. If the good citizens of this town knew just how thin the blue line was spread tonight, they wouldn't sleep. Which reminds me. Where's Harries? Dossing in Jubilee Street?'

'I don't know. He failed to make his five-thirty contact.' Peter looked at his watch. 'It's coming up to eleven. I told him to check in with Ben Gummer before closing time if he couldn't make the tobacconist's.'

'Let me know if he's stumbled across anything.'

'Will do.' Peter reluctantly moved out of his chair. Every muscle in his body ached. It had been a long day. Too long.

'Collins?'

'Yes?'

'It's not the same, is it?'

'What's not the same?' Peter demanded irritably.

'Quarrelling without Trevor around to act as peacemaker.'

Peter relaxed his facial muscles into a semblance of a smile. 'I suppose it isn't.'

'Let me know about Harries.'

'Will do.'

Chapter Twelve

Restless thoughts worming through his mind like maggots in meat, Peter left Bill's room. He walked across the passage into the incident room. Looking neither left nor right, he headed for the door directly opposite. Half-way down the longest corridor in the station, he came to a small room scarcely bigger than a cupboard. A uniformed girl, slim, brown-haired, attractive enough in a youthful sort of way, sat at a desk surrounded on all sides by a computer and computer peripherals.

'Want to get yourself a cuppa, Constable?' Peter asked.

'That's kind of you, sir.' She smiled at Peter. When she'd been posted to the station everyone had tried to warn her that Peter Collins was a hard, unforgiving bastard, but he'd never been anything other than cool and businesslike in his dealings with her. His attitude, coming after the lewd suggestions she'd received from some of the men at the station, had been more than welcome.

'Run along then. I'll mind the shop for you.'

'Shall I bring one back for you, sir?' she asked shyly.

'Yes, thanks.'

As soon as she'd left, he sat in her chair and began to punch buttons. A thin-line map of the town appeared on the screen before him. He carried on punching. With a tardiness that irritated, dots slowly appeared like a neon rash. They disfigured only three areas of the town. He checked, then double-checked both the computer and the notebooks on the desk. Once he was certain he'd left no margin for error, he pressed the print button. He tore off the sheet the moment it spewed out of the printer. Then he began the laborious series of movements and countermovements necessary to offload and secure the programme he'd been working on.

'Black, no sugar, sir?' Bright, cheerful, the girl reappeared at his elbow.

'Just the ticket.' Peter folded the print-out deftly into his pocket. 'Thanks. Constable Merchant, isn't it?' he asked, turning the swivel chair to take the coffee from her.

'Yes, sir, Sarah Merchant.'

'Do you trust me, Sarah?' She found it an odd question. If it had come from anyone other than Sergeant Collins she would have taken it as a prelude to heavy suggestions of after-shift rides, and parked cars in laybys. But there was no seduction or lechery hidden in Peter Collins' cold, calculating eyes.

'I meant professionally,' he added, as if he'd read her thoughts.

'Of course.' She stammered in embarrassment, not thinking too hard about what she was saying.

'I'd rather you didn't show anyone the trace programme on the computer, not for the moment anyway. I've put a security coding on it. The back-up banks as well,' he informed her, in case she doubted his ability. 'There's no easily accessible record left of the trace on Harries, or of any checks you made on his progress. In short, according to the open programmes on this computer, Harries never went undercover.'

'Sir . . .'

'Please,' he interrupted, putting his coffee down. 'Don't ask me for an explanation. I'm not even sure I understand what's going on myself. You'll have to take my word that it's important. If you don't – ' he looked at her earnestly ' – you could find yourself in trouble.

316

Believe me, what I'm asking you to do is for your own good.'

'Yes, sir.' She sounded unconvinced.

'Sarah?'

'Sir.'

'No matter who asks you, you don't know anything about this conversation, or the trace.'

'But, sir, you're asking me to lie,' she protested.

'All I'm asking you to do is some forgetting. And I'm not exaggerating when I say it might save your life.'

There was a sinister undercurrent in Peter's voice that made her realize how serious he was. She considered for a moment. She'd never heard anyone in the station knock either Sergeants Collins or Joseph. And it wasn't just because of Collins' reputation as a hard man. As Stephen Harries had once told her, 'Mulcahy, Collins and Joseph are on the level.' She had to look back only as far as her previous posting to remember bent coppers and what they could do to a force. Rumours had abounded there, and most of them had concerned the drug squad. Complicity, blackmail, policemen working hand in hand with pushers, taking cuts, on the make – but she'd never picked up a whisper of it here. And then again, this case wasn't even drug squad business. It was linked to the motorway murder enquiry, though she'd never figured out how Stephen Harries going undercover into Jubilee Street fitted in with the rest of the facts. The whole thing was odd. Peculiar.

'I'm straight, Constable Merchant,' Peter said quietly. 'I realize I'm asking you to stake your career on this. But I am straight.'

When she looked at him, he didn't seem at all like the pushy, cocksure man who usually strutted around the station. He looked tired, exhausted, as if he of all people had been bested by circumstances.

317

'I'll do it, sir.' She struggled to subdue her final remnants of reluctance.

'Good girl.' He pulled himself out of the chair.

'Just one thing, sir?' she asked timorously as he was half-way out of the door. 'Stephen . . . Constable Harries.' There was a tremor in her voice, slight but definite. 'He is all right, isn't he?'

So that was it. He should have twigged earlier. Both young, keen, ambitiously eager to please.

'He's fine, Constable Merchant. I'm going out to pick him up now.' She blushed crimson. 'You'll see him tomorrow,' he reassured her as he closed the door.

Bill Mulcahy carefully scanned the computer print-out Peter had handed him.

'There's no mistaking the location?'

'No.' Peter paced uneasily to the window. 'What do you say to a warrant now?'

'It'll take time.'

'We haven't any.' He left the window and walked back to Bill's desk. Flattening the print-out on the only clear corner of the surface, he sketched out the main landmarks with his forefinger. 'The sea, the headland, the town centre. The girl was very thorough with her checks, bless her. She placed Harries every quarter of an hour to the second. As you can see, the markers are clocked, small print, but legible. The first cluster of markers, from eleven forty-five to one o'clock are in the day-centre.'

'The next lot are in Balaclava Street,' Bill continued thoughtfully. 'As far as I can make out, within the outline of the Grand Hotel.'

'Now that's a name to conjure with.'

'What hotel did that junkie have his medical in?'

'Trevor said it was the Grand.'

'Harries was there until four forty-five,' Bill continued, preoccupied with reading the print-out. 'At five he was on the road that leads out to the headland, and the final cluster, which finishes at six o'clock, are inside the perimeter fence of the Holbourne and Sherringham Clinic. Why on earth would he go there?'

'Go, or was taken?' Peter rubbed the area between his eyes. He'd been up too long, hadn't had enough sleep for days. Just one more push. 'Transplants? Richard Sherringham specializes in treating rich, important people. If they should need a transplant and there's no organ available through the usual channels, who better to look to for supply than a healthy down-and-out whose life isn't worth a great deal.'

'I'd rather go for transmitter failure,' Bill observed caustically.

'Well, what's for sure is that Harries didn't keep the arranged rendezvous. That means he was either on to something, or he couldn't meet me because something or someone stopped him. And the last place he was at was here.' Peter slammed his finger down on the sketched outline of a building close to the clinic.

'You're sure monitoring continued?'

'I double-checked on that before I security-coded the programme. The monitoring continued routinely every fifteen minutes until eleven o'clock.'

'Then either the transmitter failed, or he moved out of the clinic,' Bill commented.

'That transmitter has a fifty-mile radius. Would you mind telling me how Harries could have moved fifty miles in fifteen minutes?'

'Then it has to be transmitter failure.'

'We've never had one pack up on us before.'

'First time for everything. At the risk of sounding foolish, have you tried the obvious, like phoning the hostel in Jubilee Street?'

'There and the White Hart. He hasn't been seen in either. I sent him undercover to investigate a disappearance. Now he's disappeared himself.'

'I sent him.'

'Does it make any difference?'

'I'm the Super, you're the Sergeant. That makes a difference.'

'We've got to go in and get him.'

'I'll get a warrant first thing in the morning.'

'That could be too late.'

'Go and see Trevor now,' Bill ordered decisively. 'Double-check if the hotel the junkie had his medical in was the Grand.'

'If it was?'

'We'll visit Sherringham tonight. Find out exactly what's in this building.' Bill slammed his finger down on the computer print-out. 'And ask his permission to search it.'

'He could refuse.'

'He'd better not.' Bill looked up from the map. 'Phone me from the hospital.'

'I'm on my way.'

Daisy laid her suitcase down on the bed Judy had made up a short time before. She snapped open the locks, and lifted out the pair of slacks that lay on top. Taking a hanger from the wardrobe, she folded them over the bar and hung them up. She tried not to notice the bleak ugliness of the room. The cheap pine-veneer, utilitarian theme of the hospital flat's living-room had been carried into the single bedroom. Strange how she'd never noticed or resented the decor, or rather lack of it, in the staff quarters when she'd visited Judy. But now . . . now . . . She clutched at the blouse she'd taken out of the case, screwing its fabric into a creased ball.

If only she could be sure she was doing the right thing. She was trying to cope with her grief by emulating Judy's independence. But what worked for Judy might not work for her. Judy'd always been cool, self-contained, self-sufficient. She never had. She'd allowed

Tim to see from the outset of their relationship just how much she'd needed him. She'd known, even then, that she needed love and other people. Judy could take relationships with people, or leave them. But she needed Tim.

Tim! What if he returned to their flat? He'd find it empty, he wouldn't know where to look for her. But he was dead! She believed it, didn't she? She kept telling everyone he was dead. Better dead than the unknown.

Shivering, still clutching the blouse, she left the bedroom and walked into the living-room. The television screen stared blankly back at her. Needing companionship, she switched the set on. A heap of bodies, limbs contorted into unnatural positions by death, came bleakly into view. An unnervingly quiet voice recounted a grim catalogue of horrors being perpetrated in the name of freedom somewhere in Latin America. She switched the set off. Silence was better.

She sank down into a chair, fighting her instinct to run along the corridor to Judy's flat. She'd barely been alone for an hour. Footsteps resounded along the corridor. Dry fear crept into her throat. Were the walls that thin? She'd never heard footsteps when she'd been in Judy's flat. She dropped the blouse and gripped the arms of her chair, fighting off a panic attack. The noise moved inexorably closer, then ceased abruptly outside her door. She sat rigid, nerves taut, senses strained until even the blood rushing in her veins became a thundering roar.

The doorbell pealed. She didn't move. No one except Judy knew where she was, and Judy would have called out her name, not rung the bell.

'Daisy.' A knocking – a male voice she recognized. 'Daisy!'

'Richard?' She walked unsteadily to the door and opened it.

'Can I come in?' He was wearing a dark grey suit,

clean white shirt and black and grey tie. Outwardly, at least, the authoritative Richard she was used to.

'Please do.' She opened the door wider, and he entered. He looked at the room and she saw he missed nothing. The discoloured tiles above the sink, the corners of the furniture where the veneer was cracking and splitting, the stains on the carpet.

'I couldn't live alone in the flat,' she explained nervously. 'Not without Tim. But I need to work. I thought moving in here would be a good compromise. Just for a while.'

'And when Tim comes back?'

'He might not,' she said bitterly. 'We have to face up to it, Richard, we may never . . .'

'He'll be back. I've paid the ransom. They have no reason to kill him.'

She went to the small kitchen area and filled the kettle. She would have liked to have argued with Richard. Told him that Tim wasn't coming back. That if 'they' existed, 'they' could be recognized by Tim, and that gave them more reason to kill him than release him. But she heard desperation in Richard's voice. He needed to cling to the hope of Tim's return. And she envied him that hope too much to destroy it.

'I want you to come home with me. If you won't think of yourself, think of Joanna. She needs you. Now, more than ever. Daisy, she's hurt . . .'

'She's not any worse?' she asked anxiously.

'No, but it would be better for all of us if we were together. Tim wouldn't want you to stay in this place by yourself. He'd want you to be with us. When he comes back he'll need all the help we can give him.'

'I . . .'

'Daisy, it's what Tim would want you to do.'

He walked over to her, folded her into his arms, and she clung to him out of loneliness, out of fear. As a child, Tim had adored Richard. As a man, he'd modelled himself on his older brother more than he realized. Even in small ways, like using the same brand of after-shave. And Richard's voice was so like Tim's.

'I'll help you to pack. You can drive home with me now. Daisy, Tim's coming back. I can feel it. He's close to me . . . he'll be back.'

'You really believe that?'

'I really do.' His grip on her shoulders intensified. 'Why torture yourself by living alone here, Daisy? We need your support as much as you need ours.'

'You need me?' She looked up into his eyes. Saw they were moist.

'You're family, Daisy. Of course we need you.'

'I'll pack my things and leave a note for Judy.' She stepped back, reluctant to leave the warmth and strength of his arms, even for a little while. Richard was right. It was what Tim would have wanted.

'You're sure Robin Dart said the Grand?'

'How many times do I have to tell you he did?' Trevor replied irritably. 'If you told me something that made sense for a change, perhaps I could help.'

'If I knew what made sense I wouldn't be here.' Peter stretched out his legs and kicked the foot of the bed.

'That damn well hurt.'

'Sorry.' Peter left the side of the bed and picked up Trevor's temperature chart. He flicked absently through it. 'Harries has disappeared.'

'From Jubilee Street?' A frown appeared on Trevor's white face.

'It doesn't look like he got that far.' Peter fumbled in his pocket for the computer print-out. He handed it to Trevor. 'I sent Harries out this morning with a brief to hang round the day-centre, sleep in Jubilee Street and report back if he saw Andy. I told him it would be better still if he managed to talk Andy into giving him a guided tour of the pier, always providing, of course, that that part of our information isn't sheer fiction. He had a transmitter in the heel of his left shoe. It's just as well. He didn't keep the rendezvous I'd arranged for this afternoon.'

'He went from the day-centre to Balaclava Street.' Trevor looked up. 'The Grand?'

'Then the headland road and the Holbourne and Sherringham Clinic. Or to be more precise, this building inside the grounds.'

'And you remembered the mark on Robin Dart's arm, and came up with the idea that Harries' disappearance has something to do with using live bodies for transplants?'

'I agree the idea's monstrous. But look at the evidence. Robin Dart had a tissue-typing mark from the same medical as another drifter who's since disappeared.'

'You can't be sure of that. And what about Tim Sherringham?' Trevor looked across at Peter. 'Where does he fit into your theory? He wasn't a drifter. He never dossed in Jubilee Street.'

'No, but he went to Jubilee Street with Amanda to look for Robin Dart. He poked around. Asked questions. Probably upset people. Doesn't it begin to make sense?' Peter asked impatiently. 'If he suspected a connection between the clinic and the disappearance of Robin Dart, he wouldn't have gone around broadcasting the fact. God alone knows what he intended to do, but even if he found positive, definitive proof, his brother, his own brother for Christ's sake, runs the clinic.'

'You're building all this on the basis of one small mark on a junkie's arm?'

'Amanda Dart, Robin Dart, Tim Sherringham – all dead or,' Peter picked up the map from Trevor's bed, 'missing.'

324

'And now Harries,' Trevor murmured anxiously. A thought crossed his mind. 'You're not thinking of going into the clinic to look for him?'

'Yes.'

'You'll never get a warrant.'

'Bill's going to try tomorrow morning. But I briefed Harries. I sent him undercover. It's my responsibility to get him out of whatever mess he's in, and by the look of it, I haven't much time.'

'You do realize that if your suspicions are correct, Harries could already be dead.'

'The trace was still operational at six this evening.'

'That doesn't mean Harries was alive at six.'

'No, but his shoe was somewhere in that clinic at six. And I intend to find it.'

'You don't know your way round the place.'

'Daisy Sherringham does.'

'You can't ask her!'

'Why not? She's involved. Her old man's disappearance started all this.'

'Peter . . .'

'Don't worry, I won't do anything until tomorrow morning.'

'The hell you won't. I know you.'

A plump, officious nurse bustled into the room. 'Visitors at this time of night,' she clucked disapprovingly. 'Really! Mr Joseph needs rest.' She picked up Trevor's wrist from the bed. 'He's very tired, you know.'

'I'll leave you in capable hands.' Peter grinned sardonically from the doorway at Trevor.

'You won't make a move until tomorrow?'

'Rest, Mr Joseph, doesn't include talking.'

'Sergeant Joseph,' Trevor mumbled as she pushed a thermometer into his mouth.

'Scout's honour.' Peter held up two fingers behind the nurse's back.

'You were never a scout!' Trevor shouted. The thermometer fell on to the bed.

'Thermometer, *Sergeant* Joseph.' The nurse shook it, and pushed it back under Trevor's tongue.

'If I were you, I'd give him a sleeping pill,' Peter whispered to the nurse as he retreated out of the door.

Peter left the hospital building and walked the short distance to the block that housed the staff quarters. He showed his police identification to the doorman and asked for Dr Osbourne's flat. The doorman pointed to the lift. 'Fifth floor,' he mumbled, before returning to his *Playboy*.

The lights were dimmed on the fifth floor when Peter stepped out of the lift. He looked up and down the corridor, debating which way to go. Then he turned left, scanning the nameplates as he walked along. Judy Osbourne's name was on the last door he looked at, facing down the corridor. He stood for a moment and listened. All was silent. He looked at his watch, twelve-thirty, hardly the time to be making a social call.

He rang the bell. It echoed disconcertingly loudly back at him. He waited. Eventually a muffled voice called from behind the door, demanding to know who was there.

'Sergeant Collins. Is Dr Sherringham with you?'

The door opened a crack, and a tousled blonde head peered at him. 'No. And before you ask, I'm not telling you where she is, unless you've found Tim.'

'I'm sorry, I've no news about Tim Sherringham.'

'Then good night. Unlike policemen, the rest of humanity, myself included, needs sleep.'

'Please, I need a minute of your time. I wouldn't be here unless it was very important.'

'How important is important?'

'Life and death sounds melodramatic.'

326

She opened the door a little wider, and looked at him. 'You're serious, aren't you?'

'Please. I need a few minutes.'

She shut the door, released the chain, and ushered him in. 'I never thought I'd hear you say that.'

'What?' He stepped into the room, closing the door behind him.

'Please.' She tightened the belt on her velour dressing gown as she walked over to the settee.

'I need to speak to Daisy urgently.'

'About what?'

'The Sherringham clinic.'

'The clinic? For God's sake. Can't you wait for Richard to give you one of his guided tours?'

'He gives tours?'

'To anyone who's interested enough to ask for one.'

'You've been?'

'Along with the entire staff of this place. He's always trying to recruit people, good people, that is, from the Health Service.'

'Then perhaps you can help me.' He pulled the print-out out of his pocket. 'If this is the clinic, what's this here?' He pointed to the outline of the building Harries' transmitter had been in.

Judy squinted sideways at the paper. 'An annexe?'

'Very clever. I guessed that much.'

'I think it used to be the staff quarters of the old clinic. When Richard built the new place, he used the old Victorian clinic to house the staff.'

'Then no one uses this for anything?'

'I seem to remember a delivery van outside the place when I was there. Possibly it's used for storage. Or . . .'

'Or?'

'Joanna might use part of that building to house her research.'

'Joanna Sherringham does research?'

'Has done for years. Into cosmetics. Skin reaction,

that sort of thing. Very lucrative, from what I understand.'

'Thank you, thank you very much indeed.'

'What have I done?'

'A great deal.' He opened the door. 'Sorry to have disturbed you.'

'Sorry and please all in one night. Sergeant Collins, you're becoming almost human.'

Peter didn't attempt to contact Bill. That would have taken time, and all he could think of was that last minute clock on the computer print-out. Its hands stuck at six o'clock. The digital clock in his car read midnight. It had been six hours since the transmitter in Harries' shoe had sent out its last signal. Anything could have happened in that time. If he phoned Bill it would take another half-hour for them both to drive to the Sherringham mansion, and even then Sherringham could come up with some excuse or other that would prevent them from searching the clinic until Bill got a warrant. He wasn't prepared to risk delaying the search until morning.

He slammed the car into third gear and overtook a van as it left the entrance to the hospital. The headland road would be clear at this time of night. Ten minutes and he'd be at the clinic.

'I haven't had any calls from the main office.'

'You wouldn't have.' Peter flicked his foot impatiently on the accelerator of his stationary car, revving the engine. 'I told you. The call came in from outside. Someone driving on the headland road saw a prowler within the perimeter of your fence.'

The young security guard removed his cap and scratched his head. Peter took advantage of his indecision.

'Have you any dog patrols loose in the grounds?'

'There's only me, sir,' the guard muttered shamefaced, awed by the police identification Peter pushed under his nose. 'And I shouldn't rightly leave the gate.'

'If you can't leave your post, I suppose I'll have to check out the call for you.'

'Would you like me to call the clinic, sir? There might be someone there who could help you.' The guard fingered his truncheon nervously. Peter'd seen the type before. Nineteen, twenty, wearing the muscles it had taken months, if not years of work-outs to achieve. He had the physique of Mr Universe and brains that wouldn't get him through the police entrance examination. There were hundreds just like him in security guard uniform everywhere. All of them dreaming of the day they'd be able to join the force.

'The report said one prowler. Not an army. Lift the barrier so I can get this car off the road, and I'll take a look around.'

'Yes, sir.' The guard leaped into his cabin and pressed the switch. 'Call me if you need any help, Sergeant,' he shouted as Peter drove through the gates.

Peter drove carefully along the drive until he was out of sight of the guard post, then he switched off his car headlights. Driving on sidelights, he continued slowly along the road that his study of the computer print-out told him led to the old staff quarters. Then, as he travelled around a bend in the drive, he saw it. A gaunt, gothic building with decorative turrets and pointed slate-tiled roofs that shone silver in the moonlight. Pulling the hood of his anorak over his head, he left his car in the shadows at the side of the house and approached the front door, checking his pockets as he walked. Torch, the bunch of skeleton keys that went with him everywhere (much to Bill's annoyance), hacksaw blade, wire cutters – nothing that could be used as a weapon. He'd just have to be a damned sight more careful than Trevor'd been on Daisy's boat.

Instead of the archaic wooden door he expected, he

found steel sheets, bolted, barred and padlocked. He walked around the building. It was the same with the windows, only the sheets that covered the windows had no locks. They were bolted on the inside. Had these precautions been taken because the building housed medical stores, or for a more sinister reason? Then, at the back of the building, he found what he wanted. A pair of metal doors sunk at ground level. An old coal chute.

He pulled out his torch. Shielding its beam with his hands, he studied the chain and padlock that had been twisted round the door handles. He reached for the hacksaw blade. Twenty minutes later he heaved open the doors and slid cautiously down into the darkness.

He was sick, dizzy from anticipation and lack of sleep. He didn't know what to expect. Bodies everywhere? Racks of boxed organs, like prizes waiting for suitable meritorious recipients? He shone his torch into the pitch-darkness. Dust, cobwebs, broken wooden chairs, steel bedsteads rusted through with age and damp. Nothing more. His tense nerve endings relaxed. Then, after relief, came a consciousness of lack of time. Of Harries!

He sought for and found the staircase that led upwards. A closed door faced the top step. It was locked. He stepped back and rammed into it with the full weight of his shoulder. It shuddered from the impact, but failed to give. He shone his torch around the edge. Close-fitting, steel-lined, no keyhole. He visualized the bolts on the other side of the door. This wasn't his way into the house.

He walked back down the stairs and shone his torch beam into the damp darkness. Rooms led into one another, rotting frames that no longer held doors, only broken hinges, marked the boundaries of what he guessed had once been the servants' quarters. Then he found a room, larger than the rest, less cluttered with rubbish. In the centre of the wall opposite him was a fireplace. An enormous Victorian effort that could easily have held a range large enough to roast an ox, and still have had room to spare. He walked over to it and shone his torch upwards. An old rusted meat hook hung down close to his head. He grabbed it and pulled. It was strong enough to give him the support he needed to haul himself up, and he began to climb.

Ten minutes later, he wished he hadn't. The chimney, wide at first, soon narrowed. He propelled himself upwards using his elbows and his feet, but soon found himself well and truly stuck. He struggled to gain a grip on the smooth brickwork. His feet slid free, while his arms remained jammed, the torch clamped in his hand a scant few inches from his face. He remembered something from his caving days. Something his instructor had said about muscles swelling to pack a space. The only thing to do was remain still and wait for his muscles to contract.

He forced the beginnings of panic from his mind, and thought of Harries. The idiot was probably safe at home right now. Bedding the prim Sarah Merchant. He wouldn't be the first undercover cop to crawl back to normality once night fell. Damned fool! But then, could he really blame Harries? A day spent among the smells and lice of the day-centre dragged like an eternity. To a newcomer alone on undercover for the first time it would seem even worse. How many times had he and Trevor sneaked off from a hard, verminous day in Jubilee Street to a cheap hotel that could provide them with hot and cold running water and room service?

And if Harries was safe and sound, and he was caught? What then? How in hell's name could he explain what he was doing here? Stuck in the chimney of an old building used to store medical supplies for a reputable private clinic.

Dear God, he deserved everything Richard Sherringham would throw at him. Trevor was right. One
mark on a dead junkie's arm and he'd flipped his lid.

Daisy paced the floor of the room nervously. She
wanted to walk until she was too weary to place one
foot in front of the other. She was trying to drive herself
into a sleep too deep for nightmares, too deep for headless bodies to creep into her subconscious, too deep for
thoughts of Tim to rise up and tear at her raw emotions
until they bled.

A soft cry disturbed her. Joanna! Or Richard?
Joanna was in pain – she at least had a right to cry
out – but all of them were on edge. Richard's expect-
ancy had heightened her sense of foreboding. Perhaps
Tim would be found, very soon, as Richard had said,
but not in the way he wanted.

She put her hands over her ears in an attempt to
shut out the sounds of the house. She needed to think,
to concentrate. She had tried to talk to Joanna when
she had arrived at the house earlier with Richard, she
had even offered to stay with her sister-in-law. But
Joanna had retreated into her customary reserve, shutting everyone, even her own husband, out. And Daisy
was too weary, too selfish to be concerned for Joanna
or Richard any more. He had lied when he had told
her they needed her. No one needed her. Not any more.

She resumed her pacing, switching on the radio as
she passed the bedside-table. Soft music filled the air,
drowning out all other sounds. Tchaikovsky. How Tim
had loved Tchaikovsky! He'd played it in the flat, loud
enough to be heard in the shower. Once the retired
Major from the flat below had banged on the
ceiling . . .

'Daisy?' Richard tapped on the door.

'Come in.'

'I heard you walking up and down. I've just given

Joanna something to make her sleep. I could do the same for you.'

'And tomorrow when I can't sleep, you'll increase the dosage?' She switched off the radio.

'There's nothing wrong with using a temporary crutch to see you through a bad time.' He sat on the window seat and looked out over the moonlit garden. 'In time the pain gets less, more bearable. You lower the dosage gradually, then one night you suddenly find you don't need help any more.'

'Was that what it was like for you when your father died?' she asked intuitively.

'Yes.'

'And Tim. Did he do the same?'

'Tim was a child at the time. He didn't understand death. Its bloody awful finality.'

'But he loved your father.'

'Yes, he loved him. We both did.' Richard turned to face her. 'Do you want to sleep?' he asked quietly.

It would be so easy to hand over all responsibility to him. Even the responsibility for caring for her own body. She switched the radio back on.

'Yes. Thank you, Richard.'

Peter had managed to free his right arm. He thrust it high above his head, hoping to make himself slim enough to slip back down the chimney, then his hand closed over the edge of an inner wall. The back wall of the fireplace on the floor above? He felt around the area carefully with his fingertips. He was right. The chimney widened above him. One more push and he'd be above the fireplace on the next floor. He kicked out wildly with his feet and pushed hard against the wall with all the strength he could muster. He moved slowly upwards, gripping the lip of the wall with both hands.

Finally, after a hard and painful struggle, he stood upright, his feet resting where his hands had been, in the larger, communal chimney. There was room to move. He took off his anorak and flung it down between the inner wall and where he guessed the fireplace to be. It landed with a soft thud. He was right. He was above the next floor. He lowered himself downwards. It was a tight squeeze. His foot, instead of encountering the empty space he'd hoped for, hit something solid. He lashed out in frustration. There was a splintering, tearing noise and he rolled forwards through a flimsy hardboard partition into unrelieved blackness.

Cursing the pain in his knees and elbows, he felt for his torch. A faint glimmer finally led him to where it had fallen, beam downwards. He picked it up and shone it over himself. Great clumps of filthy soot hung from his clothes, his shirt was ripped and splashed with blood. He'd scraped the skin from his hands and arms, and by the feel of it, his knees too. He looked down. His trousers had fared no better than his shirt. Trembling from shock and the cold, he slipped his anorak back on and shone his torch around the room.

Racks of medical records towered around him. Shelves thick with dust held file after damp, decaying file. He shone his torch on the floor. The dust lay thick there, too. The room hadn't been opened in years. He walked down the aisle closest to him, looking for a door that would lead into the rest of the house. He walked along a wall shelved with yet more files, turned a corner, then another, only to find himself back at the fireplace. He carried on, and at last found the door he'd been searching for. Locked. But this time it was an ordinary wooden door, without a steel sheath wrapped around it.

He tried the doorknob. It failed to move. He studied the lock. An ordinary, old-fashioned household lock, which would be easy to pick. He felt for his skeleton keys. A couple of minutes later he was in the outside corridor. He closed the door softly behind him and begàn his search.

He turned his keys in lock after lock. Inspected rooms filled with more current medical records, rooms filled with discarded furniture, rooms filled with stacking chairs, candles and oil lamps. He opened door after door, only to be met with the same disappointingly utility contents. Disposable pressed cardboard bed-pans, incontinence pads, paper sheets . . . Finally, having exhausted the ground floor, he tried the first.

Unlike the rooms on the ground floor, they were unlocked and empty. Dust, cobwebs, torn linoleum, rolls of rotting carpet. No laboratories. No organs wait-ing for transplant operations. No dead bodies. He walked back downstairs, and sat on the bottom stair. He'd broken the law, skinned his knees and arms, stuck himself in a chimney, and all for bloody nothing!

He looked up, seeking the door that led down to the cellar. If he could open it from this side he would, and to hell with being found out. Anything had to be better than climbing back into that chimney.

Ahead of him were a set of double doors. A heavy black and red sign warned:

NO UNAUTHORIZED ENTRY. DANGER
RADIOACTIVE MATTER

and below it in thick red letters:

DISPOSAL POINT FOR RADIOACTIVE WASTE

Peter closed his eyes. He saw once again the computer screen, a small cluster of neon dots centred in a sket-ched outline of the clinic. Harries! He'd sent Harries out. He had to find him. He took out his skeleton keys and attacked the lock. It was more by luck than judgement that he succeeded in turning the ratchet after five minutes of sweating, concentrated effort.

He pushed the door and walked into a tiny hallway. A row of grey aprons, gloves suspended above them like fingered heads, hung directly opposite. Another sign:

APRONS AND GLOVES TO BE WORN AT ALL TIMES WHEN HANDLING WASTE MATERIAL

He heeded the message and tied an apron round his waist, then pushed a pair of heavy gloves over his bleeding hands. There was a door to his right, and one to his left. He opened the door on the right and noticed a light switch. Remembering the steel plates that guarded the doors and windows, he risked turning it on.

Bright red plastic bags, bulging with what looked like screwed up paper, clearly marked 'Danger. Contaminated Medical Waste'. Clean-scrubbed brilliant-white tiled floor and walls. A door set in the far wall, steel-lined like the others. He guessed that it opened to the outside. He went back into the passage, to try the door on his left.

It was locked, and it took him a long time to open it. Eventually he turned the handle, and flicked on the light switch. The same blank white-tiled walls glared back at him. He stepped into the room and turned. A row of half a dozen tall, cylindrical containers were ranged along the same wall as the door. All were heavily marked with warning signs of skull and crossbones, and a reiteration of the sign outside.

THIS DRUM CONTAINS RADIOACTIVE MATERIAL

He took a closer look. The containers were lidded but

not sealed. He hesitated as an ugly thought entered his head. If he searched here it might put more than his career at risk . . . but the nagging demon that had tormented him since Harries had disappeared forced a decision on him. He knelt down and lifted the lid off the first lead-lined drum.

Chapter Thirteen

There was blood splattered over the grey apron Peter wore. He tried not to look at it, or the rust-coloured stains that slicked like dried oil over his lead-lined rubber gloves. He felt as though he'd been crouched in the cramped space of the small room, surrounded by bins, blood-soaked rags and jagged lumps of meat, for an eternity.

All around him lay segments of skin and flesh, and lengths of splintered, bloodied bones. He found it difficult to equate the mess he was delving into with the concept of a living, breathing body. There were so many small pieces, perhaps . . . perhaps it was nothing more than the labels suggested. Medical waste. By-products of the operating theatre. The leftovers of amputations, corrective surgery and animal experimentation.

Then, at the bottom of the last lead-lined barrel, he found a pair of shoes. Stained, scuffed, broken black shoes. One had sock inside it. Its shabby heel held a secret he knew only too well. He twisted the sole sharply and the transmitter he'd planted only hours before fell out on to the floor. It lay there, surrounded by shredded flesh and pools of congealing blood. His first concrete piece of evidence. And it had cost Harries his life.

He was too bloody late! Harries was dead, and this – he picked up the transmitter – was all that was left. He looked around for something, anything he could recognize. The pieces were so damned small. He couldn't even make out what had earlier in the day been Harries' head. There was an eye, part of a scalp with hair the same colour as Harries' ... .

He cradled the shoe, wiped it free of the gore that was smeared over it. Then the fog cleared from his mind. He had to clean this mess up. If he didn't, someone would realize he'd been here. It would take time to get a warrant and return with Bill and an official search party. Time which could be used by whoever was responsible for this to clear away the evidence. There was so much to do. He had to refill the bins. Clean the floor, relock all the doors, get out the way he had come in. He took off his anorack and wrapped it round the shoe. Then, mechanically, trying not to think too hard about Harries, or about what he was doing, he scooped the butcher's mess back into the bins.

When he'd finished he rose stiffly from his haunches. The floor was like a battlefield. He looked around. There was nothing in the room he could use to clean up the blood. He walked out into the hallway. Nothing there either, and when he looked down he noticed that he'd left a trail of bloody footprints. He took off his shoes and socks, and, barefoot, began a systematic search of the storerooms. Eventually he found a sponge and a bucket of cleaning fluid under an old sink in a cloakroom.

He carried them back to where he'd left his shoes. He cleaned them first, then he began to mop the bloodied floor vigorously, searching out the small shreds of flesh and stains of blood that would offer proof that the bins had been tampered with. When he'd finally done, he wiped the bins and hid his apron, gloves, and the bucket and sponge in the last bin before closing the lid.

He'd have to get himself screened for radiation contamination at the General. The signs were probably a blind, but it was as well to be careful. He picked up

339

the bundle he'd made of his anorak and began to lock all the doors.

'I was just about to telephone the clinic, sir. You were gone so long I thought you might need help.'

'The report warranted a thorough search.' Peter switched off his car headlights and shrank down in his seat as the security guard approached his car.

'Of course, sir.'

'I found everything in order, and I do have other calls to make.'

'Yes, sir.' The guard jumped back smartly to his post, and raised the barrier. He was too alert for Peter's liking. Far too alert. If he should spot the dirt or the blood that Peter knew lingered on his clothes . . .

'Good night, sir.'

'Good night.'

Peter stamped his foot on the accelerator and drove out on to the road. He'd done it! He had his evidence. All he had to do was get it to the station and Bill:

Silence lay thick and heavy over the second floor of the Sherringham mansion. Daisy lay deep in a dreamless, drugged sleep, oblivious to pain, oblivious to feeling. The curtains hung limply at the window, the air was warm and still on the gallery outside the bedrooms. Downstairs the grandfather clock ticked dully on in the hall, marking off seconds that held no meaning in the quiet house.

Richard lay awake in his darkened bedroom. He stared at the hard masculine lines of his mahogany furniture, studying them as though he were seeing them for the first time. Around him the stillness of the house was eerily oppresive. No matter how he struggled to concentrate on other things, his thoughts insisted on returning to Tim. Where was his brother? What was he doing at this moment? Was he trying to sleep, bound

340

hand and foot somewhere in locked isolation? Or was he stowed away in comparative comfort, close to a television or radio where he could hear of the efforts that were being made to find him?

The sound of a board creaking in the room next to his interrupted his gloomy reverie and put him instantly on the alert. He quietly eased open the top drawer of his bedside-table and reached inside for the gun he kept there.

The connecting door between his room and Joanna's swung open, and she stood before him, a silhouette framed against the muted light of the dressing-room beyond. She walked towards his bed, and a shaft of moonlight fell on her through the open window. Her white silk negligé and cropped blonde hair gleamed silver, giving her an oddly chaste appearance. Almost like that of a choirboy.

'Richard,' she whispered. 'Richard?'

'I'm awake,' he replied tersely, thrusting the gun back into the drawer, annoyed with himself as much as with her. She hadn't set foot in his bedroom for over six years. Not since her miscarriage. But that didn't excuse his neurotic behaviour. He was becoming terrified of his own shadow.

'I'm sorry.' She stood beside the bed.

'For what?'

'For disturbing you.' She turned to leave.

'I couldn't sleep either, Joanna. You may as well stay now you're here,' he replied ungraciously.

He switched on the bedside light, and looked at her. She was clutching her elbows with her hands, Bent and trembling, her whole body shook, racked by shuddering spasms. He left the bed and caught at her arms, leading her back to the warm place he'd vacated. She lay down unprotestingly. Covering her face with her hands, she curled into a tight little ball, shutting him out, yet again.

'Try to sleep,' he suggested, folding the duvet around her. He hitched up his pyjama trousers and reached for his dressing gown. 'I'll go into the dressing-room.'

'No. Please don't leave me alone,' she begged, her voice muffled by her arms. He sat next to her on the bed, and took her pulse. She reached up and pulled herself even closer to him. 'Please, Richard. Stay with me. Just for tonight. I know you don't want me. But please, just for tonight.'

He lifted the bedspread from the empty half of the bed and laid it over her, then he swung his legs up and stretched out beside her. She was right. He didn't want her. Perhaps he never had. Only the package that had come with her. The opportunity to buy into the clinic, the position in English society she offered, the home she made for them both. But then, she'd never wanted him for himself either. She'd married him because he was Theo's son. Possibly they deserved one another. It was just so bloody hard to live with a woman without any kind of mutual understanding, or what was even worse, without the desire or the energy to create one.

What had happened to his dreams? Had his father's death, or his own compromises led him to this state of cynicism? Twenty, even ten short years ago he'd believed himself capable of so much. Now . . . now . . .

It was dark when Richard woke. He was confused at first by the body that lay alongside his own, and he unconsciously looked for the outlines of the furniture in the cottage. Then he remembered – it wasn't Judy who lay alongside him, but Joanna. He was in his own bedroom, with his own wife. The irony of the situation wasn't lost on him.

He stirred, and her grip across his chest tightened, then he realized she wasn't asleep.

'Stop fighting, Joanna,' he murmured irritably. 'You

need to rest. If you relax the drugs will take over and you'll go to sleep.'

'I'm sorry. I'm trying as hard as I can.' He felt her tears trickling over his chest. Joanna, self-contained, unemotional Joanna was going to pieces. Even after her miscarriage she'd remained stoical, the epitome of the stiff-upper-lipped Englishwoman. It had to be more than just the cracked collarbone, and the discomfort of the tight bandage. Perhaps it was delayed reaction to Tim's disappearance?

'It's all right to cry,' he murmured, automatically employing the standard medical response to tears. Her hold on him intensified, then he felt her lips, trembling and moist, brush across his neck. His initial reaction was indifference, then as a familiar warmth stole through his veins, he thought 'why not?'

She was another being, someone to cling to in the dark. He lowered his face and returned her kiss, tasting her salt tears in his mouth. The sharp edge of grief added spice to their lovemaking. At that moment he used her, and she him. Love and compassion didn't come into it. They were two lonely, miserable people who needed someone to cling to in the dark lonely hours.

'Bloody clever ploy,' Bill commented caustically, staring at the shoe on his desk. 'Who in hell would think of looking for human remains in a barrel marked "Radioactive"?'

'I did.'

'You're a fool, Collins. But I hand it to you, you're a clever fool.'

'I didn't want it to turn out this way. Harries . . .'

'Harries was a copper. He knew the odds.'

'He was a kid.'

'A kid who was old enough to join the force. If you

beat yourself over the head with that one you'll be carried out of here in a strait-jacket.'

'Bill, I want in on the search. I'm ready to leave whenever you are.'

'You're ready to leave for the hospital. Get one of the duty officers to drive you there.'

'Later. Not now.'

'Look at the state of you. First things first. We'll get you checked out for radiation contamination. If you are contaminated, the whole bloody station and the force will have to be scrubbed. Now you don't want to delay that any longer than you have to, do you?'

'I could be clear.'

'Of radiation contamination, but God alone knows what else you could have picked up in the way of infections when you delved into those bins.'

'It could take hours to screen me for every bloody thing under the sun.'

'Who's arguing?'

'I want to go into the clinic with you.'

'And I'm telling you, even if you're clean, it's bed for you. Twenty-four hours' rest, and that's an order.'

'Damn you.'

'No arguments.'

Peter knew when he was beaten. 'You'll at least let me know.'

'I'll keep in touch. Now go. If you could see yourself from where I'm standing, you wouldn't wait a minute longer.'

'No evidence of exposure to radiation. But the casualty doctor, who clearly doesn't know you as I do, believes you to be in shock.' Judy clipped the small torch she'd been shining into Peter's eyes into the pocket of her white coat. 'Tell me, Sergeant, are you capable of being shocked?'

344

'We're all capable of being shocked, Dr Osbourne. Even inhuman policemen like me.'

'In that case, I defer to his diagnosis.'

'I take it I can go,' Peter countered sourly, buttoning his shirt.

'I said you were in shock.'

'I've been shocked before. I'll survive.'

'Clinical shock, Sergeant, is not quite the same as your ordinary common or garden shock.'

'What's that supposed to mean?'

'It means that you should rest. For a couple of hours at least. Somewhere warm and comfortable. Like the spare bed in Sergeant Joseph's room.'

'I have my own bed, thank you.'

'In that case I suggest you go to it.'

Peter stood up to fasten his trousers. He pulled his belt, and as he did so he swayed slightly.

'I wouldn't grab hold of that trolley, Sergeant. These floors are quite slippery. If you put your weight on that you could find yourself in Sergeant Joseph's room suffering from something more than mild shock.'

'Thank you for your advice, Doctor.' He sank back down on the chair.

'You really are in a state. I could quote your pulse rate, the increased . . .'

'Spare me the medical details. I don't need a doctor to tell me I feel lousy.'

'Same old Sergeant Collins. Polite and charming at all times. Well, what is it to be? Do I call your colleague in and ask him to escort you home?'

'As I'm here, I may as well see Trevor.'

'Would you like me to order you a wheelchair?'

'You're enjoying this, aren't you?'

'Not at all. Merely being sensible. If you try to walk out of that door you won't get half-way down the corridor.' She took a paper cup from a roll lying next to the sink and filled it with water. 'Sip it slowly, and breathe deeply. Not, I hasten to add, at the same time.'

'Thank you.' He watched her warily over the rim of the cup. 'Is now a good time to ask you if you're any closer to finding Tim Sherringham?'

'Now's as good a time as any to tell you that we're following leads.'

'I see. I suppose it's just as pointless to ask you why you wanted to be checked out for radiation contamination?'

'I poked my nose into something that had a warning sign plastered on its side.'

'That was stupid of you. May I ask what it was?'

Peter studied her reaction as he answered her question. 'A barrel marked "Radioactive Waste".'

'What kind of barrel?'

'A round, white one, just like the ones they use for medical waste.'

'Have you any idea what goes into those barrels?'

'I have now. What happens to them?'

'Sealed in concrete, dumped in an area set aside for radioactive waste.'

'Which is?'

'Out at sea, buried in the heart of the English countryside. Like you, I only know what I read in the papers.'

'The perfect place to dispose of a murder victim,' Peter mused quietly, watching her eyes. 'And if no one misses the victim, you have the perfect crime.'

'You think Tim Sherringham . . .'

'Did I say anything about Tim Sherringham?' His voice sharpened. 'How many of those barrels does an average hospital get through in a week?'

'I have no idea.'

Peter's voice was rough with delayed shock. 'How would a doctor kill someone?'

'Doctors are in the business of saving lives, Sergeant Collins, not taking them.'

'But supposing a doctor wanted to dispose of someone humanely,' Peter persevered. 'How would they do it?'

'In any one of a dozen ways.' Judy didn't want to continue with this bizarre conversation.

'Would such a death be painful?' Now he'd begun his questioning, Peter couldn't leave the subject alone.

'Not necessarily.'

'But before, if the victim knew what was coming?' he pressed.

'If you're talking about mental anguish, you know as much as I do,' she answered bluntly. 'Why do I get the feeling you know a great deal more about Tim's disappearance than you're telling anyone? Daisy's suffering all the torments of hell not knowing what's happened to Tim, and you're sitting there grinning like the Cheshire Cat. You don't give a damn.'

'That's where you're wrong. I do give a damn. Very much so.'

She turned her back on him, walked over to the sink and washed her hands. He could have kicked himself. He'd said much more than he'd intended to, but he couldn't stop agonizing over the possibilities that he wanted her to translate into bare facts. Harries locked in a closed room, listening, waiting for death. Harries helpless, strapped to a trolley, his mouth gagged with a bandage, his eyes wide open in terror as a doctor walked towards him with an empty syringe. A slow, excruciatingly painful, lethal injection of air that took aeons to percolate through veins made sluggish by restricting bonds . . .

He could stand his imaginings no longer. 'How would you go about killing someone?' he demanded, wanting her to tell him it was possible to die without pain. Death was a spectre every policeman had to live

347

with. But not torture, not experimental procedures that put the same value on human life as it did on laboratory rats.

'I can only tell you the basic medical facts,' Judy replied grudgingly. 'If you halt the flow of oxygen into the brain, even for a comparatively short time, you can cause brain death. And that process, in itself, is generally painless.'

'Generally painless.' The horror evoked by her calm, matter-of-fact explanation outraged Peter. What about the blind panic felt by a man fighting for his life? The gruesome soup of human remains he'd delved into?

'A doctor would know how to kill someone pain-lessly,' she continued, 'if that's what you're trying to find out from me. A couple of fingers pressed on the right spot on the neck would induce unconsciousness in seconds, brain death in minutes. Or an anaesthetic could be administered. Couple the patient to carbon monoxide instead of oxygen for a short time and you kill them.'

'Painlessly?'

'Painlessly,' she reiterated. 'Are you going to tell me why you're asking these questions?'

'Later, when I'm sure of my facts.'

'In that case, I have other patients to attend to. I'll get a porter to bring a wheelchair.'

'I can walk to Trevor's room.'

'Not without a porter with a wheelchair walking alongside you,' she said firmly. 'The last thing the Health Service needs is a lawsuit for negligence from someone who's too arrogant and bloody-minded to take medical advice.'

Trevor moved awkwardly around his room, opening cupboards, pulling out drawers, gathering together the few belongings Peter'd brought in for him. Flinging them on to the bed next to his case, he began to pack.

He checked his watch for the tenth time in as many minutes. Twelve-thirty. Peter'd told him to be ready at twelve, but then Peter hadn't looked too well himself at six that morning. He'd wait another half-hour, then he'd call a taxi.

'Good morning, or is it afternoon?'

'Morning will do.' He smiled at Daisy. She stood in the open doorway of his room, deathly white, her hand shaking as she offered him a steaming mug.

'I made coffee in the ward kitchen. Would you like some?'

'Yes, please.'

'I didn't bring any milk or sugar,' she apologized, setting the mug down on the table next to the window.

'That's fine, I'll drink it as it is.'

She slumped into the easy chair. The expression in her eyes froze the smile on his lips. He'd seen strain and misery reflected in her face before. But this was something new. Something different.

'Are you feeling all right?'

'I'm the doctor, you're the patient.'

'Not any more.' He held up his discharge papers.

'Going home?'

'As soon as Peter gets here.'

'Judy said something about Peter coming in early this morning . . .'

'He found some barrels that might have contained radioactive material,' Trevor interrupted quickly, trying to sidestep a discussion on what Peter'd discovered last night. 'He wanted to get himself checked out. Just being cautious.'

'I see.' She picked up her coffee cup and toyed with it.

'Did you take anything to make you sleep last night?'

'I thought you were on sick leave, Sergeant?'

'I don't deserve that,' he said quietly. 'I'm concerned about you.'

349

'You sound like a policeman who works on the drug squad.'

'I meant to sound like someone who cares.' He flushed crimson under her steady gaze.

'I'm not sure I could cope with anyone caring for me, not right now,' she mumbled, struggling with the depression that had lain heavily on her since she'd woken up in Richard's house earlier that morning.

'I'm trying to help.'

'You can help by finding Tim. I need to bury him,' she lashed out with uncharacteristic savagery.

He turned away from her and resumed his one-armed packing of his suitcase.

'I'm sorry. I shouldn't have said that.'

'No apologies necessary.'

'I don't know what I'm doing, what I'm saying.' She began to cry, weakly, quietly. Damn Richard and his sedatives! She'd coped until now without resorting to drugs. She hadn't even wanted to take his blasted pills.

Trevor abandoned his packing and walked over to her. He sat on the edge of the table next to her chair.

'I really do want to help.'

'I don't even know how to help myself.'

'What I'm trying to say, though not very well, is if you need anything, anything at all, I'm at the end of a telephone. And thanks to this,' he moved his slinged arm awkwardly, 'I have all the time in the world to spare.' If she understood what he'd said, she gave no sign of it.

'I miss Tim so much. I love him, I'll always love him,' she murmured dully, more to herself than to him.

'Feelings can't be switched on and off to order, and even if they could, I don't think you'd want to,' he said quietly.

'I don't think I'll ever be capable of feeling anything for anyone other than Tim again. It's just like being dead myself.'

'That's only natural. The last few days have been hell for you.'

'Don't you understand? I don't care about anyone.' Her voice rose precariously. 'Richard, Joanna, Judy, Alan, they could all die, and I wouldn't give a damn.'

'It's all right to feel that way.'

'But it shouldn't be all right,' she shouted furiously.

'You can't be angry with yourself for what you don't feel. You're numb, shocked. It's a natural reaction. Believe me. I know. I've seen it time and again.' He took her hand in his. She was icy cold. 'A policeman's job can be a lousy one. I've watched people react this way to grief before. I'm not going to tell you it will get better in time. I'm not sure it does. But I do know that people go on. Resilient beings, people,' he added, leaning forward and taking the weight of her head on his uninjured shoulder. They sat quietly while she struggled to regain her self-possession.

'Thank you for the use of your shoulder.' She moved away from him, back into her chair.

'Any time,' he smiled.

'You're a special person, Trevor. That girl of yours must have been an idiot to leave you.'

'Perhaps not.' Uneasy that he'd said too much, he turned aside and looked out of the window.

'Don't underrate yourself. You've a great deal to give.'

'To the force, perhaps.'

'No, not to the force. To the right person.'

His eyes met hers. He wanted to tell her he loved her, but he held back. It was neither the time nor the place. But he clung to the hope that there would be a time for them. When all of this was over, and forgotten by all but a few people.

'You'll remember what I said about calling me if you need anything?'

'Yes.'

They continued to sit in front of the window, together, yet separate. Trevor's presence forgotten, images flowed through Daisy's mind at breakneck speed, disconnected, confusing. Tim as she'd last seen him, pulling his shirt over his head in their bedroom. Robin Dart lying on a slab in the mortuary. Richard sitting in the gloom of the cottage's badly-lit living-room. The look on Superintendent Mulcahy's face when Richard had told him about the kidnap demand . . .

'Sorry I'm late.' Peter burst in through the door.

'Don't worry about it. I haven't even finished packing.'

Trevor left Daisy's side and went to the bed. He snapped his suitcase shut. He felt in his pockets and found an envelope, a circular that had come through his door. He hadn't even opened it. He thrust it at her. 'My address. The telephone number's in the book. I do a terrific Irish stew,' he gabbled, conscious of Peter standing behind him. 'Should you want to call in any time, you'd be more than welcome.'

'Thank you. But what I do for the next few days will very much depend on Richard and Joanna and what they want.'

'Of course.'

'But should you find out anything?'

'I'll ring you. I promise.'

'Thank you.'

'See you around, Dr Sherringham.' Peter took Trevor's case.

'Yes, see you around.' She turned her back on them and continued to look out through the window. She shouldn't have come into the hospital. She was too tired, too miserable to work. She should have stayed at Richard's.

If only they could find Tim. She drew a deep breath and imagined the scene. She'd have to arrange his

352

funeral – there'd be things for her to do. For Tim. Arrangements to be made, people to see and contact. Services to read through. Hymns to choose. Flowers and wreaths to order. She'd want to write his obituary. 'Beloved husband of . . .'

What was she doing? When her mother had died, she'd hated the paraphernalia of death. The sombre church service. The hushed relatives sitting around her father's living-room, occupying her mother's kitchen. Heavy words of comfort and solace from priests and black-garbed friends that were anything but comforting. The laughter of relatives and neighbours hastily silenced whenever she'd entered the room. The ghastly, never-ending, post-funeral ham tea, where her mother had been discussed as if she'd been dead for years. Now she was actually imagining those selfsame ceremonies laying Tim to rest.

She put her head down on her arms on the table. She was behaving as if she wanted Tim dead. Who loved Tim more? Richard, who hoped with every fibre of his being that Tim was alive? Or her, already planning out his funeral before they'd even found a body?

It was no use. Try as she may, she could not adopt Richard's hope. She needed to act out the public ritual and display of grief for Tim. It would provide her with a marker she could use to define the limits of his existence. Without it, there was only this cancerous uncertainty, sapping all that was worthwhile from her life.

Trevor followed Peter into the lift. He'd never felt so impotent, so utterly useless. He'd tried to ease Daisy's pain, make her smile again, but all he'd done was make it worse for her.

'Lost a girlfriend and found a wife?'

'Leave it, Peter.'

'That was Dr Daisy Sherringham, the light of your

life, in your bedroom at . . .' Peter glanced at his watch, '. . . one forty-five in the afternoon.'

'She came to see if I wanted anything before I left the hospital.'

'Sorry I spoke.' The lift doors closed in on them. 'Aren't you going to ask where I've been, and what I've been doing?'

'If you've any sense, you've been in bed.'

'Unlike you, I didn't have any company.'

'You bastard. If we were anywhere else, I'd . . .'

'In your one-armed state. Never.'

Trevor turned his back on Peter in disgust. He didn't speak again until they were in the car.

'There's something very wrong with you, Collins. If you were standing in the middle of a rosebed you'd see only manure.'

'From where I'm standing right now, I can't see any roses, and that's for sure,' Peter said grimly.

'That's because you're not looking.'

'No doubt.' Peter slung Trevor's case in the back, and started the car. 'All right if we stop off at Ben Gummer's place on the way to yours?'

'Why?' Trevor demanded suspiciously. He'd heard that deceptively casual tone in Peter's voice before.

'Bill won't let me near the clinic. So I thought I'd do a little investigating of my own. Pity to waste the whole day.'

'What kind of investigating?'

'I'd like to ask Ben if he remembers any more about finding that knife.'

'For pity's sake, the man took his dogs for a walk on the beach. The dogs found a parcel of food washed up on the shore and started playing with it. He rescued it and found a knife that may or may not be the murder weapon. What more is there to know than that?'

'The dogs found it trapped in the barbed wire under

the pier, together with the sleeve of a pierrot costume. And that pier and the pierrot costumes bother me.'

'They bother us all.'

'I went down there this morning at first light. Rotten boards apart, there's no way anyone can walk on to that pier from the promenade. The search squad replaced those barbed wire barricades if anything more securely than they found them.'

'Then perhaps the food parcel didn't fall from the pier. The dogs could have dragged it from God knows where. It could have fallen from a boat.'

'I don't see how, unless the boat was the seaward side of the pier. I checked the currents and tides for the past few days with the harbour master this morning. That's why I was late. There's no way that parcel could have been carried to where it was found if it was dropped from the marina sea traffic.'

'Then it could have fallen from a boat that was close to the pier,' Trevor agreed irritably.

'Exactly. A boat manned by a pierrot. Possibly even the same one that had a go at you. And although the pier's barricaded on the seaward side, it doesn't look anything like as formidable as the other three sides.'

'How do you know that?'

'I checked from the headland.'

'You drove out to the headland?'

'This morning, when I left the hospital.'

'When did you sleep?'

'I didn't,' Peter replied abruptly.

'Aren't you rather discounting the fact that the parcel could have been carried to the beach and dumped close to where Ben found it.'

'By who?'

'Sailors, down-and-outs . . .'

'Sailors carry their food to the docks or the marina. That's where their boats are. And if it had been found by down-and-outs, they would have left a lot less than Ben's dogs.'

'OK. Say it did fall from the pier,' Trevor conceded. 'You searched the place. Tell me, why would anyone go there?'

'Nostalgia? Hidden treasure? How in hell would I know? And then again, we didn't search any further than the theatre.'

'You said you'd seen everything you wanted.'

'Perhaps I missed something.'

'My God, you're admitting that you might have botched a search. I never thought I'd live to see the day.'

'I've made a list of things I want to check out with Ben.' Ignoring Trevor's comment, Peter drew his notebook out of his top pocket and tossed it into Trevor's lap. 'The theatre layout. The position of the parcel when he first saw it. And most important of all, I want to ask if he remembers seeing a boat yesterday when he found the parcel. If he did, there might have been a marker painted on the side. Name of a yacht, wharf number, anything that might lead us somewhere other than a dead end.'

'Surely if Ben saw something more he would have already told us about it?'

'I can't sit back and forget what I saw last night.' Peter's face darkened in anger.

'Bill's working on it.'

'The more people who look, the more chance we have of catching the bastard behind all this.'

'Bill's working on it,' Trevor repeated. 'Let's face it, neither of us are up to much.'

'What do you want me to do? Leave it?' The brakes of the car screeched in protest as Peter heaved it rapidly around a corner. 'Forget Harries? Amanda Dart? Your junkie? Who, incidentally, died of a poisoned dose. Enough cyanide to kill half a dozen men, and no sign of a struggle, no bruises. Just a smile on his face. We're dealing with clever, rotten people. And you expect me to lie low, let them carry on scheming, murdering, doing whatever they want. Damn it, Joseph, we can't sit back and do nothing.'

'At the moment I feel justified in doing just that.'

'And while you're lying back, you're going to say, "to hell with the victims, let them suffer"?'

'I have to. I'm sick, remember.'

'Only in the head.'

'I'll go with you to Ben Gummer's. But that's it. No more, Peter. Not until I'm fit again. I'm sorry about Harries. I liked him. I'm sorry about Amanda and Robin Dart. And God knows, I'm sorry for Daisy Sherringham. But I'm sick, Peter. Sick, and tired. I need the leave I've got coming up.'

'To chase Daisy Sherringham?'

For once Trevor didn't rise to the bait. 'Perhaps. If she'll let me near her. For the first time in years, I've something on the horizon that's worth going for. And I'm not risking that. Not for you. Not for your crazy notions of revenge. And certainly not for an investigation that's going nowhere. I'm taking this leave. I want you to understand that.'

'I understand, all right. I just wonder how you'd feel if it had been Daisy Sherringham instead of Harries in that barrel last night.'

Chapter Fourteen

The pager twittered irritatingly in Peter's top pocket.

'Someone wants you.'

'They can wait,' Peter muttered tensely. He turned, yet again, to the deaf, obdurate old crone who was washing down the tables in the bar in the White Hart. 'If you don't go upstairs and wake Ben I'll . . .'

'And I tell you he's locked in and won't come out until he's good and ready. And that won't be until the bar opens in an hour. So go, pedal your bike, Mister.' The pager trilled again, adding to Peter's irritation.

Trevor walked over to the back window that overlooked the beach. He was finding it increasingly difficult to hide his amusement. Bruisers, bouncers, pushers, junkies on the rampage – Peter could cope with them all. But give him one obstinate old woman, and he was as helpless as a baby. This was a story he'd enjoy spreading round the station.

'Sod it!' Peter switched off the pager, jumped over the bar and grabbed the telephone. While he was busy swearing at the girl who operated the police switchboard, Trevor took the opportunity to speak to the old woman himself.

'Like I said,' she shouted loudly in Peter's direction, 'the guv'nor won't be down until just before opening time.'

'Bill wants me in the station right now.' Peter turned a serious face to Trevor. 'He won't tell me anything over the phone.'

'That's hardly surprising after what you found last night.'

'I'll drop you off on the way.'

'Ben should be down in half an hour or so. If you like, I'll stick around and wait. I can always take a taxi home.'

'Are you sure you want to?' Peter stared at him in surprise.

'I've got nothing better to do. And a drink would go down nicely.'

'If it's nothing vital, I'll be back soon.'

'Fine.'

'I'll remember you for this.' Peter paused at the door.

'Sooner you go, sooner you'll be back.'

'See you.'

After Peter had left, Trevor almost pulled himself a pint of beer. Then he remembered the cloudy dregs he'd been presented with the last time he'd drunk here, so he prised the top off a bottle of lager instead. He collected the loose change from his pocket and carefully counted out the correct money, leaving the coins, together with the bottle cap, on top of the till. Nodding to the old woman, he walked out of the bar and down the passage into the beer garden.

He looked out over the beach. The gaunt iron skeleton of the pier brooded grim and forbidding in the glittering sunlight. The beautiful spring weather did nothing so soften the outline of its rotting hulk. Rather, it seemed to blacken its shadowy depths, reminding him of noisy, sunlit days. The unpleasant truth, that he, like all things mortal, would eventually become nothing more than a blurred image, consigned to stained, crumbling photographs, and a grave in the family plot in an overgrown churchyard.

He shuddered, wiped the top of the bottle and drank, his memory flicking from the distant past to last summer when he and Peter had worked the beach. In August it had been a pusher's dream and a copper's nightmare. But even as he'd stretched out on the hard, baking sand dressed only in his swimsuit, he'd noticed that the solid carpet of sun worshippers thinned out long before it reached the pier barricades. Perhaps the decaying structure hid more ghosts than even he knew about.

He lifted the bottle again, downing half its contents. On an empty stomach the drink made him feel pleasantly light-headed. Daisy's dark-smudged eyes no longer gazed reproachfully into his, as they had done earlier. Instead, he remembered their conversation. She'd talked to him, really talked to him, not of mundane everyday things, but of her private thoughts.

Daisy was all he'd ever wanted or imagined in a woman. It had to be a plus that he could talk to her. Proof that there could be something between them. Not now, of course, but in the future that lay ahead of them both. She needed time. He accepted that. And he would wait for her. For years, if necessary.

A quick movement beneath the pier caught his eye. He stared until his eyes hurt. Then he saw. A shambling figure was swinging down inside the wired-off structure, like a monkey in dense jungle. He ran down the path to the beach, tossing his empty lager bottle behind him. Earth gave way to soft, shifting sand beneath his feet. It wasn't easy to move forward. Each step he took needed the effort he normally expended on ten. The twisted wires of the barricade drew nearer, and still the figure swung precariously downwards.

His arm bumped painfully against his body. He panted, his chest heaving for air, his lungs straining to bursting point, his head swimming dizzily from lack of oxygen. The impregnable barbed and knotted wires loomed closer. He didn't pause to think what he was going to do once he reached them.

The figure turned sharply, sliding sideways into the barricade itself. It stopped. Saw him. Then beat a hasty retreat. Upwards and backwards, the way it had already travelled.

Never losing sight of the ape-like figure, Trevor ran on, directing his steps to the point where it had seemed to enter the barricade, somewhere above the low tide line. He waded knee deep into the water, then as he watched, the agile figure swung upwards, and disappeared through the boards on to the pier itself.

The barricade . . . There had to be an overlap in the curls of barbed wire that allowed a man to slip through to the inside of the supporting structure. He splashed up and down, his eyes following the lines of bent and contorted wires, searching for a break in their tangled continuity. It was not until he was almost waist deep in freezing water that he found it. The corner. The break was almost at the corner. Two parallel barricades, not one, overlapped for twelve yards or more. Impossible to spot unless you knew they were there. He inched his way forward, tearing his anorak on the piercing barbs. The gap was narrow, too narrow for comfort. Then he saw a ladder. Virtually upright, leading upwards. A ladder that hadn't been used by whoever he'd been watching.

Cursing his broken arm, he began to climb, hooking his legs around the rungs to get a firmer grip, and sliding his good hand up the side, too afraid to relax his hold for an instant. Water that made his shoes and trousers dangerously slippery squelched down from his body. Powdery rust coated his hands. He welcomed it. It gave him something to grasp hold of, and the metal beneath the covering was surprisingly strong. He looked up. Solid wood. Not rotting. Solid. There had to be a trap door. He'd worry about that when he reached the top.

He looked down. He saw a larger gap than the one he'd walked through. A gap in the centre of the seaward side. A gap high and wide enough to sail a small boat through. He swayed precariously. Mustn't look down. He hated heights. The water swirling dizzily below made him feel sick. Must close eyes to everything except the rung in front. The rung above. Up – up – up.

He remembered the pierrot. The strength in the clown's grip. The agonizing crunch of his own arm breaking. Being tossed aside on to the deck of the *Freedom*. The mutilated bodies in the mortuary . . .

Don't look down! He closed his eyes and clung tightly to the ladder. Concentrate on the rung at eye level. Open eyes. That was it. Look at the rung above. Not down. Don't look down. A dull clunk beneath him. Vibrations in the ladder. Something large hitting the metal legs of the pier. Imagination? Had to be. A throat-drying, mind-numbing fear pushed him to the brink of endurance and sanity. He wouldn't survive if he looked down. He knew it. He heard the sound again. Put it out of his mind. It wasn't there. Music – he'd think of music. Of Daisy. 'She walks in beauty like the night.' Damn it, that wasn't a pop song. That was poetry. He hadn't read that poem since school. He hadn't read any poem since school.

Climb on. Slowly, one step at a time. One leg at a time. Think. Think of Daisy, the pierrot. Had the pierrot come this way last night?

His head hit the top. A trap door? It had to be. It moved. He felt it move. Ignoring the pressure on his head, he pushed with the crown of his skull. He dared not release his one-handed grip on the ladder. The trap door was giving way. Opening. He climbed on slowly, painstakingly. He ran out of ladder. Bending at the waist, he crawled out, undignified on hands and knees, into the darkened room above, and crouched there, sweating, exhausted by fear and effort.

In time he breathed easier. Then, feeling like the Jack that had climbed the beanstalk, he looked around. A skylight. A pathetic square of blue that did little to illuminate the room. Shapes in the half light. A bench.

362

A generator. Not old, but new, covered in oil that gleamed dully in the gloom. A stack of cans. Petrol cans for the generator? An ice chest. Rusted. Still plastered with ragged stickers advertising icecream. Square cornets, wafers, plain orange lollies. None of today's chocolate and raspberry sauce-covered delicacies.

He rose shakily to his feet, testing the boards tentatively with his weight. The floor held. He couldn't see any pin-points of light, the first tell-tale signs of rot. Plain wooden walls. No stage. No auditorium. No theatre with the dust-covered deathtrap floor Peter'd described. Yet he could have sworn he'd entered the pier at the back. Unless . . . unless there was a room beyond the theatre, and this was it. A room Peter'd missed.

He pivoted on his heels, searching for a door that led out on to the pier itself. There was none that he could see. He walked from the seaward wall to the wall that adjoined the rest of the pier. A small dark tunnel, no more than four feet high opened up in front of him. He crouched down, crept forward, only to find himself confronted by solid planking. He ran his hand over it, starting at the top, working down. His forefinger slid into a hole. A key hole. He felt the metal edges. He thumped his fist hard against the wood. A scurrying noise scrabbled from the other side. Rats? Or a single human rat? The one he'd followed?

Weary of straining his eyes into unrelieved blackness, he crawled back. Squatting beside the pile of cans, he opened one and sniffed the contents. He'd been right. Petrol. Probably for the generator. He felt the side of the machine. Still warm. It had been running, and not that long ago. He turned to the ice chest, and threw the lid back. Cold air wafted out as he peered inside and saw only darkness. He reached inside the chest with his good hand. His fingers met something soft,

stranded. He knotted his fingers tightly round the
strands . . .

Peter Collins was stuck in an interminable traffic queue
in the town centre when the call came in over the police
radio in his car. The numbered code for life and death
emergency, followed by a plea for assistance. Location
– the pier. The damned pier! He shouldn't have left
Trevor. It wasn't even as if the man was fit for duty.

An orchestrated symphony of blasting horns, supported by motorists' curses accompanied the sudden
U-turn Peter negotiated in the middle of the High
Street. White-faced, he pressed his foot down on the
accelerator and sped back along the road he'd just
crawled along.

Ben Gummer slung the loaded shot-gun over his
shoulder and whistled for his dogs.

'Don't let anyone in except the police, Mary,' he
ordered.

'I wouldn't go out there if I were you. You don't
know if that man's dead.'

'I'm only going to take a look round. Remember to
lock the door behind me.'

'I was going to.'

Ben stepped out into the beer garden. The body
Mary had seen fall from the pier was floating in the
water behind the wire. He narrowed his eyes, trying to
get a clearer focus on the dark huddled mass. Damn
old age. It certainly didn't come by itself, as the saying
went. He used to be able to see a pigeon half a mile
off, and, more to the point, hit it. Now he couldn't even
see a bloody handkerchief when he held it under his
nose.

The dark mass in the water separated into two indistinct units, then merged again. Were there two men in
the water, one helping or pulling the other? They

364

moved away from him, then, miraculously, emerged from the deep water at the far end of the pier into the open sea.

'Bloody Mary,' he swore angrily under his breath, as he shoved a cigarette between his sleep-numbed lips. She'd yanked him out of a beautiful X-rated pornographic dream with a crazy tale about policemen. One of them going to the pier. Then a body falling. Old bitch! She probably spent the time he paid for looking out of the window instead of cleaning the place. No wonder the pub was in the mess it was. But he'd called the police anyway, just in case.

'What's up, Ben?'

'You got here bloody quick.' Ben glanced at Peter, then lit his cigarette.

'I was stuck in a jam in the High Street. Where's Trevor?'

'If that isn't him down there, I don't know. Mary woke me with some cock-and-bull story about a policeman climbing up on to the pier and a body falling. She was right about one thing, there is something down there. Behind the wire. See it?'

'I see it.' Peter ran headlong down the path Trevor had taken such a short time before.

'Hey, wait for me. At least I've a gun.' Ben called his dogs and followed as fast as his wheezing, creaking, body would allow.

'I brung him out for you, Mister. He's hurt. You can see it's bad. I had to drop him down through the hole, but he landed in the water. Didn't hurt himself no more, I swear it. I had to do it, Mister. Honest. The clown was up there. He would have got me as well if he could have. So I brung him down.'

Andy pushed the sodden mass he'd towed through the wire barrier towards Peter. Peter stretched out his arms to take the burden. Kneeling in the shallows, he

365

lifted Trevor's shoulders tenderly on to his lap. He brushed the shock of dark hair away from the pale face, stared into the half-open eyes, ran his fingers over the parted lips.

'Trevor, you can make it. You know you can,' he whispered. 'A few steps more and you'll be on the sand. The ambulance will be here soon.' The terrifying lack of response turned his pleading to cursing. 'For Christ's sake, Trevor, stop lying there. Move. Shift yourself, man.'

'It's his head, Mister.' Andy stood, arms flapping, a ragged scarecrow pegged to a pool of white-crested waves.

Peter concentrated on Trevor. He ran his hand lightly over Trevor's cheek, then, as his fingers travelled upwards, they slid into a bloodied dent above the left ear. He withdrew his hand and stared at his fingers, red-tipped, trembling. For the first time he saw the pink foam on the sea around him.

He choked back the words of encouragement. Sliding his arms beneath Trevor, he rose from his knees, lifting Trevor's body clear of the water. He forced one reluctant leg in front of the other and moved forward on the beach. Even with the added mass of water clinging to Trevor's clothes the man was a lightweight. Damned fool. He never would eat enough.

'Here, I'll give you a hand.' Kicking his dogs back with a sharp word of command, Ben came towards him.

'I'll manage,' Peter muttered tersely.

'Oh God!' Grey-faced, Ben turned sideways and heaved his breakfast into the sea. Peter ignored the wretched display. He stepped on to the dry sand, and crouched there miserably, his tears mixing with the blood-splattered spray that clung to Trevor's face and body.

366

'His hand.' Ben grabbed Peter's shoulder. 'Look at his hand.'

Peter looked. Trevor's fingers were twined into a head of hair. Black curly hair. Wide, staring blue eyes, parted lips, white face, clean-cut at the neck. A human head.

'Tim Sherringham had black curly hair and blue eyes,' Peter observed coldly. 'We never did find his body.'

Even in her nightmare world, Daisy was berating herself for allowing sleep to overtake her. She could see gloom, not darkness, and patches of shadowy light struggling in through thick, grimy glass. And the noise, the endless crashing of hollow sounds. Water. She was above water, and the corpses were there. The damned headless corpses. She could sense it. See their shadows, poised, waiting in the background, behind the crouching man. He was lifting the lid off a chest, looking down into it. He couldn't see them.

She cried out to warn him. But if he heard her cry, he ignored it. Then she saw the plank. A huge, thick wooden plank. Jagged at one end where it had been torn from the wooden wall. Massive six inch nails protruding through the wood at intervals, and, even as she watched, it rose above the head of the crouching man, wielded by hands encased in stained, encrusted gloves.

She tried to look beyond the hands, but she could see no further than the gloves, and a black silk sleeve. White pompoms. She screamed. The plank moved, the man in front of the chest turned. She recognized him, tried to warn him. Then the plank crashed down and obliterated everything.

'No! No!'

'Daisy, it's me, Richard. Wake up.'

She was sobbing on the sofa in Richard's living-room. His arm round her shoulders.

367

'We did debate whether or not to let you sleep. But you were so tired. Come on. Calm down, you're here. Safe with us.'

She looked around wildly for the wooden plank, the injured man, but there was only Joanna lying back on the *chaise-longue*, a tea tray set out in front of her.

'The phone woke you,' Richard explained. 'It was Alan Cummins. He wanted to tell us that the hospital's been put on emergency stand-by. He's volunteered to go out with the ambulance. The police have sealed off the area around the pier. He hasn't found out why, but he does know that the police are armed.'

'Trevor Joseph's hurt. He's been attacked. He was hit by a massive wooden plank. It had nails in it. They crushed his skull. I saw it . . .' She shuddered.

'It was a nightmare,' Richard soothed. 'Nothing more. I have to go to the pier, Daisy. I'll leave you with Joanna. Would you like a sedative before I leave?'

The crashing sound. The sea. The wooden planking. Wooden walls. Wooden floor . . .

'I'm coming with you.' She was out of her chair in an instant, searching frenziedly through her handbag for her car keys.

'I'll drive.' He looked across to where Joanna sat. She looked up at him, white-faced, drained.

'I'll wait here,' she said.

'I want the bridging boards brought up now. On the double.'

'Sir.'

'Four armed men inside the wire, covering the foot of the ladder. Get the boat that's tied to the pier leg outside the wire perimeter, and circle the whole area with our own craft. Have you ordered the dog handlers up yet?' Bill peered intimidatingly into the young constable's eyes.

'Constable Pitson saw to it ten minutes ago, Sir.'

368

'Then jump to the rest, lad. Jump to it. You know the objectives same as everyone else. That clown has to be brought out of the pier. Preferably without killing or maiming anyone else. And perhaps we can do it in the next hour or so. We don't want to be here all bloody week, do we?'

'No, sir.'

'On your way then.'

Bill watched the constable jog off the beach and back to the pub. He deliberately skirted the spot where, head bowed, Collins crouched over a white-sheeted stretcher, surrounded by ambulance men. A thick-set, ginger-haired doctor was shouting orders while a nurse rigged up a drip. What the hell were they waiting for? Trevor was hurt. Hurt badly. Surely to God it would be better to get him out of here and into the hospital as quickly as possible. Squaring his shoulders, he walked over to Peter.

'I'm sorry it had to be Trevor.'

'Are you? Are you really bloody sorry?' Condemnatory anger blazed fiercely in Peter's eyes.

'Look, you can't help here, come back to the pub with me.' Bill shuffled awkwardly, conscious of the attention focused on them. 'We'll have a drink together. Please, there's a good lad.'

'We're all good lads when there's dirty work to be done, aren't we, Bill? Him,' he pointed at the bloodied, unconscious wreck that was Trevor, 'Harries, me, we're all good lads. And we'll all end up in the sodding graveyard before our time. How many more, Bill? How many more?'

'Peter, you're tired. Upset. Go back to the pub, get yourself a brandy.'

'I'm not moving from this spot until Trevor leaves,' Peter asserted vehemently. 'And then I'm going in there,' he pointed to the pier. 'To get the bastard who did this.'

'I wouldn't bet on that if I were you, Sergeant Collins.'

One of the men Trevor and Peter had collectively referred to for years as 'upstairs' came over to them. 'We're all very upset about Sergeant Joseph, Sergeant . . . Sergeant . . .'

'Collins, sir,' Bill chipped in.

'Ah yes, Sergeant Collins. Look here, man, none of this shouting is going to help. I sympathize with you, I really do. Lost a colleague myself some years back under similar circumstances.'

'Trevor's not dead yet.'

'Face facts, man.' He thumped Peter hard on the shoulder. 'It doesn't look good. I think I'm being fair in saying that we've made all the allowances that can be made in this case. As of now I'm relieving you from duty.'

'And to hell with you, too.' Peter turned on the senior officer. 'I've done what you lot have been telling me to do for years. And look where it's got me.' He lowered his voice to a whisper. 'And where it's got him. He might be just one more bloody sergeant to you, but he was my friend. And . . . and that . . .'

Bill nodded to the officer, who turned his back and left him to it.

'Sir?' Another young constable ran hotfoot towards them. 'Sir?'

'Yes, Constable?' Bill snapped.

'Some people are up at the barricades, sir. One of them is asking about Sergeant Joseph.'

'I'll be there in a minute, Constable. Tell them to wait.'

'Very good, sir.'

'When the ambulance crew leave, I think you should go to the hospital with them. That's not an order, Peter, it's a suggestion.'

'I won't leave here.'

'I saw the stretcher. I'm a doctor.' Daisy ran breathlessly towards them. When she saw Peter she stumbled to a halt.

'Sorry, Super, I tried to stop her.' A constable and Richard Sherringham appeared close on her heels.

'Well, if it's not the virtuous Daisy Sherringham,' Peter jeered.

'Daisy?' Alan looked up from the stretcher, where he was doing his utmost to keep alive the faint flicker of life that still burned.

'It's Trevor, isn't it? I tried, so help me I tried to warn him. But he just turned and looked while the clown brought the plank down on to his head. And the nails. . . .'

'You were there?' Bill stared at her incredulously.

'A nightmare. Nothing more than another nightmare,' Richard said irritably.

'But I saw it all. The pier . . .'

Peter stared at her through narrow embittered eyes. 'He loved you. Worshipped the ground you walked on. And you couldn't give a damn for him. You can't even spare him a tear now. Not one single solitary tear.' He contemplated Daisy's white, dry-eyed face. 'Well, if you won't cry for him,' Peter picked up a bundle that lay on the ground beside Trevor, and divested it of plastic sheeting, 'try this for size.' He thrust the decapitated head towards her.

It gained the effect he desired. Horrorstruck, Daisy remained silent for only a moment. Then hysteria took hold of her.

'In God's name, Collins.' Bill grabbed the head, but he didn't succeed in covering it before Alan Cummins and Richard saw it. 'I'm sorry you had to see your husband's head this way,' Bill apologized to Daisy. She didn't hear him. She was sobbing wildly into Alan's shoulder.

'That isn't Tim Sherringham.' Alan struggled to get

371

the words out. The head wasn't Tim's, but he'd known the man it had belonged to. Laughed with him, worked with him, drunk with him. Liked him, even.

'It fits Sherringham's description,' Peter insisted illogically.

'It is . . . or rather was Tony Pierce.'

'But he want to Arabia,' Peter protested.

Alan nodded agreement. 'That's right,' he muttered brokenly, as the full horror of what he'd seen sank into his mind. 'He went to Arabia.'

Bill stood back and watched the ambulance crew carry the stretcher away: From start to finish this whole affair had been a shambles. A shambles that had cost him the life of one good man, and now probably Joseph. And Joseph would be near impossible to replace, not least for the tempering effect he'd had on Collins' irrational behaviour. Who in hell could he get to work with Collins from now on?

'Sir, the bridging boards have arrived and the armed officers are in position inside the wire.'

'Thank you, Constable.' He shook himself free from maudlin thoughts. It wasn't finished yet. He had to deal out the short straw. Pick the lucky man who'd climb on to the pier and bring out the murdering lunatic holed up in there. He breathed out slowly and looked along the beach. The ambulance was driving away, and the men were locked into a respectful silence for Trevor. Even Peter. Peter? He wanted to reach out, offer him something. He owed him for Trevor..

He clapped his hand on Peter's shoulder. 'How about you and me signing gun chits and going up on the pier?' he asked harshly.

'That's fine by me.' Peter's voice was rough with suppressed emotion.

'Sir. Sir.'

'What now?' Bill demanded irritably.

372

'Sergeant Scott told me to tell you we couldn't stop him.'

'Stop who doing what?'

'Dr Sherringham, sir. Dr Richard Sherringham. He broke through the cordon just now. He got through the barbed wire and climbed up the ladder. Sergeant Scott says to tell you he thinks he's on the pier.'

'He thinks he's on the pier.' Bill glared furiously at the nervous constable. 'He thinks he's on the pier? Why in hell can't you lot do the job you were asked to do?'

'Sorry, sir.'

'Sorry? Your bloody incompetence has given us exactly what we don't need. A stupid bungling amateur fumbling around a murdering madman . . .'

'He can't do any worse than we have,' Peter interrupted dryly.

Bill thrust his mind into top gear. 'The dog handlers arrived yet?' he asked the constable.

'Not that I've seen.'

'Dismissed. Go on, clear off. And try to do better next time.'

'Yes, sir.'

Peter took off his jacket and rolled up his shirtsleeves. He bent down to a squeeze the excess water out of his trousers, calling Ben over as he did so.

'Your dogs?'

Ben understood Peter at once. 'They're as good as army trained,' he boasted proudly. 'If you shout "attack and hold", they will. And that's what you'll need up there.' He jabbed a fat forefinger at the pier.

'Climb ladders?'

'Never tried. But if you drive them I don't see why not.'

'Worth a try?' Peter asked Bill.

'I'll get the guns,' he replied briskly.

'Sergeant Collins, about Constable Harries . . .' Sarah

373

Merchant waylaid Peter as he checked the gun he'd drawn.

'Constable Merchant,' Peter managed a grim smile, 'I'm a little busy right now. Could we talk later?'

'Of course, sir. It's just that . . .' Undeterred, she voiced the suspicions that had been tormenting her since early morning. 'Something's happened to him, hasn't it? If he'd been all right he would have telephoned me, I'm sure of it.'

Peter's first reaction was to hand her the usual platitudes, but the sun chose that moment to disappear behind a bank of cloud. The brilliant beach scene faded into a dull colour-bled shade. The sea turned to pewter, the temperature dropped, and a chill penetrated through his damp clothes. He simply couldn't tell her anything other than the truth.

'We've all had more than our fair share of misery in the last twenty-four hours, Constable,' he admitted bluntly.

'Yes, sir.' His uncompromising professionalism made no allowances for her grief. 'I'm sorry about Sergeant Joseph, sir.'

'Thank you.' Even to his hardened eyes, she looked pathetic. 'Constable, do you see that lady up there?' He pointed to the promenade step where Daisy sat huddled under a blanket that someone had thrown around her shoulders.

'Yes, sir.'

'Do me a favour, go and see what you can do for her. Something tells me she's going to need all the support she can get before today's over.'

'Yes, sir.'

Bill strode purposefully between them. 'The boys have cut through the barricades at the front end of the pier. We'll give them a couple of minutes to push across the bridging planks. If he's at the land end, they'll flush him down for us.'

'And we go up the ladder and corner him in the theatre?'

'That's the idea.'

'Richard Sherringham?'

'If he's still alive, try not to shoot him. Dead civilians don't look good in the papers.'

Daisy took the plastic beaker of hot coffee and cupped her hands round it, siphoning off its warmth into her freezing fingers.

'Thank you,' she murmured to the young woman who had given it to her.

'Can I get you anything else, Dr Sherringham?'

'No, this will be fine.'

'Do you mind if I sit with you?' the policewoman asked.

'No. I'd be glad of the company.'

The policewoman sat next to her, self-contained, silent. Daisy was grateful for what she took to be tact on the constable's part. She shivered under the blanket as she looked across at the pier. What on earth had possessed Richard to go in there? Did he really think Tim was there? That the kidnappers had left him alive? She wished she could have believed that. She really did.

Chapter Fifteen

'Up you go. Go on. Up.' Peter lifted the dog's paws on to a rung of the ladder.

'Myrtle will catch on quicker than Cyril.' Ben caught hold of the second dog by the collar, and waded through the sea towards Peter and Bill.

'You're not supposed to be here,' Bill snapped.

'They're my dogs.' Ben spat the cigarette butt he'd been chewing out of his mouth. 'Here, Myrtle. Up.' The dog got the message. Slowly, after a false start and a few hesitant pauses, the bitch reached the open trap door. 'In, Myrtle.' Ben shouted. The dog complied. 'Your turn, Cyril.'

'Bloody stupid names for dogs,' Peter observed wryly.

'Bloody stupid names for people,' Ben retorted.

'Right, Mr Gummer, thank you for your help. Now you can step back behind the wire.' Bill commanded.

'The hell I will. Those are my dogs.'

'Bullets might start flying around soon, Ben.' Peter patted the gun in his shoulder holster.

'They missed me in the war.'

'They might not this time.' Peter put his foot on the ladder. 'Go back, please. Call it a matter of insurance.'

'As far as the wire, no further,' Ben conceded.

'Behind it,' Bill demanded.

'Second dog in,' Peter called. He began to climb.

'I'm next, Collins.'

'No you're not.' Peter continued to climb, quickly, steadily, without any visible trace of fear. He looked up at the open trap door. If anyone flung a knife or fired a gun down at him, he'd be a sitting target, he reflected philosophically, but then again, close encounters of a grappling kind were more this clown's style. He figured that he had a more than even chance of making it all the way.

At the top he placed his hands firmly either side of the trap door housing and swung himself up into the room. The dogs were whimpering and scratching around an alcove in the wall directly in front of him. He reached for his gun, flicked off the safety-catch and rolled tightly into a corner, the seaward wall at his back.

He took his bearings carefully, noting the position of every item in the room. The ice chest and the generator would afford some protection if bullets started flying. The bench and oil cans might prove useful in a fight. Shouldn't be too difficult, provided the clown had nothing more than a knife. The dogs continued to scratch at the wall. No sign of Sherringham.

Bill's head popped cautiously up through the trap door.

'Clear,' Peter hissed.

Bill rolled alongside him into the room. 'In there?' He gestured with his gun. Peter nodded. They rushed the alcove. One either side. Peter darted out and pushed. The wood gave, but only fractionally. He crawled in amongst the dogs.

'Small door. I'd say about four foot. Keyhole. Open bolt this side,' he whispered.

'Shoot the lock?' Bill suggested. Peter nodded agreement. He put the nozzle of his gun into the hole and pointed down. The explosion was quickly followed by the acrid smell of cordite.

'Now.'

Peter kicked in the door at Bill's command. The dogs bounded through. There were shouts, a scream. Dogs snarling, growling, worrying at something. Holding the

gun out in front of him, Peter bent double and negotiated the small gap.

Light poured in through the ragged holes in the
ceiling and floor. He was on a stage. A heap of wriggling people and snarling dogs to his right.

'For pity's sake, call the dogs off,' Richard Sherringham, a bleeding arm stuffed into Myrtle's mouth,
appealed to them hysterically.

'Myrtle, Cyril, heel!' Peter ordered sharply. To his
amazement they slunk off, crawling behind him.

Richard bent over a body on the floor. Peter could
only see black silk trousers, white pompoms, silk
slippers.

'Who is it, Sherringham?' he called out suspiciously,
instinctively lifting his gun. He sensed Bill moving in
behind him, but he didn't move a muscle. Richard
looked up, tears diluting the blood on his face.

'My brother, Sergeant Collins. My kid brother Tim.'

'Can you tell us what you found in there?'

'Is it true there's a freezer full of heads?'

'Have you caught the motorway murderer?'

'Is there a connection between the murders and the
Sherringhams?'

'Why did Dr Sherringham . . .'

'Please, boys.' Bill threw his hands up in despair.
'You should know better. Press conference in two hours
at the station. Until then I have nothing to say.' He
slapped his fingers over the lens of a camera that
pushed in too close to his face. 'Two hours at the
station,' he repeated.

Peter passed unnoticed through the tight knit group
of pressmen. Exhausted, he leaned back against a police
van and closed his eyes.

'You look about done in, Collins. Want some of this?'
A constable who'd started in the force about the same
time as he had handed him a flask.

'Thank God for a copper who doesn't call me "Sir".' Peter took the flask gratefully. He unscrewed the top and swallowed a stiff dose of brandy.

'Rough in there?'

'Not as rough as I thought it would be.' Peter slipped the gun holster from his shoulder, and rammed it in his trouser pocket. He'd have to turn it in later, but for the moment it could wait.

'Watch out, here comes trouble,' the constable warned. Peter handed back the flask.

'Peter,' Bill hailed him. 'If you arrest . . .'

'I'm not arresting anyone. I'm not doing anything. I'm finished.'

'You look finished,' Bill agreed. 'Want the rest of the day off?'

'Not the rest of the day. As of now I'm taking extended leave.'

'Oh no you're not. There's all the loose ends to tie up.'

'Tie them yourself.' Peter picked up his jacket from the floor of the van. 'I've things to do.'

'Such as?'

'Caring for an old friend while I still can.'

Peter walked away. He didn't look back. Not once. If he had, he knew he'd get sidetracked. Involved. With Daisy, with the slobbering, jibbering maniac he'd helped strap into a strait-jacket. With finding the villains who'd killed Harries and turned him into so much mincemeat.

'Damn them all!' he cursed loudly, climbing into his car. He'd drive to the hospital. Find out the truth. Then he'd have to make a phone call. One he didn't want to make. To Axminster.

379

Chapter Sixteen

The room was perfectly still and quiet. Daisy sat fixed, immobile. Only her eyes were alive as she gazed lovingly at Tim's long body stretched out on a bed next to her chair.

The past few days had taught her to cherish the times when Tim slept. She'd learned to deceive herself, pretend normality. He'd had an appendix operation, concussion, collapsed lung – anything but the truth. Anything rather than face the fact that beneath his beautiful, relaxed features, insanity raged hideously through his broken mind.

Or did it? Wasn't there something left of the old Tim? A tiny part? The part that had reached out to her from the darkness. Triggered her nightmares, shown her the full horror of what he'd seen and done. And was conversely nurturing within her now the faint flicker of hope that given sufficient time and care he would recover.

Supposition and hope. Foolish, stupid hope. All she had left to cling to. The wild hope that belonged in the realms of fantasy. Tim would wake up. Slowly open his eyes, smile, reach out to her with his hands. Whisper, 'Darling, I've had this crazy dream.' Hope, almost but not quite as ethereal, that Richard or Joanna would walk into the room and cry, 'We've identified a drug. There's an antidote.'

'Daisy?'

She looked up, half expecting to see a figment of her imagination.

'Richard. I'm sorry, I was miles away.'

He sat in a chair alongside her own. 'He hasn't woken?'

'No.'

'Probably just as well.'

'We can't keep him sedated for ever.'

A small dry cough from the other side of the room reminded her that they weren't alone. They were never alone. A few days of living with a police shadow and she'd learned to ignore the presence. Proof that it was possible to get used to almost anything.

'I've come to take you to lunch.' Richard rose from his chair.

'I'm not hungry.'

'Doctor's orders. If you don't eat, you'll collapse, and frankly that's an added burden I couldn't cope with right now.'

'Put like that, how can I refuse?'

The constable nodded to Richard as they left the room. A nurse slid into the chair Daisy'd vacated, and silence closed in on the sick-room once more.

'About bloody time, too. We'd just about given up hope of seeing you again.'

'Well take a good look while you have the chance,' Peter retorted. 'Because as of ten minutes from now, I'm taking the rest of the leave that's owed me.'

'Oh no you're not,' Bill blasted. 'You're not taking another minute's leave until this case is closed.'

'As far as I'm concerned, this case is closed. It was closed yesterday.'

Peter threw himself on one of the familiar hard chairs in Bill's office. Familiar. But wrong. No Trevor sitting opposite. No Harries rushing in and out like an eager puppy dog. Sitting in the hospital had been a pushover compared with this. For the first time, Harries' death and Trevor's absence moved out of their separate, seg-regated compartments, and bit deep into his normal routine. And it hurt. More than he would have believed possible.

'I'm sorry. I meant to ask how Trevor is.' Bill cleared his throat in embarrassment.

'He has a machine to do his breathing and eating for him. The doctors are arguing amongst themselves as to whether or not he'll ever see, talk or think again,' Peter said flatly.

'How are his family taking it?'

'His mother cries all the time. His brother tries to keep a stiff upper lip. Some of the time he succeeds.'

'Where are they staying?'

'In Trevor's flat. I offered them mine. It's cleaner, but no better. They prefer to put up with Trevor's mess.'

'Anything I can do?'

'Not unless you're a miracle worker.'

'I've been meaning to call in and visit him myself,' Bill insisted a little too doggedly. 'But it's been like a zoo here. The brass called an end-of-case conference late yesterday afternoon and it finished at midnight. I couldn't get out of it. There are so many loose ends to tie up, and with the family of a government minister involved . . .'

'Don't apologize. His family don't know you, and Trevor's about as alert as a cabbage waiting to be picked,' Peter added brutally. Tight-lipped, he looked across at Bill. 'I'm not blaming you for any of it. Not any more. Harries and Trevor chose to be coppers. They knew the score.' He pulled a cigar out of his top pocket and lit it, remembering, in spite of the sentiments he'd just expressed, the conversation he'd had with Trevor in the hospital on that last morning. 'For the first time in years I've something on the horizon that's worth going for. And I'm not risking that. Not for you. Not for your crazy notions of revenge. And certainly not for an investigation that's going nowhere.'

For Trevor it had certainly gone nowhere, he reflected grimly. And it was his fault. Trevor had been sick. He should have been home in bed. Not hanging around the Hart waiting for Ben. Then afterwards, on the beach. Peter shuddered as he recalled the way he'd treated Daisy Sherringham. Trevor would have hated him for that. At least Daisy had given Trevor some cause for happiness, which was more than could be said for him.

'Peter, Trevor wouldn't want . . .'

'For Christ's sake, Bill, don't start piling on the platitudes. I couldn't take it. What happened, happened. Harries is dead, and Trevor is as good as dead and I'm responsible.'

'That's crazy.'

'Is it?' Peter drew on his cigar. 'I briefed Harries and sent him out. I took Trevor to the Hart. I'll have to learn to live with it. All I want to do now is to go home and drink myself into a stupor. I didn't call in here for a dose of paternal sympathy. Trevor's desk has to be cleared out and I couldn't bear the thought of some copper who didn't even know him chucking his things into a box. And as I'm here, I'm telling you, purely out of courtesy, that I'm taking all the leave that's owed me. Now that you know, I'm going into the main office . . .'

'I'll make a deal with you,' Bill offered. 'Give me twenty-four hours of your time and I'll add a week's leave to whatever you've got coming.'

'No.'

'You've got to be mad to turn down an offer like that.'

'This job doesn't make for sanity.'

'That doesn't say very much for the rest of us,' Bill replied evenly, only just managing to keep his temper under control.

Peter sat back in his chair, drew heavily on his cigar and looked carefully at Bill.

'Tell me,' he asked in a softer voice. 'Why am I suddenly so important? This place is crawling with "yes boys", ready to jump the moment you click your fingers.'

'You started the case. I thought you'd like to finish it.'

'I'm drug squad, not murder. I never wanted any part of this dirty mess. You were the one who pushed us out of our field.'

'Steady, Collins,' Bill warned. 'You've always been bloody difficult. Don't turn impossible on me now. You carry on this way and someone will have your stripes.'

'Fine. If it's my job you're after, you can have it.'

'For Christ's sake, I don't want your job. We're going to be stretched to the limit over the next couple of days. I thought you'd like to help out. Make the formal arrest. Nail the bastards who put Trevor where he is. Wrap up the ends.'

'By serving a warrant on Tim Sherringham?' Peter sneered. 'Forget it. Even I felt sorry for the poor bugger once he was strapped into a strait-jacket.'

'Not Tim Sherringham,' Bill said quietly.

Peter's jaw dropped. 'Then who?'

'Those two down-and-outs. Andy . . .' Bill fumbled at his desk, eventually putting his hand on the notepad he was looking for '. . . and the one they call Gramps.'

'But they didn't kill anyone,' Peter protested.

'I've two warrants here that say different.'

'I take a couple of days off and you have a brainstorm?'

'It ties in, Peter. They had access to the pier through the hole in the wire. They used the place as a base, dressed in the old pierrot costumes and make-up they found in the theatre.'

'Forty-year-old make-up?' Peter queried logically.

'They saw Tim Sherringham in the hostel. Saw him give Sam the cheque. They figured he had money and drew up a plan. A bit Hollywood 1930s, but a plan that almost worked.'

'Give over. Those two couldn't organize a piss-up in a brewery.'

'Together or separately,' Bill continued, unflustered by Peter's remarks, 'they travelled from the pier, by boat, upriver to the motorway. Wearing the clown costumes, they flagged down Tim Sherringham's car . . .'

'How did they know he'd be travelling along the motorway at that time in the morning?'

'They made the call that got him out of bed.'

'How in hell did they know about the Hawkins case?'

'They overheard Tim Sherringham and Amanda Dart talking about work when they visited Jubilee Street.'

'And Tony Pierce?'

'He was a mistake. They flagged down his car on the same night they flagged down Sherringham's. I figure he drove along the motorway about an hour earlier. Realizing their mistake, they stabbed him to death. Then they dragged his body to the side of the road where they removed his head and hands, which they hid in the old ice chest on the pier.'

'Why keep the head and hands?'

'Make it difficult for anyone to identify the victim.'

'You just said he was flagged down by mistake.'

'And so he was.'

'Let me see if I'm getting this straight. You believe, really believe, that those two dog-ends of humanity thought all this out, so they could kidnap Sherringham. Then, overcoming Tim Sherringham, all six foot six inches of him, and clutching Pierce's head and hands, they made off in their victim's car for a joy ride? Even if I bought it, which I don't, where's Tony Pierce's car and the boat now?'

385

'Tony Pierce's and Tim Sherringham's cars have been traced to a breaker's yard in the dock area, so Andy or Gramps must have gone back for whichever car they left first time round.'

'And Amanda Dart?'

'They picked her up on the marina.'

'Come on. Two scruffy down-and-outs that anyone in their right mind would cross the street to avoid, persuaded Amanda Dart to go off with them to Sherringham's boat?'

'They're insane, but like all down-and-outs they're streetwise, cunning. Amanda was a nurse. They probably told her Sherringham was sick, that she was needed on board his yacht. We know she was fond of Tim Sherringham, and that he tried to help her find her brother. If she'd thought he was in trouble she would have gone running to him, down-and-outs or not.'

Peter took a deep breath. It was all so bloody plausible, provided you didn't know Andy and Gramps the way he did.

'You still haven't explained away the boat.'

'They worked in pairs. One of them drove the victim's car, the other took the dinghy, rowing boat, whatever, back to the marina. They probably "borrowed" it from there in the first place. There are dozens of small craft moored amongst the larger yachts, and we're constantly getting calls that one or two have gone missing. They invariably turn up later. After all, two down-and-outs are hardly likely to go out and buy a dinghy.'

'No. But according to you, they must have saved their social security to buy the petrol for the generator that fed the ice box. And all for the fun of building up a nice little collection of frozen heads. Not much of a motive, by any standards.'

'Crazy people don't need motives. Will you arrest them, or not?'

'I'd sooner arrest the real killer. Or Richard Sherringham.'

'Richard Sherringham?'

'You did search the old staff quarters at the clinic?'

'I've been wanting to talk to you about that.'

'I'm listening.'

'The place was clean.'

'Clean! For Christ's sake.'

'We found everything exactly as you described it. Dust, cobwebs, old files.'

'Bins of radioactive waste.'

'Bins of radioactive waste,' Bill repeated. 'Holding pellets of spent radium, and human waste that had been removed during operations on cancerous tumours.'

'There's got to be some mistake.'

'The Home Office pathologist was with us. He went through those bins at considerable personal risk. He found nothing.'

'But surely to God you confronted Sherringham, showed him Harries' shoe?'

'How in hell could I? Be reasonable. What was I supposed to say? By the way, one of my colleagues broke in here last night. He snooped around your old staff quarters, rummaged in the bins marked "Danger. Radioactive Waste" and came up with this shoe with a transmitter inside it.'

'Exactly that.'

'Sherringham didn't even come along to see what we were doing. One of the porters opened up the place for us. That's how important it was to him.'

'He must have found out I was there. He could have talked to the security guard who let me into the place. He had plenty of time to move out the evidence, replace those bins.'

'I'm not saying I don't believe you. But you know as well as I do that we need firm evidence before we can make a move.'

'Sherringham owns that place.'

'And at least a hundred people work there. More, if you count the domestic staff.'

'How many of those have keys to the old staff quarters?'

'The keys are kept on a board in the head porter's office.'

'Including the key to that back room?'

'Yes.'

Peter sank his face into hands.

'It will take time, Peter, but we'll get to the bottom of it, I promise you.'

'And in the mean time?'

'In the mean time, we formally arrest Andy and Gramps. Tie up one case before moving on to the next.'

'They're connected, for God's sake.'

'How?' Bill slammed his fist down on his desk. 'Tell me how?'

'I wish to God I could.'

'Here.' Bill tossed a couple of plain brown envelopes at him.

'What's this?'

'The warrants for Andy's and Gramp's arrests.'

Peter stared at them for a moment, then picked them up and stowed them away in the inside pocket of his anorak. 'I won't be able to catch up with Gramps until the hostel opens this evening,' he warned.

'I wasn't expecting you to.'

'I don't know about Andy. He often sleeps rough.'

'If you don't find him, someone soon will. I've had coppers on the lookout for Andy for the past three days.' Bill left his desk and walked over to the map of the town that was pinned to his wall. 'You'll bring them back here?'

'Where else?'

'You'll need help. Pick your own men. Just leave someone capable to cover as duty officer.'

'I can cope with mass murderers by myself, thank you all the same. Now if it was a pusher . . .'

'Get out of here, Collins.'

Peter left his chair. 'You know they're innocent, don't you?'

'You come up with hard evidence and I'll listen.'

'I'll start looking.'

'Not until after you arrest those two.' Bill stared at Peter. 'Think about it, Collins. Just think about it, that's all I ask. It begins to make sense after a while.'

'To you, perhaps, and the London boys,' Peter commented scathingly as he left the room. 'Not to me.'

'Daisy, this is Phillip Hardwick.' Richard indicated a tall thin man who was standing with his back towards them. 'I believe his reputation speaks for itself.'

'I'd rather Dr Sherringham made up her own mind about that.' Hardwick switched off the illuminated board he was using to read a series of X-rays, and offered Daisy his hand. 'Pleased to meet you.'

'I've read some of your papers,' Daisy replied politely, trying to peer over his shoulder at the board.

'Thank you. Most flattering to know one's work is reaching an audience.' He ushered her towards the button-backed leather chairs that were grouped around a heavily-carved oriental coffee-table in the corner of Richard's office. 'Shall we sit?' he suggested, as if he, not Richard, were the host.

Richard opened a drinks cabinet that stood unobtrusively in a corner of the vast room. 'Brandy?' he asked.

'Am I going to need it?' Daisy enquired nervously.

Richard didn't reply. He poured three measures into

389

balloon-shaped brandy glasses and carried them over to where she was sitting, next to Hardwick.

'Thank you.' Daisy picked up the glass and wrapped her fingers around the bowl. It gave her something to do with her hands.

'The first thing you must understand, Dr Sherringham . . .'

'Daisy, please call me Daisy.'

'The first thing you must understand, Daisy,' he smiled at her in an attempt to put her at ease, but she recognized the professional detachment in his manner and shrank from it, 'is that diagnosis is a very personal thing.'

'Not at your level, Mr Hardwick,' she corrected coldly.

'You flatter me.'

'Not at all.'

'So little is known about the brain and its functions, that even we so-called experts know little more than the African witch doctor who treats his patients according to tradition and superstition rather than from any soundly acquired knowledge. What I am about to tell you about your husband's condition is no more than my considered opinion.'

She sipped her brandy slowly. The strong liquor, coupled with her nervous state, weakened her limbs and blurred her vision.

'I am of the belief that the damage to your husband's brain has been caused by drugs.' He slipped into the authoritative tone he usually reserved for the lecture room. 'As to the type of drug, I'd hazard a guess at a hallucinogenic, but in thirty years of practising medicine, I've never seen damage as severe, or as extensive.'

'Is it reversable?' she demanded.

'Before I answer that question, I'd like you to look at this.' He left his chair and walked over to the X-ray board. Richard remained seated. Daisy was certain that Richard knew what was coming, but her brother-in-law refused to meet her gaze. Instead, he finished his drink, and poured himself another with an unsteady hand. Eyes averted, he held out the bottle to her, but she shook her head and carried her glass from the table, going over to join Phillip Hardwick.

Hardwick switched on the board's lights and sat on the edge of Richard's desk. Daisy remained upright, tensing herself for what was to come.

'These are the X-rays that I ordered to be taken this morning. Side angles, top and front view of your husband's head.' He sketched out the sequence with his forefinger.

'I see.'

'If you look here, and here, and here,' his finger moved damningly from one negative to another, 'the extent of the damage becomes quite clear. These areas,' he pointed to the blanked-out central parts of Tim's brain, 'show where the cells have been destroyed. Eaten away, as it were.'

'Dear God.' She thrust her fingers into her mouth. 'There's virtually nothing left.'

'I agree. What little remains of your husband's brain has shrunk back to the edge of the cranium.'

'There's always the possibility of a cell transplant,' Richard declared loudly from the corner of the room. Daisy looked expectantly to Phillip Hardwick.

'Richard wants to try a brain cell transplant, using the techniques that are being pioneered in Mexico as a treatment for Parkinson's disease,' Hardwick explained briefly.

'Would it work?'

'In my opinion,' he looked at Richard, not her, 'it would be a futile exercise. The damage is far too dramatic and extensive to expect a positive response to that form of treatment.'

391

'You're saying that Tim will remain as he is. There'll be no alteration in his condition?'

'No, I'm not. Unfortunately, his condition is far from stable. These pictures were taken a few hours ago. These,' he switched on the lights to a second X-ray board, 'were taken the day your husband was admitted to the clinic. If you compare the two, you can trace the progress of disintegration. Even one week ago the damage was by no means as extensive as it is now.'

'What are you saying?'

'The life support system he's on is not a temporary measure. His respiratory problems have arisen because his brain has ceased to control even the involuntary functions of his body. It may be possible to keep him alive on a ventilator for a while. But what you and Richard have to face is the fact that you'll soon be keeping alive a body without even a semblance of a brain.'

'I think it's worth trying a transplant.' Richard had finished his second brandy and was pouring his third.

Hardwick switched off the lights, and returned to his seat. 'I can't stop you.'

'I want you to do it.'

'I wouldn't be the best person. You know better than anyone that a surgeon has to believe in what he's doing.'

'And you wouldn't?' Daisy asked succinctly.

'I wouldn't,' he replied.

'Then we'll have to find someone else.' Richard picked up the brandy bottle and half filled his glass. 'Salen is flying in from Mexico this afternoon. You'll wait until he gets here?'

'Of course.' Hardwick put his hand over the top of his brandy glass to stop Richard from refilling it. 'That's the least I can do.'

Peter checked the time as he drove through the town.

Eight forty-five. If he went to the hostel this early he would run the risk of being seen by Andy or Gramps, or both, and that might put them off the idea of coming in for the night. There were nooks and crannies in the docks known only to the dossers. If they went to ground he wouldn't stand a chance of picking them up. Not tonight, at any rate. But that left him with the problem of what to do for the next hour or so.

He could go and have a drink. The problem was where? The Hart was out. He didn't want to set foot in the damned place again. In fact, thinking about it, he didn't want to go anywhere where he'd be recognized. He couldn't face people, no matter how well-meaning. Not yet.

He drove past the largest hotel in the town. A characterless place, part of a chain that had spawned replicas in every sizeable centre of population across the country. He'd once stayed in one of its brother edifices in London. They all had the same fittings and fixtures, the same furniture, the same stained glass and blackened pine, even the same flowered wallpaper. Wendy had loved what he'd called the 'plastic ambience'. She'd dragged him into the place on more than one occasion, and he'd never seen anyone in it he'd known. Which was why he turned the wheel of his car and drove into the car park at the back of the building now. Just as he'd hoped, it was empty apart from half a dozen cars. Even plastic pubs served their purpose.

The main bar was as deserted as it had promised to be. He walked over to the counter and banged on it with his knuckles. A white-coated barman appeared from the back. Peter ordered a pint of draught beer, then, leaning on the counter, he looked around. A couple of elderly ladies sitting in a dark corner eyed him slyly as they sipped at their port and lemon. He knew the generation. They probably thought themselves little devils for daring to venture into a pub.

'Slumming, Sergeant Collins?'

Judy Osbourne stood at his shoulder. She was wearing dark slacks and a plain grey mohair sweater that hid most of her figure. Her blonde hair was tied back in a severe ponytail, and her face was free from make-up, giving her an oddly youthful appearance despite the shadows beneath her eyes.

'Thought I'd look at how the other half lives.' He took his drink from the barman and turned to face her.

'A campari and soda,' she informed the barman briskly. 'In a long glass, plenty of soda, and a slice of lemon, not orange.'

'The lady knows what she wants.' Peter threw a couple of coins on to the counter.

'I'll pay for my own drink,' she snapped.

'Of course. That's to pay for mine.'

He took his pint and walked over to a table set in the opposite corner to the one occupied by the two elderly ladies. He stared moodily into the depths of his glass as he supped his beer. It tasted strange, fizzy and antiseptic, after the rich tang of the Hart's real ale. He heard Judy Osbourne talking to the barman, then, to his amazement, she joined him.

'You're an out-and-out bastard,' she said coldly, standing in front of him. 'Not least of all for what you did to Daisy Sherringham down on the beach the day Tim was found.'

'Thrusting Tony Pierce's head at her,' he said, remembering the events of that day. 'I'm sorry, I shouldn't have done that.'

'Alan said you were deeply shocked by what had happened to Trevor Joseph, but then Alan always looks for the good in everyone, even bastards like you.'

'I've said I'm sorry. I don't know what else I can do.'

'You can tell me what you're doing to get the animals who turned Tim Sherringham into a cabbage.'

394

He kicked a chair out from under the table. 'Why don't you sit down?' he suggested mildly.

'I don't want to drink with you.'

'You wouldn't be drinking with me. You've bought your own. And I've no intention of carrying on with this conversation until you do sit down. Even policemen study basic psychology, Dr Osbourne. You either lower yourself to my level, or leave.'

'Are you doing anything to put Tim Sherringham's kidnappers where they belong?' she demanded, reluctantly setting her drink on to his table and taking the chair he offered.

'We hope to make an arrest shortly.'

'Are you bulling me?'

'I wouldn't dream of it.'

She studied him for a moment. 'I'm sorry about Trevor Joseph. He, at least, was human.'

'He was, and I'm not?'

'He's in a mess,' she said slowly, ignoring the inference in Peter's words. 'I suppose whoever kidnapped Tim attacked Trevor. It's strange you didn't find anyone else on that pier. I can't understand why Tim didn't try to escape. The pier was rotten. He could have broken through the boards and climbed down, but then if they'd drugged him from the outset . . .'

'I can't talk about a case that's still under investigation,' he said firmly.

'Then you haven't given up on it?'

'Far from it.'

There was a pause for a moment while they both drank.

'I've just come from the clinic.'

'Sherringham's clinic?'

She nodded. 'I saw Daisy and Tim.'

'How is he?'

'As well as anyone can be with severe brain damage.'

'Is there any news on how he got that way?'

'Your lot have taken enough statements and made enough reports during the past few days to sink a bloody battleship.'

'I haven't seen them.'

'I thought policemen never stopped working.'

'I've been with Trevor's family. Taking the odd shift at the hospital so they can rest. They don't trust the hospital to phone them if anything happens.'

'That must be bloody awful.'

'It is.'

She sat back in her chair and played with her glass. She'd never credited Peter Collins with human feelings before. He was obviously more skilled than most people at keeping them well hidden.

'The damage to Tim's brain is drug induced, according to the latest specialist that Richard's brought in,' she revealed. 'As he's the third to come up with that prognosis, I suppose it's somewhere near the truth.'

'What kind of drugs?'

'If it means anything, hallucinogenic.'

'LSD?'

'It does mean something.'

'I work on the drug squad.'

'Richard wants to try a transplant.'

'A transplant?'

'Brain cell transplant. You know, like they're doing in Mexico.'

'I don't know.'

'They're surgically implanting brain cells culled from aborted foetuses into patients with brain disease. The idea is to slow down the progression of brain cell disintegration. It's caused one hell of an ethical row, but no one can deny that it appears to be working. People with Parkinson's disease are responding to the treatment in a dramatic way. The transplants are not only taking, but it's claimed that after the operation the transplanted cells can stimulate the production of new brain cells to replace the damaged ones. It's hoped that the technique will eventually have similar results on patients with Alzheimer's disease. And the damage to Tim's brain is similar to that caused by Alzheimer's disease.'

'Alzheimer's disease?'

'Senile dementia to you.'

Peter's mind clicked into gear. He remembered the tissue-typing mark on Robin Dart's arm. Daisy Sherringham's voice, heavy with sarcasm, saying, 'Brain transplants, Sergeant Collins, are still in the realms of fiction.'

A down-and-out disappearing without trace. Harries cut up into so many small pieces. God alone knew how much of him remained, or what, if any, part of his body had been taken. Amanda Dart's and Tony Pierce's heads stored in the ice box on the old pier.

'It's so damned cruel.' Judy Osbourne's voice pierced his thoughts. 'Richard's had to put up with so much. His father committed suicide, now this business with Tim.'

'Sherringham's father killed himself?' Peter struggled to concentrate, file his thoughts in some semblance of order.

'Yes. Apparently some experiments of his went wrong. I don't know the details, only that there was a scandal that forced Richard to close down his father's hospital and research projects in America, and set up over here. Richard's never mentioned it to me, but you know what the medical world is like for rumours.'

Peter didn't know, but what he did know was that for the first time the removal of the victims' heads began to make sense.

'What was this research project of Sherringham's father's?'

'I don't know much about it, only what I've heard tenth-hand.' She finished her drink. 'I came here to get away from medical talk. What's left of Tim Sherringham is a mess. Daisy's devastated. She's trying to put a brave face on it, but she's failing dismally. I know it's a vicious thing to say, but it would have been better if they'd killed Tim outright, rather than leaving the mindless husk that Daisy and Richard are trying to cope with.'

'You don't think he'll recover?'

'The experts are arguing over the answer to that one. I'm only a simple houseman.'

'You're a doctor.'

'A very junior one.'

'But you have an opinion?'

'For what it's worth, I've already told you what I think. I'm on duty in half an hour.' She left her seat and held out her hand. 'Goodbye, Sergeant Collins. I sincerely hope I don't see you again.'

'That, Dr Osbourne, is very unlikely.'

'Perhaps. Perhaps not.'

She walked quickly out of the bar, her tall slim body weaving confidently in and out of the tables. He forgot about her and the arrests he was supposed to be making in the hostel in half an hour, and concentrated on the information he'd gleaned. He had to find out more about Sherringham's father, and there was one person who could help him there. A reporter who had access to newspaper archives, and what was even more important, owed him a favour or two.

Chapter Seventeen

'Andy and Gramps?'

'Gramps hasn't come in, but Andy's upstairs in the front bedroom. Peter, this is the first night we've seen him in weeks. Do you have to talk to him now? You know what he is. He could get upset, and then he'll leave. The man's sick and hungry, he needs to be here.'

'I'll try not to upset him, Sam. Perhaps it would be better if you got him for me.'

'What will you be wanting him for?'

'Talk, Sam, that's all. Just talk.'

Peter followed Sam up the stairs. He was blasted by a current of heat-laden air as Sam opened the door to the dormitory. It was crowded. Twelve narrow beds were packed into a space barely large enough for four. There was a strong smell of unwashed clothes and sweating bodies. He caught a glimpse of Andy lying half asleep on a bed next to a window glued shut by layers of old paint.

Sensing antagonistic eyes staring at him, Peter stepped back and allowed Sam to go in alone. Sam spoke gently, quietly to Andy. After a few moments, Andy followed Sam meekly out of the door.

'Mister, what do you want me for, Mister?' Andy spoke in the familiar grating tone that set Peter's teeth on edge.

'I want to talk to you for a few minutes, Andy. That's all,' Peter replied in a strained, softened voice that bore an uncanny resemblance to Trevor's.

'Let's go into the kitchen,' Sam suggested. 'I'll put the kettle on, and we'll all have a cup of tea.'

Peter made no objection, so Sam led the way downstairs. He switched on the kitchen light, and took the kettle from the chipped and rusted gas stove across to the sink to fill it with water. Peter hauled a rickety chair out from under the table and placed it carefully in front of the door. He'd learned his lesson from his last visit. He waited until Andy was well and truly into the room, then he closed the door, and sat with his back to it. This time no one was going to escape.

'What do you want me for, Mister?' Andy whined. 'I didn't do nothing. Not me. I tried to help the other Mister. Honest I did. It wasn't my fault he wouldn't move. It wasn't my fault. It was the clown that did it. The clown, Mister. He did it all. And you took the clown. I saw you take him.'

'Why didn't you wait, Andy? We wanted to talk to you. We looked for you afterwards, but you'd gone.'

'Wait for what, Mister? You were angry. You're angry with me now. And I didn't do nothing. Not me.'

'I want you to tell me about the clowns, Andy.' Peter pulled some money out of his pocket and laid it on the table. 'You can have that in the morning. Father will look after it for you.' Andy looked to Sam.

'It's all right, Andy, I'll take care of it, I promise. I'll keep it for you.'

'How many clowns were there, Andy?' Peter asked.

Andy stared at him for a moment, debating whether to talk or not. He looked from Peter to Sam several times, then finally, realizing that his only exit was blocked, he answered Peter's question.

'There were two clowns, Mister. The big one. The big one you took away. He was there for a long time. He hurt the other one. The thin one that fell into the water with a splash. I was there. I saw it.'

Peter remembered the food parcel. Had someone carried food to Sherringham? He held back and said nothing, waiting for Andy to continue.

'I hated the thin one, Mister. Once it hissed and

400

stamped at me. And it chased me. I fell. I hurt myself.'
Andy clutched at his arms and sang in a crooning
voice. 'I hate it. It hurt me. I hate it. It hurt me . . .'

'Here you are, Andy, a nice, cup of tea with lots of
milk and sugar, just the way you like it.' Sam placed
the mug in front of him. 'Would you be having one
with us, Peter?'

'No. No thank you, Sam.'

Andy grabbed greedily at his tea. He sipped it slowly,
eyeing Peter over the rim of the cup.

'The pier was kept locked, Andy. Tell me, how did
you get in and out of the place?'

A sly, cunning look stole into Andy's eyes. 'I climbed
up. There's holes in the floor. Big holes. If you cling
to the poles you can slide along, Mister. All it takes is
time. Watch, be careful, don't trust the wood. The
wood cracks and breaks, but not the poles. The poles
are strong. But always have to watch the holes. And
the sea. The sea's a long way down. Have to be careful,
Mister. Bodies fall. Bodies fall down deep.'

'And you saw a body fall?'

'I did, Mister. Fall a long, long way down. Hit the
waves, there was a big splash. The water hit me, but
no one saw. No one saw. Not even the tall clown who
threw down the clown with the keys.'

'The clown who fell? He had keys?'

'Keys to unlock the door. He had keys.'

'You seem to know the pier well, Andy. And you
saw a lot.'

'Saw a lot, but no one saw Andy. I'm too clever to
let anyone see Andy.'

'This other clown. The one you hate. When did this
other clown come?'

'In the night. With keys. It kept the big one locked
in. Andy saw. Andy heard the howling. No one else
heard. But I did. The tall clown howled. Howled like
a dog.' Andy's eyes glistened, two glowing coals in the

yellow light of the dingy kitchen. 'Howled and howled like a dog. Beat his head against the door, too. But the door wouldn't move. He couldn't get out. Not like Andy. The tall clown wasn't as clever as Andy. He didn't know how to get in and out.'

'How many clowns did you see, Andy?' Peter pressed again.

Andy held up his fingers. 'One, two,' he said slowly. 'But one went into the water with a big splash. And the tall clown. You took the tall clown away. The tall clown was bad. He hurt the other one, Mister. Andy saw. And he hurt the other Mister. Andy tried to mend the head.'

Peter closed his eyes against the scene on the beach, Andy pulling Trevor through the waves.

'Trevor, is he hurt?' Sam demanded. 'You should have told me, Peter, I'll pray for him.'

'The doctors think he's past praying for, Sam.' Peter rose stiffly from his hard seat, and turned his face away from Sam. 'He's not expected to recover.'

'I am sorry, Peter. But whatever happens, he's not past prayers. I'll pray for him tonight. God will take care of him.'

'I wish I could believe that, I really do. Now I've got to get this man to the station.'

'No. Not me, Mister. You're not taking me away. Not me, Mister.'

'You'll be arresting him, Peter? On what charge?'

'The charge doesn't matter. He won't be inside long.' Peter clamped his hand firmly on to Andy's shoulder. 'We'll find you a nice comfortable cell, with a warm bed and a meal. Fish and chips, perhaps. You'd like that, wouldn't you, Andy?'

'You'll hurt me.'

'No one's going to hurt you. I promise you. Not this time. All you're going to get is a good night's sleep, and a meal.'

Andy looked at Peter, then at the door. He knew when he was cornered.

'I'll go if you find me a bottle, Mister,' he whispered, his craving for a drink making him suddenly brave. 'I'll go with you for a bottle.'

'Then a bottle it is.' Keeping his hand on Andy's shoulder, Peter opened the door.

'Do you know what time it is?' Bill shouted, marching up to Peter's desk.

'Eleven o'clock,' Peter replied absently, tossing some papers into his top drawer.

'I sent you out hours ago.'

'And I told you then that I'd have to wait until the hostel closed. If I'd moved in earlier they could have run off.'

'You've brought them both in?'

'No. Gramps wasn't around, only Andy.'

'Where is he?'

'In the cells with a fish and chip takeaway and a bottle of cider.'

'You've charged him?'

'No, I've put him in the cells with a fish and chip takeaway and a bottle of cider,' Peter repeated irritatingly.

'You gone soft in the head, Collins?'

'No. I just feel sorry for the poor old bugger. You know as well as I do he didn't kidnap Sherringham. Or murder anyone. If you want to carry on with this damned farce you can charge him yourself.' Peter left his desk and walked out of the door of the main office.

'You knocking off duty now?' Bill demanded, following him. 'Because if you are, it's an early start. Seven o'clock sharp tomorrow morning.'

'In that case you'll forgive me if I go and get my beauty sleep.' Peter stopped and leaned against the doorway of Bill's room. 'By the way,' he said casually,

403

an inflection in his voice Trevor would have recognized at once, 'did we get any pathology reports on the heads we found in the ice chest on the pier?'

'On what?'

'The heads we found in the ice chest on the pier,' Peter repeated patiently.

'Some reports have come in.' Bill pointed to his in-tray. 'I haven't had time to read them. What the hell do you expect to find?'

'Nothing. Nothing much.' Peter walked into Bill's room and picked up the file. 'You don't mind, do you?'

'I thought you said you were leaving.'

'A little light bedtime reading wouldn't go amiss.'

'Put it back before you check out,' Bill shouted irritably, moving towards the canteen. 'And when you come in tomorrow, make sure you're in a more co-operative frame of mind.'

Instead of retiring to the small bedroom that opened off his office, Richard Sherringham showered and changed into fresh clothes. Discarding his suit jacket, he sat at his desk in shirtsleeves. His secretary kept in constant touch with Hare, and between them they took care to ensure that Richard was presented with meals at regular intervals, and that the small wardrobe in his office was kept well stocked with clothes. Richard himself hadn't made a decision, or given a direct order to any of his staff, medical or domestic, in days.

He hadn't left the confines of the clinic since Tim had been brought in. And he had no intention of leaving now. Tomorrow – so much hinged upon tomorrow. The operation. Would it work for Tim? He picked up the notes Salen had left on his desk.

The intercom buzzed loudly. He pressed the button. 'Yes?'

'There's a Sergeant Collins to see you, Dr Sherringham. He says it's extremely urgent.'

'Send him up,' Richard answered briefly. Damned policemen. Were they never going to let go?

He waited for footsteps to sound along the corridor outside his office. When they did, he left his seat and opened the door.

'Dr Sherringham, it's extremely good of you to see me.' Peter was cool, professional, but undeniably polite.

'I could hardly do anything else, seeing as how you're already in the building.'

'May I come in?'

Richard stood aside and allowed Peter to walk into his office.

'It's late, Sergeant, and I'm tired, so would you mind coming to the point quickly.'

'May I sit down?'

'If you must,' Richard muttered ungraciously.

Peter walked across the room and sat in one of the chairs grouped around the coffee-table. He leaned back, making himself as comfortable as he could.

'The point, Sergeant Collins,' Richard repeated tersely.

'The point, Dr Sherringham, is that you decided to recreate your father's experiments here, in England. And several people, innocent people, have died as a result. That makes you a murderer.'

Peter turned to face Richard. If Richard was shocked or surprised at the allegation, it didn't register in the expression on his face. Instead he walked calmly over to the drinks cabinet and opened it.

'Brandy or whisky?' he enquired hospitably.

'Neither, thank you.'

'Then you're on duty?'

'No. This is an informal call.'

'I hate drinking alone.'

'We all have to do things we dislike from time to time, Dr Sherringham.'

Richard poured himself a brandy, then he joined

405

Peter, sitting in the chair opposite him. 'Are you basing this accusation on anything more substantial than a mental aberration, Sergeant Collins? Because if you are, I'd be extremely interested to hear what.'

'The facts are incontestable. I have all the evidence I need. What I don't have is a motive. And as I've worked out the solution to this case without any assistance from you, I was hoping you'd supply me with that much. Why? In God's name, why?' Peter's professionalism broke down as he remembered Trevor's unconscious face. And Harries – young, keen, enthusiastic, and incredibly proud to be given his first plain clothes assignment. 'Why did you insist on repeating a series of experiments that cost so many lives twenty years ago? Wasn't there enough damage done then?'

'What makes you think that my father's experiments have been repeated, Sergeant Collins?' Richard asked quietly.

'Please don't insult my intelligence.'

'I wouldn't dream of it. Although you apparently insist on insulting mine.'

'I asked a friend of mine to carry out some research into his newspaper's archives for me. He came up with twenty-year-old stories about a Dr Sherringham. A group of students were apparently driven insane after a drink and drugs party organized by the man. One that produced a uniformly bad trip. My friend even discovered a follow-up story that had been written by an investigative reporter ten years ago. The reporter had attempted to trace all the students who'd been at the party. Apart from three exceptions, they were all dead. And those three exceptions were incarcerated in mental asylums, their bills paid for by a kind and charitable benefactor who signed his cheques anonymously. Is that where you intend to put your brother, Dr Sherringham? Or do you have a private room set aside here for your failures?'

'Old newspaper articles hardly constitute evidence, Sergeant Collins.'

'That newspaper article was all I needed to fit everything into place.'

'Everything?' Richard raised his drink to his lips.

'This case began with the filing of a missing persons report on your brother. Of course, we didn't know then that you'd fed him hallucinogenic drugs that had turned him into a raving lunatic. And, naturally enough, when headless bodies turned up on the motorway, we assumed that he'd be one of the victims. Not the perpetrator.'

'Surely to God you can't believe that Tim is responsible for the motorway murders?'

'I said he was the perpetrator, not the murderer. You and your father are responsible for the motorway murders, and as your father is dead, I suppose that leaves you.' Peter pulled a cigar out of the inside pocket of his anorak. 'Do you mind if I smoke?'

Richard shook his head.

'It was very clever of you to organize two killings. While we were out looking for a deranged serial murderer, we were too busy to even contemplate the idea that the victims had been carefully selected. Take the first victim, for instance. Tony Pierce. He was driving home from a party at your house. He'd stayed behind to play cards until four o'clock in the morning. You knew the make, model and number of his car, the time he'd left your house and the direction he was taking Enough to forecast where he'd be at a given time, plus or minus a few minutes. All you had to do was prime someone to waylay him. And that someone was your brother.

'I worked out the how, but not the why. Then, earlier this evening I ran into Judy Osbourne in a pub. She told me about the brain cell transplant scheduled for your brother tomorrow morning. She answered the question that every copper on the case has been asking. Heads? Why would anyone cut the heads and hands off a body?'

'I would have thought that was obvious. It's difficult to identify a body without hands or a head.'

'But we found those particular heads stored in a freezer. An ice box that was kept running at the cost of a great deal of time and trouble. Again I asked myself why? Why would anyone take petrol to a deserted pier to keep an old generator running in order to keep human heads fresh in an ice box?'

'Cannibalism?' Richard suggested derisively.

Peter chose to ignore the remark. 'If the murderer had wanted to get rid of the heads, he could have done so straight away. We know he had a boat. He used it to gain access to the pier. If he'd wished to dispose of the heads, he could have sailed that bit further out into the bay, weighted his load and dropped it to the seabed. No one would have been any the wiser. Then tonight I read the pathologist's report on Tony Pierce's head. If Tony hadn't been murdered on the motorway he would have soon been in an asylum. He was suffering from brain decay. Senile dementia. The same disease Judy Osbourne told me your brother's suffering from. The pathologist also noted that Tony Pierce had been subjected to a recent brain operation. A small circle had been surgically removed from his cranium, and something had been introduced into the area most affected by the disease. He found evidence of decaying cells and a mass of dead foreign tissue.'

Peter noticed that Richard was gripping the stem of his glass tightly. He took it as a sign of guilt, belying the calm relaxed attitude that the doctor outwardly presented.

'There was one other head in that ice box. It, too, had been tampered with. It was also minus sections of brain tissue.'

'Removed, no doubt, in the clinically sterile atmosphere of the old pier,' Richard sneered. 'Whoever tampered with those heads was a maniac.'

'A maniac you created. You wanted Tony Pierce's head for analysis. By studying the mistakes you made during your first operation, you hoped to avoid repeating them in the second that you have planned for your brother tomorrow. Which brings me to the question of the donor tissue you need for that operation. Judy Osbourne told me that foetal brain cells are usually used. I don't know why you didn't use them. Perhaps you couldn't lay your hands on a supply. But what you could lay your hands on was an abundance of down-and-outs. The dregs of humanity. People with no homes, no hope, no friends or relatives to ask questions if they're wiped off the face of the earth. You needed a fit and healthy donor. You looked around, ruled out the junkies and hardened dossers, and settled on a young kid. Fit, healthy and no fixed address, and, as you thought, no one to miss him when he disappeared – without trace. He told his mate he was going to Saudi Arabia. Where is he now, Sherringham? At the bottom of the sea, feeding the fishes?'

'I don't suppose it would make any difference if I told you I have no idea what you're talking about?'

'None at all.'

Richard took his drink, left his seat and walked over to the window. He opened the blinds and looked out over the sea.

'One of the people you screened as a possible donor was a junkie. You rejected him. Later, unbeknown to you, he disappeared.' Peter's voice filled the room. 'And when he disappeared, his sister went down to Jubilee Street, accompanied by, of all people, your brother Tim. The two of them searched the dock area. They met people, asked questions. You found out about it, took fright and eliminated her, not realizing she posed no risk to your bloody experiments at all. You used your brother Tim to kill Tony Pierce. The junkie's sister, Amanda Dart, you either killed yourself, or had your insane brother do it for you. But what you didn't know was that the junkie who failed your screening was in a rehabilitation centre. His name was Robin Dart. Of course he's dead now, but before he died, he walked into the police station. He spoke to a copper, and he told the copper about a strange "medical" he'd had for a job. A medical that included a tissue-typing test. He hadn't passed muster. Hardly surprising, he was a junkie. But not your ordinary everyday junkie. He was an actor who'd used heroin by injecting it into the veins at the back of his knees. Three hours after leaving the police station, he was dead. The pathologist put the cause of death down to an overdose. Mainlining heroin through the vein in his arm. A vein he never used. And Robin Dart was clean. Had been for a while before he died. It didn't add up. Particularly when the pathologist later found enough cyanide in his body to kill half a dozen men. You got crude on that one, Sherringham. There's no refinement in using cyanide.'

Peter screwed the stub of his cigar out in the onyx ashtray on the coffee-table in front of him.

'And your last donor. You picked him up in the day-centre in Jubilee Street, but he wasn't a down-and-out. Stacko was an undercover copper. A young kid on his first plain clothes assignment who ended up as so much mincemeat in one of your bins of radioactive waste. I know, because I found him there.' Peter's face was white, strained under the harsh lighting in Richard's office.

'You went through the bins of radioactive waste? Here in the clinic?'

'Yes. Your security guard let me in to search for a prowler. I broke into your old staff quarters and combed the place thoroughly. I've got to hand it to you, bins of radioactive waste make the ideal place to dispose of an unwanted body. I wouldn't have dreamed of looking for Harries there if I hadn't been the one who'd sent him out. But then I felt responsible for the boy. Tell me, what's in that old house? Concealed video cameras? Or did your security guard tell you I'd been snooping around?' Peter looked Richard squarely in the eye. 'Aside from your bloody experiments, you've engineered the death of one copper and the destruction of another. And I'm arresting you for murder. Now.'

Silence pressed into the room once more.

'You have no warrant. No evidence other than what, on your own admission, you've gathered illegally.'

'I can still take you in.'

Richard left the window and walked back to his chair. He sat down in front of Peter.

'What you're calling evidence won't stand up in a court of law, and you know it.' He looked intently at Peter. 'I'll make a bargain with you. If you leave me here until tomorrow morning, I'll write out and sign a full confession detailing everything. All I'm asking for is a breathing space of a few hours. Once Tim's operation is over, I'll come with you.'

Peter said nothing.

'There's a policeman posted at Tim's door in the intensive care unit,' Richard suggested persuasively. 'Tim's on a life support system, he's hardly likely to get up and walk out. Why don't you telephone your colleague?' Richard handed Peter the phone. 'Ask him to come up here. He can follow me everywhere I go until you return tomorrow. He can remain in the same room as me. I give you my word, I will be here in the morning. And I'll have my confession signed and waiting.'

Peter knew Richard was right. He had very little evidence that would stand up in a court of law. He looked at Richard Sherringham, then he took the phone.

'You have until eight o'clock tomorrow morning.'

Joanna walked past the guard who was sitting in the ante-room of the intensive care unit of the clinic. She donned the obligatory mask and gown, and crept into the startlingly white antiseptic environment of the cubicle where Tim lay surrounded by the tubed and chromed high-technology apparatus of a life support system. Daisy was sitting next to him. Gowned and masked like Joanna, she was holding one of Tim's hands and looking into his face, trying to see past the paraphernalia of the machinery that was linked to his body.

'There's no change?'

Daisy glanced at Joanna and shook her head.

'If you'd like to take a break, I'll sit with him for a while.'

'Thank you. But I'd prefer to stay. I thought I'd never see him again, and now,' Daisy stared intently at her husband, 'I don't want to leave him. Even while he's in this state.'

'He won't remain in this state. Salen's preparing to operate first thing tomorrow morning.'

'I didn't think it could be organized that quickly.'

'We've managed to put together everything that's needed. It's all ready and waiting in the main theatre.'

'You've found compatible brain tissue?'

'Yes.' Joanna leaned back, closing the cubicle door behind her.

Daisy increased the strength of her grip on Tim's hand, trying to blank out the image of foetal brain cells that insisted on intruding into her consciousness. Ethics aside, there was so little of Tim's brain left. She couldn't help feeling that even a successful operation carried with it a risk of complete personality change.

How much of the Tim she knew and loved would remain after tomorrow?

'Daisy. It will be successful.'

'I wish I had your faith.'

'I've given Salen the notes Tim made six months ago when he carried out similar surgery on Tony Pierce. We have adult brain tissue as close to Tim's as we can get.'

'Tim operated on Tony Pierce?'

'Here in the clinic. He's a brilliant surgeon, Daisy. He has to pull through. He simply has to.' Her voice thinned into silence when she saw Daisy staring at her.

'I assisted Tim at the operation.' Joanna walked around the bed until she faced Daisy. 'Of course Tony's condition wasn't as serious as this, and the operation was less traumatic. Tim injected the cells into the affected area with a syringe, after removing only a small area of the cranium. But the principle is the same. And Salen has had a great deal more experience than Tim had. It's going to work this time, Daisy. Believe me.'

'Do you know how Tim got into this state?' Daisy demanded harshly.

'Yes.'

'He was part of some bloody experiment.'

'Not an experiment. He was finishing the work his father began.'

'What work?' Daisy kept her voice low, controlled, but the pressure she was putting on Tim's hand increased. Her knuckles whitened as her face grew tense. 'What work, Joanna?' she repeated.

'Theo was a great man. A great doctor,' Joanna revealed emotionally. 'When he died, I kept his papers. I hoped that Richard would carry on where his father had left off. But Richard didn't have Theo's breadth of mind. Theo's vision. Tim did. When I showed Tim Theo's research about a year ago, he understood exactly what his father had been striving towards. I've

413

worked with Tim now for nearly a year and we're close to completing what Theo began.' Joanna moved closer to the bed. 'He has to come through this.' Her voice lowered to a whisper. 'So much depends on his recovery.'

'Tim's work was at the hospital. If he'd been involved in anything else I would have known about it.'

'You knew only what Tim wanted you to know,' Joanna contradicted cuttingly. 'Tim's work at the General meant nothing to him. It was no more than a stopgap. It was you who wanted to work for the National Health Service, not Tim. He lived for the day when he'd be able to publish his father's findings. He took Theo's notes with him wherever he went. The hospital. Your flat. You never asked him what he was working on. You never looked to see if it was his patients' notes he was studying so intently. I know, because he told me.' Joanna flung the secret she and Tim had shared in Daisy's face.

'Tim and I told each other everything. We loved one another,' Daisy countered.

'He might have loved you, but he didn't trust you with the most important thing in his life.' Joanna reached out and touched Tim's cheek. 'He's so like his father. He has Theo's mind, Theo's way of working out problems. He has that special quality that can change attitudes, our whole way of thinking, our perception of the world. Call it what you will. Genius, brilliance. Whatever it is, I recognized it in him as I did in Theo.'

'Tim's a dedicated doctor. Not a genius. He had to work hard for what he got. The same as the rest of us.'

'You're forgetting how well I know Tim. Richard and I practically brought him up after Theo died. I've always thought of Tim as the son I've never had.'

'Tim's too old to be your son,' Daisy snapped

414

viciously. She wanted to lash out, hurt Joanna. Tim was hers. No one else's. He was reliant on her now, in his present state, more than ever, and she had no intention of abdicating that responsibility. Least of all to Joanna.

'God help us, do you think Tim and I were having an affair? It runs deeper than that, Daisy. Much deeper. We were colleagues. Tim achieved so much in the short time we worked together.' Preoccupied with the past, Joanna bit her lip. 'I've given Salen Tim and Theo's notes. I suppose they'll be made public now, but not in the way we wanted. We were working on ways to alleviate personality disorders. Give someone a controlled dose of hallucinogenic drug and hypnotize them out of character and out of unacceptable behaviour. It had never even been thought of seriously before Theo conceived the idea. The early results were promising. Think about it.' Joanna's face grew animated, positively glowing with enthusiasm. 'It is possible to hypnotize people out of character. We did it, and we proved it. Time and again. In the early stages we had government funding and access to long-term prisoners in gaols across America. Theo reprogrammed rapists and murderers, redesigned their entire personalities. The applications of his theory were limitless. He foresaw a time when prisons would be obsolete. When there'd be no need to lock people up. Simply treat them in a clinic. But then the authorities grew frightened. There were side-effects. So we took the experiments back to the laboratory. Tried the drug and hypnosis combination on volunteers . . .'

'Including Tim?'

'Tim was a child when Theo carried out his experiments. But when he began his own work a year ago, he insisted on actively participating in the experiments. He knew the limits of his own character. Exactly what he was, and was not, capable of doing.'

'My God!' A horrible suspicion dawned in Daisy's mind. Her nightmares. People crawling around without hands and heads. 'You turned Tim into a murderer. Tim really did kill Tony Pierce. That girl. He attacked Trevor Joseph. He knew what he was doing, and he hated it. That's why he tried to reach out to me. Why I saw the things he'd seen and done. He was mad, but not mad enough to lose his conscience.'

'I turned Tim into nothing. I advised him not to use himself as a guinea-pig. His father would never have countenanced the idea. I would have brought in volunteers from outside, but Tim wouldn't hear of it. He wanted to keep the experiment secret. Apart from Tony Pierce, of course. And Tony helped, in the beginning that is, until he became too ill to work. It was the drug that did the damage. It's so difficult to gauge the correct dosage. Tony was ill, and getting worse every day. He needed treatment and that meant finding donor cells. Tony and I set it up, and Tim operated, but it was too late. The whole thing was useless, futile. Tony didn't improve. We tried, we really tried, but if anything the rate of Tony's deterioration accelerated.'

'So you murdered him.'

'He was going to Arabia. We couldn't risk him dying God knows where, with some foreign pathologist poking and prying into his skull. Tim programmed himself to kill Tony. He made tapes. Took the drug. We set up in my laboratory, and we made use of the old pier. It had the reputation of being haunted and I decided to build on that. I thought no one would investigate reports of pierrots flitting about there during the night. I knew about the access in and out that my father had left when he'd wired off the place. Then, when Tim became totally deranged and the police had taken your boat, I locked him up on the pier. Tried to organize time in which to reverse the damage by pretending Tim had been kidnapped. At first I hoped

I could treat Tim myself by using the tapes Tim had made. But the more I tried to reprogramme him, the worse he got. I didn't know enough. I searched for, and found a new donor. I had the money Richard had paid to ransom Tim. It was sufficient to buy the services of a competent brain surgeon. I began to look for one I could trust, but in the mean time Tim needed looking after. I took food and drink to him on the pier, but he was deteriorating rapidly. He attacked me. I tried to calm him, keep him here, but he had a knife. He forced me back and I fell . . .'

'From the pier?'

'Yes.'

'That's how you broke your collar bone?'

'It was a small price to pay.'

'It wasn't small for Tony, that nurse, or Trevor Joseph,' she whispered. 'And donors? Where did you get the brain tissue?' she demanded.

'Tony knew the risks. Tim told him,' Joanna replied emotionally. 'Great discoveries have always been made at a price. The others, the donors, they were homeless. Down-and-outs. They had no life, no future, nothing to look forward to. They didn't matter, Tony and Tim did.'

'And the nurse?'

'She cried on Tim's shoulder. As luck would have it, she worked on the same ward as him. Tim asked us about her brother. I couldn't even remember him. He tried to smooth things over, help the girl. But she kept on looking for her brother, asking questions, stirring up trouble. Tim ran into her down at the marina the night after he'd killed Tony. He was ill. He hadn't come round after the dosage he'd taken the night before. He'd had the sense to hide out on your boat, but he was no longer in complete control of his actions. Amanda must have said or done something . . .' Joanna shrugged her shoulders.

417

Daisy dropped Tim's hand abruptly. She felt strange. As if she didn't know him. Had never known him.

'It all just happened, Daisy. It wasn't anyone's fault. It just happened. You have to try to understand. Tim wanted to do so much.'

'I understand. I understand only too well.'

'Joanna.' Richard tapped on the glass wall. 'Joanna,' he repeated irritably.

'If you should need me for anything, anything at all, I'll be here in the clinic.' Joanna laid an icy hand on Daisy's shoulder.

'Richard needs you more,' she replied, shrinking from Joanna's touch.

Daisy heard the click of the door as Joanna left the room. She looked down at Tim. At the hand she'd been holding. Then quietly, softly, she began to cry.

Chapter Eighteen

'Do you want to come in?' Richard demanded of the policeman who'd dogged his footsteps like a shadow since Peter'd summoned and briefed him.

'I'll take a look round for a moment, sir. If you don't mind.' The policeman brushed past Richard and walked into the office.

He opened all the doors, thoroughly checking out the small bedroom and bathroom. Then tried, and failed, to open a window.

'Hermetically sealed,' Richard explained irritably. 'The clinic's temperature is carefully controlled by a central system. An influx of outside air would adversely affect the atmosphere.'

'I have to make sure.'

'We're twelve floors up, Constable, and my wife and I would like to go to bed. With your permission, of course.'

Nonplussed by Richard's impatience, the policeman opened the wardrobe at the far end of the office. Taking his time, he brushed aside Richard's clothes and the row of surgical gowns. Then he inspected the boots ranged along the floor of the cupboard. At last he pushed the clothes clear of the locks and slammed the wardrobe shut. 'I'll be outside if you should need me.'

'How thoughtful,' Joanna murmured cryptically, throwing herself down into one of the chairs.

The policeman left them, closing the door quietly behind him.

'Drink?' Richard turned the key in the lock, then went to the cabinet.

'I would have said you'd had enough.'

'Joined a temperance society, Joanna?'

'Make mine a brandy,' she said blandly, trying to avoid a head-on confrontation.

Richard poured the drinks. He carried Joanna's to the table, then, undoing his tie and the top button of his shirt, he walked over to his desk. He unlocked the top drawer with a small key he kept on his watch chain. Joanna picked up her drink, then leant back in the chair and closed her eyes. She heard Richard searching for something, but she was too preoccupied with her own thoughts to wonder what he was doing.

'What were you discussing with Daisy?' he asked abruptly.

'Giving her moral support.'

'Or your apologies for turning Tim into a cabbage.'

Something in the tone of his voice made her sit up. She looked at him. She saw a gun barrel, long, slim, dark, pointing directly at her.

'It's the same one my father used to kill himself. Poetic justice, don't you think?'

'Richard, you don't understand . . .'

An explosion of light shattered her consciousness. Her final thoughts were of the brandy. Its wet stickiness spreading to her legs through her skirt.

The policeman sitting outside the door heard two shots fired in quick succession. He tried the handle, but it failed to give. He depressed the button on his radio and shouted the emergency code. Without waiting for a reply, he put down his radio and heaved his shoulder into the door.

The lights in the cubicle flickered from their night-time half-strength on to full. Daisy blinked away the effect their harsh glare had on her sensitive, sleep-heavy eyes, and moved out of her chair. She looked through the glass screen. A nurse was walking down the tunnel of windows that hemmed in the intensive care cubicles. She was carrying a kidney dish. A few more minutes and they'd be coming to prep Tim. She turned to look at her husband. He hadn't moved. He remained the same soulless hulk he'd been yesterday, and the day before . . .

'Daisy.'

'Alan. I didn't expect to see you here this morning.'

'I had nothing better to do.' He lied badly. The strain of his wakeful night sat heavy on him. Since Peter Collins had called him in the early hours of the morning, he'd made decisions that he was all too conscious weren't his to make. But there'd been no one else to call on. No one except Daisy. And as he looked at her – and Tim – he realized he'd had no choice. Daisy was barely coping with the misery she knew about. The horror of what Richard had done to himself and Joanna would have broken her in her present frame of mind.

'Have you been here all night?' he asked gently.

'Yes.'

'You know it's almost time?'

'Yes, I've been expecting Richard and Joanna.'

'They won't be here,' he said abruptly. 'I came to tell you Salen's ready. Judy's here with me. We'd like to stay with you while Salen operates.'

'Thank you, but there's no need.'

'Daisy, please. Don't shut us out. Not now.'

'Alan. Do something for me?'

'If I can.'

'Leave me alone with Tim. Just for a little while longer.'

'They'll be here in five minutes.'

'I know. Would you wait for me outside?'

'Judy and I'll be in the corridor.'

'Thank you.'

*

421

She looked down at Tim, seeing him not as he was now, but as he'd been the last time they'd stayed with Richard and Joanna. Leaning against the doorway of the bathroom in the bedroom they'd shared, mischief glowing in his deep blue eyes.

'Shall we shower together?'

'I've just dressed. Joanna's expecting us downstairs.'

'Joanna can wait.'

'Dinner . . .'

'Dinner will have to be delayed. I want you. Now.'

'Not now, later.'

'Now.'

'I couldn't bear the embarrassment.'

'You hard-hearted creature. Very well, but not too much later. We'll leave before dessert.'

'Tim, they'll guess.'

'What? That we're in love? It's not a crime, you know.'

His strong arms wrapped warmly around her waist, his lips on hers. 'I'll make the excuses. I'll say I have a headache. Don't all new husbands suffer from headaches?'

'You're an idiot.'

'Not for marrying you.'

'Some people might disagree with you.'

'I can't imagine who. You're the best thing that's ever happened to me. What did I do with all this love before you came along?'

'Perhaps you gave it to someone else.'

'Never. Only you. There'll only ever be you. And when I'm old and bald, I'll pull on my toupee, put my teeth in, press the button on my electric wheelchair, and kiss you, just as I'm going to now . . .'

She looked down at the bed. At what was left of him. Then, very slowly, very deliberately, she reached out towards the plug that fed the supply to the life support system.

When Alan and Judy burst in moments later, they found her staring at Tim, the plug still in her hand.

Epilogue

Autumn winds scoured the beach, drawing fine patterns across the rain-whipped sands. A grey drizzle merged the grey skies and the grey sea into one. Only the white frothy tips of the waves crashing on to the beach lightened the brown and pewter tints of the cold, unwelcoming scene.

Peter left the shelter, pushing the newspaper he'd been reading into his pocket. Bill had been right all along. Robin Dart's death had been retribution from a drug dealer. He'd moonlighted for a pusher while he'd been in college. Acted as carrier and distributer. Only one day he'd got greedy, sold stock that wasn't his to sell, and pocketed the money. He'd tried to disappear, and didn't get quite far enough.

No wonder Richard Sherringham had stared at him blankly when he'd mentioned Robin Dart's name. The pusher who'd given Robin Dart his last injection had got twenty years. With good behaviour, he'd be back on the streets in eight. Not much to pay for a life.

He walked along the deserted promenade towards the pier. Its gaunt skeleton stood proud no longer. The structure had been stripped naked, its shell plundered. Iron girders lay on the sands, their metallic branches spread upwards into the air. A huge man-made monster agonizing in the indignity of its final death throes.

Peter watched the blackened silhouettes of tiny men fighting against the wind and rain as they loaded the pier, now just so much scrap metal, on to cranes that winched upwards and outwards. A mile or so down the promenade, a patient line of lorries queued, waiting for their loads.

'You couldn't stay away either.'

Daisy Sherringham stood beside him. She was wearing a long black coat and scarf. Her hair was loose, the first time he'd seen it that way, but it was tangled. The wind whipped it savagely around her pale face and dark, smudged eyes.

'Sticks in your guts, doesn't it?' he commented bitterly. 'Never enough money for these damned things until something happens.'

'You know Trevor's going to make it. It'll take a long time . . .'

'And you doctors say you hope he'll be the same. But you don't know.'

'We can't give guarantees. With anyone's life.'

'Pity. I'd like a thirty-year warranty on mine.' He hunched his shoulders deeper into his anorak and pulled up the zip until the collar met his chin. 'I heard that you refused to take over the clinic.'

'The clinic was Richard's and Joanna's. I wouldn't have run it the way they'd have wanted.'

'Close on a million pounds is a lot of inheritance to turn down.'

She looked him coolly in the eye. 'The estate belongs to Joanna's father.'

'Richard Sherringham's will was quite clear. Everything to his wife, and on her death, to Tim. Joanna Sherringham died before Richard. Tim was the last to die.'

'Only technically. I really don't want to talk about it.' She turned her back on the pier and walked down the promenade. He walked alongside her.

'I heard about your promotion.'

'It's hardly a promotion. They asked if I'd take over Tim's job at the hospital until they could appoint a replacement registrar.'

'I hear they're not looking very hard.'

'I've already handed in my notice. Hedley's applied again. Perhaps this time he'll be lucky.'

'For the sake of the future of the General and medicine, I hope not.'

She smiled at him. 'He's not a bad doctor. He just lacks a bedside manner. He really suffered when he was suspended during the enquiry about the work he did for Joanna. It'll be a long time before another doctor at the General moonlights in private practice.'

'If you're not going to stay on at the General, what are you going to do?'

'I'm going abroad. They need doctors in Africa. I've applied. I don't know what I want to do with the rest of my life. Not yet. But I do know I don't want to stay on here.'

'You're going to be missed.'

'Not for long. The General's a busy place. People come and go all the time.' Her grey eyes were misty. He couldn't tell if it was the rain, or tears.

'Perhaps we could see each other before you go. Have a drink or something? Gratitude for what you've done for Trevor.'

'Thank you, but no, Sergeant Collins.'

'You're probably right.'

'Goodbye.' She held out her hand. He took it.

'Goodbye, Dr Sherringham.'

He stood by the rail and watched as she walked towards the lights of the town. A shambling figure crossed her path. He put his hand in his pocket and pulled out some loose change. He held it in his palm, ready. Then he followed her.

J

MYSTERY

John   John, Katherine

Without trace

$24.95

004579297

DUE DATE

✓ MSS
EW